Published by Amazon

Copyright © 2021 R.K. Atkin

All rights reserved. No part of this publication may be reproduced, stored in a retrieval system, or transmitted in any form or by any means, electronic, mechanical, photocopying, recording, or otherwise, without the prior permission of R.K. Atkin.

Cover designed by Troy Lourens

For Delva and Susan

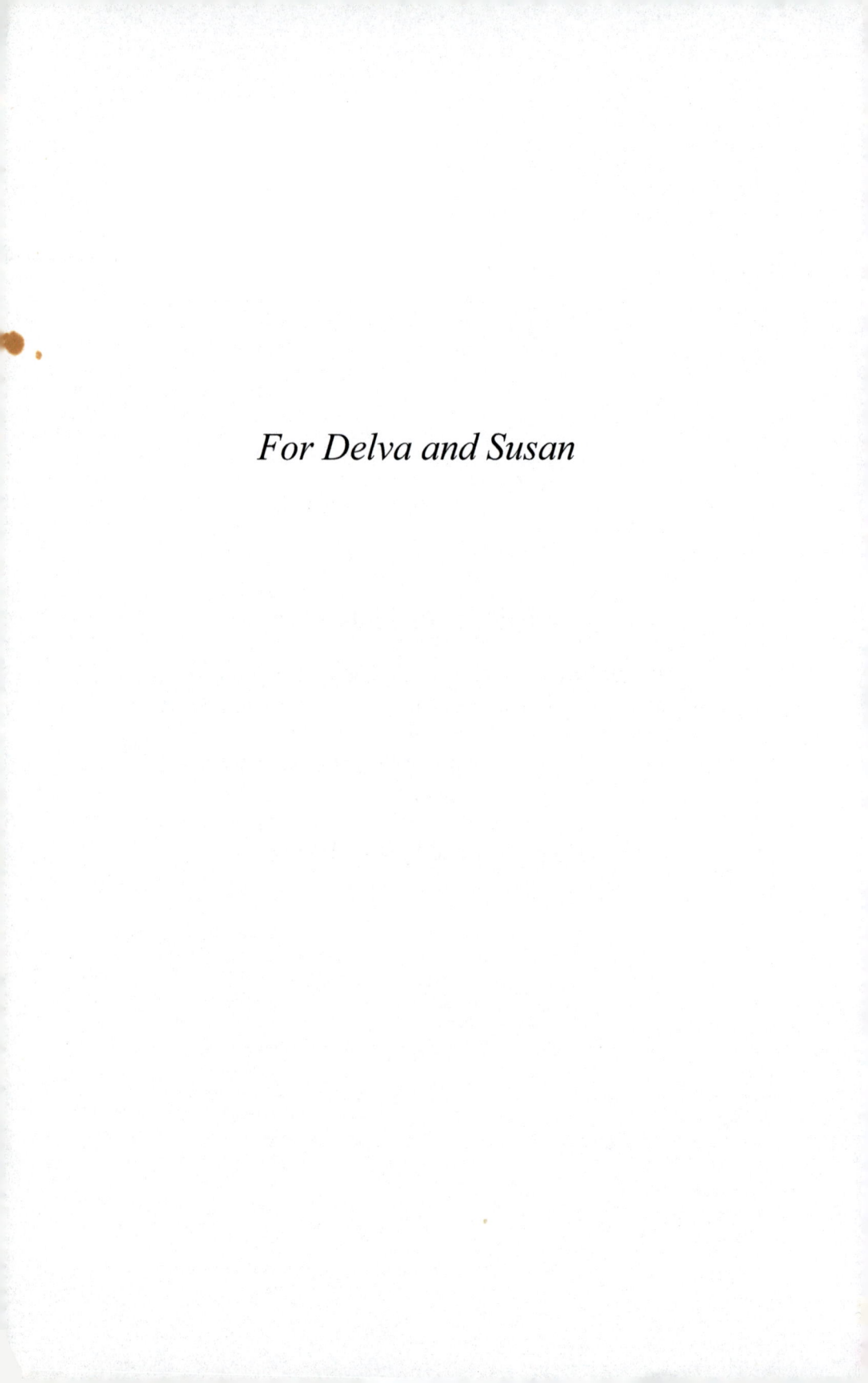

The Phantom Syndicate

By R.K. Atkin

Chapter 0
Prologue

It starts as a dark light. In the vastness of empty white space, it exists only as a single point, shimmering into life. A black sparkle. An idea. Its shadow grows and shines. A shade as gradual as it is unnoticeable, turning day into night. The dark light breathes a flame of life. A force now mobilizes behind the shadow, moving surreptitiously as it gathers momentum. Advancing in no discernible direction and leaving no memory or trace of its existence. It Strikes as fast as lightning with a bright black flash, then vanishes into thick obsidian smoke, ever present and yet untouchable. But the trail of absence cannot go unnoticed for long, and the inexistence develops an actuality in the form of myth. A myth that becomes increasingly notorious for its insidious mystique. The Presence of such a force pierces fear into the hearts and minds of the unsuspecting as it moves past everyone and through everything. All the while remaining unassailable, intelligent, and cruel.

"When did this start, Joel?" The agent asked sternly.

Joel was still feeling a little shaky. He didn't have the energy to lift his head all the way. "What do you mean?" he asked groggily.

"Everyone else is saying it started with you. Now, when did it start?"

Joel thought for a moment. A particular day stood out in his mind. "I started to investigate them myself, early this year," he said, pinching from his temples to the ridge of his nose. "I guess it started the day I called MI6. The interview that day gave me what I needed to... set things in motion."

"Were 'they' watching you back then?" asked the agent.

"No," Joel shook his head weakly, "I don't think so. There's no way..."

Chapter I
Out of the Dark
Hampton, England
17:25 GMT, Sunday, 13th March 2016

The moment they pass through the doorway of that house the clock will start. Every second will be critical from that moment onwards. In that house, where the answers are.
Where the questions are.

They didn't know it yet but that's where it all began. It wasn't a special day, in fact, it was just like every other day in England; a grey sky casting a dull gloom over the quiet afternoon. The house hid to the right in between its attached neighbours, all connected and identical, side by side to each end of the road. He could see it hiding, and she knew it.

Elizabeth Spear elected to go on the trip with him because she was still a newbie finding her place at MI5. Any opportunity she could get to prove her work initiative to the officers at the security service - such as experience shadowing another officer in an interview - would be accepted without question.

However, Joel Masier had provided this opportunity by arranging an interview with a girl who has already been interviewed, for a case that has already been closed. On a Sunday.

Similar to the unusual occurrences at MI5, Joel's intentions remained unexplainable. Elizabeth was as bewildered as Joel's colleagues when he told her about it and offered to take her. Since he arranged the interview in his spare time for what he called his "own case of interest", nobody had a problem with it. During the drive from London, he gave her tips for giving an interview in an attempt to avoid explaining what he was looking for. All he would say was he wanted to be sure. Sure about what she was yet to find out.

    Joel had offered a few of these opportunities to her in the past and she gladly took them. This one was different because it felt pointless, but she went along anyway because, admitting to herself, she looked up to him. He was taking the time to investigate something outside of MI5, the kind of work initiative that Elizabeth aimed to replicate. Joel's passion for life-saving responsibilities was unparalleled. It couldn't be bought or swayed. There was never a moment Joel wasn't thinking about what he considered important, which she figured is what made him such a good officer in investigations. Even looking into things that nobody else gave a second thought. He kept an eye on whatever political party was in London, or the United States. He even kept up to date on whatever the peacekeepers in the Middle East were blowing up and what threats the North Koreans were feinting. Whether it was about one person or everyone, Joel was in on it, even though he could not do anything about it.

    As much as Elizabeth admired the way Joel took an interest in anything potentially hazardous to other people, this time he had gotten carried away, and now they were about to make some poor young girl relive the trauma of her kidnapping. As soon as it was time.

    Elizabeth watched the clock in the car with her seat back. She looked from the clock to Joel's face. He was monitoring the house as if someone was going to come out and give him the signal to go in. His hair wasn't as neat as it usually was at work, but it hadn't changed much from its natural light-brown, except for the grey she now noticed coming through on the sides. The suit he wore was meant to make him appear more professional and it looked better on him than on most men. She thought of it as a workaholic's casual attire.

"Did we come here just to look?" she said lightly. Friendly as Joel was, he still outranked her enough to make her consider her words more carefully.

"Time to go," he said as he opened his car door. Elizabeth got out slowly so she didn't look too eager to get it done and go home.

"And when we go in, you're definitely not allowed to talk," he added strictly. His usual mix of serious but not serious. Elizabeth wasn't sure if he ever went further than that.

Joel rang the bell. Elizabeth could hear muffled footsteps approach the door. The lady that answered looked up at Joel with a bitterness that suggested they had come to hurt her daughter. Elizabeth couldn't shake the idea that, in a way, they had.

"Mrs Woodstrom, hi, I'm officer Masier. We spoke on the phone last week." Joel spoke with a practiced kindness. Mrs Woodstrom opened the door all the way. Although she was a little rounder in the middle, she looked fit for a mother in her forties.

"Yes, hello. You can come right in just… take a seat in the lounge." She gestured to a room on the left of the hallway. Remnants of a traumatic ordeal soured Mrs Woodstrom's welcoming voice with fear.

Past the threshold, the clock has started, let the games begin.

"This is Elizabeth Spear, she's shadowing me and will be joining us in the interview. I hope you don't mind," Joel said as he took his seat. His kind and polite manner was clearly working because with every word that he said, Mrs Woodstrom's cold shoulder got a little warmer. Elizabeth sat beside him and tried to position herself just as business-like as he had. She watched him take some papers out of his folder. They could not all have been from the same case.

"Mary-Ann! Could you come down sweetheart?" Mrs Woodstrom called up the stairs. A teenage girl, no older than 15, came step by step down the stairs and into the lounge. The bags under her eyes brought out her sunken expression. They took their seats together, both facing Joel.

"You have no need to worry, Mary-Ann. I'm not here to make you recall everything that happened, I only want to hear more about your escape," said Joel. Mary-Ann's shoulders rested as she sat further back in the couch. Joel smiled and looked down at his first page. Elizabeth found herself enjoying it; watching Joel make them feel more relaxed. She took mental notes of every detail of his performance.

He reread the file more for accuracy than for the details. The case at hand could not be simpler: Teenage girl, one of many kidnapped by small-time human traffickers, found after a rival gang supposedly wiped out the captors, leaving her and the rest of the girls a chance to escape and no more traffickers for MI5 to investigate. Case closed. Simple. But when was simple ever good enough for Joel? Nothing that endangered people's lives was ever simple as far as he was concerned, and he was always concerned.

"I have your previous statement here," he said, looking up to Mary-Ann's eyes. She could only manage to stare at the document. "You gave a good description of the men who fought with your captors. You mentioned how they looked "more official" than the kidnappers and "a guy in a hood". Is that right?" He asked.

"Yeah," she replied, speaking as softly as could be expected from someone thinking about their worst experiences.

It had been a few months since her escape. Making her remember it all had clearly caused her to regress into a post-traumatic state, remedied only by Joel's calming smile.

"Would you say that these men looked, almost, military?" Joel asked.

Mary-Ann looked aside for a moment, avoiding eye contact with him. "Yeah," She nodded with a small degree of confidence.

"With that in mind, would you say that they looked or acted as though they had had some training?" He asked. Elizabeth could tell that he was getting to some point but she still knew as little about it as she did during the forty-minute drive from London.

"Yeah, I guess so," Mary-Ann replied. The questions were far enough from her own personal experience that she began to engage with Joel. That's when Joel gave a shock that left even Elizabeth in awe.

"They weren't just there for your kidnappers, were they? They were there to set you free as well?" He asked more sternly now.

Mary-Ann froze for a moment looking into Joel's eyes. Red rushed to her cheeks as she looked fearfully from Joel to Elizabeth, who kept quiet as instructed. Mrs Woodstrom simply watched with the same level of anxiety as before.

"It's ok, Mary-Ann. Please, tell me the truth," said Joel.

Heart beating faster now, Elizabeth tried not to look impatiently at Mary-Ann.

"I dunno'," she mumbled. All of Joel's effort to make her feel less nervous had been undone.

"I know you were all kept in a room. Just tell me what they did and how they did it," Joel requested politely. Elizabeth thought he was being a little too direct with this. So much for the kind and friendly performance he was giving.

Mrs Woodstrom shifted in her seat. Mary-Ann hesitated, then she began to explain: She heard the sounds of fighting outside the room. Gunshots and screaming. When it got close, they all hugged the far walls to get as far from the door as they could. Mary-Ann thought it would be the police, but when the door of the room broke open there were men wearing masks (Previously identified by one of the other girl's descriptions as paintball masks) peering in, aiming assault rifles with flashlights at her and the rest of the girls. She could not see much with the bright lights in her eyes, but once they turned away, Mary-Ann watched as the men in masks lowered their weapons and walked away.

"Just walked away? Got up and walked away?" Joel asked her right after she finished saying it.

"Yeah, they left and didn't come back," she finished.

Elizabeth looked to Joel to see what he thought of it, only he had the last expression she thought he'd have. He was not even slightly surprised.

"They left the door open?" He asked more kindly now.

"Yeah," She replied with as much surprise in her voice as Elizabeth could feel.

"And, after it had gone quiet for a while, you all sneaked out?" He asked.

"After a while, yeah," she said.

Elizabeth couldn't keep it in any longer. "You encountered no one else? No obstacles or anything preventing you from escaping?" She asked.

"No. It was kinda easy after that," Mary-Ann replied.

Joel smiled pleasantly at her. She smiled back only for a moment, flashing small dimples in her cheeks. Joel didn't appear to notice that Elizabeth had said anything. She knew that was the kind of question he was going to ask and he likely didn't mind because he was too focused on Mary-Ann's answer.

"Mary-Ann," said Joel. He had become stern again, and the interview plunged back into a sort of interrogation. "That building was like a maze with your room in the middle. How did you find your way out?" He asked more in the form of a statement. Elizabeth thought he sounded like he already knew the answer but just wanted her to say it out loud. Mary-Ann's bottom lip began to quiver; she crossed her arms, but Joel's look was unrelenting. His silence built the pressure against Mary-Ann's internal resolve until finally, it cracked.

"They told us not to say anything," she half cried. Elizabeth finally realized why they were there; the rival gang that killed Mary-Ann's captors had actively set them free in secret.

It didn't change the case being closed but it would have major implications on the investigation into the rival gang itself. Suddenly this became the most interesting interview she had ever been a part of. Questions they don't train for began to swim curiously in her mind. What gang kills every member of a small organization for nothing? And helps the 'merchandise' escape? There's a lot of money in human trafficking, hundreds of thousands of pounds sitting in a room, and they let them go. They could even have claimed responsibility for saving the girls and been called 'heroes' all over the news. There's some money in that too, as well as some celebrity status. But after killing the kidnappers and setting the girls free, they did nothing more. No profit.

"When did you see the hooded man?" Joel said out of nowhere, making Elizabeth suddenly sit upright again. Mary-Ann tightened up and her eyes began to water.

"I think that's enough," Mrs Woodstrom said sternly.

Elizabeth could tell that the simple mention of the hooded man had reopened an entirely separate wound in Mary-Ann's mind.

"Please, Mrs Woodstrom. This is important. Anything she can tell us would be of great value to our investigation," he said carefully. The kindness in his voice was back again.

In her mind, Elizabeth was begging Mary-Ann to keep going. She wanted the interview to be over so she could find out what it all meant, and so Joel could answer all of her perplexing questions.

Mrs Woodstrom held her daughter's hand as she continued. "It's complicated…" Mary-Ann struggled for words.

"It's ok, whatever you can tell me, no matter how strange," Joel said gently.

Up to this point, Elizabeth had thought that Joel was just acting like he wasn't surprised by any of this, but now she could see that he really wasn't surprised. He knew what she was going to say, he had been expecting all of it, even that whatever she knows about the hooded man is strange. Too strange for her to tell it to the last officer who interviewed her.

"He was… different." Mary-Ann's voice trembled slightly.

"His clothing was different?" Joel asked expectantly.

"Not just that. He…" She paused. "There was just something about him." Her pitch was getting higher. Her eyes shined with unfallen tears, looking anywhere but up.

Elizabeth began to feel the conversation turn cold. She could not describe it with words, but an unnatural foreboding began to grip her, sending shivers through her nerves and constricting her stomach.

"He wasn't normal. He just stood there but like, not quite a normal or human way. Everything was - *darker* around him," she said, trying hard to fight the choke at the back of her throat.

"I couldn't see under his hood - it didn't look like anything was there. I know it sounds weird but…"

Before she could finish, Joel's warm voice returned to console her. "I understand."

Joel spoke slowly and gently. Elizabeth actually believed that he did understand, and the goosebumps began to settle in her arms.

"And I'm guessing that he left with the other men?" Joel asked as he looked through his folder again.

"Yeah, he went first. No gun or anything, just some stick in his hand," said Mary-Ann. For the first time, Elizabeth saw Joel's eyes widen slightly.

"I'm sorry?" He enquired.

"Well, he didn't have a gun like the rest of them. Just some stick. I couldn't see anything else, it was just a silhouette or a shadow or something."

"A shadow"

"You're sure?" Joel asked, much less gently. His austere tone made Elizabeth's heart beat faster still. Joel sounded like a different person.

'He can be serious' she thought. Poised as he may be, he was at attention now.

"Um, yeah," she said, more to Elizabeth than to Joel, looking for someone calmer to explain what it meant.

Elizabeth was equally as taken aback, so they looked to Joel for what he would do next. He looked up from skimming his case files. "Thank you very much I appreciate you taking the time to talk, I hope it wasn't too uncomfortable for you." He tried to sound kind but the rush made it emotionless.

He knew something. Elizabeth followed as he got up and started towards the door, not even bothering to put his documents away.

The strange new information. The paranormal description. Nothing, no reaction from him but when she mentions a stick, it's suddenly the most unbelievable breakthrough. On top of the intriguing development, Joel's sudden upheaval made Elizabeth rush alongside him all the way to the car and give him an enquiring glare over the top.

Without noticing her, Joel got in and looked through his case files on the wheel.

"Well!?" Elizabeth popped.

Joel looked at her and smiled. He handed her the documents and started the forty-minute journey back to London.

She scanned through them looking for answers. "What am I looking for here?" She turned to him.

"Highlighted in green are several descriptions given in statements," he said calmly. He didn't take his eyes off the road. By now he could recall the documents from memory.

Elizabeth fumbled through them in seconds. 'This is it' she thought, 'he's going to explain what the hell he's investigating.'

"Ok, I have them," she said.

"Can you find a pattern?" He asked. She skimmed through five statements until she found the one given by Mary-Ann Woodstrom in her first interview.

"They describe the same gang?" She asked, more from the context of his questions in the interview than from the pattern they revealed.

"And?" He continued.

Then it clicked. Elizabeth could see that all of the statements were given by victims of criminal organizations. All of which were completely unrelated to one another. In fact, the cases dated as far back as a year and were situated in various locations across the country. Not only had all the cases been closed, but each case had been closed in no more than two days. Years of investigating any given organization, and all associates turn up dead overnight without leaving a single thread to pull on. She could see what Joel had put together and came to the same conclusion: "It's the same gang, doing the same thing, in all these cases?" She asked.

Joel could hear that she was struggling to believe it and began to fill in the rest for her.

"And in that group or gang or whatever, the same man in black appears. It's a little different each time but they all end up describing the same hooded man." He didn't try to hide the excitement in his voice.

"What about the stick then? What's so special about that?" She asked.

The stick. Not a stick, a pole, or more of a staff perhaps. It had come up once before. The mercenaries appeared all over Britain, closing cases and replacing them. The new cases never make it anywhere of course. It wasn't easy to notice how they connected. Joel identified the pattern after looking through old case files from his previous (official) investigations. When the case he was working on suddenly got dropped, and when he found out why, the pattern took a hold of him like a python crushing him into obsession. All those cases being mysteriously killed off until it landed right on his doorstep. He was the most recent victim of the vigilantes.

For the last week, he had spent every moment he could spare, at home or at work, investigating the pattern, until he found a case that was both mysterious and full of witnesses. Mary-Ann Woodstrom is one of two people to actually see *him*. More than just a glimpse or a rumour. The other had described a demonic/shadowy man. "Abnormal" was the word she had used. After that, Mary-Ann's description confirmed Joel's suspicions beyond a reasonable doubt. It was the same man. It was the same group.

The hours he spent scanning old case files had finally paid off. The mess in his apartment was no longer just a mess. Joel threw his documents onto the floor with some of the others. The one he needed now was in the kitchen somewhere. One night earlier that week, after hunger had taken over his desire to work, he browsed a particularly interesting case file as he cooked. The Parker case.

It was still there. Similar in description but one of many cases that was too ambiguous for him to confirm. Until the stick was mentioned. The stick was unique to the Parker case, but now it was a strong link to the rest of pattern. Timeline? Checked out. Matched all signatures of the mercenaries? Somewhat, but nothing to suggest it was different.

The more he looked through it the more convinced he became: The case was a part of the pattern. However, the case had been taken over by the secret intelligence service - MI6 - taking a national security threat to an international level. Joel's excitement grew with the implications. Tomorrow he would take it to his Head of Department and open the case himself. 'Unless MI6 have already figured this all out from the Parker case, this could explain what's happening at MI5. It could become a serious investigation for both agencies.' he thought with an uncontrollable feeling of giddy pride in his chest.

The clock is running. The game is on.

London, England
08:36 GMT, Monday, 14th March 2016
(*The next day*)

A fortress of stone with little defence. Prepared for battle without an armoury. The Thames House, home of the Security Service, MI5 Headquarters. Combating the hidden plagues that eroded the country from within. Parasites that live off the light of good people, leaving them corrupted and hollow. The invisible struggle against organized crime.

Something of a bad streak had taken over. Over the months many cases had been shut only to be replaced by dead ends. Rival gangs killing each other, clients killing sellers or sellers killing clients. Each case meeting their own gruesome end with nothing but loose theories as to who, how, or why.

Despite having a rather large pebble to throw into the glassy surface of MI5s investigation pond, Joel knew he had all the time in the day to prepare his homework for presentation. Nobody likes the idea of the Security Service in a rut of cold cases. Their central purpose was to make all of their work go away. Joel, more than most, hated that they could not get anywhere. It was the wrong kind of peaceful. He knew it could not last. He would have to disturb the peace if he could. At least a country-wide investigation was interesting enough to raise the depressing standard.

The mysterious nature of the case allowed Joel to re-familiarize himself with the earliest hours of the morning, during which he pondered his many questions. This was no issue for him. After he finally got some sleep, he had extra time in the morning to wake up. The journey from his apartment to the Thames House building felt shorter than usual. Last week was the same. On Thursday Joel realized it was because he was in no hurry to get to work, and that he was probably the only one in London to care so little.

Now that he had a strong reason to go, it took much longer. He made his way through the pleasant fortress, up the stairs in the lobby, and down the hallways towards his desk. He helped Elizabeth when he could because he knew she was being deprived of the genuine first-hand experience she should have been getting. Hopefully, in light of his new information, she could take part in the investigation that would inevitably follow. She was ambitious enough, he had always facilitated that, and she was the only one who knew about the case besides him.

Upon reaching his workplace, Joel was met by the regulars sitting at their desks. They were side by side against the walls with some in the middle separated by dividers. The rest of his team could be confused for an accounting office, if that accounting office had lost their previous clients because they turned up dead one morning. The typical friendly greetings were exchanged by skipping them entirely and starting with "Are you guys actually doing work?" from Joel.

"Yes. You would be too if you showed up on time," said Thomas.

"Funny, because I've been doing some work of my own," said Joel. He looked over to see what Thomas was doing. Standard paperwork, nothing exciting.

"We know. Taking Spear on an adventure to find the ghost of killer's past," came a voice from ahead of Joel. Being the head of the team, Paige would typically go unchallenged, unless she was speaking to Joel.

"It was a kidnapping case," Joel corrected. "And I have a lead."

"What's a lead?" Thomas commented sarcastically.

"Joel, I know you have trouble with this fact, but we

don't have any immediate calls. What we do have is making digital copies of written reports," said Paige.

"For now, but I have a meeting with Lawrence," Joel lied. He knew if he said he wanted to take his investigation to the head of department that they would sooner let him work from home than let him go. Instead, they watched with only mild interest as he continued walking by.

Joel made it out before Paige could protest and stopped at an office at the end of the hall. A tight feeling spread in his chest and dropped into his stomach. The head of department's office. He held his file close and knocked on the door.

"Yup," came a voice from inside. The feeling in Joel's chest was relieved by a sudden austere confidence.

"Mr Lawrence, how are you?" Joel said as he closed the door behind himself.

Mr Lawrence was sitting in his office chair, arched over his desk. Papers were falling off from all sides. His reading glasses glowed with the white-blue of his monitor. Joel could see a wall of text in the reflection.

"Well, Masier, the only work I have is the tedious kind, and for reasons I can't explain I have a lot of it so whatever you're here for had better be good," said Mr Lawrence.

"Not good, but definitely worth your time," said Joel. He raised the file for Mr Lawrence to see.

"Talk," said Mr Lawrence, looking Joel in the eyes. Joel could tell that, although Mr Lawrence would never admit it, he would humour anything to get away from admin work, especially the tedious kind.

"About a week ago our case was closed after every one of our suspects turned up dead at once," Joel began.

"Strange as that may be, I did know already," said Mr Lawrence.

"I know who killed them. And not only that, they've done it before," said Joel. Mr Lawrence leaned back in his chair slowly. Joel knew this to be his way of being stunned, even if his expression hadn't changed from tired concentration.

"I guess if anyone was going to find something to stir things up it would be you," he said. "Keep talking."

Joel began to place documents from his file onto the tablecloth of papers that covered the desk.

"*Twenty-four*. Twenty-four cases in the past year have all been closed because the suspects or culprits were killed. All by some separate gang or group. Parties unknown with enough training to kill off any criminal organization in under two days, and then vanish. No evidence and no leads. One by one they have the same descriptions: unusual cases of quick, efficient and highly effective attacks. No survivors except for any innocent parties that happen to be involved. Fortunately, they get set free," said Joel.

Mr Lawrence raised his hand to stop him.

"Set free?" He asked as though he had misheard it.

"Yesterday I spoke to a victim from one of the human trafficking cases. They threatened the girls not to say anything about being freed and I believe they did that in all the other cases as well," said Joel.

"Who is *they*? What makes you think that it's the same group of people?" Mr Lawrence asked.

"Descriptions of trained men given by the witnesses that were set free. Reports of 'brutal deaths' and 'torture' given by the response teams, the details of which match more often than not. And in eight of the cases, all of which are trafficking cases, there is mention of a man in black. Witnesses always recall him with fear as some sort of fiend or demonic man, like encountering a paranormal entity. I don't think he's a demon...

but when a shadowy man dressed all in black with a wide hood and a long overcoat is described by eight different witnesses in eight different parts of England, it's no coincidence," Joel finished.

Mr Lawrence looked over the summary that Joel had placed in front of him. Knowing that it would only be enough to appear crazy, Joel continued to explain the pattern in further detail while using the file for references. Mr Lawrence examined them with increasing concentration.

Upon first glance, you can never truly tell how much the iceberg hides beneath the surface. There was a time, however brief, that the first man with Spanish flu was just a single, sick man.

When Joel finished, Mr Lawrence looked up at him, and he knew what he was going to say before he said it.

"Alright, there's enough evidence here to open an official case. Since you apparently have nothing better to be doing, take this to Paige, I'll take care of the rest. It'll give me something to do that isn't this crap," said Mr Lawrence. He gestured to the wall of text on his monitor.

"There is one last thing," said Joel. Mr Lawrence tilted his head down to look over his reading glasses.

"One of the cases was taken over by the SIS. There's a chance these 'mercenaries' extend internationally. I tried to contact MI6 about it but they refused to share their side," said Joel.

"If that's the case, this could be a career-changing discovery for you, Mr Masier. So don't go and do something stupid like contact the SIS without executive permission! How many times must I remind you where your job ends, and someone else's begins? Take the case to your team, and if there's grounds for it, then I will take it up with our friends at

MI6. Is that clear?" Asked Mr Lawrence.

"Yes sir," Joel responded. He was used to being restricted by every one of his superiors but it hardly had any effect on him. If he was going to do his job to the best of his abilities, then he had to have some freedom. The Bureaucracy and the rules just slowed everything down, and he often had to work against the clock.

Joel took his file back to the team. They were no different to how he left them. That was about to change. Paige was in her own office at the other end of the room. She allowed Joel in when she saw him walking over.

"We have a new case," said Joel. He put the file on Paige's desk and fell into a chair. She pursed her lips but picked up the file.

"What did Lawrence say?" She asked.

"To open the investigation officially," Joel said matter-of-factly.

"What investigation?" Asked Paige.

"The reason we lost our last case." Joel said with a hint of smug satisfaction that made Paige shoot a scorning look at him. "Mercenary vigilantes," said Joel.

Beira, Mozambique
19:34 CAT, Thursday, 24th March 2016
(*10 days later*)

What a waste of time. Four days and the contact was dropped. Not only that, but the supposedly 'high value' tradesmen had all been eliminated by an unknown third party. If it was done by a task force then surely GCHQ (Government Communications Headquarters) would have told the active senior operative? It couldn't have been London. In fact, there's not a lot that it could have been.

By the time she figured out what happened, she was the only one left. Her contacts had left town and the surrounding areas of the scene were abandoned. Any attempt to follow up on the anomaly was met by distaste. The locals - even law enforcement - seemed spooked. It began to explain why everyone involved who wasn't killed had jumped ship. Everything was dissolving. How could a thing like that happen over a few days and then her request to look into it further be denied? She was there already; she may as well make use of the trip.

Caitlin slid her sunglasses back against her high ponytail. The brown frame and dark lenses blended into her chestnut hair. She pulled the zip of her duffel bag closed, leaving a jacket out for her arrival in England, where water fell out of the sky instead of just floating humidly in the air like it did in the streets of Mozambique.

On the brighter side, Beira had been a pleasantly warm place. The city was still developing but she knew Ben would have enjoyed it all the same. She wished it weren't illegal to tell him where she went on her 'business trips'. That way she would feel less guilty when she told him anyway. Its only fun to have a secret agent girlfriend if you get to hear about her 'adventures', just as long as MI6 never finds out that she releases classified information. Caitlin was confident enough not to care, she had been bending the rules since her earliest days in the military and she had known Ben since before she enlisted.

He would be the first image to form in her mind whenever she looked at the C-17's. The heavy-duty transport aircrafts that were used to fly soldiers to and from home. They looked exactly like commercial Boeings that had been painted with Airforce-grey. To Caitlin, they were symbols of home. Everything that waited for her back in Oxford would live in the C-17's while she ran in drills and missions. In the primarily male barracks, she could see the spirit of her older brother come out every time the other infantrymen played basketball.

The face she never used to see was her father's. Probably because her father was the kind of figure that couldn't be matched by any high-ranking military official, all of whom lacked any sense of positive encouragement when barking orders down the chain of command. Even as a furniture salesman, her father was more of a hero to her than any first-class general. Hence, she left the military for good after her second tour. She couldn't bear the thought of being so far from her real home, not in klicks, but in months.

Over a year later she had finally gotten what she asked for; MI6 calling her back to London after only four days of being away. Just one more taxi to the airport and she would fly home. All the while imagining she was back in a C-17 with more leg room than she knew what to do with.

Ben would not be waiting at the airport like he used to years ago. The unpredictable nature of an operative's location meant that farewells and welcome-backs would have to be done over the phone, if at all. Caitlin looked back at the last few days and wondered if they had been interesting enough to risk telling Ben. Perhaps if they run out of things to talk about then she could resort to high treason. Besides, all she did was talk to the contacts on the rim of Beira, nowhere close to the tradesmen who were rumoured to be dealing in cattle as well as their regular business of exporting high calibre ammunition to the coast of England. The operation never even made it to the fun stage that allowed her to utilize her old combat training.

Caitlin could recharge from her frustration once she got

home, where Ben had a talent for defusing it. She was going to need that from him. Especially after eleven hours of trying to stretch her legs under the seat in front of her. Then, of course, the inevitable report that she would have to write about her uneventful week. About how her operation had been made redundant by whoever was able to neutralize her targets and vanish with no more than dead ends in their wake. Who would even be so daring when there were foreign intelligence operatives monitoring the scene?

Chapter II
Forerunner
Unknown, Unknown, North Korea
01:23 PYT, Tuesday, 29th March 2016
(*5 days later*)

Past the dead of night. The devil's playtime. A blanket of shadow covered the valley, yielding to steep, curvaceous hills. At the bottom, an array of geometric shapes lay at the base of the concave jungle, generating the only white glow beneath the stars. The forest breathed with an eastern wind. Rustling leaves gave way to chirping crickets after every gust, just loud enough for the predator's crawl to be lost in the cacophony. Watching from an eagle's distance, unwavering eyes studied the sources of light from the crest of the neighbouring hill. Two lookouts nested high up in a tree. The other three remained on the sloped floor below. Position Zero.

"It's going to be three hundred meters down the hill," said the scout. The lead was holding onto some branches next to him. They had positioned high up the hill for a good view of the facility below. "The lights at Entrance Two are still on but we need to leave now if we want to reach it in time."

"Let's go then, and don't leave anything behind," Lead replied. They packed their binoculars away and used the winch to return to ground level. Each of the four men that made up Unit 2 put their masks on. Night-vision goggles were folded over the top of their heads. Jagged lines on their masks replicated a long skull-like shape, with four ripped lines from nose to chin. The rest of their on-hand equipment was standard for infiltration: All matte-black in colour, no grenades, and nothing capable of making a full sound.

"How do we tell him that we're going?" Cover asked as he nodded to the Korean. There was no verbal communication with the Korean, he didn't speak Japanese, but they needed a local guide with the balls to get them out that far.

"We don't," replied Lead. He began walking down the incline with his radio out. "Lieutenant, this is Lead 2, we're making our way down, ETA: Twenty minutes." He slid the two-way radio back onto the strap of his chest. Scout went first. Being Scout meant that he was Point Man as well. Lead relayed commands from the Lieutenant, he went second. Heavy was the one with the equipment, so he needed to fall back to third. Then Cover last, watching over the Unit and covering the rear. They made their way down the forest floor toward the next position. The trees were thick and spaced about 2.5 metres apart but the rest of the foliage provided ample cover.

They immediately identified the Lieutenant, Tadao's voice over the radio: *Make it fast, the Commander is here and he's in charge. As soon as he's cleared the path, we move in,*" he said.

"The Commander?" Heavy said from behind. "That's that Shadow Man, right?"

"Yes," said Lead. He sounded as confused as they all felt. The thought of asking why the 'Commander' was in command was dismissed by their knowledge of Tadao's loyalty to rank. For him, they would acquiesce to the new arrangement, just as he would ask them to. Rules aside, they couldn't help but wonder why the position had been given to the Shadow Man and not Tadao. He had been their leader since they joined. His military experience made him a good team captain, even if he insisted that they call him 'Lieutenant'. Tadao had an almost perfect mission success rate with them over the past two years. Because of the reputation he had built for the team, the Grandmasters expanded their operations into China and Korea.

They had hit some of the most profitable scores of their lives since he inflicted a military-style discipline on their missions. Although he hated the military, Tadao could never let go of it. He lived for the practice of it - the terminology and protocol. It proved to be an efficacious influence on the organisation.

Tadao had refined them from a larger group of mindless mercenaries into a first-class kill-squad. One of a kind. Nobody else would come to admire their grandeur, of course, the organisation itself was practically made of secrecy. 'The best reputation is one that doesn't exist', and so they don't. Tadao would say that he didn't leave the military to become a warlord, but that he just traded in one life of crime for another. Nobody understood, but who was going to argue with the man in charge of making them money? And it was always Tadao who lead them down the path to riches. Not the 'Commander'. They had heard about *him* through Tadao and others in the organization. He was like another lieutenant but with a sinister reputation. Everyone just seemed to fall in line for him, although scarcely anyone had actually seen him.

The Unit reached Position One in good time. Just inside the tree line with a direct path to the outer fence. The facility was a couple hundred meters long so for security purposes it was fenced off twice around.

Unit 2 radioed Tadao once they reached the position. Units 1 and 3 were entering the facility from other angles and would link up with them inside. The transport crews followed them in.

"The Commander is on the inside. When the lights go out, stay low and move fast," Tadao said over the radio.

"Why is he in charge now?" Came the voice of Lead from Unit 1.

"He has always been in charge. He planned all of this. Without him here, we would not get far," said Tadao.

"Since when?" Asked Lead 1.

"*Since his name means* Commander, *so don't embarrass me,*" Tadao said sternly. If they had known that his name was English for 'Commander' then they would have been more respectful.

"How can he just take over? We've never met him before," Cover asked Lead.

"How am I supposed to know why they put him in charge? You can ask the Grandmasters themselves when this is over," Lead replied sarcastically.

The lights around the fence ahead of them went out. They switched off the safeties on their rifles. "Suppressors on, safeties off," said Scout.

"Lieutenant, the lights are off but what about the patrol?" Lead asked into his radio.

"*Taken care of, now move!*" Tadao pressed. They walked as quickly as they could at crouching level. The white lights in the depth of the facility made them feel exposed. Heavy reached the fence and took out the bolt cutters. With each snap and click, their grips on their G36 assault rifles got tighter. Heavy made sure to leave a side of the fence intact so he could fold it like a door. As instructed, they moved inside, leaving the fence looking untouched, and hugging the inside of the boundary to the right.

In front of them was a two-story building followed by a row of one-story rectangular structures. Their preselected path felt more daunting than it looked on the satellite image, but just as promised, they encountered no resistance. The rendezvous point was an alleyway with minimal chance of detection from the outside. Cutting the right lights meant that the centre of the alley became an abyss. A simple task that the first entry unit had seen to. Unit 3 was at the rendezvous first. Unit 1 arrived in sync with Unit 2.

Position Two.

Tadao walked around the corner of the alley right on time and the units straightened up. "With me," he said. His voice was as light and calm as always. He never shouted. No matter how much he raised his voice, there was always a tranquil authority when he spoke.

"The Commander is up ahead clearing a path for the transport teams. Don't stray from the plan and we won't have to improvise," Tadao said as he walked by. He put his mask back over his face. It was the same design only with more jagged lines detailing his features. Following him with rifles half raised - just the way he had taught them - they moved towards the next position. Tadao kept an eye on a watch on the inside of his left wrist and changed their pace accordingly. From the way he held his rifle he could switch between his sights and his watch. Just the way he had been taught.

The units began to see movement - flashes of motion on top of the structures and down alleyways. The Commander's men were moving parallel to them. Perfectly aligned and advancing in unified silence. They could see men on the rooftops climbing from building to building, taking out any lights that would not leave the area noticeably dimmer.

Tadao was moving on a pathway between the structures. There were no guards, not even on the rooftops. All at once, the Commander's men stopped and ducked out of sight. The ground units backed up against the darker spots near the walls. Tadao gave them the signal to halt.

"We'll clean up if we have to, otherwise just ignore them," he said back to his units. He then began leading them down the next section of alleyways, where they first started seeing the bodies. Tucked away in dark corners, behind barrels, and lying against walls. The blood was hard to see in the dark but there was just enough light to reveal the gleam of glossy dark-red splatters around the bodies. The closer they got to each crime scene, the more violent they appeared. There were no bullet wounds, only lacerations. Blood decorated each deformity with its own unique, monochromatic Pollock replica. They tried to ignore them but the idea of meeting the Commander now made their skin feel cold. Today was not the day to embarrass Tadao.

Position Three. The entire operation came to a soundless halt once more. A ten-meter gap separated them from the open side door of the opposing building. A single light high above the door shone a cone of white around the infinite black of the doorway. They all watched as a pair of shins and boots were slowly dragged into the abyss beyond the doorway. They had caught up to the Commander at last.

"From this point there will be guards in our way. Don't fuck this up, or *he* will leave you behind, like them," said Tadao. They could sense the artificial tone of humour in his voice. The idea of being a part of the Commander's gruesome art project made them walk extra quietly to either side of the door. Footsteps came from inside the warehouse, then white light flooded the inside, forcing the units to back away from the doorframe. Lead saw Tadao press in his earpiece; he was listening to the Commander.

"Adjust eyes for a dark breach," said Tadao. They lowered their rifles with one hand and enclosed their eyes with their other hand. Looking into the black grips of their gloves, their eyes adjusted to the lack of light. There was a swishing sound inside, then a snap, and the lights were out.

"Now!" Tadao hissed. They funnelled through the doorway in their pre-arranged order. The warehouse floor was no bigger than a basketball court. Three soldiers were standing in shock on the catwalk at the far side. Before their eyes could adjust to the dark, white flashes filled the warehouse as the units neutralized them. The suppressed rifles were hardly silent, but the walls kept the sound from escaping. One of the victims filled the subsequent void with writhing and moaning. They could not risk shooting him in case they hit something else that would make a loud noise, but it wasn't necessary, as an object flew to his body from above, making the room go quiet once more.

Tadao led his units through the warehouse. They passed the Korean soldier and the long silver object that had finished him off; a throwing knife. They began to feel the source of Tadao's inflamed resolve. That fear. Their diaphragms felt heavy. The surface of their skin was fluctuating between hot and cold. Their nerves were spiking with adrenaline. All possibility of the North Korean military finding and arresting them was suddenly at the back of their minds, leaving the rest of their brains to comprehend the thing that was now in charge of them all. Tadao kept them at a reasonable (Safe) distance away from *him*, taking corners much more slowly than he usually did.

Risking moderate sounds of impact, they eliminated multiple guards before they reached Position Four. Tadao stopped them suddenly on a catwalk inside the third warehouse. There were no guards except for a single soldier who was hanging by his neck over the opposing railing. Once the twitching stopped, he swung gently with blood running from his neck to his toes and dripping into a puddle on the floor. The chain around his neck was a complex set of mechanical pivots that allowed the blade-links to bend like rope, which suddenly disconnected, dropping the soldier into his own blood with a splat. The units froze. They watched as the chain links glimmered and tinkled up onto the catwalk like a silver snake. It slithered around the doorway, and out of sight. Scout 1 suggested that it could have been the source of the swishing sound from earlier. A steel whip with the Commander at the controlling end.

They followed Tadao, who followed the Commander. They couldn't see *him*, only the flashes of dark silhouettes when his blades darted in and out of view. It didn't feel like he was one of them. The Commander seemed to take the form of an animal, killing for sport rather than purpose. The way he took his time with his prey. The way he played with them. A vehement display of intimidation to drown them in fear before their execution. He was delicate. Every kill was quick. There was little pain in their wide, unblinking eyes. Only fear.

They stopped in the fourth warehouse with the Commander still ahead. Position Five.

"Number four is clear," Tadao said into his radio. "*We're outside; open the main doors,*" came the reply. The two doors were large, heavy, and had squeaking wheels to roll them aside. The teams lifted them to reduce the sound, but the noise still gave everyone goosebumps. Any loud sound is unwelcome in a stealth operation.

There were lookouts on the rooftops of the surrounding buildings. To everyone's amazement, they had all arrived at the checkpoint on schedule. Multiple teams comprised of forty men all arrived at their own positions at the scheduled time.

The transport team's casual entry made Tadao's men breathe naturally again. They immediately started to unload crates from around the warehouse. Tadao left his men as sentries before making his way to the rooms on the side of the warehouse. He needed to speak with the Commander privately.

The game is stealth. If your opponent finds out you're playing, you lose.

The crates were heavy. High value at the price of great effort. The payoff had been guaranteed. A high-security military facility in one of the most desolate regions of North Korea, containing some of their most valuable hardware.

Investing extensively in the facility's security would have been a senseless expense. There was no reason to anticipate a ground attack on any one of the bases inside the restricted zones. Solitude and confidence made them weak, but no reward comes without risk. The imminent threat of the Commander's wrath could paralyze a man. Fortunately, Tadao was acting as a liaison. The assumption being that it was because Tadao spoke English and the Commander didn't speak Japanese. Whatever the reason, everyone was thankful that *he* wasn't watching them directly.

Tadao came back while the last few crates were being stacked on the trailers. Walking in alone, his entry filled the room with relief. There were no vehicles to pull the trailers so it was up to the collective strength of the transport crews to push them. All four wheels on each trailer had been modified to make as little sound as possible. Not that they were concerned about being caught. The path that had been cleared begged the question of whether or not there were any soldiers left in the facility. That's when Lead 3 noticed a new set of eyes watching them work.

"Lieutenant!" He called. They all turned to where he was pointing. First, they spotted a single camera, but looking around, they were everywhere. Cameras had been recording every square metre of the facility since before they arrived. Their rising panic was held at bay by Tadao's indifference.

"Don't worry about the cameras," he said as casually as ever. They looked at him for a moment then around at each other. Without a choice, they followed Tadao past the trailers and left the thought of cameras behind.

One moment it seemed like the mission would be as straightforward as they predicted, making it the first of its kind. The next moment it was time to make use of themselves. The path of the trailers had to be wide enough but still secluded. This meant passing through a denser arrangement of buildings.

The transport crews pushed the trailers and started on the path that the Commander had left for them. Every other available man was moving either alongside or parallel to the convoy. The haul was bigger than most; twenty-seven crates, each greater than a metre in length, had been divided on to the four trailers. A single crate was worth more than they got from some of their earliest scores.

For the next 142.87 metres, they were to neutralize any military personnel they encountered. Although the guards in the facility could barely see their figures in the near-moonless night, there was enough light to see the trailers. The date of the infiltration was selected to provide them just enough moonlight to see the figures of hostiles in the night. Since the North Koreans' dark-green uniforms were easier to see than the mercenaries' all-black attire, it was a matter of finding the sweet spot of moonlight for the visual advantage. It made a small difference, but their collection of small advantages made for almost ideal mission conditions.

With such extensive consideration, they could stride through the streets and alleyways with reassuring simplicity. The units felt cautiously hesitant whenever an obstacle appeared, but the force of the Commander behind them prevented anyone from slowing down. The splendour of the resulting motion was like liquid gold. Marching, smoothly and steadily, in perfect synch. They neutralized the guards without slowing or missing a stride. Men swept the rooftops with athletic prowess and eliminated the lookouts. The sound of their suppressed rifles, like muffled snapping, barely slowed their rhythm. There was no scuffing of boots, every step had to be planted in order to be strong against the kick of the recoil into their shoulders.

Second-floor balcony on the left, three shots to the chest and a finishing blow from one of the roof units. No matter where they shot the soldiers, or how many times, the kill had to be confirmed so that no dying men could scream the facility back to life. Darts of silver shot ahead of them as knives and throwing stars silenced lookouts before they could react. Rows of men on either side of the convoy moved at a fast-walk pace and aimed with identical focus on the area ahead. Hive minds sharing unspoken communication were felt and obeyed:

'Leave him he's too far, better for the rooftop units to-'

'Wait until we're alongside' before killing him, so that his fall doesn't alert the-'

'Target on the right of the road heading this way, eliminate him before he reaches the last pillar.'

'You have the best shot from in front of him.'

'Wait for us before taking out those two, better to do it at the same time so-'

'You take right and I'll take left.'

'I'm ready when you are.'

No number of soldiers that crossed their path could challenge them. Even after the facility's early-morning rotation started a dozen new shifts. They had cleaned through the streets once, they could do it again. The units acted as a single wave that washed in between and over the buildings.

Somewhere in black of the night, a glint of spinning steal struck at unsuspecting soldiers with august accuracy. Up to four meters long, it whipped majestically from soldier to soldier, reflecting their last sight of the stars before it glided through them. The chrome serpent would then slither out of existence. Gently, the sound of steel against stone would tear at the stillness that proceeded each kill.

It wrapped around a soldier's ankles and pulled them up and out, slamming his face into the pavement with a hollow crack. Then it dragged him away to his end. A glint caught the eye of another guard before the blades of the whip enclosed around his neck. The living shadow made an arc over him and off the building, leaving a silver tail to yank his head towards the edge and embed the corner in his vertebrae. With a flick, the magnetic lock disconnected and left the soldier's head to hang from the flesh in his neck. Hearing the scratch of steel, a guard looked up towards the source. But his view froze at the oncoming advance of unknown silhouettes in the street. He tried to raise his gun, but a strange and shiny chain struck and magnetized to it, pulling it away. Shock muted him for his last few living moments.

The hair stood up on the backs of their necks as the chain's mag-lock released the rifle and rose towards its master. Tadao caught sight of it in the corner of his eye. The Commander was playing with them again. Tadao could imagine the sadistic smile that would grow with each creative kill.

A high-pitched whistle came from behind the next guard. Something began to spin loosely around his neck. Panic tensed up his body which only made the damage worse when the commander pulled the chain. It suddenly switched direction and tore its way back around. The guard's spinning corpse ejected a pinwheel of blood from around his neck.

Apart from the sprinkling of brass cartridges and smell of gunpowder, nothing was left behind that wasn't already there. Every magazine had been strapped to another for faster reloading, then were put away after use. Tedious methods of recycling resources had long since been drilled into them. Only those that had submitted to Tadao's style were able to remain in the organisation long enough to reap the rewards.

Positions Six through Ten were met and passed like signs beside a motorway. They reached each position on time which allowed them to effectively cover each other. On any other day, they might have called it serendipitous. But second-by-second planning suggested calculation. Every member had once come to the unanimous opinion that this overcomplicated operation would never meet the demands of both objectives and times. The proposition of the plan first appeared too simple and therefore too easy. Once everyone had been caught up on the extent of the plan in all its detail, it appeared too complicated, and therefore too difficult. By the time they had reached the final checkpoints, Tadao would not have to save them from the Commander. They had done exactly what they were predetermined to do exactly when they were predetermined to do it, and the precision of the plan took it from there. Like putting a puzzle together all at once.

Their trail of red footprints came to an end at the exit position where the trailers had entered with the Commander. The last phase of the plan was getting the trailers to the dirt road that led from the base to the nearest roadway. From there, the Korean guides would drive them back to the land of the unknown, where the eyes of satellites could not follow. In order to avoid detection, they would have to take an indirect route down a pre-made path in the forest, beneath the shadow of the valley. Time was on their side. They had hours of darkness left.

Unit 3 was the last to pass through the two fences. They covered the others by looking inward at the facility. The exit was next to the highest buildings on the perimeter. As the best available cover, it minimized the possibility of anyone seeing them cross the grass.

When it was their turn to cross, with cover from Units 1 and 2 in the tree line, they found that their focus was directed at the Commander instead. They had all left the same way, so they had been anticipating his approach. They would finally see *him*.

Each second passed as peacefully as the last. No more sound than the regular chirping from the jungle. There was no light other than the overhead canvas of stars. They watched the corners of the buildings for only a few moments more before the radio crackled with Unit 1's signal for 'all clear'. Reluctant but somewhat relieved, they ran for the tree line, kicking at the grass to cover the footprints and tire tracks. All kill squads then transitioned from hostile-neutralizing to bush-moving. The path they had made for the trailers had been covered with branches and bushes to avoid detection. They lifted the obstructions from the 'road' and replaced them once the trailers had passed, slicing their way through the jungle and sowing the wounded earth behind them.

The convoy hummed with light chatter. The thrill of success crowned the plan with admiration.

"Did you see him? I only got a glimpse," said Heavy 3. Several other men confirmed the same.

"He was too busy leaving bodies, we practically walked in and out," said Cover 1. "We need more plans like that. Where's the Commander been all these years? The Grandmasters should have put him in charge sooner."

"Lieutenant, where is the Commander?" Lead 1 whispered to Tadao at the front of the convoy.

"He can take care of himself. Go find the Koreans, they should be waiting for us at the road," said Tadao. Lead 1 began running ahead. They reached the road on schedule and hooked up the trailers to their off-road vehicles. Scouts at the ends of the roads confirmed that no cars were coming in. Not that any were expected to at that hour. They were far enough from the facility not to be heard, and so they vanished.

It would be hours before the crime scenes were discovered. The facility fell into respite, generating a dimmer glow wherever it had been hurt. Stained red walls scarred them with failure. The architects of the ghoulish infiltration could be anywhere. Agents of darkness swimming in the depths of the trees. Behind the rise and fall of the surrounding hills. Ebony specs lost to the vast expanse of the night sky. Lost, but not forgiven.

Chapter III
Calm Before the Storm
Virginia, United States of America
14:52 EST, Wednesday, 20th April 2016
(*22 days later*)

Peace of mind. They went there to find it. To cry for it. It was a peaceful room. It was quiet, like they were far away from the world outside. In a glum, isolated room. Sounds of footsteps outside were so distant they may as well have been coming from a different dimension. One sound ruined the room's potential for total tranquillity. He blocked it out. Blocked them out. The litany would pause sometimes, blessing the room with a moment of sudden relief. The ceiling was a sunset orange. Quite plain. The light in the middle wasn't on because there was plenty of sunlight coming through the windows. Such a nice colour.

"Mr Bradford," said a women's voice.

Owen was staring upwards. He snapped out of his mental block and let his head fall to meet her gaze.

"Are you still with us?" She asked sweetly. There were twelve of them looking his way, each with their own seat in the circle.

"I'm here," said Owen. Even to himself, he sounded like he had just woken up. Felt like it too. He squinted as he looked over to the window. The sun was making its way down but its light still glared off of the windowsill. The colour distracted him from the dejected feeling in the room. The feeling that was infecting him.

"This won't interest you until you participate," she continued.

Such a consoling tone was wasted on him. He had

always thought it, but he couldn't tell a therapist to 'cut the crap'. It was her job to be that way.

"No thank you," said Owen. Sounding tired was better than sounding frustrated. It was best not to come across as angry in any way, especially in front of her. As sullen as he felt, he couldn't let himself make his situation worse.

"Mr Bradford, try to remember why you're here. I need to know that you're making progress," she said.

Owen closed his eyes. He knew that the others would react with solemn looks at the floor. Only Owen knew what she was really referring to. How sneaky of her. After a sigh of defeat, Owen sat up in his chair. "Ok," he said, finally capitulating to the concept of group therapy.

"Alright, why don't you start off by telling us who you lost," she said.

Owen rubbed his eyes until they began to go red, inadvertently making him fit in with the rest of the group.

"My fiancée," he said dryly. The feeling of the word in his mouth started to take effect. The lump in the back of his throat emerged from its months of hibernation. His cheeks began to burn as red as his eyes. As long as he could keep his eyes from watering he didn't care what else happened. The therapist recognized his reaction and continued with a professionally gentle tone.

"How long ago?" She asked.

Owen paused, looked at his watch, then crossed his arms and looked back to the space on the floor he was concentrating on. "Two years, four months," he said.

"Do you–"

"Nine days, Eighteen hours and thirty-four minutes."

The room was blessed with its longest period of silence since they started. Most of the other group members had joined

Owen in staring at a space on the floor. The therapist looked at him without words. She didn't dare say anything. The silence spoke for them all. Owen could feel dampness on his lower eyelids. He was not going to cry, but the effort was making the back of his jawline ache. The resistance in his face was nothing compared to the forces in his head. Sorrow and anger clawed their way up into his mind. He could feel them pushing against his brain, making it throb with the strain of keeping them down. He could not let either one prevail; they had already landed him there.

"Do you mind if I ask how?" She asked so gently that she looked at him with more caution that consolation.

That had done it. Anger was beginning to take a lead. Owen could feel the twitch in his right eye. He didn't think he could answer without growling it. He wondered if he even had to say it. Then he remembered why he was there and clenched his jaw into submission.

"She was murdered," he said in a low voice. His earlier disinterest was forgiven by the circle. They could feel the indignation emanate from him. All they could do was join in on his hate.

From there they moved on. The room settled with new discussions. Once the spotlight was removed from him, it took a few minutes for Owen to calm himself down. By the time the session ended, only frustration at his vulnerability remained.

The hour ended shortly after that. Walking outside, Owen was met by the refreshing spring air. It helped him shake off the experience with deep, rewarding breaths. There was one last thing he could do to cleanse himself of it, so he made a call.

"*Yes Mr Special Agent sir?*" Answered a deeper voice.

"Henry, it's that time of the week again," said Owen. He could already feel his remaining tension releasing.

"*Oh I'm well aware,*" Henry quipped.

Owen could hear him grinning over the phone. "The only time of the week I care about," he laughed.

"*Alright, I'll be there later. I just gotta pick up the VIP first,*" said Henry.

"*I'll see you there at seven then,*" Owen replied.

"Alright. Here he comes, I gotta go," said Henry. With the call over, the radio in the car came back on, and Henry turned it down keeping his eye on the side-view mirror. The VIP opened the back door and Henry put on a straight face. "Mr Busher. Where to, sir?" He asked, professionally monotone.

"Home, dad!" Replied the boy in the back.

"Home *Please*," said Henry, watching his son buckle-up in the rear-view mirror.

"*Home pleeease,*" his son repeated with childlike emphasis.

Henry smiled and pulled away from the school's parking. "What did you do today?" He asked. A hopeless question, but they had plenty of time to talk in the after-school traffic. For a seven year old, James could speak well, he just didn't speak often.

"Nothing," James said simply.

"Didn't you do that last week?" Henry asked.

"No," said James.

"Well that's too bad because last I checked, boys who do nothing don't get to play soccer," said Henry.

"You just don't want to *lose* again," James laughed at him.

"OH is that what you think? Save it for the field, quick feet," said Henry. He reached his house a half hour later and parked in the garage. The house was average size. Humbling compared to his previous place. James instinctively threw his bags in the same spot beside the door to the garage and went to his room to change. Henry did the same. They wasted no time getting ready for their traditional weekly afternoon soccer match. It was the highlight of both their weeks. Everything else could wait.

"Come on James! Its game time!" Henry called from his kitchen. He had changed from his suit to a pair of blue jeans and a pale blue shirt. James came running from his room and Henry threw him an apple.

"We can eat these on the way. Put all your stuff in the trunk and I can take you to your mom's house from the field," said Henry. He took a bite out of his apple with the soccer ball under his arm.

"We're not coming back here?" James asked shyly. Henry noticed him hesitate with his bags.

"It means we can play for longer. Afraid I can beat you with the extra time?" Henry asked in an attempt to distract him.

"No!" James exclaimed.

"Then let's go! Go! Go! Go!" Henry said as he steered him back into the garage. "And eat your apple. Did you tell your mom to buy you some fruit?" He added.

"Yeah," said James. He jumped into the back and put his seatbelt on without being reminded.

"Good. You gotta make sure she gets the right stuff when she buys groceries alright? But no candy!" Said Henry.

"Daaad!"

"Alright a little candy, and get some for me too." He turned around to face the back seats. "You ready?" He asked with his fist pointed at James.

"Ready-er than you," James smiled. They performed their ritualistic handshake; fists alternating up, then down, then slapping their palms together. Henry backed out of the driveway and drove to their regular park.

The screen changed from men marching in perfect sync to high-ranking officers standing and talking. There was no volume but there was no need for it. The discord was no secret. It had been an increasingly popular story on the news. Updates and developments were consistently broadcast to the entire country like they were scheduled programs. Not the most popular series, until a few weeks ago when activity suddenly began to spike.

Upon losing interest in the North Koreans, Owen took a sip from his beer and turned back to face the bar. Henry put his phone away and looked up at the bar as well. The only bartender was cleaning glasses on their left. The rest of the seats in the row were mostly empty; the majority of people were at tables behind them. They were used to the sound of conversations in the background. It was even nicer now that the heaters weren't making their own humming contribution.

It was getting lighter and warmer every day. Owen's dark blond hair was getting lighter. It usually never got so dark in the first place, but without exposure to the usual brand of tropical sun, the east coast winter had enough time to take effect. Having it short and centred made him look even younger than he already did. His clean-shaven, pointed jawline and bright blue eyes attracted a lot of looks from around the bar.

Henry still had the look of a married man. His hair was shorter and sensibly cut. He looked as old as Owen was despite being as old as Owen looked. When they met, Henry was bigger than Owen, with broader shoulders and more muscle in his arms and legs. Over the years, Owen hadn't changed much but Henry had fallen behind. There was even a bit of belly hanging over his belt.

"So why are we here so early?" Henry asked without turning to him.

"Had group earlier today," Owen murmured.

"That bad?" Henry asked, turning to face him.

"Worse than usual. They're making me contribute," said Owen, finishing his beer. He kept his gaze on a space at the back of the bar and ordered another.

"Sounds like a bitch of a day for you. How many have you got left?" Henry asked.

Owen straightened up a little and his sunken expression lifted. "Not much. Just until the middle of next month. Then I'll have my Wednesday afternoons back."

"Does it even help?" Henry asked. Then he got the answer he expected.

"It is a complete waste of my time," said Owen. "Still, I have to go. Keeps the suits-and-ties happy, and they let me keep my job."

"I wear a suit and tie. And you only get to be casual when you get to go to hot countries and tan in your shorts," said Henry.

Owen squinted at him. "So did you!" He said with and indignant expression.

"Not any more. It's official now. I've made a full transition to the desk job. No more field work," Henry said proudly.

"I gotta say, I never thought I'd see you take a desk job," said Owen.

"And I never thought I'd see you in group therapy. But I got a son who needs me to stay in the country because his mother is still trying to drink her way out of it. And you," Henry dropped his voice to a whisper, "beating that wife-killer was probably more therapeutic than all of your group sessions combined."

The beers were starting to take effect on Henry. Owen knew he was wasn't usually so forward. "And yet I have to go to group anyway," Owen said as he finished another beer.

"Well yeah, you were only supposed to arrest the guy. The punishment could have been worse than just compulsory time wasting," said Henry.

Owen ordered another beer. He wanted to change the subject and knew just how to do it. "How is the 'VIP'?" He asked.

Henry chuckled and the weight of the conversation was lifted. "When I picked him up, I asked him what he did today. You know what he said?" Henry asked, grinning.

"Nothing?" Said Owen.

"Not a damn thing," Henry laughed. The combination of alcohol and Henry's laughter lifted the last of the tension from Owen's mind. Lingering thoughts of the group session had faded from his mind. He could finally just laugh.

"He's getting good at soccer," said Henry.

"I bet he kicked your ass," said Owen, finishing another beer.

"He's getting *really* good at soccer," said Henry. They laughed some more and Owen ordered yet another beer.

"You know, when I dropped him off at his mom's place, she wasn't even there! So I took him to that fast-food place that he loves," said Henry. His volume rose but he didn't sound surprised.

"Why don't you take him home to stay with you then? It's not like she would notice," said Owen. They had talked about James' custody for so long that the proposal was more of a genuine idea than a joke.

They laughed about it anyway and continued to talk for a couple of hours. They drank until they had to call cabs. Almost as early and sober as they promised themselves, they returned to the aversion of solitude that awaited them at their houses.

Virginia, United States of America
07:40 EST, Thursday, 21st April 2016
(*The next day*)

The spring sunrise had given the day a warm start. Morning rays of light struck through a thin layer of mist from the east. The active life of the suburbs would disturb the stillness soon. For now, the air seemed to give way to her. She felt like a ship breaking through the icy surface of a flat sea - running against no resistance. Her legs ached with their own strength. Each quick breath was as warm as the sunlight on the side of her face. The stitch in her abdomen remained subdued. She began to slow down at the end of the stretch. The cooling breeze faltered and she felt the heat on the surface of her arms. Amy was approaching from behind. Her strength was fading and every muscle was desperate to relax.

Sophie slowed to a walk. Her breathing was far less audible and the pink in her cheeks was paler next to the prominent shade of diluted red that covered Amy's face and neck.

"Let's – Walk - from here." Amy huffed between gasps of air. They continued at a comfortable pace with their ponytails swinging lightly behind them.

"Okay. I can't have you too tired to run again tomorrow," said Sophie. Her voice was sweet yet strong. It had a smooth quality that offered gentle reassurance with confident authority.

"I'm happy with - four out of five days. I don't have – lungs like yours," said Amy. She was recovering through quick breaths now. Sophie's chest heaved steadily, stretching her support bra as far as it could go.

"You can't give up with only a day left," said Sophie.

"I've got the family life as well. We'll see if you still have this much energy after *you* have kids," said Amy.

Sophie shook her head and smiled. "*If*," she said.

"*When*. Come on, Sophie, becoming a parent is the next great adventure," Amy said joyfully.

"I've still got a few years left of my current 'adventure', there's no room for husbands or kids," said Sophie. As she said it she knew that she was bending the truth a little. If she cut her exercise and training time down then there would be considerable room left over, but that was not time she was willing to let go of yet. Unfortunately, Amy knew that as well.

"It's not going to end your career. Only pause it. Besides, didn't you say things were boring now anyway?" Amy asked. Sophie couldn't say no. She wanted to say that work was slow. That would make more sense than to say 'boring'. But yes, it was boring. Somehow, they found themselves between a rock and a hard place at every turn. All work turning cold and dead leaving more questions than answers. Nothing that came up ever stayed there for long. It gave Sophie more time to spend at home which - after a period of doing more of the same exercise routines – she got bored with as well.

They reached Amy's house and were welcomed by the familiar sight of two school uniforms and a suit. Sophie jogged forward to hug her now ecstatic nephews.

Jenny and Franklin looked neat in their elementary

school uniforms. They ran to Sophie and she lifted them both up in her arms and walked them back to the car in a great long hug. It left them laughing every time how much stronger she was than their father. On weekends they often attempted gymnastics in the back yard. The more concerned Amy's reactions were, the more points they would get. They could get away with a lot more when Aunt Sophie was around.

Over the years, Sophie had never stopped trying to become better. The way her father taught her. It started as a way to combat having two older brothers, but her self-improvement wasn't for the same reasons since she moved away. Eddie, the eldest sibling, moved west with his girlfriend years ago. Christmas and Thanksgiving would always be spent up in Maine with their widowed mother. And with no sibling rivalries left, Sophie regularly saw her other brother and his family. The extension of the Mercer family.

"Hi, Duncan." She stood up straight and looked up at him with a nostalgic feeling of supremacy.

"Hey Sophie, You two have a good run?" He asked.

Amy walked by, glistening with sweat. "The only thing I ran was out of breath."

"Would you stop trying to kill my wife with your exercise? Think of the children, Sophie," Duncan pleaded.

She looked back at Franklin climbing into the large four-by-four where Jenny was already sitting patiently. Hands on her hips, Sophie followed Amy inside.

"I'll see you tomorrow, Dun," she smiled back at him. Morning was the busiest part of their family schedule. There was little time to talk and catch up. Not that there was much to tell every day.

Sophie enjoyed what little she saw of them then changed and left for work. It had become part of their morning schedule when Amy had taken to running as part of a New Year's resolution. As a result, Sophie's runs had become sluggish. She didn't think she would be able to accommodate Amy in such a significant (and private) part of her life. It came as a pleasant surprise when she started enjoying them in a whole new way, and getting to see her beautiful nephews each morning was a bonus. Their part in her life had become increasingly significant since then. She never imagined that she would get so involved.

She had been welcomed as part of the family over the past few months. What she couldn't figure out was why she was enjoying it so much. She traced it back to work. She had become lost without genuine stimulation. Nowhere to go and no major purpose to fulfil. Now with both of those revitalized by family, she almost didn't want the quiet to end.

Sophie knew it would end. Sooner or later, something was going to stir it up again, and everyone at the CIA would return from their monotonous tasks to the world where nothing existed.

Every morning was like Sunday morning. The cogs turned lazily and the clocks ticked in their own time. The unseen energy that kept people moving was in drought. Offices that worked to the beat of ringing phones had lost their rhythm. The flow of intelligence had become stagnant, leaving a collective apprehension in its absence. The secrecy had lost its extraordinary status, but that was far from a downfall.

To the government, foreign intelligence was of great importance. Any and all information possessed value. Intelligence was the key to a functioning defence against potential threats. Secrecy and espionage advanced with anything that cast a shadow. The *Information Age* existed in an expanding digital city, under which a vast network of dark tunnels spread. Every day the city became the largest it had ever been. The Central Intelligence Agency existed in the ground, separating everything below from everything above. Only, they had reached the ends of the tunnels. The rats were scattered. This phenomenon could mean only one of two things:

The hidden world rests in an uneventful era…

…Or they cannot see the threat approaching.

Blissfully ignorant and untouched by concern, those excluded from the intelligence network made use of rare opportunities. The CIA still functioned but there was a slight lacking in operations being conducted. The time and resources that would be spent could then be reallocated. Funding was distributed well to all departments so that everyone could reap the rewards of their efforts. They were prepared. Should anyone challenge them, they would gladly demonstrate the full force of their improvements.

Sophie could feel herself almost looking forward to it. She didn't care how insensitive it sounded. She was excited to get back in the game. She pushed on the revolving glass door and entered the lobby of the CIA. It was a wide, open space like a hall, with a staircase to the left, and second-floor walkway around the inside. To the right, a path led past a series of offices until it reached a smaller open area. Apart from both entrances on the sides of the lobby, the only all-glass wall was one that ran along the far end of the smaller area. The rest of the open area was filled with desks, each with their own layout of folders, office supplies, and computer equipment. It all came into view as Sophie walked out of the hallway and into the open room. On the left were the more significant offices.

It had a new feeling to it. A new atmosphere, calm and dull. Sophie got to familiarize herself with the networks of hallways and offices over the past few months. Yet another part of her life to change. With the changes forcing more overly-extensive work, she found herself all around the building, with all kinds of other people. In the past, she only needed to know the other agents and officials in charge of her department. One of them was up ahead, Special Agent Bradford. He was leaning on a divider and looking over a desk. Once she got close, Sophie could see Agent Busher behind the divider. The two of them were only a little older than she but the difference in fitness certainly showed.

"Morning," she said behind Owen. He turned slightly to reply and Sophie could see the bags under his eyes were bigger than usual.

"Hey," Owen said in a dry and weak voice.

"Morning, Mercer," said Henry. He was in better condition but still showed the same symptoms.

"What happened to you guys?" She asked.

"Late night," said Henry.

"Not that late," Owen added.

"Drinking?" Sophie asked without hesitation.

Henry looked at Owen with the same expecting look as hers.

"So I'm on trial now? Shouldn't you be busy elsewhere?" Owen directed at Sophie.

"Shouldn't you?" She shot back.

"Bradford!" came a shout from behind him. Owen looked around and up. The head of department, Nathan Dawson, was looking down at them from the second floor walkway with his trademark scolding expression. The wrinkles in his face emphasized his look of repressed rage. He was bald apart from the dark grey hair that still grew around the sides and back of his head. Below the neck, he could be confused for Owen. Tall and slender with admirable strength. Dawson glared at them for another moment before turning away and returning to his office.

Owen knew what it meant. Sophie and Henry looked at him like school children watching an unlucky fellow classmate going to the principal's office. Owen could relate to the feeling as well. He gave Sophie a reprimanding look before making his way over to the stairs.

It wasn't as bad as it looked. Owen had known Dawson for a number of years longer than the others. He knew full well that Dawson was just an angry man by default. He was never really as angry as he looked or sounded. Owen estimated that – whatever his offense was – it was about as bad as leaving the front door unlocked.

Dawson had a corner office on the other side of the second floor. Owen saw him through the blinds. The outside of the office was glass but Dawson kept the blinds half closed at all times.

"Yes, sir?" Owen said as he walked in innocently. Dawson gestured to the chair opposite his desk. Owen sat down but Dawson remained standing with his hands on his hips.

"I'm glad to see that you're keeping busy, despite not having an assignment," said Dawson. Owen wanted to feel reassured but he knew there was no way he could stay sufficiently busy those days.

"So I guess you took it upon yourself to help the FBI? After all, there's nothing to do here, is there?" Dawson asked rhetorically.

Owen's innocent act caved. His offense had become apparent now. It was hard to detect the sarcasm in Dawson's deep, aged voice, but it was there.

"Do I really have to tell you again, Owen? Leave that case alone. If you want to take part in it then join the damn FBI! But stop using our resources for your own investigations!" Dawson finished and sat opposite him.

Owen had nothing to say in his defence so he just sat quietly and sighed with a blank, defeated expression.

"Owen, you got excused last time because it was still soon after her death. That was two years ago, there's no excuse now. I managed to keep you afloat after that incident in January by getting you therapy rather than fired. Am I wasting my time?" Dawson asked.

Owen's guilt felt worse with the truth behind it. "No, sir," he lied.

"I can't keep covering for you. I could suspend you but there's not much to suspend you from. Owen," Dawson looked at him earnestly "I need your head to be with us, here on earth. Let the FBI do their jobs."

They sat in silence for a moment as Owen thought about how Dawson could have found out. He had covered his tracks, left no obvious evidence. Dawson must have assumed the connection. With years of experience and Owen's history, he must have been looking for it.

They both knew that letting the FBI do their jobs wasn't going to help anyone. If they couldn't find the killers after two years then there was almost no chance of the case ever being concluded. Owen would have to live alone, unmarried, without knowing who or what or why. No explanation. No justice.

Dawson spoke up before the thought could properly land in Owens mind.

"You know, it's funny, I heard the FBI's going cold as well," he said.

"Really?" Owen asked. He wasn't sure how felt about it.

Dawson looked mildly surprised. "I don't get it. Dead ends on everything? I mean the North Koreans look pretty antagonizing..." said Owen. He hoped the joke would lift the weight of the mood in the room.

Dawson gave a light shrug.

"They're not just keeping more secrets from us?" Owen asked.

"Careful, Bradford. You sound like you're about to ask questions up the ladder. And you know if you ask questions up the ladder-"

"-You're only going to get a load of shit in return, I know, but its possi-" Owen was cut off by the ringing of Dawson's phone.

"Go on, get the hell out of here," Dawson said, dismissing Owen with a limp wave of his hand as he picked up the phone. "Hello?" He answered.

Owen walked past the office window and out of sight.

"*Hi, Mr Dawson?*" Asked the caller. A young man. Not a voice that he recognized.

"Yes this is Special Agent Dawson, what's this about?" He asked.

"*Ok, uumm, my name is Mark, I'm from a technical support team, FBI. We just want to ask you about a man by the name of Jacob Henley,*" said Mark.

"Never heard of him," Dawson said abruptly.

"*Ok, well, umm, we found records on his phone. He made calls to you, to the CIA that is, this morning at around seven-forty. Do you know anything about that?*" Mark asked timidly.

"Why the hell would I know anything about that. You think every call goes through my phone first? What's so important about this guy?" Dawson asked.

"Well, he was shot and killed shortly after. He made outgoing calls to the police, us at the FBI, and you," said Mark.

Dawson paused for a moment. Strange as it was, the man was likely desperate for help and decided to call every kind of law enforcement office he could think of. "So? He was probably just scared and desperate. We get a lot of those kinds phoning us."

"*He was shot twice by a sniper from over seventy yards. Cops were on the scene. They saw the whole thing,*"

Dawson leaned forward in his chair. He was a little more interested but only in one specific detail: If the police were already on their way, why would he still call the Feds as well? "Where did this happen?" He asked.

"*Just outside Chicago,*" said Mark.

The fleeting potential that it was as important as the Feds thought motivated Dawson to act out of professional courtesy.

"I will see what contact he made and if anything stands out then I will have someone send it over," he said.

"*Umm, ok thank you, bye,*" said Mark, hanging up the call.

Dawson thought for a moment. He was certain that it would not concern him. It was in federal territory after all. Anything within the United States was their business. Nevertheless, if he could help, he should, and with that in mind he made another call.

For once, they didn't waste his time. Somehow he had said the name too many times and it had summoned them. Whoever put the Feds through to him had not done so with the express purpose of pissing him off. For once, he was bothered with something that actually might bear some significance.

Dawson saw the breakroom beyond some pillars at the end of the hallway. The clean white walls lit up the room with natural light coming from the windows on the other side. Haw saw Grace Credette by the coffee machine. A short, stout woman with shoulder-length hair falling down either side of her round face. As usual, her suit looked half a size too small.

"Miss Credette," Dawson said to announce his presence.

She shot a sideward glance at him from under her curtain of dark brown hair. "Hello, Nathan. What is it you wanted to tell me?" She asked with an aged and husky voice.

"It's about that guy this morning. I went down to I.T. - he made one call to us at seven thirty this morning," Dawson said, leaning against a pillar.

"Oh yes, anything interesting?" She asked without looking up from the machine.

"Yes, actually," Dawson said in a low voice.

She turned to him with her coffee in hand.

"He wasn't asking for help. Apparently he sounded like he was trying to warn us of something," said Dawson.

"Warn us of what? Why wasn't this flagged?" Grace asked.

Dawson shrugged. "He sounded very out of breath. Kept going on about someone 'coming back', it was hard to understand him. Some, uuh, well 'they'. He just said 'they'. Then the call ended suddenly. No trace, nowhere to go from there," he finished.

Grace looked at him curiously. She pursed her lips and stepped forward. "So he was being chased?" She proposed.

"Maybe, he made the same kind of call to the Feds, but not to the cops. Chicago P.D. claims he spoke only of someone trying to kill him, no warning of any kind," said Dawson.

"You think they killed him so he wouldn't talk?" Asked Grace, her look of curiosity returning to normal.

"Whatever he was trying to say was directed at us and the Feds, and was valuable enough to get him shot - out in public - right in front of the cops. Not by any gang, by an assassin, and a good one at that." Dawson sounded more convinced the more he spoke.

Grace appeared to be considering it. What he said made sense but it was yet to be confirmed. He continued to look at Grace as she thought about it. He knew she would likely trust him because of his record and their good history, so it came as no surprise when she arrived at the same conclusion that he did.

"Keep an eye on it, make sure the FBI updates you on any breakthroughs in the case. Chances are it's not as bad as we think, *but*, we shouldn't make assumptions. That man died for something, we should take that seriously," said Grace.

Dawson nodded in agreement. He looked sullen, or normal to anyone that knew him. Grace started down the hall to her office, followed by Dawson.

"First decent lead in weeks and it goes to the Feds," he said gruffly. "My agents are restless. They're looking for trouble on the news."

"They should be careful what they wish for," Grace said in a half laugh. "You know, we caught sight of something in China. An item of value, a tape, resurfaced recently. I think it was one of your old cases," she said as she reached her office door. "If it comes up again and I need one of your agents, I'll give you a call."

"Please do," said Dawson. "God forbid they should be put to work."

Chapter IV
And Into the Light
Cape Town, Western Cape, South Africa
11:28 SAST, Wednesday, 18th May 2016
(28 days later)

 A calming warmth rested over the city. The south-east breeze mercifully lifted heat from the ground. Clouds spilt over the edge of Table Mountain like a slow avalanche of pure white powder, vanishing into dry air. A constant flow of cars funnelled into the streets, diverging from the motorway like capillaries pumping life into the surrounding buildings. Traffic moved with the beating heart of the city. Endless queues of cars in the streets drifted by after so long waiting and melting on the hot tar. The ocean stretched in a wide arc of beaches leading away from the city. The same weightless sunlight pressed down on it all. The city breathed, slow and steady, unsuspecting.

 White pillars and walls glowed in defence against the unrelenting sun. Windows with red-brick frames yielded to white rays that diffracted into the hallways and offices of the Houses of Parliament. Men and women walked past each other with their own unique destinations and purposes. Guards stood idle at their posts. Some sat at desks outside the main hall, listening to the suppressed litany of political debates coming from behind the tall oak doors.

 Outside, a boy ran across the grass. His eyes darted to either side of the building. He shook the can he held and a ball bearing rattled against the insides. He was forced to squint in front of the great white wall. His dark complexion exposed him against it. Taking the cap off the can, he looked around once more to check for any sign of life. He was alone. The wall had plenty of space to complete the project. He reached up above his face and started spraying.

Elsewhere, a regular four-door sedan broke from the traffic and charged at a police station. People walking nearby watched helplessly as the car broke through the gate and rebuilt momentum for the front doors. Glass windows and steel frames shattered and warped against the bonnet. The officers inside jerked aside from the sound of falling glass. Tires screeched with a piercing pitch against the floor. The vehicle stopped in the centre of the reception. The tips of four assault rifles peaked out of the opening doors.

Two heavy-duty vans drove over the broken gate and parked with their sides facing the building. A third van pulled away from traffic and scratched against the outside fence until it blocked the entrance. Two more did the same at the side entrance. A small army swarmed from the vehicles and surrounded the building, taking up assault positions behind the vans. They were covered from head to toe in military-grade, pale desert gear with matte-black paintball masks to match their M16A4 assault rifles.

Further away, the Ysterplaat Air Force base was suffering an amplified assault. The militia pressed the attack on all sides using vehicles for cover. They took their positions around the main buildings and blocked all exits.

Multiple other police stations mobilized into defensive positions. They armed themselves with shaking hands and took aim at the attackers through doorways and windows. At the Air Force base, one man from the militia took aim with an RPG and fired. A sound like a high-pressure firework filled the area as the rocket screamed forward and lit up the first tandem-rotor helicopter. The subsequent explosion boomed across the grounds sending a cloud of smoke up from its expanding flames.

The air was then filled with a series of suppressing shots fired at the entrances of the buildings, sounding low and metallic, familiar yet unfriendly. Lead rained sideways forcing the occupants to press against the walls for cover. A few members of the militia in each assault broke away and began setting up their defences. Metal barricades from the vans were unfolded and placed around them. Blockades at the entrances were reinforced with beams that anchored the vehicles in place.

Officers inside the stations winced at the cacophony of high calibre gunshots. Then a new sound took over at the Air Force base. An M2 Browning, set up by a barricade, started putting dents into the walls of the main building. The force of the bullets shattered the brick, blowing rubble and dust across the firefight.

Fleeting hope drained down crackling lines as the military's communications were scrambled. They pressed against the walls, gripping their rifles, yielding to the concussive force of the militia's besiegement. The smell of sour smoke filled their lungs as burnt gunpowder was caught and carried by the breeze. They were stuck in their selected positions, crouching beneath the lethal wind. They soon reached an equilibrium between return fire and overpowering onslaught. The militias slowed their rate of fire after sufficiently subjugating the buildings and their occupants. They conserved ammunition but punished retaliation. Each assault party held their ground with intention to stay.

The tranquillity was broken by motion outside the window. A boy was running across the grass towards the edge of the grounds. The security guard's mild concern tripled as a ladder was lifted and angled over the fence. He watched with wide, unblinking eyes as the boy climbed over and vanished into a passing bakkie. In a matter of seconds, they were gone.

The guard grabbed his two-way radio as he ran. His adrenaline slowed when he reached the double doors but before he could grab the handle, the doors exploded and blew him back into the opposite wall. Smoke gushed over his body from the splintered doorway. The explosion rang through the halls, drawing eyes and ears to the source. The nearest security guards came sprinting to the scene where a few workers were still staring at the destruction. The echo continued to spread and bounce off the walls to every end of the building.

Workers evacuated the scene while guards took aim at the smoke from the front and sides. The hallway burst into life with a barrage of shots from beyond the smoky doorway. The guards instantly began to spasm and recoil from the force of lead puncturing their torsos. Spikes of smoke protruded from the cloud following the paths of the bullets. Then the firing came to a sudden stop. Dark, desert-beige silhouettes swam in the restless cloud: military-grade outfits, matte-black gas masks, M16A4 assault rifles with grenade launcher attachments, and steady aims. They advanced from the doorway, two on either side kneeling with their sights toward the left and right hallways. The rest moved with a collective momentum down the centre.

Any flash of motion ahead was subdued with shots from the two leading gunmen. The shots were far louder in the hallway. They morphed into reverberating pops that dominated all other sounds. Everyone behind the first four gunmen would stop and crouch against the walls on either side. They lowered their rifles, watched, and waited. Once the four front-men reached the two open doors at the end of the 30-metre hallway, they came under fire from guards inside and jumped to either side of the door. The shots scratched the rough surfaces of their vests. The two men closest to the doorframe whipped their rifles inside to return fire. Here, both forces met equally hard. Then the back end of the hallway turned cold.

The silence behind the militia grew louder. They kept their eyes forward and centred their aim, feeling a tingle in their spines. The hair on the backs of their necks stood up. The scene went still. The guards, the militia, everything froze in anticipation. A shadow appeared in the clouded doorway, growing taller and wider. The smoke stretched out as *he* broke from the cloud. A 1.84-metre tall, smooth, pure black figure with glints of steel underneath.

The air pressure in the hallway seemed to increase. The lights appeared dimmer as details of the custom attire came into view. His one-piece outfit was tight against the defined curves of his muscles, yet he moved without resistance. Besides the silver of metal pieces, the outfit was violent-black with thin purple lines that lightly detailed it from top to bottom, decorating him with tribal graphics that curved and swirled, into sharp, wavy patterns.

His open overcoat ran from the top corners of the lapel to the outer ends of his collar bones and up to the peak of his hood. Inside the sloping triangle of the hood, darkness gave birth to a thick mask that covered everything below his eyes. Long tears in the mask ventilated air through thin wire grids, forming a crooked smile of jagged columns side-by-side to each ear. Light, metal pads on his knees and elbows stretched away from the rest of the material to allow full articulation. Two military-grade knives in holsters hugged the sides of his calves, above which were two black pistols in thigh holsters. Two more pistols gleamed with an aged and scratched platinum finish beneath his coat. Above the mask, two bright-green eyes locked onto the far end of the hallway. His pupils dilated and his expression grew with sinister desire.

Weighted steps marched with low, metallic springing sounds. He walked with a mild limp, as though his left leg was slightly heavier. He advanced to a man in the middle of the hallway on his right. Eyes remaining locked on the targets ahead, he glided forwards. The man put his rifle down and produced a long metal staff from the side of his backpack. It was dark grey, titanium, with long rubber grips from both ends meeting a hexagonal block in the middle. On the end, bolted into the cubic head, was a large, double axe with half-meter long curved blades. *Divider.*

The man held Divider, handle up, out to *him*. The immense weight was lifted as *he* took it swiftly in his stride.

The game is speed. You need not outrun time, only your enemy.

He accelerated toward the open doorway where his men and the local security met in a stalemate. The men standing on either side saw him approaching and swung around for covering fire. One man used his rifle's grenade launcher to arc a flash grenade into the middle of the room. The guards were stunned by the flash of bright white and tensed up behind pillars and desks. Shockwaves from the gunfire deflected off *him* as he passed through the doorway.

The first guard watched the others recover around the room. Then a sudden quiet granted him the opportunity to peer around the column. A gleam of silver swung in a wide arc speeding towards his head. The column exploded from the destructive impetus of Divider. Concrete shattered across the side of his face. The metal rods inside the pillar had split, letting the blade continue to force its way into the side of his cranium. Blood, skull, and powder all made an equal arc in the wake of the blade being pulled free. The rest of the guard's head swung away as he pirouetted and fell to the ground sending a chilling crack echoing through the hall.

Using the axe's momentum, *he* swung it around, ready for another go. The rest of the guards had recovered and were looking for an opportunity to counter. The militia moved in behind *him* and killed off those opportunities with more covering fire. Dragging Divider behind, *he* swung it clockwise into a pillar on his right. The guard standing there had no time to react. The blade split through his vest, under his ribs, and broke through his spine before becoming embedded in the concrete. Without stopping, *he* kicked the upper handle with his right boot to eject it from the wall.

Any attempt to counter made by the remaining the guards was shut down by the supporting militia. Two of them were shot down for revealing themselves, however, their final return fire came uncomfortably close, hitting two members of the militia. The last living security were those behind the desks at the end of the hall. Bright green eyes surveyed them. They could feel his hot gaze through the wood. The silence was louder than ever. They could almost feel him getting closer.

An uncomfortable screeching began to approach them steadily. *He* had crouched low and was dragging Divider over the tiled floor. The screeching whipped into a higher pitch before silence took hold of the room once more. Then a deep whistle fell through a desk and split it apart. The blade narrowly missed a guard underneath. The wood splintered and sprayed over him. Divider retreated slowly for another go. The guard's guns clattered against the floor. Shaking hands rose, followed by heads and shoulders. Their eyes were closed, their faces contorted with fear. Tense with apprehension, they awaited execution with tears in their eyes. All four of them winced when the militia grabbed their hands and bound them with thick zip ties. Their eyes were then covered and their mouths sealed with duct tape.

At several other entrances of the building, militia walked over the security in minutes and made their way further inward. Like a starting pistol, the first explosion was followed by the rest in almost perfect synchronization. Half of the explosive breaches were found to be vacant. Decoys meant to weaken security responses sent guards in all directions. Having arrived before most of the workers that morning, the militia were glad to escape their hiding places. There would be no more hiding. It was time to give the world something new to fear.

A pair of guards heard shots and explosions ahead of the surveillance room. They pulled a pair of bolt cutters and a small explosive charge from a duffel bag, then placed the charge on the centre of the wall and backed away. The detonation rang in their ears. Past the smoke, they saw the cables in the hole and used the bolt cutters on each one in turn.

The monitors inside the surveillance room went black while the security guards watching them struggled against the blocked exit. A sudden heavy crack made them jump away from the door. They looked in confusion, watching a tall blade retreated into the void on the other side.

Going to the control room first forced *him* to stray from the main target, but removing Parliament's ability to call for help bought them a lot more time to deal with only the minimal amount of security forces. So with units moving in from every direction, he could take an obscure route down the path of least resistance. The faster they moved, the easier it would be. They had to maintain the element of surprise - at this point shock - for as long as they could. He checked the watch on the inside of his left wrist: They had four minutes and seventeen seconds to reach the next checkpoint.

After too few opportunities to wield Divider, he threw it past a guard hiding behind a corner where it became embedded in the wall. In the moment of distraction, *he* broke into a run and delivered a rib-cracking knee to the centre of the guard's chest. A pistol lolled in the guard's hand, so *he* gave it a hard kick and wrenched Divider from the wall. Then he let his arm fall under its weight. Retracting his bloodthirst he only knocked the man unconscious with the flat sides of the blades, but later… later he could do anything he wanted. The thought floated in his mind. He remained stationary, staring into space. Some of his men watched him stand unnervingly still over the unconscious man as if a demon that possessed him had left and gone elsewhere. But he was only waiting. They were ahead of schedule. Timing had to be resynchronized.

"Sir," one of them called. His mind must have drifted back into reality because he looked around slowly and curiously. Then he turned his torso, revealing the broadness of his shoulders. The path ahead was empty so he strode forward without hesitation. He was still limping, but it didn't hinder his speed. They could hear him ahead by the springing sound in his strides.

All the units reached their next checkpoints simultaneously. They immediately set up blockades at their preselected positions. Chain-locked door handles, barricades, and some men even set sections of the building alight with petrol and oil. The oil was to prevent the fire from being put out with water. The extinguishers were then taken from the area and thrown into a room, out of reach. A circle was forming around the target centre of the building like an arena. The predator had boxed in its prey.

They fell back into synch as they converged on the main hall. There was no slowing and no accelerating. They moved at a sufficient pace between fast-walking and jogging. They identified each other in the halls by the desert colour and personalized paintball masks. It reassured them to see each other pass by. It meant that every second was going according to plan. Delays had been accounted for and were eliminated within the allocated time. No one was surprised when they all reached the central checkpoint at once.

He was looking down at his watch, standing as still as a cast iron statue.   "Sir, the funnel is ready," said one man.

He looked up, in front of him was the entrance to the main hall. It was almost time. The next phase was going to start soon. Right on time – when it was time.

He stared at the great oak doors, admiring the craftsmanship one last time. He was listening to the clicks of assault rifles being reloaded behind him when the calm of his focus was disturbed by the muffled cries of a woman. Without looking at her, he turned and walked to where she was sitting. A dozen soulless masks followed his motion across the room. He walked slowly. His heavy boots echoed in the tall room.

She could hear a metallic spring stretch as he knelt down beside her. His bright green eyes met with hers. She made no sound through the duct-tape but could not control her shaking breath. He took his right hand and – with a lover's touch - stroked the side of her face. Too afraid to move away, she turned her eyes from his burning gaze. The feel of his fingerless glove was warm and wet against her skin. The stroke of his fingertips as soft as the rays of a setting sun. He ran his fingers slowly and gently to the tip of her chin, leaving four red smears

...er pale cheek.

She began to feel her heart slow and her muscles relax. She was no longer breathing quickly. Following the lead of his fingers under her chin, her head leaned forward from the wall behind her. Then with a single quick thrust, he gripped her throat beneath her jawbone and slammed her head against the wall. Her head lolled over his hand as he withdrew it just as slowly and gently as before.

He rose to full height, his back straight, and gave the pointing indication with two fingers to the door. His men began to mobilize, then he turned his left wrist over.

There was nowhere to look. Worried faces scanned their surroundings. Hundreds of politicians were glued to their seats or cowering under their desks. Trapped in a bowl. The main hall was shaped like an oval lecture theatre. The second floor was identical but ended halfway to the centre of the room. Forest green carpets and neat, dark wood desks circled in layers around the hall. Everyone fell quiet when the gunshots got near enough to hear. Without knowing what else to do, the security teams took defensive positions at the entrances. The President's Close Protection Unit surrounded him. Everyone else could only watch, only wait for the threat – whatever it may be – to show itself.

It started with a thud. Loud, metal on wood, at the main entrance's double doors. Every pair of eyes looked around to the source of the sound. Then another thud. Many of the women wailed and ducked behind the desks. The third thud made the second floor of the left wing jump. It came from their door. Then another from the right wing ground floor. One by one, every entrance was hit hard, except for one of the emergency exits. The thuds stopped suddenly. Then it was drumming. It didn't sound like drums, it was still metal on wood, but there was a beat. One every two seconds, then one every second and getting faster. The thuds got harder and started cracking doors. Once it got fast, nobody was left on their seats. Everyone was shaking beneath their desks. The entrances shook on their hinges as violent thuds and crashes came from the other sides. Then it stopped, all at once. Security took aim at the doorways. The Close Protection Unit guided the President over to the untouched exit with their pistols at the ready. Fearful apprehension took over the hall. All they could do was wait for the silence to end.

      He watched, patiently unmoving, at the motion of the big hand.
    Tick-tick-tick-tick-
    The entrances exploded in a single collective *boom* that continued to ring in everyone's ears. Smoke flooded the hall from the blasts. It floated in past the doorways remaining too thick to see through. The guards that recovered fastest opened fire into the nearest clouds. The Close Protection Unit couldn't hear each other over the gunshots. They opened the exit and began running the President to safety.
    Something stirred at the main entrance. The double doors hung loosely on their hinges. The flow of smoke had stopped. A wide rectangular shape was only visible because of the effect it had on the smoke it passed through. Before it could emerge into full view, guards turned their fire at it from all directions. The shape had only just made it through the doorway and the glass was already cracked. But it didn't break. Painted on the bullet-proof glass, splintered with gunshots, was a face.

Red, smiling, and ever so innocent. A simple face that became less and less visible.

The back-to-back shields of glass were not meant to last the entire fight, only long enough to reveal the positions of the guards for the rest of the breaching party. At the opportune moment, the rest of the militia poured in from the entrances and began eliminating the security teams. Bright flashes and gunshots gave away the positions of all guards still shooting at the main entrance. Most of them were shot and collapsed within seconds. They lived for only a few more moments in the chaos. Blood soaked into the carpets and spilt over the railing of the second floor. Those who lived long enough to moan and cry out in pain were found and terminated. The hall erupted with painfully loud firefights, and at the centre of it all, *he* stood, indifferent.

He walked leisurely through the smoke and chaos, taking in the fresh smell of gunpowder. Divider cut a trail in the carpet behind him. Swinging it up to the right, *he* left a guard's head with a fine split in the side. The sound of cracking skull barely breached the surface of the gunshots. Spinning to *his* left, the blade got stuck in the back of a guard's neck, forcing *him* to step on the corpse's shoulder to pry it free. With each whistling swing, Divider would spray an arc of blood, painting red curves across the carpet. Finally, he dragged the axe over to the politicians cowering in the far corner. He scanned them and selected his targets. Then he reached out with a damp red hand. Slowly, it got closer to them, and slowly, they recoiled. His eyes shined with desire. The ecstasy of power. He savoured the moment and pulled some of them aside for execution.

The last of the guards gurgled from drowning in their own blood. Only a few of the militia were lost. Those that were injured were pulled from the fight and taken away for medical attention. Then the focus turned to the politicians. A select few were collected from around the hall and lined up in the centre. Those too afraid to move were killed by impromptu firing squad. The runners would kill themselves faster by provoking the grand swing of Divider. Two targets remained. One had not left the hall.

He walked up the green steps on one side. Divider left a glistening red river.

The Defence Minister crawled to the end of the row. The frequency of gunshots had died down but he would not look until they had stopped completely. *'Please!'* he begged in his mind, the air could not escape his lungs, *'please God, help me, please God.'* He kept his whimpering as quiet as he could. Then there was a thud behind him. He froze. Then there was another. He kept his head down and stared at the green of the carpet beneath his face. He felt that he couldn't move any further, his own body had given up. He turned over, shaking violently. His neck was soaked with sweat. *'Please God, let there be nothing, please God, please God.'*

The figure looked down at him. Tall, pure black, and slender. Towering over him with a perfectly upright posture. *His* silhouette pulled light from around him, drawing it into darkest black the Minister had ever seen. The great width of *his* shoulders curved gracefully into his sides, where they expanded to each leg standing on the desks. In the shade, he could see two wide, green, predatory eyes staring down at him, watching. He tried to verbalize his begging but his throat closed up, leaving his lips to tremble soundlessly. The figure's arms rose to reveal a staff with two enormous curved blades. An executioner's axe. With some effort, the figure hoisted it over its shoulder. The sight of the dripping blades made the Minister's body produce a shot of adrenaline.

"W-w-we told you e-everything! WE DID W-WHAT YOU A-ASKED!" The plea faltered under *his* gaze and died at *his* feet. Desperation settled into the defence ministers bones. He turned and began to crawl hastily towards the end of the row. There was a whistling behind him, then a crash of wood as the desk splintered across his legs. He felt a sharp, stabbing pain cut into his calves. He managed to crawl halfway onto the stairs whilst crying out in agony. Then the wind came rushing into his lungs as the weight was lifted from his chest. Without clemency, the figure lifted him and flung him down the stairs like a sandbag. He landed with new sources of pain rising from multiple parts of his body. The air that filled his lungs ejected with spittle and blood that oozed onto the floor. He struggled to lift his face. All movement was resisted by the throbbing in his joints.

The Axe balanced upright on *his* hands. It was difficult to keep it standing. The weight alone was too much. Feeling it become unstable, *he* angled it to fall forward. The bottom of the handle left his hands and the blade fell onto the centre of the Minister's back between his shoulder blades. Creases in *his* cheeks spread to each end of his face and peaked over his mask.
A little fun never hurt anybody.
It was over, but time was still going. He checked his watch and made his way towards the funnel; the exit that they left for the President's 'escape'.
"Sir, they've trapped the President at the next checkpoint but reinforcements have broken through the barricades. He won't be around for much longer," said a man following on his right. Their window was thinning. He handed Divider to the man, then signalled for the others to follow him. He looked

around for the man with the yellow mask and signalled for him to come as well. The man hesitated but did as he was instructed.

They followed *him* out. The rest of the politicians were tied and gagged. Many of the guards had panicked and fled. Within the confines of the blockades, they surrendered upon being found.

The next checkpoint was alive with firefights. As ordered, they did not shoot to kill, only to delay. Reinforcements made loops outside the blockades, rerouted to long and unfamiliar paths where they became lost and helpless. A single elite task force had broken through the blockades and was closing in.

He heard them beyond the door ahead and took out his pistols. In his right hand, a standard IMI Desert Eagle handgun. Black and red with a length that gave it an oversized quality. In his left was something unique. Similar in design yet larger, longer, and packed with metallic muscle.

His focus locked. Distant gunshots sounded further away. Time slowed to a manageable pace. The task force was advancing in the hallway, just on the other side. The door was thin, the walls were not. There were five – six – seven – eight stepping feet on the other side. Eight unsuspecting victims. Eight beating hearts.

He waited until the last man reached the door and synchronized aim with focus. His arm remained parallel to the ground. He turned side on with his back straight. The first shot of the Desert Eagle blew the silence away. Through the hole in the door, he could see a spray of blood on the opposing wall. He repositioned and took aim before anyone could react. Shouts from the squad were dominated by the following three shots as *he* moved to the right. From his angle, he could shoot through the door with maximum cover. The back two men were hit and fell away. *He* moved up against the wall and signalled one of his arriving men to throw a flash grenade. The task force watch it hit the opposing wall and bounce on the floor in front of them. Then there was white. They rubbed at the feeling of needles in their eyes as their paper-white vision decayed back into focus.

He stepped through the doorway, mega-pistol in hand, and took aim at the line of dazed heads. The shot was like a cannon blast. The gun recoiled over his own head. The first man's helmet exploded with blood, plastic, and bone. The second man was blasted into the third, who immediately went limp. The three of them fell like dominoes onto the two men at the end. Two subsequent shots from the Desert Eagle left two red splatters behind them both. The militia didn't need to stop. It was over before they passed through the doorway.

Time resumed its regular pace. The final act was ahead. His men followed and they approached the scene. The familiar sounds of bangs, cracks, and snaps grew louder when they saw the firefight over the edge of the second-floor railing. The floor below was covered with pools of red and sprinkles of smoking cartridges.

There was no hesitation, no slowing down, only speed. He broke into a run and kicked off from the railing towards the nearest target. With practised precision, he fell and spun his weight around the man's neck. The victim's head twisted as two jet-black arms gripped it like pythons, then his body collapsed and folded under the weight.

With his arms still folded around the guard's neck, *he* gripped the pistols from his thigh holsters. He slid them out letting the man fall to the ground at his feet and began relentlessly eliminating the closest threats. His arms remained parallel to the ground. His back remained straight.

Always moving, never hesitating. Each shot was less

than a second apart. No bullet went astray. The room shook with the boom of the hand-cannon, which nearly struck back at him from its own force.

He continued forward looking for the target but his ephemeral assault left the room empty. Many of the bodies were his own men. They could not be saved. The magazines fell from his raised pistols and were replaced.

"He's gone! That way, to the parking bays!" One man said, pointing to the hallway on the right. To maintain speed, direction would have to change.

A new phase was in effect. A small collection of guards stood between the predator and his prey. There could be no delays.

Smoke grenades landed at the end of a hallway. A dozen barrels monitored the growing cloud. *He* took back the element of surprise for his men by flanking.

Two hits to the first guard's face in under a second. Then a swipe of a knife and the second guard fell to his knees. *He* avoided the blood squirting from the dying man's neck and stole the position of cover. The rest of his men were fighting their way into the hall from either side of him. He counted two possible exits and kept track of his distance from both. The man with the yellow mask was ahead; he could not be allowed to die.

Without hesitation, *he* broke into a run. Right shoulder first to fire ahead with his left side reserved for close quarters. Any potential threats were blown away by either the power of the Desert Eagle or a well-placed fist. In the time it took for the guards to aim at him, he would flick his wrist and fire first. Headshots only. But he kept moving, avoiding the guards' shots by returning fire and ducking into a room.

He counted every shot. Once his magazine was empty there was no time to reload, so he put the gun away and switched to using his bare hands. The steel mould in the knuckles of his gloves tore through the already weakened material with every punch. Bloodlust drove him to overtake his men. He reached the end and retreated to a man on the right. He then took three grenades from the man's belt and pulled all three pins out at once. One grenade to the end of the hall, one around the left corner, and one ahead of the man with the yellow mask. Just far enough not to kill him. The blast knocked the man back where his head was struck hard into the wall by *his* thick, black forearm. The yellow mask cracked and fell with its unconscious owner. One of the other men produced a syringe and injected him for good measure.

Everyone else watched the rise and fall of undulating black shoulders, of *his* deep and powerful breaths. His face was spotted with blood. It ran from the tears of his mask in lines. The metal moulds over his knuckles were exposed through the torn material. The black of his gloves had a maroon hue where more blood drained down the backs of his hands. It dripped and flowed from the tips of his knuckles and fingers. He stared into space once more, inserting a new magazine into the Desert Eagle. Then he listened.

At the parking bays, security struggled against the attacking forces. Some of their own men had blocked them off with obstacles. The President made it to the *Evac* cars alive but at great cost. None of the attackers took shots at him. By request; no-one was willing to take the heat for such a high-profile kill, but they pressed the assault none the less. The President's car was dented and shot but made it out, only to be met by a great blockade of cars and trucks that forced it to turn right, parallel to the Parliament building.

After being told that the target had reached his vehicle, *he* clenched his fists, squeezing out more blood. Then he turned and stormed away without further hesitation. He reached the end of the hallway at full speed, pulled himself up the stairs to go faster, turned right, and ran alongside the windows to where his contingency unit stood at the ready. They retreated from his powerful gaze. The pressure in the room felt strong. Divider was being held out by one of the men. *He* took it and swung at one of the windows. Without stopping he broke through the rest of the shattered glass and dragged the axe behind him.

Outside was an open balcony decorated with chairs, tables, and various potted plants. He ploughed through them like a ship breaking through ice, sending furniture skidding aside. Divider carved a line in the concrete as he dragged it towards the end of the balcony. Over the edge, two floors down, he could see his riskiest opportunity. Speeding once more into a run, he held the handle of Divider firmly. By using his diaphragm he forced his breath under control. He kicked off the railing while using what strength he had to swing the axe up and behind himself. His body curled into a D-shape against the long handle as he descended to the road below. His arms could not bend any further back. Gripping the handle with both hands, he swung Divider back over his head in a great arc where it crunched into the front of a moving car.

The blade cut through the metal like dough and split into the front tire. The axe was jerked from *his* hands so he tensed himself to roll with the force. The car swung right uncontrollably and collided with the side railing. At such a high speed, it concertinaed and rebounded hard, spraying debris in all directions before rolling twice and coming to an upright stop. Another car ahead screeched to a stop and four members of the Close Protection Unit made their way to the wreckage. The two cars that were following did the same.

He kept his focus on the target and stood up straight. His own blood now drained from the tears of his mask. Beaming green eyes locked onto the wreckage with a raging determination. It was the only car with the Presidential flags, both of which were lost in the carpet of glass and steel that snapped and crunched beneath *his* feet. There was a new limp in his stride that produced a stressed springing sound with each step.

The Contingency Units up on the balcony rained down on the two cars behind *him*. Using grenade launcher attachments, they nullified the use of the cars for cover.

He limped on, indifferent. Divider lay in wait between him and his prey. One of the axe's blades was torn and bent from contact with the speeding wheel. With one hand, he swooped the handle off the floor and began to drag it behind. With the other, he slid the Desert Eagle out of his thigh holster. A sequence of equally spaced shots suppressed the Protection Unit on the other side of the crash. They had moved from their vehicle into the open road. The punishment of such a mistake was death.

With no one left to slow him down, he holstered his pistol and reached his final target. The two security members in the front had streams of blood running down their motionless faces. In the back, the target was belted to his seat. Through the broken window, *he* could see it; the look in his victim's eyes that he loved so much. Such an important man, a President. So much effort, so much blood, so many lives dedicated to his protection. All to no avail. The president's lips quivered with blood from his nose. His wide eyes took in the tall, black figure that approached.

He hoisted the axe onto his shoulder, let it fall back, and gripped the bottom of the handle with both hands. Then with all his strength, he swung the undamaged blade for the last time in a round arc over his head. It tore through the top of the car and delivered the coup de grâce.

The road was empty by design, like the rest of the plan. Two four-wheel-drives pulled up beside him. He threw Divider into the back seats of one and took over as driver.

His men were retreating. Only one was left behind. Several common, commercial cars arrived on schedule around the outside of the Houses of Parliament. The exodus was swift and unchallenged. They vanished into the surrounding city. The life that flowed in the streets bled from the wound they left behind.

Red streaks continued to run down the walls of Parliament and gather in puddles on the floor. Bodies lay peacefully still. Smoke dissipated from the hallways. Gun barrels and cartridges began to cool.

Far away, police looked over the devastation. No casualties, but extensive damage to the stations. An uncountable number of bullet holes decorated the walls in pointillist styles. The Ysterplaat janitors would sweep empty cartridges into gleaming piles of brass. Soldiers and officers hung up their sweat-soaked vests and retired to the barracks.

People on the beaches looked in fearful wonder at the column of smoke that rose at an angle from the city.

Chapter V
The World's Stage
London, England
16:44 GMT, Friday, 20th May 2016
(*2 days later*)

Over the first forty-eight hours since the attack there had been no arrests. There were no suspects. With each passing hour the nations of the world grew restless and afraid, for with each passing hour, the new threat covered more distance in any direction it pleased. An expanding circle of possibility grew from Cape Town, covering more of the globe every second. In a world connected like never before, people still believed that distance was safety. It had been two days. The circle had covered the globe.

Chances of the terrorists going to England were greater than most. They could be anywhere – which meant the number of possibilities was at its max. But recent developments suggested they were a more likely target. They had no choice but to fall into the same pattern of security as the rest of the world. Systems were being put in place to try to look out for *him* and his small army. Airports, borders, and shipping ports were clamping down on the populous. Every available resource was now dedicated to search and security. They would not make it into the country - unless they already had.

Someone came asking enquiring long ago. Naturally, he was turned away, but recent events had created extenuating circumstances. In a case with no leads an answer presented itself to them. The investigation was a stone-cold dead end for the longest time. Then hundreds died in a matter of hours and the world was left with more questions than answers. The clock ticked in an infinite spiral with no end approaching.

Dennis was walking with haste. He hadn't looked up from his phone. The file in his other hand was thick with documents threatening to slide out at any moment. His suit was restricting but he barely noticed it.

Hopefully, the man himself could shed some light. The man who came enquiring. The idea was an oddity, but these were desperate times. Dennis got a text that the man was in a waiting room, so he made his way there. Stanley Martin saw him from his office and ran to catch up. Dennis' light-brown complexion and thin beard was instantly recognizable by anyone on that floor.

"Knight!" Stanley called after him.

Dennis glanced at him but didn't slow down. "I'm a little busy right now, Martin." Dennis could feel himself almost out of breath as he spoke, as though age itself was creeping into his body.

"We're running the search you ordered. You were half right, the Parker case does sort-of match that Israel Op," Stanley said quickly.

"Half is more than enough," Dennis said eagerly, "Keep looking."

Stanley gave him a nod and turned back. The case felt accelerated. Dennis slowed down as he reached the waiting room and scanned for a familiar yet unknown face among the seated. The man was sitting in the far corner of the room. He couldn't have been more than a couple of years younger than Dennis. He wore a stylish, pale grey suit. His hair was cut short and neat. He looked like he was staring into space but anyone could tell that he was deep in thought. Dennis walked over to him calmly.

"Mr Masier?" Dennis asked lightly. The man looked up

at him and stood up to his height.

"Yes, hello," said Masier. He sounded unsure of himself. Dennis could understand why; he hadn't exactly been told much about his summon.

"My name is Dennis Knight, I'm the one who called your office."

"Joel Masier, and you didn't call *my* office so why am I here?" Joel asked courteously.

"Your head of department said you were the best man on the investigations team."

"I *was,* until your guys took the case."

"Yes, and that's why I'm taking you as well." Dennis led Joel out of the waiting room and back the way he came.

"I'm guessing that's because you came to the same realization that I did," said Joel.

Dennis looked sideways at him expectantly.

"This case has been trying to be a dead end for a long time."

Dennis found himself pleasantly impressed. They were on the same page, so now they could move on at a better pace.

"Perhaps it's not dead any more. The attack in South Africa matches your descriptions. I was hoping you could tell me what you make of it," said Dennis.

"I take it you've read everything we had on the case?" Joel asked.

Dennis held up the thick folder. "Okay, then I'm going to need everything you have on the attack."

"You will," said Dennis "I want you to remain here as a consultant."

"Why? Everything I know is in that folder," said Joel.

"Because the Parker case has been an equally dead end for six months. There was just nothing to go on. Nobody else noticed this group and then two days ago they appear out of nowhere and dismantle a government," said Dennis. "Clearly we could use your help."

They stopped outside an office door. The nameplate read 'Operations Officer Dennis L. Knight'.

Joel looked like he was back in deep thought. "I can help. But I'm going to need everything you have, not just about the attack, but the Parker case as well. And you will want to check all other operations and investigations from the past two years. You may have encountered them before."

Dennis entered the office before Joel and immediately threw the file down before grabbing the phone on his desk. "I think we have. I'll get it all for you, but first I'm going to assign one of our own officers to you. She'll work with you while you're here." He dialled her work number as he spoke.

This was not how Joel expected the visit to go. After the frustration of losing his own case, he found himself working for MI6, consulting on his own investigation. Strange as it was, it felt right.

"You're right," Dennis said suddenly. "We need more information about the attack." He had just finished the call.

Joel was so caught up with processing the last few minutes that he didn't realize what was going on around him.

"If we find a link then maybe we can find out what they were doing here," said Dennis.

"You assume it's the same group of mercenaries," Joel replied absentmindedly.

"Isn't that what your investigation implies?"

"My investigation implies there is a group here just like

them. But yes, it seems likely that they are all the same," Joel admitted. "There will be tell-tale signs that give it awa-" Joel was cut off by a knock at the door.

"Come in!" Dennis called. The door opened and a slender women stepped in. She was younger. Joel had to look up at her slightly. She wore pale jeans with a white buttoned shirt tucked in. Joel noticed her eyes had the same chestnut-brown colour as her hair, which was long enough to reach the small of her back. She looked curiously from Dennis to Joel.

"Sir?" She asked simply.

"Cait this is Officer Joel Masier from MI5," said Dennis. He then turned to Joel, "Mr Masier, this is Caitlin Harper, one of our senior operatives."

"Just Joel is fine," he said as he shook her hand. The strength of her grip felt disproportionate to her size. She was muscular but still maintained a feminine physique.

"Ok, Joel, what's this about?" She asked. Her voice was smooth and sophisticated. Joel found it admirably intimidating.

"Well, Joel here was part of a team who were looking for a mercenary group operating across England," said Dennis. "That investigation is ours now." The phone on his desk rang and Dennis indicated to Joel to continue.

"Where did this group show up to make us take over?" Caitlin asked before he could start.

"South Africa," said Joel. He let it sink in while he took the file from the desk.

"The terrorist attack?" Caitlin asked with her eyebrows raised.

"Yes. They were here at least three months ago," said Joel.

"How do you know?" She asked.

"They killed a *lot* of people. Here, see for yourself." He

handed her the file and she began paging through it.

"And where do you fit into all this?" She looked up at him for a moment before concentrating hard on the file.

"I'm the one who put *that* together," he said firmly, pointing to the file in her hands. Confidence in his own laudable achievement made him defensive but Caitlin seemed unconcerned. "I started this investigation myself a couple of months ago, now I'm here as a consultant I guess. Apparently we're going to be working together," he said.

Caitlin reached a point in the file and her eyes widened. She flipped through the last pages with a puzzled expression. "There's nothing in here about connections to South Africa," she said.

"Not yet," Joel smiled.

Just when Dennis didn't think it could escalate any higher, he got a call. Arthur Euwin was leagues above him, above the department heads, above everyone. There was rumour he was a secretary of some kind. A secret advisor. Euwin was many things, most of them classified, so there was little to no reason for him to visit the Operations Department personally. Dennis had only spoken to him a few of times before, so when he saw the name on the landline, he was quick to pick up.

"Mr Euwin, how can I help you?"

"*Your new case, Mr Knight. I'm moving it up, it takes priority from now on. Tell me, what have you got so far?*" Euwin asked. The ascendency of his deep tone made Dennis' thoughts abandoned him.

"Well, the uuh, the case from MI5 has no more strings to pull on. There hasn't been a single lead in the case since it was started. But, there's bound to be something at the site of the attack. So far that's our only option," he said. There was barely a moment of silence before Euwin spoke again.

"Have officers sent to Cape Town to investigate the scene as soon as you can. I'll see to it that you get whatever you need," he said.

"Thank you. I also want to contact the States, I think we've encountered this group before while alongside the CIA. They may have information we need," said Dennis

"I see. With our limited knowledge, we need to explore all our options. A collaborative effort may be necessary," said Euwin, *"I'm going to bring in a detective to consult on the investigation. From what I've read we're going to need a psych profile on this 'Man in Black'."*

"Good idea, I have a couple of officers here with me who I want to-" Dennis stopped as soon as he heard Euwin's voice again.

"I want those officers in South Africa by tomorrow evening. From now on you report to me directly. I want updates on all developments as and when they happen. And let me know once you've made contact with the CIA," he said.

Dennis was taken aback again and forced to recollect his thoughts.

"I read the case file. This group has been right under our noses for years and we only found out that they exist two months ago. Now the whole world knows. They're in the spotlight on their own terms. They've entered the world's stage, showing everyone just how powerful they are. They went from background noise to the greatest terror threat in fifteen years, over the course of a day. If they were here before then they might come back, we cannot afford to let that happen," said Euwin.

"I understand, sir. I'll send my guys as soon as I can," Dennis replied. He heard the click of the call ending and looked up at Joel and Caitlin. They heard him mention them and were looking at him expectantly.

"You're going to South Africa. Tonight," he said.

"Yes-sir." Caitlin spoke out of military muscle-memory.

"What about me?" Joel asked.

"You're going as well," said Dennis. Joel looked at him with puzzled surprise. "Your record is good, and you're best equipped to figure this out. I want you there. Is that a problem?" Dennis asked.

"No... sir," Joel replied, and suddenly, everything faded into the past. MI5 became a distant memory like school or college. All became insignificant next to the responsibility that now lay ahead of him.

"Good. Now go, both of you. Be packed and ready to leave by tonight," said Dennis.

Caitlin left and Joel followed. They talked all the way to her office.

Dennis felt confident with his decision; Joel seemed dedicated. The fact that he started the investigation himself – and in his own time – made him a reputable and trustworthy representative.

Dennis picked up the phone again and used his computer to search for the right number. It was an old contact. One he hadn't used in almost a year. Typically he wouldn't be the one making the call, but given Euwin's instruction, he couldn't afford to wait. The phone rang a couple of times before Dennis recognized the same old gruff voice on the other end.

"*Hello?*" Dawson answered.

"Hi Nathan, its Dennis."

"*Dennis. It's great to hear from you again, what can I do*

for you?" Dawson asked. A familiar cheer lifted his voice into a friendlier pitch.

"What makes you think I need something?" Dennis teased.

"*This is the first time you've called in months and it's during work hours, I think. I hope. Come on, you have a request, something interesting. What is it?*" Dawson asked.

"Do you remember an operation we ran together back in twenty-fourteen? Rahat, Israel?" Dennis asked. He waited a moment as Dawson racked his brain.

"*Yes, what about it?*"

"It was a failed Op. Didn't amount to anything; we thought there could have been a third party but there was no trace of one," said Dennis.

"*Yeah it was a big mystery, where are you going with this Knight, get to the point.*" Dawson spoke with his typical pissed-off tone that was never really how it sounded.

"Alright look, it's still in the air but we're on to something new here. The terrorists in South Africa have shown up before, they've been around England for the last couple of years," said Dennis.

"*Why has nothing been done?*" Dawson asked seriously.

"We only found out a couple of months ago. MI5 had lost all their major cases to them. And it's not just here, I think we've encountered them abroad as well," said Dennis.

"*Rahat.*"

"There was a man there. Do you remember? Some local ringleader with a dark reputation." Dennis tried hard to remember the details but his memory was escaping him.

"*The Prince. In the hood,*" said Dawson. Suddenly the memory clicked into place.

"Yes! We have reason to believe that someone of his

description is at the head of this terrorist group, and if they were in Rahat they could have been anywhere," said Dennis.

"You think I might have met them before as well? They don't exactly sound familiar," said Dawson.

"I know, that's how they've stayed under the radar for so long. They're practically untraceable. And if I'm right then you have met them before in Rahat. We both have. I know how it sounds-"

"I understand. It's a long shot but on the off chance we've encountered them before then it would be in our best interest to work it together. I'll look into it and get back to you." Dawson spoke with an unusually supportive spirit.

"Great, I'll send you some details to help with the search," said Dennis.

"Thanks, I'll keep you posted," said Dawson.

After the call ended, Dennis couldn't help but think that Nathan was dodging the warning. He didn't seem bothered much by the possibility of being involved. He was hiding something. Dennis sat quietly and thought hard on the day's events.

Virginia, United States of America
12:23 EST, Friday, 20th May 2016

'Fucking hell I swear to fuckin god!' Dawson thought as he stared down at the phone. 'This had better not turn out the way I think it will'.

He waited, collecting his thoughts of the call.

Shown up before. Only found out two months ago. We've met them. Hooded man… like in Rahat.

Dawson felt stupid like he was the only one not laughing

because he didn't get the joke. The wrinkles in his face contorted with fury. Someone had been making fools of them. MI5 struggling with work sounded painfully familiar.

A notification came through his phone. He put it away and checked his computer. An email from Dennis. There were basic descriptions of the mercenary group; their style, as well as a few eye-witness statements. Again, it all sounded painfully familiar. They were like copies of his last few operations. His last few failures. Descriptions like symptoms of a disease they didn't know they had. The English realized, so it was time to catch up.

There would be no more second-guessing. No more theories. No more doubt. Dawson looked through a directory and pulled a number from the page. Then he yanked the phone across his desk and dialled. Each press of a button pushed the phone along the desk.

"*Hello?*" Answered a woman's voice.

"Where is Mark!?" Dawson yelled.

"*Umm, he's just-*"

"Get him!" Dawson demanded over the women's timid voice. He waited for a minute while pacing as far as the phone's cord would allow.

"*Hello?*" Mark said.

"Mark! It's Nathan Dawson. You called me about that umm, that fucker, what's his name!" A vein began to grow on his temple.

"*Jacob Henley?*" Mark asked nervously.

"Yes! He called us about someone – some people – coming back. What do you know about that!?" Dawson asked. Every second that passed made him want to pull Mark through the phone.

"*Uuuh, well, his statements to police mentioned a*

hooded man returning and people after him," said Mark.

"Man in a hood!? Are you sure!" Dawson's impatience was reaching critical mass.

"Well... I can check the official-"

Dawson could hear scuffling in the background. *"NOW, MARK."*

"Y-Yes! Yes. 'Hooded man' is what he said." Mark blurted Shakely.

Dawson clenched his fists. "Speak to no-one about this, Mark! You understand me!?" Dawson asked.

"Yes but-"

"Speak to no one!" Dawson shouted. He slammed the phone down and sat to calm himself and think clearly. Yet another identical description. He stood up, making his chair roll across the floor, and stormed out of his office. It wasn't Mark's fault. Nobody was trying to put the two together. It was the FBI's case. They focus their attention inside the country. But it wasn't their case anymore.

Dawson marched all the way to third floor, speeding past the slow working day around him. From the Catwalk, Sophie saw him burst out of his office like someone had pissed in his coffee. He had to find Grace, but her office was empty. She could be getting coffee, in a meeting, or on an errand. Picking up speed again, he walked past the boardrooms on his way to the coffee machine. He saw her in a meeting in the room at the end.

Barging in was rude but he had little consideration for anything that would slow him down at that point.

"Agent Dawson?" Said a man at the end of the table.

"Afternoon gentlemen, sorry to interrupt. Miss Credette can I borrow you for a second?" He asked as politely as he could manage.

"Can't it wait?" She asked, as wide-eyed and perplexed as the others.

"Absolutely not," Dawson said plainly, "In fact, you all might want to hear this." The room went quiet with anticipation. "The terrorist group that attacked South Africa isn't new. I just got a call and MI6 has records of them from the last couple years, inside *and* outside the country, led by a 'hooded man'. Last month a man named Jacob Henley was shot while trying to warn us, and the Feds, about a 'hooded man'. I just got them to confirm." Dawson finished and looked around at their reactions. Just as expected, it sounded a little crazy.

"How can you be sure it's the same man from such a vague description?" asked one of the men.

"The Brits sound pretty damn sure of the reoccurring identical descriptions, I don't have time to get into detail. I'm telling you it's almost definitely the same for us. There is plenty of evidence to confirm it because MI6 have already done so and they are moving forward with their investigation. We need to catch up," Dawson said vehemently.

"What do you need from us?" Grace asked.

"They'll likely be sending agents to South Africa. Let me do the same. They have a lot more information than we do. We need a rapprochement with them," Dawson pleaded.

"Done," Grace said suddenly.

Admittedly, Dawson was a little confused; he didn't expect the pitch to work so quickly. He figured he would have to prove it and confirm it through miles of red tape before they allowed him to open it officially.

"He's right. Clearly, we're behind. Do what you need to do to get us on top of this." Something in the way Grace spoke sounded strange, shaky, like she was suddenly perturbed. Dawson was thankful that she was taking it seriously. She trusted him enough to understand the magnitude of his desperation.

Dawson left before he could get trapped in the discussion that followed. There would certainly be a discussion but he could trust Grace to speak on his behalf. She was stubborn enough. Dawson was glad she was on his side for once. He marched all the way back to his office and sat at his computer.

Sophie leaned over the desk closer to Owen. He had a sandwich in his one hand and was checking emails with the other.

"Seriously, he was angry about something," said Sophie.

"Nathan? Angry? Noo waay," Owen said through a mouthful of his sandwich.

"I can't imagine what he must have been like as a field agent," Sophie said as her mind attempted the thought.

"Better than us," said Owen.

Sophie caught movement in the corner of her eye.

"Here he comes," she whispered.

"Brace yourself," Owen remained apathetic and continued to eat his lunch.

"Everybody listen up!" Dawson yelled as he approached the centre of the room. Everyone working at their desks or walking by stopped and turned their full attention to him. "I sent a memo out to all of you, containing some of the information we will need for our new case! Whatever you're busy with, drop it. This comes first!" His deep, gruff voice gripped them. "I want a comprehensive profile of this group by the end of tomorrow! Analyse the data and look through our operations from the past two years for anything that matches their M.O."

Dawson then turned to Busher and those sitting around him, "Contact all other agencies and make sure they do the same!" Everyone watched as he turned back around. Owen could tell what he was going to say.

"What are we waiting for people!? Let's get to work! Now! Come on!" Dawson's shouting filled them with a new energy. The room exploded into life with everyone rushing to get started on a case they knew nothing about. The sounds of paper, computer mice, and fast-moving footsteps overlapped as the work force started up again. Dawson walked over to Owen's desk, where he sat quietly eating his lunch.

"You have a job for me," Owen said calmly as Dawson reached the two of them.

"Vacation's over, you leave this afternoon," said Dawson.

Owen grinned and wiped his hands. "Where am I going?" He asked pleasantly.

"Cape Town, South Africa," said Dawson.

"Oh," Owen said with blank surprise.

Sophie saw her chance and interjected. "What about me, sir?" She asked.

"You go too since you're here," said Dawson.

"What's going on?" Owen asked, putting on his blazer.

The two of them walked with Dawson as he explained. They listened carefully and tried to put it all together but the concept seemed vague.

"So you two must link up with the British agents and find out what you can about the attack," Dawson finished.

"You want us to find out what they know?" Owen asked. One of the many questions he now had.

"Yes, this is not a competition Bradford. We know

nothing about this. All our information is from MI6. We need their help and they're going to need ours, so play nice. I'll arrange the collaboration from here," Dawson said sternly.

"How do we know it's the same person, and people, if we've never actually seen them before?" Sophie asked.

"The SIS have never actually seen them before either, yet somehow they were able to put it all together. When you see the memo you'll understand," said Dawson.

As they got to his office they tried to fit in more questions. By the time he had gone inside, they had only half the answers they wanted. The rest of the day was spent getting ready to leave, distracted by the sudden quantity of information they were forced to accept and understand. Luckily, the flight to Cape Town would have enough time for them to study the case files. What they didn't know was how many questions they never even thought to ask.

Chapter VI
The Red Dawn
Cape Town, Western Cape, South Africa
13:31 SAST, Saturday, 21st May 2016
(*The next day*)

Many people had gazed upon Pandora's Box in wonder, but few ever got to look inside once it was open. To see the home of chaos itself. To feel the heat of hell at the bottom of the devil's vault. What questions one might ask. What answers one might find. Rewards to be reaped through tragedy and sacrifice. Only the wake of devastation could pander to this fascination.

Charred windows and shattered glass. Chunks of the walls were broken and exposed. Metres of crime-scene tape bandaged the wounds. The buildings looked dead and unoccupied. The autopsy was in progress.

Caitlin couldn't count the bullet holes. As the car turned into the entrance, she could see them everywhere. She had only once returned to the scene of a firefight - one she had been a part of, trained and prepared for. This was not the same; this besiegement was exaggerated. Evidently, overkill was paramount. By the time they arrived almost everything had been cleaned up, leaving only scars and trauma.

Joel sat beside her looking through the same window. Representatives from the South African Secret Service picked them up from their hotel just as Dennis had arranged. They hardly had time to unpack and judging from the state of the Houses of Parliament, they would not get to see rest of the city.

Cape Town was beautiful from above. From the plane, they could see flat, urban areas suddenly break upward into dark, towering stone. Table Mountain connected everything; the city, the ocean, and the clouds all appeared to be drawn to it. When they landed they could see only mountainside. It wasn't until they reached their hotel that the illusion was revealed. From the ground, the random collection of mountaintops aligned - implausibly flat – into the table for which it was named. A rare natural wonder as Joel had pointed out.

They had left it all behind. Navy blue oceans and pale gold beaches would have to remain a hopeful dream. So far yet so close. Even Table Mountain became an overwhelming rocky monstrosity. Tall and wide, looking down on the city with superior might.

The roads and walkways outside Parliament looked clean and fresh. The air was filled with a soapy chemical smell. A sharp scent of sanitizers stabbed at Caitlin's nostrils. Joel absorbed every detail of the scene.

A man emerged from the entrance of the building heading straight for them. He was a skinny guy in a thin suit who wore a curious grin as he approached.

"Are you Agent Harper?" He asked with his hand stretched out.

His Afrikaans accent took Caitlin by surprise, like a warped kind of Australian-English. "Officer Caitlin Harper, and this is Officer Joel Masier," she said as she shook his hand. With her other hand, she produced her SIS badge, but the man ignored it and went to shake Joel's hand.

"Officer Masier, welcome," he said joyfully.

Joel stopped staring at the holes and dents long enough to greet him.

"You can call me Julius. Come, let me show you around." He gestured for them to follow him and led them inside with an energetic alacrity. The soapy smell only got thicker as they entered.

"So you're from MI6?" Julius smiled back at Caitlin.

"I am, Officer Masier is-"

"From MI5, yes, I'm actually from the National Intelligence Agency. It wasn't until we started finding foreign bodies that the Secret Service got involved." Julius sounded unusually upbeat.

Caitlin could see by his perplexity that Joel thought so too. Julius was one of the few white men that they had seen since they were picked up. The rest of the working staff were black. Caitlin thought that if she couldn't see much of Cape Town then at least there would be some cultural diversity in her work.

Joel appeared more interested in the hallway. It was clean, and they both knew what that meant. Caitlin learnt long ago that blood, like wine, was not such an easy clean. They passed a crew of crime scene investigators and entered a reception hall. The tall ceiling echoed with the discussions of the men below. Only a couple of them wore suits, the rest were in standard navy-blue jackets as part of the investigative crew.

"Nigel!" Julius called.

One of the larger black men broke from discussion and walked to meet them. "You must be the English," said Nigel. His voice was deeper and had a slight Nigerian accent.

"Caitlin Harper, MI6, and Joel Masier, MI5." Caitlin pulled out her badge again.

Nigel ignored it and immediately started to walk and talk. "I have been told that you two can help us on this investigation, that you have information to offer. This is good because we have no idea what we're looking at here. Let me show you." Nigel stopped at the far entrance to the hall. "We will answer all your questions. Then you will answer ours," he said.

"Okay," Caitlin agreed, nodding slightly. She could hear something of a quiver in his voice.

"This was one of the entrances to be attacked," he began.

"One of how many?" Joel asked in surprise.

"Nine parts of the building were attacked but the terrorists only came through five. They used high-calibre weapons, smoke, and grenades to get through the security. Multiple blood trails converge to the centre of the assault - the main hall. That's where the executioner was seen the most." Nigel walked them to the main hall.

Julius followed them with the same quirky smile.

The hallways were decorated with the same collection of bullet holes as the outside. Ghosts of old bloodstains marked the walls. Joel couldn't take his eyes off it.

"They cut through our security," Nigel explained, "They left some alive and tied them up. We killed hardly any of theirs, but we managed to capture one."

"You have one of them alive?" Caitlin asked abruptly.

"We will need to speak to him," Joel said sternly.

His sudden presence and authority caught Caitlin's attention.

"We can give you some of the past interrogations. We've prepared a full informational package with everything you need to know in order to help us," said Nigel.

"Yes, why don't I fetch that for you guys," Julius interjected, "I'll be back now-now." He turned away and hurried back to the reception.

"We will still need to see him ourselves," Joel said, making firm eye-contact with Nigel.

"I'll put a request through but it'll have to be approved before you can go near him." Nigel slowed down as they approached a smaller reception hall.

Two large, splintered doors were being taken apart at the far end. The damage to the room was minimal but there were tracks of devastation beyond the broken doorway. Caitlin noticed a small spherical dent at thigh-height in one of the walls.

"Naturally, when the attack began the alarms were triggered for reinforcements and extraction, but the alarms didn't work. They had been cut - every single one of them. When the SOS did finally go out there was no response. All the police stations were incapacitated by terrorists. Same thing with the two air force bases nearby. Ysterplaat couldn't get a helicopter here until the day after. They were helpless and outnumbered," Nigel said gravely.

"They're much larger than I anticipated. The effort put into this job is extensive," said Joel. He was looking intensely at the two broken doors. Great, dark brown and blown to pieces, which had obviously been cleaned up.

"Through there," Nigel pointed to the main hall beyond the doorway. "That's what they were after. The executioner came from in here. You can see the marks of his axe on the floor." Nigel guided them into the main hall.

"Executioner? With an axe?" Caitlin asked vaguely.

"It's *him*. It has to be, but I don't think he's used an axe before," Joel trailed off as he passed through the shattered doorway.

One of the most haunting images Caitlin would recall would be that of the main hall in the Houses of Parliament. Not so much worse than anything she had seen in Iraq, but in a place like this – somewhere that shouldn't see violence of any kind - was all the more horrifying. Her first thought was of a monochromatic paintballing scene. Stains all over the hall were exaggerated as if vandalized with red paint. The green carpets were spotted with brown and maroon puddles every few metres.

Dried rivers ran over the balconies and down the stairs. Gunshots had chipped away at the wooden desks and bannisters until they were breaking apart. Even over the clean and soapy scent, Caitlin recognized the harsh iron-coppery smell of blood - old and dried. A few men were still cleaning up the last of the cartridges and detritus.

Caitlin could almost see them, the victims, places where bodies once lay. Her experience around crime scenes had granted her that skill, but this was ghoulishly amplified. She stood, mouth ajar and eyes wide, at the centre of the massacre. Turning slowly to take it all in she suddenly caught sight of Joel in the corner of her eye. He wasn't as shocked as she was. She had seen the pictures he had of the old crime scenes and they were nothing of this scale. Yet he remained focused on the floor.

Caitlin looked to where he was staring. There was a single line carved into the carpet –stopping and starting again until the middle of the hall. Something had cut deeply and perfectly straight. Where it stopped, the blood splatters started, whipping left and right at all sorts of angles and spreads. The stains of slashes had sunken into the carpet, preserving them well enough for Joel to evaluate. Caitlin watched him follow the path of the blade and note the direction of each swing. Finally, he reached the empty space on the floor at the end of the hall.

"This is where he executed the politicians," said Nigel, indicating to the line of overlapping blood puddles that had long since turned brown.

Caitlin couldn't put it to reason - the idea of such an advanced terrorist group using medieval and gruesome methods like execution by axe. It was not the most effective weapon against armed guards so they must have been trying to convey a message. Some fucked up message.

Nigel continued to talk, giving details about the attack.

Caitlin could see the cogs in Joel's head turning as he tried to comprehend the new-found scale of the investigation. She could hardly understand it herself. A week ago, they didn't exist. Now they were climbing the ranks of the world's most-wanted list, and there she was, at the front line.

Joel paced alongside the dry puddles. Caitlin could only stand with her arms crossed and try to make sense of it all. Clearly, the staff were used to the smell but for Caitlin it was nauseating. Joel's focus, however, remained undeterred.

"Then he dragged them here. The rest of them escaped out the sides," said Nigel.

Joel stopped and turned to him with full attention. "They just escaped? How many politicians were killed exactly?" He asked. His eyes scanned the exits again.

"Only a select few. Twelve I think," Nigel shrugged.

Concentration furrowed Joel's brow. He focused hard on the exit routes. Somehow Caitlin knew he had found something.

"They can't have just escaped, in the middle of a firefight. His targets were chosen selectively. He let the rest go," said Joel.

"I agree," said Nigel, pointing to a desk in the middle.

Joel's eyes locked onto the desk. "That one is destroyed, not by gunfire but by a blade. Who was there?" He asked.

Caitlin noticed that the desk he was pointing to had been broken in the middle. The break was hefty but it had only been hit once. Thinking about the size of the axe – and what it must have been like to see it coming – made her nerves go cold. A small shiver let her shake the feeling free as she followed Joel to the stairs.

"That desk belonged to the Minister of Defence, Mbaki Uthalo. He was found with lacerations on his calves and a crushed spine. The cameras in the room could not see much through the smoke and were shot out before it cleared. But some of the microphones were still on, and his picked up something very interesting," said Nigel.

Caitlin looked up at Joel, who then turned away from the desk to look down at her. For once it felt like a lead.

The walk to the control room was more of the same. Cleaning crews still had a lot of work to do but most of it was just repairing the damage. At one point they walked around a corner and saw a long, thin indentation where the axe was once embedded in the wall.

During the walk, Julius caught up and brought a reasonably thick folder which he handed to Caitlin. She skimmed through the first few pages before handing it to Joel for a more thorough evaluation.

The control room had been cleaned up, leaving Caitlin to wonder how there was even footage at all since the terrorists had obviously been there and made a mess. It wasn't until she was inside that she realized the door to the room was missing as well.

Nigel stepped behind the technician at the computer and started speaking a language that Caitlin couldn't identify.

"This was recorded from the Minister's microphone," he said as he turned to them both.

The audio was scratchy and there were a couple of gunshots overpowering the sounds of footsteps, shuffling, and screaming. Then in a moment of brief quiet, they heard him:

"*W-w-we told you e-everyth-! WE DID W-WHA- Y- A- ASKED!*"

Joel's brow furrowed with further concern. They listened to it twice more but despite the poor quality, it was reasonably easy to tell what he was saying.

"They had met *him* before," Joel said lightly, "Show me

all footage you have of the Man in Black."

After a nod of agreement from Nigel, the technician got to work on the video feed. There he was. After so long only hearing from witnesses. A hooded black figure, slender but defined. He was striding down a hallway. Calm and unaffected by the chaos of the battle around him.

Caitlin's first thought was that he had been edited in – the footage tampered with. The Man in Black was dragging an enormous axe without a care in the world. And he was dark - extremely dark. Darker than she thought to be possible.

Joel was staring intently at the screen with the same expression of awe that Caitlin had in the main hall. They both watched as *he* swung his axe into the abdomen of one of the security guards. Then he swung it around himself in a full circle that nearly cleared right through the guards back.

Caitlin recoiled. She turned her eyes away from the screen and towards Joel. His eyes were wide and shaky. She decided to break the silence to avoid the discomfort.

"That axe must weigh a ton! He can barely hold it up. What's the point of using it?"

Joel rubbed at the stubble on his cheeks with his hand over his mouth. He was shaking his head. "He's insane," he said with dismay. "But from a certain angle, the handle of that axe might be confused for a staff. How could they see the handle but not the blade?"

Clips of the Man in Black played one after the other. They were quick, he never slowed and never stayed in the same place for long. There were periods of him dragging the axe around and performing gruesome executions. Then there were periods where he would use two handguns. Large, powerful, and clearly aged judging by the state of the steel shine.

"Why is he so dark?" Caitlin asked. She wasn't sure if

she was seeing it or if it was a trick of the light, but he looked unnaturally dark.

"I've been asking the same thing for a long time but that's even darker than I imagined," said Joel.

"Yes, well we have an explanation for that," Nigel began. "We picked up some residue off the bodies. A compound so dark it absorbs ninety-eight per cent of all light. It's called Vantablack, pure carbon Nano-tubes made by a company in England-"

Joel stopped watching the footage and stood up straight.

"-Called Surrey Nano-systems," Nigel finished.

A defeated expression sunk into Joel's face. "That's why you let us in on this," he said.

Nigel nodded.

Caitlin admired his brain. Something in the way Joel thought allowed him to see beyond what was in front of him. His dedication was admirable. It was relieving. She felt glad to have been teamed up with someone so acutely aware of the subliminal details. Being so new to the case she did not trust herself to see them as well as he did.

"It's the darkest material known to man and not very easy to come by. *He* has it on every solid piece of his outfit, and the S-VIS spray-on version covers the rest of the material, with the exception of the purple patterns," said Nigel.

"So dark it looks unnatural, paranormal, demonic even. I guess the witnesses weren't exaggerating," Joel said with a hint of guilt in voice.

"Actually our witnesses said the same thing. They think he was sent by the devil from hell to punish people for their sins."

"What did those people do to deserve something so cruel?" Joel asked, avoiding the obvious implication of them being politicians.

"Many of them have been accused of crimes. Corruption, bribery, and several other offences none of which were ever taken to court. We didn't even know about some of them. It wasn't until the day after the attack that we found evidence of all their crimes. Every one of them could have been prosecuted with the evidence against them," Nigel explained in repentance and shame. "Then there were the guards."

"The guards as well?" Caitlin asked with growing disdain.

"Some of them helped the attackers. They blocked their own men to prevent any support from getting to the President. Two of them cut the cables in that wall so they couldn't see the feed through the monitors." He was pointing to a collection of blank screens hanging on the far wall.

Caitlin made eye-contact with Joel, his eyes were bright and meaningful, but he seemed to have a thought of his own. He then switched to eye-contact with Nigel, who still looked ashamed. Caitlin could only guess it but she knew the two of them were forming some kind of mental connection.

"Your service has been compromised," Joel said in a half whisper, lightly, almost consoling.

"That's why we need your help," said Nigel. His voice was quiet and secretive.

Caitlin recognized his kind of tone instantly.

"It's impossible to do this with the internal investigations going on. We don't know who to trust anymore. We cannot do this. The government is collapsing and there's nothing we can do about it. None of the survivors will come back. No one wants to take up the positions. They're afraid of *him*, afraid he'll come back. Especially after what was written on the wall outside." Nigel explained dejectedly. Helplessness was crushing his spirit.

"Why?" Joel asked sternly, "What was written on the wall?"

London, England
16:37 GMT, Saturday, 21st May 2016

The sun had started its decline. The city settled into a cold afternoon. Plain grey clouds stopped the warmth and light from illuminating anything below. From that point of view, that is.

Other parts of the world saw the same sun in a completely different light. More or less cloudy, more or less sunny. Some were in the dead of night, some were at the peak of day. Here, the sun still had a few more hours before the end of another spring day. In Southern Africa, the sun would soon be setting as the autumn day came to a close. The difference was perspective. The difference between everyone was perspective. No two people are the same. Similar, yes, but not the same.

This perspective was on the third floor, looking out the window over the city of London, waiting for him to come. There again at the SIS building. The headquarters. The big-time agency of secrecy.

Christian knew he was there because of his perspective. His knowledge, sure, but he was not the only criminal psychologist in England. His perspective, however, was the only one of its kind. Euwin had brought him in a few times over the years as a consultant. But never before had his cases ever been on more than just the local news. The whole world was looking at Cape Town, and he was about to do more than just look. This was just the backstage tour before he became a member of the crew.

The case was... interesting, to say the least. And yet that

didn't quite do it justice. Individually, *they* were almost unheard of. Once put together, every occurrence and event became a piece of a far greater puzzle. One which Christian would help put together. How could he not? To take on a puzzle of that magnitude, that complexity, he had to excuse himself from work. Perhaps Euwin knew he would. Oh yes, he definitely knew.

"Detective Taylor," said a deep voice. The voice of authority itself.

"Mr Euwin," Christian said in automatic response. He wondered how many times he had done that; looked up at Euwin and waited for him to start. He never knew what to say first.

"Follow me," Euwin said after a brief hesitation. The way he said it and turned away was typical of people like him.

"I take it since you're here that you are interested in joining us for this investigation?" Euwin asked, his accent as posh and stern as his posture.

"How could I not? This case is incredible. The years of secrecy, the calculation, this organisation is unparalleled." Christian ran his fingers through his slick blonde hair, leaving it off to one side with unintentional style.

"You read all of it?"

"Yes."

"Good." Euwin relaxed his shoulders a little. "Since you've read everything we know about them then you know why you're here. I might need you to do a psych profile as well," said Euwin.

Christian was uncertain, as usual, but he thought Euwin sounded less formal than usual. He followed closely but remained a step behind.

"Tell me, what is your first impression of these

terrorists?" Euwin asked.

"Well, they're not necessarily terrorists. But apart from that they're organized, experienced, an efficient group of vigilantes under tactical and intelligent leadership. I have a lot to say about some of your theories, plus some questions of my own,"

Euwin stopped him by a door. They were outside a board room with no windows.

"I'd like to know what you have to say but there are a few others who will need to hear it as well." Euwin opened the door to let him in.

Cautiously, Christian made his way inside where three new faces sat around an oval table. The projector screen at the far end of the room was on but blank.

"Detective, I'd like you to meet Operations Officer Dennis Knight, Officer Stanley Martin, and Officer Elliot Spencer." Euwin indicated to each of the men as he called them out.

Dennis had a tanned-brown complexion and a close-cut hairstyle to match his beard. Stanley had a bright face, angled jawline, and vivid blue eyes. Elliot must have been South American by origin, judging by his tanned complexion and dark hair. He had a sharp expression. His thick brows were angled with concern.

"The only people to know everything about this investigation are in this room," Euwin continued. "In a few moments we're going to call the two officers in Cape Town. Earlier today they visited the Houses of Parliament where the attack took place. They should have a great deal of information to share with us."

Christian took his seat at the back of the table. Euwin sat opposite him. For the next few minutes, they engaged in a light discussion about what they knew so far. Christian remained silent. He observed the conversation from outside. The others had a lot of questions. There were a lot of the wrong questions. Each of their different perspectives viewed the case as something routine. They were used to some form of criminal format. Christian figured it might be why a new kind of enemy would be able to avoid them for so long.

Euwin could see him pondering and asked if he had anything to add. Without much to say for certain, he would rather wait to hear from the officers abroad, who called fifteen minutes later.

Officers Harper and Masier called from their hotel room in Cape Town. Christian couldn't see them. It was only an audio call, but Stanley had set up a connection with their computer so that they could display their own images through the projector. It took a minute of introductions and establishing a connection before the slide show began. They started by giving an outline of the attack; how it was done, the steps that were taken, and all necessary details. The room was bright with images of the devastation; the outside, the inside, and the main hall. With each detail, and each image, Christian grew increasingly impressed.

"And now no one is willing to go back to work there. Their government is dysfunctional because of what was written on the east wall," said Masier.

The next image showed a great white wall draped in shade. Red spray-paint was used to make the shape of three swirls converging and connecting at their centre. Next to it on the right were two words written as largely as possible: Who's next?

"Grammatically correct, charming," said Euwin.

He was right. Christian tilted his head as he examined it. He knew of the type to be so considerate.

"Well at least we know for certain they're going to strike again," said Dennis.

"*The image has been leaked online as well. It's on the news already,*" said Harper.

Christian could see Euwin in the corner of his eye, glancing at him every so often.

"*The symbol is called a Triskelion. A Celtic symbol associated with motion in the form of progress or a cycle, like a revolution. It also happens to be on the flag of the neo-Nazi nationalist party - Afrikaner Weerstands, uuhh, here.*" Masier put the name up on screen. Not one of them attempted to pronounce it.

Afrikaner Weerstandsbeweging.

"*The twenty-one highest ranking members of the party turned up dead just a few days before the attack. They were slaughtered in a manner similar to that of the members of Parliament, during a meeting at their headquarters in the North West Province.*"

The room fell quiet as the crime scene images were displayed. If Christian didn't know better he would have said they were both from the same attack.

Finally, they showed footage of *him*. Christian had read about him from Joel Masier's notes. He was like a fiction. Something out of legend. Christian wanted to see the truth for himself - to see the reality.

The reality was no different. His own eyes were being deceived in front of him. The man was Caucasian, but he wore an outfit so black that none of them could really tell what they were seeing. He was armed well enough yet dragged an oversized axe around. Christian had thought it might be the most interesting case he had ever investigated, but now he was sure of it.

"We're not sure what the axe was for. It's heavy, slow, and doesn't really serve much purpose," said Harper.

"Of course it does," Christian blurted out, "for fun. Look at it, there's no real purpose there, there's just... sadistic value. I mean the rest of the attack was easy, they went to great lengths to make sure of that. Using the axe was a challenge, made it interesting. Every kill is different - like he's being creative. Like its game."

"So he's cocky? Stanley asked.

"No. He was confident with his plan but he still wanted to play." Christian was still engaged with the footage.

"You don't sound so sure. What is he, Detective?" Euwin asked.

"He's a psychopath. You don't need me to tell you that, but there are so many discrepancies that I can't piece together. You said evidence of his victims' corruption came to light right after the attack. I think *they* released that evidence, but not for credit, otherwise why only go public now after all they've done? They're killers, yes, but they've achieved some great things." Christian smiled slightly as he wiped his reading glasses.

"I'm glad you're a fan but we still need to stop them," Dennis said with mirth.

"And if they're such dedicated vigilantes then why steal that dark material from the company in England?" Masier added.

"I don't know. His motives are... I don't know." Christian felt his internal frustration build with the randomness and inconsistency of logic. He decided to start over. "He spoke with the Defence Minister before, got information from him, got him to do... something, then decides to execute him and the rest of them in broad daylight. Also warning everyone that he will do it again."

"Maybe they were trying to stop their arrangement from coming to light?" Elliot suggested.

"If they wanted them silenced they wouldn't need to go through this much effort. Plus, *they* revealed the corrupt nature of the politicians. They brought it to light," said Stanley.

The room waited for Christian to complete his thought when he suddenly came back into focus with a new sense of clarity.

"They had to prove it. They released the evidence of the government's crimes to prove that they had done wrong. It's intrinsic in vigilante mind-sets to feel the need to prove that their victims have done wrong so as not to be compared to them." Christian began to worry they didn't understand when Joel Masier spoke up again.

"*It makes sense since they were the only targets not openly in the wrong.*"

The reply gave Christian a sort of supportive confidence to keep going. "*He* is clearly an experienced fighter. Definitely has a military background. Leadership position I bet."

A simultaneous 'Agreed!' came from both Caitlin and Dennis.

"Yeah, he's obviously in charge," said Elliot.

"The axe slowed him down but he used it anyway, despite having something wrong with his left leg." Christian paused as the others re-watched the footage in confusion. Now that he had pointed it out, it was obvious.

"He has a sort of limp in his left leg, like its heavy, but he's perfectly balanced. His outfit and weapons are symmetrical in both weight and position. He has no trouble walking or running. It might be an old military injury. That should be enough for a search shouldn't it?" Christian directed the question at Euwin but quickly adjusted to look at everyone else.

"I think it will," Euwin concurred. "Keep going with the profile, any more information we could use."

"Fearless. Sadistic. This is not a man we can afford to underestimate, and he's still ahead of us," Dennis pointed out.

Christian rolled his sleeves up to his elbows and began taking notes on his phone.

"Cait, have the Americans arrived yet?" Dennis asked.

"No-sir," she answered quickly.

"That's a good idea." Christian said suddenly. The room was once again facing him in anticipation. "Working with other countries I mean. They could have additional information."

"And if they don't?" Masier asked.

"We could still use their help," Dennis replied.

"And they could use ours," Harper added.

"A rapprochement with the CIA provides an ally. Something we could certainly use," said Euwin, ending the debate.

"So play nice. That goes for the locals there as well," said Dennis.

"That's a bit more complicated..." Masier responded.

"Since some of the politicians and guards worked with the terrorists, internal affairs have been all over them. The question of loyalty has tied their hands for now," said Harper.

Christian made notes as the conversation went along. Sometimes Euwin would glance sideways at him.

"If that's the case then be careful around them. If they're questioning loyalty then so should you," said Dennis.

The room went silent and Christian looked up to Dennis. He had a grave expression as he looked at the images on screen. The change was evident in each of their faces - the addition of foreboding, severity, and a little fear. They were beginning to understand their enemy.

Number after number: 201, 202, 203, 204. Their muffled footsteps were the only sounds in the hallway. It was late. They were late. The visit would have to be quick. Sophie counted the doors ahead to calculate the one they were looking for. They found the right room and straightened up. Sophie had an odd feeling as Owen knocked on the door. A nervous guilt. Turning up so late was not a good start.

The door opened with a taller woman sizing them up. "Hi," she smiled. Her accent was posh and satisfying.

"Hi, I'm Special Agent Bradford," Owen smiled back and showed his badge, "this is Agent Mercer. We're from the CIA."

The woman checked both their badges before opening the door and stepping aside to reveal the rest of the room. The inside was neat and tidy except for the side table in the middle. Sophie could only see the legs of the table and a laptop on a bed of papers. The man behind the laptop had some grey hair but not much age on his face. With his glasses on, though, she figured he must be older than Owen.

"I'm Officer Harper, SIS," the woman said as she closed the door behind them.

"Officer Masier, MI5," said the man. He was the only one in the room still wearing a suit though he had removed the blazer and tie.

"MI5?" Owen asked in confusion.

Sophie stood next to him trying not to look too awkward.

"I know what you're thinking," Masier said. "I've been thinking the same thing." He took off his glasses and stepped over to them. "And call me Joel." He smiled and held his hand out.

"Owen." Owen smiled back and they shook.

Caitlin did the same and then finally Sophie joined in. Now that they were all acquainted with first names, the stiffness melted away. Joel seemed immune to the initial awkwardness. He opened the conversation by asking about their flight and where they were staying.

They talked for a while about the abrupt nature of the job, and how they all became involved on the same day. Except Joel.

"So you've been on this case for months?" Sophie asked.

"Yeah. I opened it myself after I lost my previous case to them." Joel smiled to himself.

"I think I lost my last operation to them as well, in Mozambique," said Caitlin.

"How long ago? Because that's not far from here," Owen asked.

"Exactly." Joel's expression sank ever so slightly as he looked Owen in the eyes. "What about you? Any history that might help?" He asked with a little less humour. The nervous edge was back. The Feds had a potential connection but nothing substantial.

"Yeah," said Owen.

Sophie's ears burned.

"They've been to the East Coast but our informant was killed before he could talk." Owen spoke with enough confidence that Sophie almost believed it, but she knew better and kept her mouth shut. It must have worked because Joel and Caitlin told them about their day at the Parliament building.

If it weren't for their professional manner, Sophie would have thought they were telling a horror story. The worst part was that they weren't exaggerating, and they had the pictures to prove it.

"We're going in again tomorrow for the interrogation," Caitlin finished.

"How did they capture one?" Sophie asked.

Even Joel shrugged.

"We'll need to talk to him as well," said Owen.

"I'm sure we can figure something out," said Joel.

They had stayed longer than Sophie thought they would. All things considered, she was happy with their first impressions. Owen agreed that the arrangement would work out just fine.

Even in autumn, South Africa was warmer at night than Virginia during the day. But the wind coming off the ocean delivered a harsh chill.

The two of them walked to their car outside the hotel. They were talking but couldn't be heard. He watched them as they got inside.

"The other two are leaving," he said into his mic. The lights of their car flashed on and they backed out of the parking bay. The reply was clean from the earpiece.

"Follow them."

Cape Town, Western Cape, South Africa
15:14 SAST, Sunday, 22nd May 2016
(The next day)

They had been waiting a long time now. Owen managed to negotiate with Joel; he and Caitlin would conduct the interrogation while Sophie and Joel observed from outside. They had been very accommodating. Maybe it was just what the British were like, or maybe they really needed the help. Not that

Owen could help. But as long as they thought he could, then they would give him the information he needed. It wouldn't have been much trouble if they weren't so damn friendly. It had only been a day and they were all getting along just fine. Gaining their trust was supposed to be the hard part. Now that they had it, they needed to be able to keep it. That's where his conscience came in.

Joel was leaning against the wall with his arms crossed. Caitlin paced past them majestically with her notes in hand. Owen simply stared out of the window past Joel. It was Owen's first time seeing Cape Town in the daylight. The sightseeing was pleasant until the house-of-horrors tour. He had never seen damage like it. After days of cleaning, there were still stains of maroon and brown all over the walls and floors. The main hall was worse.

The memory was suddenly denied by distraction as Sophie returned with a cup of coffee. Her hair hung loose to just below her shoulder blades, a lighter shade of blond than his. Caitlin had tied her hair up neatly which made more sense to him since it almost reached her belt. He was thinking of asking her why she let it grow when Nigel came around the corner. Joel was no longer the only one in a full suit.

"Alright, follow me," said Nigel.

Owen could only just catch up with his accent. Nigel led them to the interrogation room where there were two doors. Guards were spread out every few metres. Anyone, especially the National Intelligence Agency, would consider an attempt on the captured man's life to be foolish. Apparently, that didn't stop the terrorists from trying a couple of times.

"Ten minutes is all I could get you," Nigel said apologetically.

"Thank you, Nigel," said Joel. For whatever reason, Joel

trusted Nigel. The SASS was supposedly compromised by men working with the terrorists but Joel vouched for Nigel. Everyone else, however, would have to be avoided if necessary. This made the tour all the more interesting when they were surrounded by potential double-agents.

Owen had never felt a tension in the presence of authority like that before. He and Sophie felt nothing but disdain for the South African agencies. Their own men betrayed their country. It made Owen and Sophie far more appreciative of their own government, and agency, and gave them a new sense of pride in their work. The problem remained; if members of the Secret Service were on the terrorists' payroll, then everything said during the interrogation would be available to them.

Nigel, Sophie, and Joel went through the door to the observation room where they would watch. Then Owen followed Caitlin into the interrogation room. The man awaited them with his hands cuffed to the table. He had an extremely dark complexion, which contrasted with his few remaining teeth. Caitlin introduced herself. Her voice was strong and intimidating yet he seemed more curious than afraid.

"We want to ask you some questions about the terrorist group you were part of." Caitlin said it slowly so that he could understand.

"I tell them already," he said. His accent was thicker than Nigel's.

Owen kept his expression stern. He hoped Caitlin could understand him better than he could.

"We know, but we have questions of our own," Caitlin replied.

The two of them took their seats. The man shuffled a little before speaking again. He spoke too fast and Caitlin had to ask him to repeat it slowly.

"I will tell you anything, just please do not let me out," he pleaded with his hands together.

Owen couldn't tell if he didn't understand or the man didn't know what he was saying. "Why?" He asked.

"If they find me they will kill me," he said.

Owen could tell that Caitlin shared his thoughts. Making a deal with the subject would allow them to get what they need without hassle, and his demands weren't going to be difficult.

"Answer our questions, and we will make sure you're kept safe," Caitlin said kindly. If he only knew how many guards were outside.

They started with the simple questions. Nothing they didn't already know from his answers to the SASS. In an attempt to get more information, they asked him to elaborate. Then after explaining to him what the word *elaborate* meant, he tried to no avail.

They ran through most of their questions with no success. The group the man came from was hired by the terrorists but all contact was excruciatingly secretive. Instructions and resources were given to them in the most basic forms. They were less experienced guns-for-hire who were likely added just for the extra numbers. Redundant for a small army. The only time he spoke to the main terrorist group was just before the attack when he was given his yellow mask. The only other interesting point was that they were all foreign.

"Did you ever see the Man in Black?" Owen asked.

"Yes," he croaked. A sunken shade fell down his face.

"What can you tell us about him?" Caitlin asked kindly in an attempt to subdue his fear.

"He was very dark, and very good with his guns," he said simply.

They paused expecting him to continue.

"That's it? He didn't say anything? You didn't see anything unusual?" Owen asked, now getting tired of his useless answers.

"Yah I tell them, the only time they talk to us was before. They tell us what to do and talk about *afgesten*," he shrugged.

"Hold on, they talked about *afgestan*? What's *afgesten*?" Caitlin asked.

"I don't remember, they talk about *afgesten* or *afgestan*," he said vaguely.

Owen made the connection, but Caitlin was quicker.

"You mean Afghanistan?" She asked, slightly louder.

"Yah, I think that was it, yah." He looked hopefully at the two of them.

Owen spent a moment trying to get him to confirm while Caitlin glanced over at the one-way glass. On the other side, the others were watching intently. Nigel took out his mobile and rushed to find the right contact when Joel suddenly stopped him.

"Don't. If their spies find out that we know, we lose the element of surprise, and we lose our only lead," he said desperately.

"I have to inform my superior," Nigel pleaded.

"We'll take care of it," Joel said sternly.

After a moment of consideration, Nigel conceded and put his phone away.

"Don't tell anyone about this," Joel said as he continued to watch Caitlin and Owen.

Sophie remained in the corner watching it happen. She had taken out her phone and was already calling Dawson but felt a strong appreciation for Joel's quick thinking.

"*Yeah? What is it Mercer?*" answered the same old gruff voice.

"Sir we're at the interrogation. The terrorists were talking about Afghanistan. They could be going there next."

"*Are you sure?*" He asked calmly but quickly.

"Yeah, he heard them mention it. That's all we could get."

Caitlin and Owen were leaving the interrogation room.

"*Get anything else you can and bring it back here ASAP!*" Dawson demanded, then he hung up the call.

Chapter VII
The Point of No Return
Kandahar, Afghanistan
07:55 AFT, Monday, 6th June 2016
(15 days later)

It was time for retaliation. They had the upper hand, a single step ahead, hinging on capricious intelligence. Covert Operations in Afghanistan had been indefatigable in their pursuit, chasing shadows only to lose them in the shade.

Two weeks had produced enough Intel to stay in the lead and yet they still didn't know where they were going. If they didn't find out soon, they were going to lose their lead, the race, and a lot of innocent lives all at once. It was time to learn more about 'the trade'.

"And you know where it's going to be." Colonel William Trauss stared at the man intensely. It was child's play – a dimly lit room, small and quiet. He was going to sing them an opera in there. "The trade is happening here in Kandahar. I need *when. Where. Go!*" He demanded.

Behind him, Major Hugo Bennett took a step forward. His arms were crossed, and his stare was equally harsh.

The man was sweating even in the rags he wore as clothes. They had let him fall in and out of consciousness up until ten minutes ago. It had been made clear that if he blacked out again, they might not let him wake up so easily. His head was heavy, and his eyelids were fighting him, but he spoke up with what was left of his voice.

"The Aquuar Square." He swallowed but kept his head up. "They said three weeks."

"How long ago was that?" Bennett asked.

"About two weeks ago…" He sounded numb.

Bennett wondered if they had given him too much anaesthetic. He had been in a lot of pain since they pulled him out of the Hot-Zone the previous day. A firefight broke out and, to their sudden immeasurable luck, this man had survived.

"Who's going to be there?" Trauss asked.

"I 'don know."

"What are they trading?"

"I 'don know." He attempted to shake his head, but it merely wavered from side to side.

With time still of great value, Bennett moved on with the questions. "The Man in Black, he was there yesterday?"

Like a pinch of adrenaline, the man's face contorted into that of a child about to cry.

"Keep it together now! Where did he go!?" Trauss pressed.

"*I don't know. I swear!*"

"He made meat bags of your friends! I wonder what he'll do when he finds out he left one behind!" Trauss leaned over the desk.

"NO! PLEASE-"

"Tell us something then!" Bennett stepped forward again as he spoke.

"He's evil! He doesn't die. We could do nothing. He was angry." He looked down, exhausted by the effort of speaking.

Bennett and Trauss didn't try to hide their amusement. As soldiers, they were trained for any challenge, and to face it with a dominant attitude.

"Sounds like he's scared you something true," Trauss huffed.

"HE HUNTS YOU DOWN!" There was a shake in his voice that wiped away the humour. "He doesn't stop! Like he's a-a-uh… an agent of hell, come to punish those the Devil or God himself cannot reach!" The man broke down into shaking sobs.

Bennett considered the man's fear but dismissed it quickly in the spirit of military passion. The man would remain in custody outside of Kandahar, by request, which no longer surprised Bennett. He had given them the information they needed. That was the deal. Bennett and Trauss left the interrogation room to set the next stage in motion.

"Three weeks; that was two weeks ago, plus or minus a few days. It will take us about up to forty-eight hours to make it to the trade site," Trauss said gruffly.

"Aquuar Square is on the edge of insurgent territory. How are we going to get close without being seen? If we spook them, this would all be for nil," said Bennett.

They marched past offices and down the stairwells until they made it to the ground floor.

"We'll think of something. We can't miss an opportunity like this. Have your squads prepped to move out soon, likely tomorrow morning," said Trauss. He then made his own way towards the Americans' barracks.

Bennett continued through the hallways towards the British barracks. Joining forces for the operation made life difficult for everyone there. It messed with the base's system and operations. No one could complain since they managed to complete their mission, which – at that point still going without saying – would not have been possible without the collaboration. That didn't mean a great big 'We told you so' wasn't being implied by the US and UK Defence Departments.

The building was full of men, both on and off duty. As Bennett got closer to the barracks, he passed the entertainment rooms; pool tables, televisions, darts, and other activities that were enjoyed to at least three different sources of music. Bennett reached the end of the hallway and passed one unfortunate man mopping the floors around the fun.

His own squad was in one of the hangars, taking up space and typically being of no use to anyone. That changed as soon as they saw him striding in their direction.

"Off your arses! Assemble around me! Move!" Bennett yelled.

With trained haste, they made a well-formed semi-circle around him in seconds. No one sat down. No one spoke up. They stood at attention and waited to be told what to do.

The other squads would be told what to do when their orders arrived, which wouldn't be until a mission was properly constructed. This squad was his responsibility; they had been for months. Spend enough time around them and they become your brothers. You no longer see soldiers. Instead, you see good men dressed as government tools. You see the extension of their lives beneath the uniforms; their families, kids, houses, careers, dreams, their best and their worst. All of it being projected above them like informational posters. Each reminding you of what that life really meant. Its scale. Its significance.

That's what made it hard to see them get caught out in the field. When they die, their projections don't go away. It hangs over their corpses like gravestones displaying a record of their life's accomplishments, defined in existence by the purpose and effect they had on the world - their own magnetic fields of personality interacting with everyone around them now extinguished.

He could see each of their projections as they stood around him. Allen Kendren: Girlfriend back home and a hopeful career as a computer technician, yet he couldn't fix the radio the previous week because it was "not his area of expertise". Isaac

Gillian: single – to nobody's surprise – but a family of six who called him all the damn time. Edward Nell: had a hot wife and a two-year-old son who may or may not have been Gillian's. He couldn't prove otherwise, and Gillian was sure he banged her before, despite having never even gone to Bristol. Jack Thawn: Committed soldier with a few family members back home and a possible girlfriend. He was a good man. Played guitar pretty well. Couldn't talk to girls for shit. Kelly Laurence: Kind of fit for an Irish gal, long-term boyfriend waiting to travel the world with her. Only been to London yet she swears she saw Gillian leaving a pub with Nell's wife.

Bennett would sometimes think about his own projection; divorced, three kids, every reason to go back home yet stayed in the armed forces because their stepdad 'Terry' was probably doing a better job than him anyway. Missed by his parents, no contact with his old friends, and all the guilt in the world for it. None of it slowed him down though - which was impressive. Everyone had people who missed them, but they still got past it.

Bennett had more reason than any to be distracted, but he never was, which Jack sort of admired. He had no trouble himself leaving his life behind. If he had three kids then he might reconsider. It was a good thing Bennett stayed; he was a great squad leader - one of Jack's favourites from the start.

"Eyes on me. Listen carefully," Bennett began.

Jack and the others did as they were told.

"We have a location and a time frame for the trade. Our window is the second half of this week which any idiot can tell means we need to leave soon if we're going to make it. The mission is being put together as we speak, but whatever it is, you can bet your lazy arses are going to be put to work! And because my squad does not waste time, you are going to prepare for that mission right now!"

Instinct took over Jack's body as he and the rest of the squad immediately started clearing the area of their stuff. Jack knew that in Bennett's mind, you should be able to do physical work and listen to instructions at the same time. So naturally, they were wasting time by standing around waiting to hear the rest of their orders.

"You will be out of here tomorrow!" Bennett had to yell so they could all hear him after dispersing to unpack and arrange their equipment.

Jack was near but still dragged his backpack closer to Bennett, who was pacing as he yelled the briefing.

"You will be ready to leave whenever you are ordered to! You will be ready for whatever the mission requires of you! Until the parameters of the mission are released, you will assume you need all of your equipment! Night and day! Long-term and short-term! We have one shot at this! Do not disappoint me!"

No one asked questions. Bennett filled in the gaps of the operation as best he could but somehow they still knew nothing about it. They would be leaving in under twenty-four hours yet they knew so little, and Jack's confidence began to suffer because of it.

Bennett seemed confident enough. That's all they needed. Jack believed that, but he was smart enough to doubt the assurance of one man. It wasn't his problem though, so he fell in line and did as he was told. Trust the system - it knows what it's doing.

"I can't wait to kill the guy and go back to our own base," Gillian said once Bennett was out of earshot.

"Might not be so easy. I heard he's ex-military, Special Ops or some shit," Nell said as he adjusted the straps on his vest.

They grouped up enough to talk while they packed. Jack sat nearby and listened as he forced rounds into a magazine.

"Not surprising. He killed a government," said Gillian.

"You don't kill a government, dumbass," Laurence said in her trademark Irish accent. She was attaching a sight to her rifle with a screwdriver. "He killed their president and dismantled their government. And he didn't do it alone. He had an army with him, which we're going to fight soon."

"Why would anyone follow a creep like him? He only comes out at night and wears all black, like some edgy, Goth motherfucker," said Gillian contemplating his night-vision goggles.

"Makes sense to wear all black at night," Kendren added.

"And he'll be easier to see in the sand tomorrow," said Jack.

There was a murmur of agreement. The rest of the conversation involved the mysteries of the mission and the fame they would get from killing the world's most-wanted terrorist.

Later that night they were called in for mission briefing. Deployment would be the following morning. Just the boost Jack's confidence needed. Trust the system; they knew what they were doing, and they hadn't let him down.

███, ███, Afghanistan
███, ███, █ June 2016

The neutral district was like a mix between hell and home. 'Houses' were damaged, chipped, and cracking. The paint was coming off in patches. There was power to the area - sometimes.

Civilians looked lost like they once had a purpose that had long since been forgotten. Remnants of a functioning civilization... if ever there was one.

They were not there to help the civilians. They destroyed more than they rebuilt. They were soldiers, not some charity case construction party. Their purpose was to kill the disease. You have to kill the disease before the body can heal. The insurgents were the cause of the suffering. Removing them was the best thing for the locals. Not many people understood that.

But that had all been put on hold. There was more important work to be done. Their mission wasn't for peace in the country; it was for peace in the world. Terrorists from their own back yard resided within the broken nation.

There was a trade taking place soon - so close to the insurgent Red Zone that you could see them with your naked eye. Limited intelligence suggested the trade was between a local group and some unknowns. The "Man in Black" and his terrorists meant to take part in some way, and so did the armed forces.

In a joint task force, squads from the US and the UK were combining their resources. The result of some cross-political, Afghanistan legislation bullshit. The point was they had double the men, double the firepower, and double the Intel.

They had to sneak to the site to avoid provoking the Taliban. That meant small numbers of ground units. Two squads - Trauss' and Bennett's. The targets were high profile and in such perilous company that ground units wouldn't be able to take them on alone. Suicide isn't an exit strategy. There would be reinforcements. Enough armour and firepower to get the job done, all of which would wait, idle, on the outside of the Hazard Zone.

Posing as reconnaissance convoys, they would drop off

the ground teams and wait in the Safe Zone. The ground teams would travel to the trade site, where they would make camp and wait for the party to begin. Upon confirmed sight of the "Man in Black", heavy-duty vehicles would move in to intercept and eliminate the targets. Evac would be imminent; they couldn't sit around so close to the Red Zone. That would be asking for death, and hell itself would oblige.

Jack had been staring out the right side-window, looking inward at the Safe Zone. On their left side was the Hazard Zone, beyond that was the Red Zone. Technically they were in the Hazard Zone. They needed to push in as much as they could to reduce their distance from the target. Time was going to mean everything when it came to the assault phase. The current phase was 'patrolling' and they would continue to 'patrol' to each drop-off point.

Jack was being pressed up against the window. He could see his breath on the glass. On his left, Kendren and Nell suffered the same. They were in the third Humvee of a four-vehicle convoy.

Dust lifted around the tires as they slowed to a stop - a checkpoint for them to 'survey' the area. Jack dropped out of the Humvee with his rifle in hand. On the right side was a small opening. Not many people, nothing to be concerned about. Just broken buildings and dust.

On the left side of the convoy was a dense arrangement of houses with thin alleyways, where half of the squad 'surveyed' while the other half got back inside the vehicles.

"See you on the other side, over." Jack heard them say over the radio. He waved to Kendren and Nell as they vanished deeper into the alleys.

Pulling away with low revs, the convoy rolled onward, considerably lighter. Splitting the squad into two meant there would be fewer of them moving through the Hazard Zone at any one time. So few in fact that they could pass through the bulk of the Hazard Zone relatively unseen. Jack wouldn't see the others again until he reached the rendezvous point deep inside the Hazard Zone.

"Possible tangos on the right."

Jack's mind melted back into focus. He had been functioning on autopilot for most of the drive. This wasn't supposed to be the hard part. Consciously present, he looked and saw the men on a second-floor balcony. They were not armed but were watching the convoy pass with great interest. The Humvees moved slowly. Speed implied a purpose, which could be considered threatening in those parts. Avoiding suspicion meant taking everything nice and slow.

There were one or two men on every block watching them pass. As the number of potential spotters went up, the number of genuine civilians went down.

"This is beginning to look hostile," came a voice over the radio.

Jack leaned away from the window and gripped his rifle properly. There were no threats yet, but spotters were often forerunners for an ambush. Men in the street watched them with blank expressions before going back inside.

"Insurgent presence doesn't start until we pass Barak."

"How much further to Barak?"

"About uuuhh… six klicks ago."

Jack shuffled further from the window and checked his helmet strap. He began to feel the heat under his many layers.

"Come on! Can we stay on the ball please?!" He heard Bennett say. *"Let's move. Get us to the checkpoint."*

The convoy was now moving too fast for Jack to get a good look outside. Bumps in the uneven road shook them from side-to-side like being off-road. Just as they were squeezing through a tighter section in the street, the convoy came to a skidding halt, leaving the Humvees within a metre of each other.

Jack leaned forward between the two front seats. The three of them were trying to look at the front of the convoy but their vision was impaired by all the dust that had been lifted by the Humvees. Jack raised his rifle, as did the soldier in the passenger seat. Jack then angled himself slowly to look out the right side-window.

"*Obstruction ahead,*" came a rough voice over the radio.

Jack couldn't see anyone yet, but he was looking for gun barrels more than for spotters. The buildings on either side were too close. He couldn't see the rooftops. They were boxed in. Silence energized each soldier with a familiar foreboding. Jack continued to lean for a better view… slowly… ready to duck at the sight of a little black cylinder. Each of them was breathing more audibly now.

Jack heard doors opening at the front of the convoy. Car doors. Confident with his view of the outside, Jack opened his door and gently leaned out to look down the road. He couldn't see any civilians, and that was almost never a good sign. Soldiers from the first Humvee were up front with their rifles raised to eye level. The rest of the squad was looking around, same as him.

Jack got out and backed up against the nearest wall. He left one leg on the Humvee to hold the door open and surveyed his surroundings. The left side was equally as barren. It felt unnaturally unfortunate to be stuck in such an inexpedient position. They were more waiting than wondering. Voices came from the front. Could have been Bennett and the others.

A sound from behind him made him look over to his right. There was an alley there. Only the second Humvee could see down it, and they didn't look worried. A figure appeared on the other side of the Humvee. Jack could clearly see the tip of a rifle. A military standard rifle held by another soldier looking down the road.

The more Jack felt like they weren't in immediate danger, the more he thought about how the soldier in front of him could be shot down in a blink. He could do nothing about it. If they were to be attacked, someone would have to be first, and whoever that person was stood little to no chance of getting up again. Three soldiers on his left, two in front of him, eight on his right. Himself. Any one of them could be first. Someone had to be first.

Motion on his right made his arms jerk around. He stopped himself from aiming his rifle at Bennett who came walking from the front. He was waving at them to stand down, which they did, then signalled to keep moving, which they obeyed. Jack saw the obstruction on the left side as they passed it; a wooden post, probably for telephone wires or something, had broken and fallen into the street. It looked like an accident rather than a sabotage. A reassuring piece of information Jack would have liked ten mikes ago. He couldn't tell if it was luck or an irrational fear. This was not where dreams were made. All you found in those streets was fallout and firefights.

Jack saw the checkpoint coming up before Bennett said it. Once again, the Humvees reached a peaceful stop. The second half of the squad got out on the left side. Soldiers staying with the convoy stood on the right side and tried to look busy. Bennett led his squad into the secluded alley. The next ten minutes went by uncomfortably fast. They advanced deeper into the town as the low rumble of Humvees faded out of earshot.

"This is Sierra-One-One; we've passed checkpoint Bravo, on our way to the rendezvous point, over," Bennett said into his two-way radio.

All four of them stopped to listen for a reply. Jack felt the weight of his gear sinking into his shoulders and pressing on his knees. Every soldier in the Hazard Zone fell into a simultaneous hush with steady anticipation.

"Copy Sierra-One-One. All units be advised: You have passed the point of no return. If you are compromised there is no guarantee that ground forces can assist and extract you. There will be an approximate one-hour wait time before reinforcements can reach the trade site. Air support cannot operate in that area without a sufficient ground force. Stay low, stay out of the way, over."

At the east end of the city, the American unit prepared to move to their own rendezvous point. The team assembled in their circle and picked up their gear. Backpacks and rifles as heavy as gold, and equally as valuable.

The captain passed his team and made his way to the roof. "We're ready to move out as soon as Longshadow confirms visual, over." Looking east, he waved an arm while holding his radio close. There was no chance he would see them. All he could see was the random assortment of deserted buildings turn to open sandy hills as the city died off.

"Copy, Jackson, I got ya."

Amongst the random assortment of buildings scattered across the landscape, one building sat atop a steep incline overlooking the rest of the neighbourhood. Fencing on the edge of the incline had broken and fallen away. Patches of dry, overgrown grass gave way to a sudden mound of pale earth.

A hollow cylinder with a square frame on the end protruded over the edge of the drop. A blink of sunlight flashed and curved around a circular abyss. The mound crawled backwards before revealing an arching back and pair of shoulders.

Captain Dax Falser got to his knees and put the spotter's scope away. On his right, the patches of grass that made up Lieutenant Matt Clerk stood up and looked around. The area was as quiet as when they arrived. "Let's move," said Dax.

Matt switched on the safety of his Designated Marksman Rifle and put a cover on the scope before swinging it onto his back. The two of them slid down the incline one after the other. Dax would drop to one knee and survey his every line of sight when at a corner or waiting for Matt. It would seem pointless in the deserted end of the city, but playing was for games, and games were for kids.

"Jackson's squad are rendezvousing half a klick southwest of here," Matt said as they passed the corresponding landmark: A set of apartment buildings tall enough to see from most angles at street level.

"Trust our bloody luck we get assigned to babysit the Americans," said Dax, grinning suspiciously into his radio.

"*Fuck you too, English motherfucker.*"

A smile grew on Matt's face. He turned to see Dax grinning with his radio still in hand.

"Oh man, was this on? Aww no," Dax said, sweating with sarcasm in the late-day sun.

The rest of the advance was a walk in the park. Never a real park though; open spaces were too exposed and to be avoided if possible. Traversing dangerous territory was easier with fewer men. A squad would be noticed. Half a squad would be glimpsed. A two-man sniper team? Invisible.

The sun began to touch the peaks of the buildings. They were three blocks away from the trade site. They hadn't seen a soul during the last hour of walking. Contrast to the predicted level of activity in the area. Orders were to avoid the local insurgents but to eliminate any if necessary. Dax had peaked around a few dozen corners expecting to see some potential threat or obstacle. Each time, he was pleasantly disappointed.

"*Sierra-Two-One, come in, Longshadow,*" said Jackson.

Dax ducked out of the street and dropped to one knee. Matt followed suit.

"Go ahead, Jackson," said Dax.

"*We have eyes on the trade site; triangular courtyard, reasonably open, your best view is a tall, white, apartment building one block west, only building with an open view, over.*"

"Copy, Jackson. Heading there now," said Dax. He tapped Matt – who was covering the rear – to signal for him to follow.

"*All units be advised: hostiles spotted in and around the trade site; proceed with caution, over,*" came the voice of HQ.

Dax stopped and turned to face Matt. Matt rolled his eyes and the two of them started their long arc around the trade site. They were passing Jackson and his squad south of the site when Dax pointed out the tall white building.

The walk was slow. They could feel the weight of their gear pulling down on their shoulders. Each of them had sweat themselves dry. They strained their necks around the last few corners until they finally reached the apartment building. Then, they searched the floors as swiftly and quietly as ever, before concluding it was undoubtedly empty.

They took to the stairs with greater peace of mind after agreeing to set up on the fifth floor. Now walking more casually, they evaluated the rooms facing east towards the trade site. Parts of the ceiling glowed orange from the sunset. There was barely any furniture left. Every sound echoed slightly around the pillars.

"Spacious," said Dax. "A lot more room than our last

place of residence."

"Man, I hope it's in our budget. Smells a bit, *but look at that view,*" said Matt.

Through nearly opaque windows, over two smaller buildings and a road, they could see the triangular courtyard in the last of the day's light, along with a few of its occupants.

"Neighbours don't look friendly," Matt said, straining to see what kind of rifles they were sporting.

"Spy on them all you like. I'm getting settled in," said Dax. He turned away and found a room on the west side for them to make camp for the night.

Chapter VIII
A Predator's Patience
███████, ███████, Afghanistan
June 2016

"Remain calm! Keep your heads on!"
"Don't Move. Don't. Engage."
"This is getting *very* complicated."

Bennett had his finger on his lips. The call for radio silence had been made. Everyone was kneeling in a circle with their heads down. Each of them blank and expressionless with their eyes wide open, seeing with every other sense. Light coming through the boarded windows striped black and white against the back of the room as the vehicles went by.

On the south side, Jackson was looking through a slit in the curtains. The street below growled and shuddered under powerful engines and heavy armour. A parade of insurgents were escorting the tanks and trucks to the courtyard.

Matt and Dax had their backs against the walls on either side of the window. Fear reflected between them as they glanced sideways at each other. Dax leaned over to get a look at the courtyard. He couldn't see the floor. Taliban were amassing into the triangle. Armoured trucks had to force their way through the throng to park on the sides.

Jack could hear footsteps on the road behind him. The scratching of dirt on tar no more than a metre away. Some of the light from outside came over his shoulder. He didn't dare move in case they somehow saw the motion through the boards. He clenched his jaw to stop the shaking, his rifle on safety but in hand. As Bennett had already pointed out, their fighting chance had left that morning.

"Another truck has entered the courtyard. That makes four in the last ten minutes," Dax said gently into his radio.

A block away, the din of foreign voices shouting competed with frequent shots into the air from the local militia.

"*Copy Sierra-Two-One, Surveillance estimates over a thousand hostiles now inside the trade site with more on the way. Over,*" said HQ.

"So, all of them, basically," Matt said, breathing hard. He crawled onto the table facing the window and propped up the DMR.

Dax sat on the edge of his chair and looked through the spotter's scope. "That tent… in the middle of the courtyard… is about two-ninety-two metres from us," he said, adjusting his scope's settings.

Matt used a small flathead screwdriver to calibrate his scope one last time, making a soft *click* sound as he adjusted the dial. The large, beige tent in the centre of the triangle flapped in the south-westerly breeze. Over his scope, he could see the surveillance drone high up to the east. The speck of a grey cross cruising under the clouds. The idea of it being spotted caused goosebumps to form on his forearms.

Jack was stretching to see what Bennett saw. Three black sedans drove by the windows and into the courtyard across the street.

"Looks like VIP's," Bennett mumbled. Cautiously, he took out his radio and moved away from the window. "Sierra-Two-One, Dax, you see three black cars going into the courtyard?"

"*Copy, Ben, I see 'em,*" said Dax.

"We can't see through the army outside our building. What's going on in there?" Bennett asked, moving to an empty room.

"They're unloading large crates from the trucks, looks like arms and ammunition. There's men getting out the black cars, they're dressed in khaki uniforms with bandanas and field caps. One of 'em looks older and well-decorated... he's gone inside the tent. Taliban captains-"

"Major, we've got some activity outside." Gillian was leaning around the corner.

"Yeah no shit-"

"It's not Taliban."

Bennett froze in thought. "Hold for a moment, Dax." He followed Gillian back to the front room.

"Where are they?" Bennett asked the circle of horrified faces that now faced him.

All of them looked up to the ceiling and pointed. Bennett tried to listen over the sounds of shouting men on the street. Lawrence was meant to be on the roof, but she was standing in front of him.

"Men on the rooftops all around us. Desert, military-looking gear," she whispered.

Bennett didn't hesitate. He pulled his radio up and broke the silence. "Sierra-Two-Three, do you copy, over," he said quietly.

Silence penetrated their ears. The response, if there was going to be one, was taking a long time. They tried to think of explanations that didn't involve lethal vicissitudes.

"Copy, Sierra-One-One, keep it nice and quiet," said Jackson.

The squad shared a suppressed sigh of relief.

"We think we've spotted the terrorists on the rooftops surrounding the trade site." Bennett looked through a slit in the blocked window. He could only see the edges of rooftops and the surveillance drone high up on his left.

"Copy, notifying HQ."

"Heads up, activity in the courtyard, the Generals are outside looking at the crates," said Dax.

Matt couldn't see them in much detail but it looked like they were just talking. He angled his scope back at the tent; it was facing left but he could see inside the door.

"Dax the terrorists are on the rooftops around the trade site! Stay low!"

Matt crawled back. Dax jerked the scope to look around the rooftops.

"Shit. Shit!" He wasn't whispering any more. Matt pulled the DMR further from the window. He didn't need the scope to see the figures on the rooftops appearing and disappearing.

"Everyone keep an eye out for the Man in Black," HQ said harshly.

Matt looked back to the trade site. Insurgents were standing around, oblivious to the new presence flanking them.

"Shots fired on the south side! Suppressors on the rooftops." Jackson snapped.

"Same in the north, either side of us." Bennett restrained his volume. There was no reaction from the courtyard.

"I can't see them anymore," said Dax.

Matt could hear him holding back his panic well.

"More shots."

"I can hear 'em but I can't see 'em."

Matt tried to ignore the calls. He focused on the trade. The generals were pointing at the crates. A little to the right, insurgents were standing around or walking casually (*"Shots, thirty yards east of us."*), packing AK-47s and RPGs as well as a few other assault rifles he had never seen before. He scanned left to right at the unique assortment of modern looking rifles (*"More suppressed shots, less than fifty metres behind us and closing in."*). They made up almost half of the firearms he could see.

Looking over one of the tanks (*"HQ please advise!"*), he could see a figure in the doorway of the tent. Tall, black, and motionless, leaning against one of the posts that held up the canvas. It took Matt a moment to focus on the figure before he could see under the hood. A black mask covered the lower half of its face, which was looking at Matt's building.

"I see the Man in Black!" he blurted out, "Doorway of the tent!" He could feel a cold rush being pumped into his veins.

Next to him, Dax looked to the tent. "Confirmed." He pulled his radio closer. "We have confirmed sighting of the Man in Black. He's in the tent in the centre of the courtyard!"

"*Say again Sierra-*"

"We have a shot on the Man in Black! Please advise!"

"Dax," Matt said with a quiver.

Dax turned to see his pale face and wide eyes.

"He's looking this way."

Dax turned back slowly. A cold flush washed the blood away from his face.

Matt couldn't have moved a muscle if he wanted to. He could barely see under the pitch black hood, but there was a face there, locking eye contact with him.

Dax swallowed. "He might not be looking this way," he whispered.

Matt watched as the figure leaned forward, revealing a tanned white face in the sun.

"*Say again Sierra-Two-One, what is going on?*" The blaring voice of HQ sounded distant to both of them.

"He's looking right at us," Matt said sternly. The shapes

of eyes beneath the hood were looking up at their window.

"I think he knows we're here," Dax breathed.

"*Stay cool Sierra...*"

"I swear to God he's looking right at us."

"*There's no way he can see you from that distance-*"

"He is literally watching us!" Matt said through clenched teeth.

"He sees us base! He knows we're here!" Dax whispered harshly. He felt exposed so close to the window. Adrenaline was telling them both to move but the hope that they were blending in was paralyzing.

The Man in Black leaned away from the post and raised his right hand up to his face. Coiling his fingers, he looked through his hand like a scope - The military hand signal for a sniper, aimed directly at Matt.

The game is patience. Good things come to those who bait.

"HE KNOWS! HE DEFINITLY KNOWS! WE'RE COMPROMISED!" Dax yelled as he kicked away from the wall and grabbed his rifle.

Taking careful note of the wind, Matt fired just to the left of the figure's chest. The two ground squads whipped around to face where the shot came from. The sound, like a hard *POW*, echoed through the courtyard and the streets, turning everyone's attention to the large white apartment building.

The shot hit the Man in Black's chest just left of the centre, shattering him into a thousand pieces that shimmered as they fell. Matt recoiled in shock and confusion. He could see the pieces of a mirror on the floor for only a moment before Dax pulled him off the table.

On the roof of the tallest building to the east, a canvas

was pulled off a large grey missile launcher. One of the men in desert gear calibrated the launcher, rotating it to aim up at the east sky, and fired. The missile jettisoned up with a thin tail of paper-white smoke.

Jack pressed his face up against the board covering the window and watched, wide-eyed, at the slim rocket that was accelerating upwards. He could almost hear it over the sound of his thumping heart.

A hush had taken over. All but one pair of eyes watched the missile soar up, as if in slow motion, in a tall majestic curve. As it gained altitude, the missile appeared to slow down, before it finally became a white speck next to the grey cross that was gliding above it. Once the long tail of smoke reached the surveillance drone, a tiny flash of red and orange swallowed it whole, leaving a cloud of dark grey to trail its descent.

Everyone on the ground dropped back into the moment. Time accelerated beyond its regular pace. Voices grew in the streets. Insurgents charged out of the courtyard into the scattering crowds. A cold, hollow feeling grew in Jack's stomach. The ground around them began to quake again.

Matt and Dax pushed away from the window to abscond. Half of their gear remained on the floor above. The building shook as the windows behind them shattered, sending glass flying across the room. They recovered from the force of the blast with their ears popping and their knees shaking. More RPGs continued to shake the building while they leapt down the staircase three steps at a time.

Jack could hear a firefight south of their position. It could have been in the courtyard or with the Americans. Either way, they were on their own. Nell aimed his rifle with one hand and turned the doors handle with the other. He opened it slightly, amplifying the shouting in the streets, then closed it carefully. Their only chance was to escape down the warren of alleyways that led out the back. The only thing standing in their way was the small army rioting down the streets on either side. Nell shook his head. "Too many."

Matt tensed up. Dax was right. There was a large crowd outside, approaching fast. He counted three mags plus one loaded. After that, there were a couple of mags for his sidearm. His tight vest suppressed his increasing heart rate. He took aim at the door, and switched the safety off.

One hand raised in the air, he remained still, staring down at the corpse under his boot. Khaki field cap with matching bandana, both stained red. His men watched him, equally as still. Taliban fought to leave the courtyard and take to the streets. It had been long enough. The Man in Black let his hand fall with mild thrust.

The sounds of muffled yelling and revving trucks vanished beneath a hurricane of gunshots. Jack flinched back against the wall. The inconceivable notion that the militia had turned on each other hovered at the top of his mind.

Nell grabbed the handle and raised his rifle. The amplified sound of gunshots burst through the opening door. He checked both roads and suddenly bolted to the next building. He stopped to provide cover and signalled for them to do the same. They wasted no time.

Jack caught a glimpse of the battle as he ran; insurgents were scattering in smoke, tripping over the carpet of dead bodies that lay in the streets. Whatever firefight had broken out, it allowed them to run north in short bursts.

Matt flinched and ducked away when the shooting started. He thought it was directed at them but the implausible collection of bodies outside suggested otherwise. He scanned his surroundings desperately. Dax ordered him to run before he could question it.

Nell peeked around the second to last corner. All Jack could see was his waving hand as he shouted "FRIENDLIES!" The response was almost immediate. Dust and chunks of concrete flew from the corner. Nell swung back clutching his bleeding arm and fell over his bruised knee.

Jack had no time to admire Kelly's speed with the bandages. He joined Kendren in throwing smoke grenades. Each of them ran through the smoke with their backs arched and their knees hitting their chests. Nell hopped with Bennett and Kelly under his arms. Everyone else returned fire on the mystery assailants. The terrorists had revealed themselves on the rooftops to fire at the militia. Nell had mistaken their desert colours for standard military gear, and the terrorists punished him for it.

News of their presence spread fast. They came under fire from new angles. Bennett yelled something about moving up and hoisted Nell onto his back. Jack was firing at the rooftops when a shot like a high-powered sniper overtook all other sounds in the cacophony. He instinctively backed up behind the wall and slid a new magazine into his rifle.

Distant cannon blasts marked the tanks positions. RPGs filled the air with smoke trails, leaving webs between the buildings. Trucks crashed without living drivers. Grenades turned into red craters. Cartridges and magazines mixed into the dirt and gravel, swimming in steaming rivers of blood.

A layer of hot sweat grew on Jack's back. The weight of his gear under the sun was prostrating. The second shot of the sniper lifted the weight for him, sending a shock down his spine and legs. It was following close behind.

Bennett had to shout in their faces over the cracks, snaps, and yelling of the surrounding firefights. "TAKE COVER BY THOSE CARS! ONE AT A TIME RUN TO THE ORNAMENT ACROSS THE OPEN THEN TURN AND COVER THE REST OF US!"

They looked over the broken cars to see a large stone ornament. To get to it, they would have to cross the road, then dash twenty-five metres in the open. They reached two rusty cars perpendicular to each other and took cover. The area ahead was mostly empty. The fighting had spilled out in every direction, diluting the activity in the streets.

Jack looked right. The militia were running away, fast and light in their shirts and shorts. The third mega-shot boomed from around the corner. The mobile sniper was closer than ever.

"CONTACT LEFT!"

Shots pierced Jack's eardrums like thick spikes. The squad exchanged fire with a large group of militia down the road. Threats emerged from the building on the other side of the ornament. Militia besieged the cars, forcing them to duck and cover in time to see more insurgents running in the alleys behind them. They shot down every man in sight before they could do the same - but the return fire got dangerously close. Jack checked himself for damage before turning his attention to the others. Gillian had a scratch on his helmet. Kendren had a hole in his vest that only went skin deep.

After a few seconds of recovery, they realized the militia weren't shooting at them anymore, but they were still shooting. Jack looked over his shoulder to see the terrorists gunning down militia in the open. A small group on the left stood their ground against the onslaught sweeping in. The ornament, some old fountain, wasn't wide enough to provide cover for six men.

Jack aimed his rifle through a window but a series of high-powered shots pounded at the car on his right, forcing him to drop down behind the wheel. Hot with frustration, he peeked behind the car to see where the shots were coming from. He only caught a glance of the black figure aiming at him before it opened fire again. He could feel the shots hitting the car when he noticed the sequence. The beat. The same eight-count rhythm he knew back from his old guitar lessons. A consistent rate of eight shots per four seconds in a sequence.

When the shooting stopped, the rhythm continued in his head. He peeked again. The Man in Black jerked his SCAR-H assault rifle anti-clockwise to flick the magazine out. Then he punched in a new one and released the bolt on the eighth beat. Shots then resumed in their sequence.

He advanced at a walking pace, planting his left foot with every stride. Jack stared, mesmerized by the contrasting black figure in the sandy-yellow street. An icon of indifference in a lethal medium.

Gillian was first to make a move. He and the others rose to engage on the Man in Black before being shut down by an explosive that blew on impact against the car.

The Man in Black opened the grenade launcher underneath his rifle and let the smoking shell bounce away. Jack shook his ringing head as another wave of insurgents appeared in the alley behind them. Reflexes took control but were subsequently overridden by the left wall of the alley blowing out. Bricks and dusty debris were thrown sideways at the insurgents before they could fire or react.

The smoke stung Jack's eyes. His vision turned cloudy white. He crawled away before he realised where he was going. He fumbled with his rifle and took aim at the street. No black figure. No militia. No men. The stars had aligned for the briefest of moments. Jack heaved himself up and bolted to the ornament. For what felt like the longest sprint of his life, he kept his eyes forward, listening to the others running beside him - their shaking breaths, the metallic tapping of their equipment.

The explosion and outcries of anguish attracted a third wave of militia, who caught sight of the squad ducking behind the ornament. The resulting storm of bullets forced them to press up against each other. Jack squinted at the building in front of them expecting more ubiquitous threats.

Then the whistling started. Above them. Starting at a low pitch and getting higher as it fell. Squealing whistles transformed into a brutal quaking of their bones. Their bodies shook violently against the reverberating earth. Every sense went numb. Rubble flew past on either side of the ornament. Then, apart from the raining debris, there was quiet.

Jack opened his eyes. Peace had filled the street. There was a door in the building ahead. A way out. Debris began to rain heavier around him. Small rocks, getting bigger and raining heavier, littered the ground around them. Some landing on them and bouncing off their helmets, worsening their throbbing headaches. Jack used the stone wall of the ornament to lift himself up to his knees and look over. The open area was filled with clouds of grey smoke that poured into deep craters. Pieces of the militia were spread in all directions.

He could see a black figure standing on a car through the devastation. It executed the recovering insurgents with robotic precision, shooting nonchalantly without looking directly at them, hitting each mark without having to try.

The Man in Black swung his rifle across the face of a man crawling beneath him and dropped down, landing on his neck. Jack heard the snap. He turned away but the screams of tortured militia filled the street more than the smoke did. The squad held themselves still. Fear crushed their windpipes into submission. Kendren lifted his hands to reveal their last pair of grenades.

"Gillian," Bennett said in a weak voice, "Clear a path." He pointed to the door ten metres in front of them. "NOW."

Kendren pulled the pins and flung the grenades over at the Man in Black. Gillian sprinted shoulder first into the doors. The doors barely cracked ajar so he kicked them open with the heel of his boot. Kelly dragged Nell first. They moved slowly. Jack aimed over the ornament to provide covering fire but was greeted by a rocket in mid-flight. His reflexes jerked him back down. The rocket hit the centre of the ornament, obliterating it. Chunks of stone flew in the shape of a peacock's tail from the ornament, narrowly missing Jack and Bennett but wiping out Kendren.

It took a moment for Jack's hearing to focus again, so he ran ahead as he began to hear Bennett's shouting. Gillian pulled him through the doorway. Their rifles were buried under the debris. Jack wanted to turn around, to cover Bennett with his pistol, but he didn't have the strength in his knees to resist Gillian's pushing. High-powered gunshots echoed through the hallway. It encouraged him to capitulate to reality until finally he stopped resisting.

Bennett didn't have the voice to tell them to run any more. He looked over at Kendren's Body, and the projection of his life: Allen Kendren, girlfriend waiting for him back home, who will only be met by a formal letter. No hopeful career, no hope, nothing.

Bennett pushed away from the wall to face his enemy. Men in desert gear walked idly by on each side. The Man in Black appeared over the stump of the ornament. His head hung low and his overcoat was shredded. Dust covered him from top to bottom with a sandy-desert hue. A line of red ran down the side of his bruised face. His green eyes were aflame with repressed rage. His long legs limped up and over the broken stone before stopping on the edge of the wall.

Bennett tried to push away from the figure of death looming over him. Wet hope bled from his chest in warm trickles of dirty red, painting a picture in the blank shell-shocked canvas of his mind; the image of fear he saw in the man he interrogated. Bennett felt it, word for word, in his nerves and on his face. Pure fear. True fear. A stronger combination of hopelessness and powerlessness than any regular person would feel in their lifetime. He hadn't the strength nor the will to push against gravity, for they had played with the fire of *his* temper, and would now burn for it.

The Man in Black stepped forward over the soldier's weak and quivering body. He kept his back straight and knelt down on the soldier's chest, letting his weight sink into his lungs. The soldier's gasping breaths weakened. The heat of shining green eyes burned into his retinas as the last image of light he would see before his mind faded into a void.

Jack only had his pistol left. Nobody spoke. Nothing needed to be said that they didn't already know. At that point, grieving went without saying.

Firefights died out in the distance. The four of them moved into the open road once they were sure the coast was clear. The street was devoid of life apart from a couple of rogue horses. The squad could camp in the hazard zone and await extraction, assuming they didn't draw attention to themselves.

Jack spun around with his pistol raised. He definitely

heard it. There was someone behind them. Gillian looked back but Jack signalled for him to keep going. Kelly and Gillian helped Nell off the street.

Jack struggled against the weight of his pistol. He spotted the black figure instantly against the pale walls. Two shots missed badly but the Man in Black took cover anyway. Jack heard voices somewhere reacting to the shots and backed up against a wooden house. Their shots penetrated the wood easily, scraping past him and sending spastic shocks down each of his limbs.

The mega-shot returned for a fourth time. In under a second, the Man in Black had drawn a large pistol and fired over Jack's head. The power of the shot broke the wood apart and lifted one insurgent off his feet. The rest of them scattered without another word. Jack aimed his pistol but the Man in Black had closed the gap between them. Jack felt the weight of his gear lifted from his legs and driven into his stomach as the Man in Black tackled him. The pistol in Jack's hand fired upon being seized. Jack's nerves abandoned him when falling backwards through the window, expecting to hit a wall.

The impact had minimal effect; there was no air left in his lungs to be expelled. He crawled away and pulled himself up to a table. Two heavy thuds on the wooden floor announced the entry of Player Two. Jack spun with a right hook. The Man in Black already had his forearm up to block it. Then he grabbed Jack's throat and swung him into the wall with a hard crack. Jack slid down against the array of new cracks in the wood. He tried to pull the air back into his lungs but struggled against a sharp pain in his side. There was a tranquil pause. He felt the warmth of the wound between his ribs.

"**Keep pressure on that**."

The Man in Black spoke with a deep and powerful voice

that seemed to come from and fill every part of the room at once. Jack turned his head away but continued to stare. He pressed his hand against the wound and held his arm down against his hand. Blood oozed between his fingers. Pain prevented him from finishing each breath. The Man in Black pulled out a small white sheet and ripped it open.

"You fought well, but it's over now."

His words were slow and precise. Somehow clean. Jack could recognise the accent anywhere.

"You're English," he said hoarsely, leaning back.

The Man in Black dropped slowly to one knee and ripped the hole in Jacks vest to fit the bandage through.

"Why?" He said through clenched teeth.

"It's over. You're done here. Don't worry, your people will be here soon."

"What are you gonna do!?"

"I'll make sure they find you, then take my leave."

"They're gonna kill you." The physical exhaustion was beginning to make Jack feel sleepy, and there were black spots appearing in his vision. The Man in Black produced a small needle, injected it, and squeezed before Jack could protest. The effect was quick, he could feel himself going slightly numb. The pain subsided.

"Even if I gave them the chance, would you trust them to do it?"

Jack didn't know what to say. The answer seemed too obvious to be questioned.

"You obey every order you're given because you trust the people in charge? Or because you were trained to?"

"BOTH." Jack could feel his frustration growing inward. It was insulting to imagine they were not the same thing, yet he found himself doing it anyway.

"What if you didn't trust them?"

"Then I wouldn't be here, listening to you."

It was like the last fifty minutes had never happened. Kind and friendly were not traits Jack was prepared for. The Man in Black tilted his head slightly. Jack looked into his bright green eyes which, despite his nature, looked peaceful and earnest. He shook off the gaze to try and remind himself who he was talking to. Yet, he felt unsure who that was.

"You have a mind of your own. How do you know you can trust them?"

"They *earned* their positions, through dedication and hard work," Jack said spitefully.

"Neither of which require a person to be good, or trustworthy."

The growing sound of a running horse distracted Jack from the words that were sinking deeper into his mind. The Man in Black slid a Desert Eagle handgun out from inside his overcoat. They could see the horse and its armed rider through the window on the right. As they passed in front, the Man in Black turned to face Jack with his gun in line with the rider, then stretched out on the other side and fired at the wall.

They heard the horse continue to run but when it passed the open door on the other side of the room, the rider was gone.

The Man in Black turned to look Jack in the eye.

"Men, who are willing to do anything for a position of power, will do anything to keep it. With enough power, one could even cover up one's own indiscretions, without question."

Jack stared at him blankly. His calm, unnerving expression hadn't changed. "What are you saying?"

"That's none of your concern, it's above your paygrade, either way, you're dismissed."

Two choppers flew overhead. The Man in Black stood up without looking away. Jack wanted to question him but didn't know what to ask. He couldn't make sense of it.

"Save your breath, Jack."

One of the Man in Black's men appeared at the door. Before *he* rounded the corner, the man yelled for a medic before following him out of sight. Jack didn't believe anyone was there until they walked past the right side window. Then it took all of his remaining breath to alert them to his presence.

They helped him to one of the Humvees down the road. How they found him was a question for later. His first priority was finding the others. He told the medics where they went and left it up to them. There were more than enough soldiers in the road to draw them out.

Once the tanks broke a path through the carnage, they could reach the trade site. Every street leading to the courtyard was littered with bodies and debris. None of the Humvees could make it over the uneven ground. The inside of the courtyard was untouched apart from a few dead men.

Colonel Trauss looked down at the glass mirror cracking beneath his feet. It was leaning against a pole in the tent without a frame.

"Colonel! Here!" There were soldiers kneeling around the dead bodies and unusual weapons with great interest. Trauss marched up to the nearest one and crouched for a better look. 'It can't be' he thought. He cursed under his breath and pulled off the khaki bandana.

"What the fuck," uttered a nearby soldier squinting down at the body.

"Get these bodies on a transport! I want those weapon crates and that anti-air loaded and ready to move! And somebody get me a radio NOW!"

Chapter IX
United We Stand
London, England
18:33 GMT, Thursday, 23rd June 2016

    Mrs Knight watched her husband with increasing concern. He was usually so good at keeping his work from affecting him at home. It became clear early on that his work had to remain as separate as could be from his family life. Neither of the girls fully understood what their dad did for a living, and to some extent, neither did Mrs Knight. The Afghan incident had been tugging on his mind for days. He said only that something went wrong during an operation, and they had some serious work on their hands. The SIS strictly forbade him to say much more… but it was even on the news.

    Dennis looked continuously distracted. He didn't seem as lively when playing with Casey and Emma. He didn't speak as much during dinner. When he did, it was short and to the point. Mrs Knight knew that he could work through it. Whatever it was. He came through for his girls whenever they needed him. He liked to believe they could try for one more. Mrs Knight wanted to believe him. As hard as he worked to prove it could be done, they both agreed that two was as far as they could go. It would be too much for her to handle when he left. Sometimes it felt like the agency required as much attention from him as fatherhood did.

    Sometimes he would be gone for days. Sometimes she wondered if he would be gone longer than he should. She would have to look into her little girls eyes and tell them that daddy wouldn't be coming home from work, ever. They're only four, but she wouldn't be able to keep it from them for years.

The phone in Dennis' study rang through the house like a call to arms. Mrs Knight stopped to watch Dennis. He lifted Casey off his lap and left hurriedly to answer. It was just a call. He had gotten calls before.

"Emma don't go in there, sweetie." Mrs Knight said, racing to stop her daughter from entering the study. She turned Emma away and caught sight of Dennis.

"I've heard enough about it today, can't this wait until tomorrow?" He said. Mrs Knight couldn't move. She told herself she was guarding the doorway from the girls.

Dennis straightened up. "Mr Euwin." He said with mild surprise. It had to be about the incident. He would have to leave for work after the call and she knew it. She began preparing herself mentally. He may not get back until tomorrow.

Mrs Knight closed the study door and returned to the kitchen, formulating a plan for the outcome of the call. She could read him well, and knew as well as he did that he would have to leave now. She was still every bit the women he married. Which made him feel worse when Arthur Euwin finished his briefing.

"I can get there in about fifty minutes." Said Dennis.

"I'm sorry to ask this of you but this is critical, and we're working against the clock. I need a reliable representative to-"

"I understand but I want Masier with me," said Dennis.

"Done." Euwin replied.

Taken aback, Dennis hesitated with the counter argument he wouldn't need.

"He can represent MI5. You'll be taking detective Taylor as well, with Officer Harper that makes four of you."

"Umm, Okay, I'll get them as soon as I can." Dennis swiped the papers off his desk looking for Joel's contact number.

"I'll take care of the detective, you get Harper and Masier ready by tomorrow."

"Yes, sir." Said Dennis. He found the number circled at the bottom of a consultancy form.

"And Mr Knight,"

"Yes, sir?"

"Time is of the essence."

"Understood. Goodbye." Dennis put the phone down. A to-do list streamed through his mind. "What first?" He said to himself, scanning the study with his hands on his hips.

Caitlin's number was on his phone already. The phone was on the dining room table.

"Have you got to go?" Mrs Knight asked when he left the study. She had an anxious yet kind expression.

"Yeah," he dropped his voice to a whisper, "To the US, I don't know how long I'll be gone." They glanced over at the girls who didn't appear to be listening.

"Are you going to miss Emma's gymnastics on Saturday?" Mrs Knight asked timidly. Dennis could feel the opposing forces of responsibility pulling at him again. Back and forth eternally. Producing only guilt. He nodded while looking down at his phone.

"Your suitcase is under the bed, take a Jacket for the plane, and tell the girls you'll bring home presents that always makes it easier."

"Okay, I just got to make a few calls." He took his phone and wallet back to the study and closed the door.

Caitlin pressed mute and answered the call. On her left, Ben froze in sudden silence, caught between watching her and the T.V.

"Hello?" She said professionally. In the corner of her eye, Ben kept himself busy with his phone. She knew he was listening but didn't care.

Dennis spoke quickly. She could hear him moving around to the faint sound of kids in the background. "When do we leave?" She interjected. Ben's attention shifted suddenly. Her tone probably told him everything he needed to know.

"Ok, I'll be right there. Ok… Sure… Bye." She looked innocently at Ben who raised his eyebrows enquiringly. She added an apologetic smile but he only shook his head in denial. Caitlin nodded. Ben's head hung in defeat.

"Not again." He said despairingly.

"I'm sorry." She said, kissing him on cheek before running to their room to pack.

"Where? When? How long?" He asked in the doorway.

"America, now, and… I'm not sure." She grabbed a handful of socks from a drawer.

Ben sighed. "I'm still going to your brother's place tomorrow night though, I'll let him know you're working." He rolled up her charger and placed it on the bed.

"Thanks." She said absent mindedly. The rest of the packing took no longer than five minutes. With her duffle bag at the door and a carry-on ready to go, she was done. Dennis wouldn't be at HQ for forty minutes and the drive there would only take fifteen at that time, granting them the rare gift of a more passionate farewell before saying their goodbyes.

Christian read down the list of flights until finally he found

Kandahar.

Suspended indefinitely. Of course it was.

He navigated his way through the throng of people looking up at the sign and checked his phone. It was the most excited he had been since the attack in South Africa. The investigation had been escalating curiously until suddenly it blossomed, becoming an even greater terror threat than before. Infinitely more significant and equally as complicated. He was just a detective, but it didn't feel that way anymore.

With over an hour until the flight, he figured he would find the others at the boarding gate. It only took a moment of scanning the area before he identified a man who looked like Joel Masier, buying coffee at a nearby stand. He walked up to the man whilst double checking for either of the others.

"Excuse me, Joel?" He approached hesitantly.

"Uhh, yeah, are you with MI6?" Joel asked hesitantly.

"Technically, yes, I'm detective Taylor. We've been exchanging notes." He swung back his laptop bag to shake Joel's hand.

"Oh yes," Joel smiled kindly, "Good to meet you detective."

"I believe you have the information I need to provide the answers you need." Christian ran his fingers neatly through his hair.

"I guess you could say that." Joel said with an air of confusion, reminding Christian to make sense when he talks.

"Sorry, it's an interesting case." He said, and with that, they began sharing their fascination. Conversing had never been so easy. By the time Dennis and Caitlin found them, they were deep in discussion.

"Glad to see you two have met." Said Dennis. He unzipped the side of his bag and produced a small folder.

"Mr Knight, Cait, good to see you." Joel said, recovering from a long yawn.

"I want to ask why we're leaving so early in the morning but I'm more interested in *that*, which I'm guessing is for us to read?" Christian asked, looking expectantly from the folder to Dennis.

"Yes." Dennis said with a tight hold on the folder, "Much to their surprise, our friends at the CIA have encountered the man in black before. More than they knew. After the events in Afghanistan they really want to make up for lost time, and the department of defence wants to continue our collaboration. So we're going to be working with them for a while. Plus there's a conference in Washington in a few days and they want us to present what we have."

"They want our Intel, they have no interest in collaboration." Christian said casually.

"Either way, we need to know what they know." Dennis glared at him suggestively.

"Sounds a lot like espionage to me." Caitlin said in a hushed voice.

"Not while it's considered collaboration." Dennis replied firmly.

"I get it. A none-zero-sum." said Christian. The added risk of high yield deception left butterflies in his stomach.

"I still don't see why we had to leave so suddenly." Joel said, yawning again.

"Yeah, we barely had time to say goodbye." Caitlin added sarcastically.

"You think I don't know that? I had to leave my family too." Dennis dropped his voice, "You should consider how serious this is before you start complaining."

"You're right." Joel took the folder from Dennis, "This

is more important."

Caitlin caught a glimpse of an image in the file when Dennis handed one to her. A street like any other in the Middle East, but packed with corpses. She imagined the main hall in South Africa would have looked similar. They had been after the Afghanistan files since they heard about it. It was only a matter of time. But the memory of Caitlin's 'brothers' in the armed forces ignited a fearful flame in her. They were the toughest people she had ever met. A country's military is its best weapon, the Taliban were their primary enemy. If neither one can beat a single terrorist group, how can anyone be expected to? The thought plagued her mind right up until take-off.

Virginia, United States of America
09:18 EST, Monday, 27th June 2016
(3 days later)

Henry couldn't concentrate. What had been a mild distraction was now an ever increasing anxiety. The British detective had requested case files from the FBI. Any and all that had been flagged as 'potential encounters'. If it tied to the man in black in any way, it got flagged. For whatever reason, they wanted them printed. That was five full minutes earlier. The printer hadn't stopped. Henry began to wonder if the FBI had even dealt with anyone else, or if they flagged every case just to shrug of the responsibility. His anxiety grew with each page. The sheer quantity. The magnitude of their influence. No-one ever knew. Suddenly, he found he didn't quite know what they were dealing with. Learning how much he didn't know did not impart confidence.

Dawson was jogging towards Henry's desk. Henry

spotted him over the edge of his monitor and pointed left with a pen. Dawson looked and saw the two of them waiting. Whatever they were discussing was put on hold when they saw him.

"Sorry I'm late," he said as he caught his breath, "The conference *has* been delayed, to Wednesday, and they would not tell me why. Bastards."

"Have you been asking questions up the ladder?" Dennis smiled.

"You know what, Knight," Dawson smiled back, "As a matter of fact I have." The two of them laughed for a moment, leaving Caitlin to watch awkwardly from the side-lines. Dawson walked back to Henry's desk and asked where Owen was. Henry pointed his pen right, towards Owens desk. When Dawson called him over, the printer next to them finally stopped. Henry let out a sigh of relief.

"Dennis, Ms Harper, this it Special Agent Bradford."

"Just Bradford or Owen is fine." He said, shaking Dennis' hand.

"This is Dennis Knight, Operations Officer at MI6, and-" Dawson was gesturing to Caitlin when she stopped him.

"Good to see you again, Owen." She smiled.

"Captain Cait." He smiled back. Dennis and Dawson looked back and forth between them with curious perplexity.

"We met in South Africa." Caitlin added quickly.

Owen saw Henry glaring up at him enquiringly with his brow raised. "What?" He said defensively.

"Hey whatever, man, what happens in South Africa – stays in-"

"Shut it, Busher." Dawson interjected. Caitlin and Owen avoided eye contact despite having nothing to be embarrassed about. Dennis asked where Joel and Christian were in an attempt to retain focus. Dawson told them about the meeting room they had been given to work in. They requested boards and an open space for something they were working on.

Henry gave Dennis the FBI files to pass on to Joel. Then Dawson sent Owen to find Sophie before leading Dennis and Caitlin away.

Since their arrival on Friday, Joel and Christian had synchronized. They sorted through a dense collection of data with inexhaustible determination and interest. But by the end, each of them had fallen victim to the stress of what lay ahead. Intrigue and mystery dissipated, revealing the true nature of their reality, and their responsibility.

Due to the encouraged transparency between agencies they had more than double the material to work with, which sparked some inspiration in them.

"They've been working in here for a couple of hours." Dawson opened the door to the meeting room. Most of their vision was then taken up by black on white. Pictures and pages were spread over the floor and tables in neat, overlapping piles. Christian was pinning something to one of the many boards that were placed side by side. He froze like a robber caught in the act. Joel was sitting on a table facing him. Once he saw Christian's reaction, he turned slowly and greeted them with a friendly smile. Caitlin closed the door behind herself and joined Dawson and Dennis in awe at the state of the room.

"Most of this is his." Joel said lightly. Christian glared at him with mild disapproval and offense.

"What exactly... is all this?" Dawson asked. He tracked the boards from left to right where a series of connections formed a sort of line.

"With years of data we formed a timeline." Said Joel, gesturing to the sequence of pictures and pages pinned across the line. Christian crossed the room with the FBI case files in his sights. He flicked through them as Joel continued to address Dawson's elevating concern.

"We're starting to fill in a lot of the gaps but there are still so many unanswered questions." He explained. Dawson considered the mess for a moment before nodding approvingly. Dennis and Caitlin followed suit, they had already been introduced to Christian's working style on Saturday when he and Joel made a mess of their hotel room.

"Joel!" Christian called. Joel watched as he pulled out pages and pinned them into the gaps on the timeline. Pieces of the puzzle fell into place. There weren't many empty spaces left on any of the boards. When he finished, the room fell into a pensive silence.

"I need to see an analyst." Christian said suddenly. He swiped a few pages off the floor and left without another word.

"So they did originate from England?" Dennis asked, stepping closer to read the timeline.

"*He* is English, but their origin is unclear." Replied Joel.

"It looks like they're spreading." Dawson waved a hand across the boards.

"What are these?" Caitlin asked. She was pointing to red lines that diverged from the central line.

"Links to other organizations." Joel answered, "They connect to pre-existing organizations and then both of them disappear."

Caitlin first thought of their vigilante streak, but notes on the board suggested their influence grew with each connection. "Like a syndicate." She suggested. Joel nodded.

"If that's what they're doing then we aren't the only ones in trouble. They have ties to over ten nations spanning as far back as a year. Russia, China, Japan, Italy, no real pattern but locations in Southern Africa and Afghanistan have clearly been proven legitimate." Joel fiddled with his reading glasses. Owen and Sophie entered with lost expressions. They skimmed over the room to catch up but remained at the back.

"I'm sorry they made such a mess." Said Dennis.

"Its good work," Dawson sounded as gruff as ever but with an added trace of admiration, "You two, front and centre." He gestured Owen and Sophie to the front then left with Dennis. Caitlin's proud grin grew when she saw Owen's wide uncomprehending eyes.

"Is it anything like your theories?" She asked Joel boastingly. He had exceeded her expectations but something seemed off about him. A sunken gloom had taken over his once lively posture. He was staring into space with an empty expression.

"It's worse."

Caitlin moved into his line of sight but his vacant eyes focused on the board beside her. "How much worse?" She tried not to sound too concerned. Joel rubbed his eyes. He had been reading and analysing for hours.

"I don't know what to tell you," He shook his head weakly, "I don't know what we're supposed to do. We still don't have much to go on. They are very good at what they do, we could be chasing after them for years."

"Who else is going to do it?" Sophie asked rhetorically.

"Exactly. This is what we do." Said Caitlin.

"Then what? We organize a raid? They would tear through us, we're not exactly their most formidable enemy to date. That's a job for the army." Joel gave a nod to Caitlin. She couldn't disagree. Sophie's point warmed up her optimism, but Joel's struck a nerve. Her most perilous missions were all during her service. The rest of the world was meant to be safer to some degree. Joining the SIS was a less hostile alternative. Yet the battle found her anyway.

Lucy tensed up as she jumped. The accent of the man was as startling as his sudden appearance behind her.

"Sorry, I'm Detective Christian Taylor." He said, holding out his hand.

"Lucy, Rei." She said robotically. She shook his hand without turning away from her computer. The man adjusted his glasses and stroked his hair to one side.

"So, are you an analyst, Lucy Rei?" He asked as calmly as before.

She wondered how she could get such a freight from someone so reposeful. "Yes."

"Perfect. I was hoping you could help me with some… linguistic anomalies." He said in a hushed voice.

"Um, sure." She said. He handed her a short list of unique words, most of which were foreign.

"I just want to know what these mean and where they come from."

It took a few minutes but it was reasonably easy. She compiled a corresponding list of details then turned to face him. He had been pacing behind her, waiting patiently in deep thought.

"So there's ten terms each in a different language," she began, Christian concentrated on the screen with a hand on his chin, "They're mostly along the lines of 'shadow' and 'ghost' but a couple of them are different. The word 'Commander' comes up twice in Japanese and Russian. This one is a phrase, it means 'prince of darkness' in Italian. And this one just means 'Angel of death' in Portuguese, could be from Portugal or South

America."

He knelt down and took a picture of her monitor so she moved aside and carried on.

"Most of these words translate to variations of phantasm, like spectre and ghost, but this Latin term literally means Phantom."

"You're sure?" Their eyes met as he asked.

She saw a flash of pretty blue in his concerned gaze. She hesitated until he looked away. "Yeah, it's all along the same lines."

"Thank you, Lucy Rei."

"You're English right?" She asked before he built up speed.

"Yes." He said simply, making time for a light smile.

"Cool," She mirrored his smile, "Call me Lucy."

She watched the back of his neat suit as he left. A mysterious English detective at the CIA, possibly the most interesting man she had ever met.

Washington, District of Columbia, United States of America
13:54 EST, Wednesday, 29th June 2016
(2 days later)

It was a garden caged in concrete. Green bound by grey. The quiet had a secluded tranquillity to it. A refreshingly natural quality. Light green grass was illuminated by the overhead sun. Five walkways connected the central structure to the pentagonal path around the outside. All of it surrounded by five great inside walls. The heart of the Pentagon, United States Department of Defence.

"Remind me why the Americans get to host this

conference and not us." Joel loosened the collar of his shirt. The summer heat was beginning to show. Next to him, Christian admired the architecture of the five entrances around the inside.

"Because our mutual terrorists have a greater presence here, and the Americans take terrorism very seriously." He said as casually as ever.

"But they didn't even notice until *we* reached out." Joel said indignantly.

"The US *is* a much larger country, so they have a greater capacity for crime. Probably why they would get more attention from vigilantes. Not to mention their pre-existing obsession with guns." Said Christian.

"Of course," Joel sighed, "Then they panicked and came to us for help."

"I'm beginning to think they're actually going to listen to us." Christian admitted.

"Of course they are, that's what I'm worried about. Entire countries are looking to us to find these guys, there are some serious officials here waiting to hear what we have to say." Joel chuckled nervously. It was something he had been pondering since their arrival in the States. Now that the case had been taken up by the departments of defence, all necessary resources were being poured into the investigation. They used to be the only two on the case. Now they stood at the front of an army of men, all working on the same problems.

"We're here to show them what we have, so let's show them. We hold all the cards right now." Christian held out his arm to let Joel go inside first.

Doing so, Joel shook his head disapprovingly. "You're getting cocky, young man." He could hear himself age as he spoke.

"I'm getting confident, and you should be too, this is all

because of you." Christian said with an arrogant smile to match his stride. They retraced their path through the building. The corridors looked no different to any other, but they had an air of elegance and respect.

"It doesn't matter who started it, Chris, we found out too late and people died. We've been working on this for months now and still don't know the full story. It's not enough. We are still no closer to finding or stopping them and when we do get close," Joel paused. He couldn't quite find the words for it. Christian's smile had faded. The truth was grounding. Where their new found authority elevated them, reality pushed down just as hard. Heroes are expected to win, if they don't, they are shamed, forgotten.

"We've come this far," Joel said with a hand on Christians shoulder, "We started it - we can finish it." He pointed at the conference room but kept eye contact. "This is all that matters now. Let's see it through."

Caitlin saw Sophie in the bathroom mirror. She buttoned the top of her shirt to hide the scars and curled the hair out of her face.

"Why so nervous?" Sophie asked, standing in front of the neighbouring mirror. Caitlin's shoulders relaxed. She hesitated for a moment before giving up entirely.

"You're usually so confident. You can hide it from them but I can tell." Sophie fixed her ponytail to look busy.

Caitlin sighed. "I'm not nervous."

"So what's wrong?"

"Joel's worried. And if Joel's worried then we should all be." She expected some counter but Sophie seemed to consider it while staring blankly at the bathroom sink.

"You sounded so positive, and you've been in the army." Sophie looked up at her with furrowed brows.

"But we never saw anything like this." Caitlin admitted.

"This is new to all of us." Sophie agreed.

"I don't fully understand. But Joel... he's instinctive about this stuff. If he's afraid then what should *we* think?" Caitlin explained.

"I don't fully understand either. None of us do. But we're figuring it out and once we do we won't be so afraid. What is there to be scared of anyway?" Sophie's smooth voice was reassuring. She leaned against the sink and crossed her arms causing her suit to become taut over her muscles.

"What happens when we try to intercept." Caitlin answered, looking down earnestly at Sophie's bright face.

"The whole world is looking for them, they can't hide for much longer. Stop worrying about everything, you need to take your mind off it." Sophie leaned in and lowered her voice, "I think Owen's taking a liking to you."

Caitlin's rosy cheeks began to burn. "You know I have a boyfriend." She said definitively.

"Yeah I just thought it would lighten the mood, you sound like you need a distraction." Sophie flashed a cheeky grin. "Plus it's good to see Owen moving on at last."

"Huh?" Caitlin felt like she knew already.

Sophie lowered her voice again, this time in a kind tone. "His fiancée was killed a couple of years ago. No idea who. They were never caught and he never stopped obsessing over it."

Caitlin's previous concern was replaced by complicated guilt. She now saw Owen in a new light that could never be switched off. It was beyond her empathetic capability. She knew the longing, the desperation of desire, the tethered feeling of loving over long distance. Every time, she would eventually be relieved of it. But what if the tether broke. Nothing on the other side. No other half. No release from solitary ache. Owen lived it every single day. The longest she had lasted was a few months. She couldn't imagine what years of it could do to a person.

Empty. Depressed. Tied to something that no longer existed. Desire lost without direction. Then the anger settles in. Owen could suppress it, manage it, but didn't always. Anger was better than the eternal longing. It could be focused, so he embraced it. Where depression left a hole, rage grew unchallenged.

Caitlin was like a revenant. Some piece of him brought back. She could settle the storm. His focus would waver whenever she was around. Just like it would years ago because of someone else. Caitlin reminded him of her. Like an ignition for his desperation. Forces of violent passion built up over the years without catharsis. She was a drug; euphoric in proximity, then devastating in withdrawal. He told himself it was temporary. Eventually the job would be over and she would be gone. Everything would return to normal. Focus was more important now than ever. Focus born of infuriation was all he had left.

Owen held the door of the conference room open. Sophie thanked him and entered, followed closely by Caitlin. Everything he felt amplified within a moment of meeting her gaze. Her kind brown eyes and gentle smile offered something he wish he didn't want. He didn't desire Caitlin, he desired what she could offer; something of a release from the tether to his past. A return signal from a connection that had long since gone cold. Sadness and anger flushed his cheeks. Then the sight of the conference theatre broke his train of thought.

Hundreds of seats looked down at a single podium, which stood in front of three large projectors. The auditorium was full within minutes. Officers and officials from both the United States and the United Kingdom were seated in their own rows.

Security members at the back watched Owen Bradford. He sat next to Caitlin Harper with Sophie Mercer on the other side. Nathan Dawson and Dennis Knight were seated next to each other with Grace Credette in the row behind them. Security took note of their attendance, and melted into the background.

The low rumbling of chatter trailed off when the Secretary of Defence – Gene A. Miles - stepped up to the podium. Then he spoke with a sudden austerity that set the tone for the rest of the conference.

It was an intimidating step up from the head of department back at MI5. Joel sat amongst the hundreds of seats bearing down on the podium. His memory of the day he took the case to Mr Lawrence numbed the butterflies in his stomach. Every muscle relaxed slowly. He could remember the feeling he had when he was told to open it officially. A bout of confidence had swept through him. A product of his unfaltering resolve. He was so sure about the case. Years of tenacity had developed a gut instinct. It was an instinct he knew he could trust. And the instinct was telling him that Christian was right. They held all the cards. The entire theatre and everyone in it would have to hang on to his every word.

When Secretary Miles called him down, he composed himself, stood up straight, and walked with purpose to the podium. Christian followed with an odd indifference to the hundreds of eyes watching him. Joel took his time with everything he did. Everyone else would have to wait for him now. They introduced themselves, and wasted no more time.

"We tracked their organization as far back as two years," Joel began loud and strong. He pressed the slide button on the podium to bring up a timeline on the projector screens. "We're still not sure how accurate the data is and we have no definitive point of origin. However, we can confirm ties to various locations around the world including Russia, China, Japan, Italy, South America, South Korea, and of course, Afghanistan and South Africa. MI5 encountered them in several parts of England over the two years. FBI and Homeland security - as well as the DEA - encountered them in several part of the US over the same period of time. Which is why we think the investigation should primarily belong to the combined efforts of the CIA and MI6, for convenience sake. A couple of the countries named have confirmed possible encounters. China has even agreed to collaborate and assist with the investigation given its similar nature to the Beijing massacre back in twenty-thirteen, although there is no evident connection between them. What we can tell from the timeline we constructed is that they moved around a lot, building their numbers and spreading out. We think their influence is divided up into each country they visit. Everywhere they go, they break up criminal organizations of all types and escape with their resources, since none are ever recovered. There are multiple cases where vigilante justice had been chosen over profit, but our current definition remains as a 'hostile syndicate'. We don't know what the Syndicate calls itself and we don't have names of any active members, but stories and eye-witness accounts describe mercenaries with military-level training and organization, often comparing them to some mention of a 'rogue militia'. At the head of the Syndicate is the Man in Black. Some evidence suggests there are members higher up than him but nothing conclusive." Joel stepped aside.

Christian took over without hesitation, switching the slide to one that showed images of the man in black during the attack in South Africa. "Caucasian male; age, uncertain, most likely in his early thirties; English Nationality; Possibly ex-military; and a violent psychopath. I say ex-military because his display of skill with firearms and hand-to-hand combat has been recognized by members of the British armed forces. The Syndicate shows discipline and organization under his command. Many of their tactics and signals are textbook military, as well as their combat style and execution." Christian brought up a slide that showed a physical profile of the man in black.

"I believe the use of black is an intimidation technique, what you see here is the substance 'Vantablack', which is one of the darkest materials on earth. It was stolen from Surrey NanoSystems in England and as you can see, was applied to sections of his outfit. Although, much of it is scratched off and faded."

Everyone in the auditorium glared intensely at the muscular black figure in the photo. Their attention glued to the intense yet tranquil expression on his face. Some of the older officials had gone pale with an almost pre-emptive fear. Joel looked curiously at their hollow expressions. He knew it was a scary concept, he felt a little afraid himself. This was different. They looked unusually spooked.

Christian began listing the arsenal of weapons the Man in Black had been seen with, ending with the axe from South Africa. It wasn't until he began naming the Syndicates general arsenal that a few people shifted uncomfortably in their seats. Especially when being presented with the unidentified rifles found in Afghanistan. Watching their fearful reactions was far from encouraging, but Joel felt hopeful. The more afraid they were, the more they would invest in the investigation. Joel could easily convince them to give him certain freedoms. His days of restrictions and limitations were over. With friends like those, no amount of red tape could stagnate his work.

"Timestamps, descriptions, and physical links suggest that this man commands all of the syndicate's operations. Every country has a different name for him when telling his legend, all of which essentially translate to 'Phantom'. The stories of the Phantom and his syndicate remained myth for years. A secretive organization with no name is hard to actualize. They're world news now though. Even gaining popularity and sympathy. The Triskelion symbol they used in South Africa – and the text 'Who's next?' that was sprayed next to it – has become a public symbol for unrest and rebellion. People all around the world are using it to express political displeasure by spray-painting the symbol around their cities. Sometimes on the walls of their Governments as a mark for the Syndicate to attack. The governments take this provocative behaviour very seriously and consider it a threat to their national security. Right now it's hard to say what the Syndicate's goal is but political rebellion is very possible. Although, their involvement with the corrupt South African officials remains unknown."

Joel took over with a list of unconfirmed Syndicate activities. Assassinations and murders in the various nations mentioned. Disintegration of other criminal empires. Grand larceny and theft. Although he could give a direction, Joel couldn't say how any of it was being achieved. They could have been using any form of transportation. Their weapons could be cargo somewhere. Without DNA or recognition, there was no way identify them. They never left anything that could be so incriminating. Their civilian identities were camouflage. The masks were their real faces.

The presentation went on for another twenty-five minutes. Hashing out the details and leads. By the end, everyone had been caught up. Secretary Miles returned to the podium once they had finished. He opened with a speech about working together. The loss of American and British lives during the Afghan incident called for a joining of forces. Christian listened with his mind. They could say 'better together' all they wanted, it wasn't going to sink in. Owen and Sophie were motivated by justice, same as the English members, but they were only a small scale team of operatives. The bigger picture was clearly a competition between Governments. Unspoken but known by all. Each side had information the other needed. That's why they were invited to the US. The Pentagon probably hoped to distract them with the honour of the invitation. The real purpose was Intel. Both sides playing for a none-zero-sum but too scared to call it what it was.

As long as they kept up the 'united' standpoint then intelligence and operation could function uninhibited. Christian figured he could claim ignorance if either side were to turn. Until then, he would have to manage the guilty foreboding he would feel when working beside them.

If he gave the CIA too much to work on, the US might pull them out and carry on independently. Keeping intelligence from agents is the epitome of suspicious. Not to mention the concept of keeping secrets from people who uncovered hidden intelligence for a living. If they found out, the dissention could jeopardize the collaboration. It would be espionage against their friends so that they could stay friends. High risk - high reward. Conversely, if he uncovered too much himself, his own Government could pull them out of the US. He would have to keep intelligence from his own institution, and from his own superiors.

Secretary Miles announced the joint task force of MI6 and CIA just as Joel had proposed. And so it had begun. The balance of intelligence to convince both parties that they needed each other. All because the men in charge want the same thing: Credit. As much as they could get for themselves. The more one man does, the more impressive it is. Sharing doesn't fast track your career. Efficient justice doesn't pay the bills as well as velitation.

Christian's attention turned back to Miles when he used the name Phantom for the first time.

"...Phantom. Every week, thousands of people around the globe claim to see the Phantom. They report suspicious and criminal activities thinking it's him, regardless of if they see him or not. The most notable witnesses place him in Russian gang wars, Italian riots, drug cartels in the favelas of Rio, even responsible for the disappearance of flight 257 in China. Most of it is false but it would be nearly impossible to tell what is legitimate, and what is background noise. They sprung the trap in Kandahar in order to escape, and although we lost the fight, we didn't let them get away. We've been tailing them, and we're getting closer, but if we lose this tail, we stand no chance of finding them until their next attack."

The news struck them like an alarm. Suddenly everyone was at attention. Their first victory – although at great cost. Just the break they needed to really put their knowledge to good use. Joel remained sceptical. He thought it was more like trying to hold onto smoke.

"Units in pursuit are following them North-East towards Tajikistan. A path that puts them closer to some of our bases. Lethal force *has* been authorized. They have military-grade equipment that can put a real dent in our side but they don't stand a chance against the full force of both our armed forces. Insurgents in our custody have admitted to knowing about the Syndicate. What they didn't know, however, was the truth about whom they were trading with." The next slide showed a line of bodies recovered from the Afghan incident. Neat, Khaki uniforms with their caps lined up above them.

"North Korean military officials. The Koreans deny their involvement in the trade of course, but we suspect it was an attempt to arm the insurgents against us. They have even gone so far as to accuse us of setting the whole thing up, claiming we stole the hardware and kidnapped the officials in a wild attempt to conspire against them and motivate military action. This is a troubling discovery that wouldn't have been possible without the good work of our joint team effort. As for the Syndicate, we are still unsure as to how they knew we were at the trade, or how the Phantom stood in the middle of the trade like he belonged there. No Syndicate members were found alive or dead."

Sophie followed the others out. Caitlin's chestnut chair swung gracefully over the arch of her back. As they filtered outside the exit, Caitlin fast walked ahead to Dennis and Dawson, who were conversing at a million miles an hour. Sophie had to jog to keep up with her effortlessly long strides.

"Are we staying on the task force?" Caitlin asked calmly. Dennis let out a peeved sigh.

"Yes, Harper, we are." He spoke with more authority than usual. The veins in his temples were throbbing stressfully. Dawson's gruff demeanour looked more annoyed with his hands on his hips.

"I don't understand, why don't we go back London? It doesn't make sense to have everyone in one place." Caitlin held back to avoid irritating Dennis further.

"We know you want to go home to your family," Dawson said suddenly, "We're disappointing people by being here too."

"That's not what I'm saying!" Caitlin said strongly.

Dawson returned her angry stare.

"Okay! We're all a little on edge from hours of sitting down," Owen stepped between everyone but faced Dawson, "We have a lot of work to do together so let's keep it professional."

Each of them took a calm breath as Christian and Joel finally made their way over. Sophie heard Dawson mumble something to Owen. It sounded like 'did you keep it professional in South Africa' but there was no reaction from Owen, so she left it. His comment about disappointing family was what intrigued her the most. Dawson was like a college professor; they never heard about or saw his life outside of work. Hearing him casually mention his home life broke the illusion. It humanized him.

"Look, we have enough agents here, you can return to London if you want." Dawson said with more control. "Joel, Christian, you two would probably be better here where you have access to anything you need directly."

Christian started to protest when Joel cut him off, accepting the offer on their behalf.

"Wonderful," Dennis clapped his hands, "Harper and I will return to London, you two can finish up here until you're ready to join us."

Joel nodded in approval. Once everyone started walking on, Sophie fell back to listen in on Joel and Christian.

"They're just using us, Joel." Christian whispered.

"Yes but they will let us do whatever we want as long as we give them some results." Joel whispered in return. It must have convinced Christian because he didn't counter or argue. Sophie wondered if she should say something. Not wanting to give herself away she thought it best to observe from the outside, so she acted oblivious.

"Gentlemen!" Said an old and familiar voice from behind. Secretary Miles caught up to Joel and Christian with a thin smile. Sophie joined the others in watching from the side.

"I just wanted to thank you for your work in protecting our nation's security. I'll make sure you get what you need to keep it going."

Sophie's heart began beat harder. The exchange gave a cynical frame to both her friendships and her superiors. Joel may have been right but he was far from innocent.

"The Phantom is a good tactician. After analysing the Syndicate's attacks I've come to notice that the core of their strategies is straight out of The *Art of War* by Sun Tzu, I suggest you read it. Might help." Secretary Miles offered his thin smile once more before turning back, followed closely by two members of security. Joel dropped his fake smile of appreciation and met Sophie's eye. She turned away cautiously, faking a vague, uninterested expression.

"Good for you." Dawson said with his eyebrows raised.

"Not proud of us, Dennis? Or does it bother *you* as well?" Christian asked lightly as he passed him.

"They're being very generous to this case." Dennis said, half genuine half suspicious. "I've never known it to be this easy."

"There's never been a case like this one." Owen added.

"They must really be afraid." Said Sophie. She needed to

shake Joel's subtle observation.

"Or they know something we don't." Christian said casually.

"Let's not jump to conclusions." Dawson spoke slightly louder so they could all hear him clearly. Dennis agreed and walked on beside him. Sophie joined Owen and Caitlin's conversation to avoid Joel, who continued to talk privately with Christian.

At the entrance of the Pentagon, members of security monitored the flow of officials leaving the building. Two guards facing opposite one another at the doors identified the task force as they left. They made special note of each member. Physical appearance, age, and rank. Once they were gone, they were someone else's problem. The security shift carried on for another few hours before the night shift took over. They gave the new guards a friendly nod and were relieved from their posts.

The day shift members got in each of their cars and left within a few minutes of each other. A select few of them drove their regular obscure routes before converging on the factory. A large, scrappy looking complex near the railway. Much of it was rusted and unkempt. Flood lights lit the grounds when necessary and a dim orange glow could be seen in most of the upper floor windows. The rest of the buildings and structures were hidden behind the surrounding wall.

The great double-gate entrance was opened by two armed men. Once inside, the guard's cars were hidden in underground parking to be searched for foreign devices. After being searched themselves they made their way upstairs. The mercenaries they passed were geared up in dark grey combat vests, with pockets for extra rifle magazines. They could hear blow torches in the garages behind them. Echoed voices and metallic clanging. Other men and women were sitting around; laying back or talking casually to one another.

They passed through a room glowing from almost twenty computer screens. An intricate network of cables lined the ceiling of each hallway. Finally they reached an open room with more computers on either side. The edges were draped in shade. Two strong lights illuminated the centre table that took up most of the room. Maps and other random documents were scattered across it. At one end, the captain saw them enter.

He asked about the conference. The propitious goldmine of Intel. Of course, *she* would want hear all about it, so he left on his own path through the factory. He passed a few mercenaries in the hallway and took the stairs to the third floor. Glancing into the open doors as he passed them, he caught sight of the projects currently under way. Mechanical frames that mimicked human skeletons. Kevlar vests filled with liquid armour that hardened on impact. Drones charging in a corner. Heavy duty helmets and masks each fitted with smoke filters and wide goggles. One man spray-painted a paintball mask with a coat of grey. The last room was filled with circuit boards and wires, taken apart from random devices and machines.

At the end of the hall was the final staircase. He knocked on the heavy wooden door at the top, and stepped back. The man who opened it had a mean look. The wrinkles in his forehead merged with a scar that went up to his jarhead buzz cut.

The man left him, so he closed the door as he entered. Tall shelves on the right held their local servers. Most of the wires from the servers ran around the edges of the room and left through a hole in the wall. The rest were connected to a row of computers against the wall opposite him. Three men wearing headphones operated the computers. What they were doing, he could not tell. Next to the door on the left was a row of tables covered with weapons. Rifles and handguns. Knives and swords. All spaced out neatly and organized into groups.

She sat, legs crossed, on a table at the left end of the room. A row of 5.56cm cartridges stood on the table next to her. She wore a skin-tight tank top that only covered her upper torso, a pair of grey combat trousers with large thigh pockets, and no shoes. Her hourglass figure was slim but well defined between her muscles. Straight, dark blonde hair cascaded down her back. He could see thick scars up her back and right shoulder. The right side of her head had been shaved down, revealing a collection of shrapnel scars that continued over her ear and neck. The rest of her hair was draped over the other side. An Exo-skeletal frame was connected to her right hand, all the way up her arm, and over her right shoulder. Deep-tissue scars covered the thick muscles in her arm, yet it moved no differently to the other; slowly, gracefully, as she handled the long, desert coloured rifle on her lap. It was a SCAR-L. Appropriate for her, he thought.

"My lady," he said clearly. There was no reaction. She continued to polish her rifle whilst looking up at the six screens on the wall in front of her.

"The guards are back from the Pentagon, they're preparing their report of the conference now."

She looked over her shoulder at him. Thin scars on the left edge of her jaw cut across her nose, eye, and temple before turning jagged across her forehead. A cut on her glassy brown eye lined up with the rest of the scar. Despite her injuries, she had mature beauty.

"*Good.*" She said in a heavenly voice. Feminine, but not girly. Her eyes wondered as she happily considered the good news.

"They finally have a name for us, you know." He said with mild glee. Her focus snapped back to him.

"I heard." She smiled and turned back to her rifle. "*The syndicate.*"

"And for *him* too." Like her, he was smiling with amusement.

"*The Phantom.*" She said seductively.

"Where did you get yours? The *Lady Danger* Must have a story behind it."

"You are dismissed, Captain." She reached for the remote on the side of the table. One of the screens was streaming security footage of the garages. The completed steel frame of a giant arrow-head ram was sitting to one side. She switched the feed to see the captain returning to the Pentagon security unit downstairs.

"My lady, we're live again." Said one of the men behind her. He walked over and handed her a pair of earphones that extended from his computer. She put them in, letting the wire fall under her mechanical frame, and listened.

The familiar voice of Secretary Miles sounded a little distant but clear enough to hear. He was speaking to someone. Then several people. The conversation went on for over ten minutes until he went into a room alone. The Lady Danger waited patiently. She was about to take the earphones out when the sound of a door opening started another conversation. Some unknown man had entered the room and was talking to secretary Miles.

He mentioned something that made her stop cleaning the scratches on her rifle. She concentrated on the conversation, staring blankly into space.

"*We have an approximate location but it's hard to track them with local insurgents mobilizing in the area as well.*" Said the Man.

"*Are they moving together?*" Asked Miles.

"*No, we think they're taking a route through active Taliban territory for cover.*" Said the man.

"Clever boy." Whispered the Lady.

"*They won't have cover for much longer. The second they step out into the open, we'll move on them.*"

"Good, don't jump the gun." Said Miles.

"Look, Mr Secretary, even if the Hunter-Killer units catch up… they're soldiers. They're just going to start a firefight. Then there's no guarantee we can stop this 'Phantom' man from getting away."

"What are you proposing?" Miles asked.

"I have a Special Operations unit that has proven very effective at hunting high-value targets. They would be perfect for this task." Said the man.

"I'd rather not wait for the Phantom to escape so you can use a Marine death squad. I'll authorize sufficient air support for the open assault and if that doesn't work, then you may call in your unit."

"Thank you, sir." The sound of his footsteps got quieter, as did his voice. "*They work better covertly. I think it would be best if we kept their existence need-to-know only.*"

"Alright, but any information they uncover must be made available to the CIA." Miles instructed.

The Lady Danger had a gleeful sparkle in each of her wide eyes. A happy yet sinister smile grew across her face. "I don't think we were supposed to hear that."

Chapter X
Hunter-Killer
Ghazni, Afghanistan
16:08 AFT, Tuesday, 12th July 2016
(13 days later)

Jack was damp with sweat again. The intensity of the unrelenting sun spread as far as the eye could see. Houses of brick and stone baked in the afternoon oven. A layer of light-warping heat emanated from the road on which they walked. The heat had seeped deep into their rifles. They were lined up, keeping to the left side where the shadows of the houses were beginning to lengthen. Without wind or traffic, the only sound was the scuffing of their boots on the sandy earth. Soon the sun would falter beneath the hills. Ghazni lay ahead. On the outskirts of the city, they were one of many sweeping units, hunting a phantom in a ghost town.

There was a lot of time to think during the walks. That was one thing people didn't expect from enlisting in the armed forces; how much nothing you actually did. Training, drills, chores, and nothing. Once the noon sun had settled in, they hadn't the breath to talk. Six of them were spaced a few metres apart: Kelly, Gillian, Jack, and three newbies. Nell was discharged on account of his injuries. Jack spent some time in the hospital, then left fresh and ready to be manipulated back into combat.

'Hunt down the sons of bitches who killed our brothers!' Capitalizing on the dead, they managed to convince most of the reserves to go jogging in the desert looking for terrorists who were too smart to move during the day. Hence why nothing had happened in the month since Kandahar. Recon had been chasing the Syndicate through hostile territories using satellites and drones. They kept getting confused between the Syndicate and the insurgents, sending soldiers into Taliban zones by mistake.

Days of tailing but not chasing were turning Jack's perspective sour. He saw their redeployment campaign for what it really was: Desperate attempts at vindication using grief as a motivator.

Never had his loyalty been so poisoned - all because he had to question it for just one second. The Phantom's enigma ran its cycle.

"That's none of your concern, it's above your paygrade, either way, you're dismissed."

It didn't mean anything. It was everything else he said that meant more to Jack than he would have liked. He shouldn't have listened. A scheming psychopath like the Phantom couldn't be crazy enough to just make friendly conversation. Phantom's men killed Kendren and Bennett, but he let Jack go. An embarrassment he would never outlive. Perhaps that was why he felt it necessary to glorify the Phantom's words with consideration.

The commanding tent was full of the highest-ranking members in Kandahar. Jack actually had an excuse to be there. He jumped on the first available opportunity when it arose - A job that sent him to the tent. All he had to do was deliver a message. It was enough.

Once there, he delivered the message and lingered for a moment, wondering how he could phrase it. Brigadier Read was the man to ask, so Jack struck up a conversation as casually as he could. Then he needed to keep up the act after directing the conversation toward his main question.

"Who decides who gets promoted in higher ranks?" Jack eventually asked, pretending to have mild interest.

"A centralized board at the Human Resources Command determines promotions. Based on service record and merit and such," said Read.

"Do they look into the records to… y'know… check that they're legit?" Jack tried to express a little concern in case Read suspected him of something.

"I don't know," said Read, "They might, although I don't see why they would have to; it's official record. Why?"

"Oh no reason," Jack kept his tone normal. "You never hear of corruption and stuff so I thought it must be a bloody strict system."

"Corruption?"

"Yeah y'know, like doing sketchy or illegal shit to get a promotion."

"No, I've not heard of anything like that in years."

"So, nothing illegal or covert? How do we know they haven't just covered it up or something?" Jack asked.

"That's none of your concern," said Read.

Jack's stomach turned over. Read was walking away but he had to be sure. "Right, sir, above my paygrade," he said normally. Meanwhile, his chest felt like it was getting tighter.

"Exactly. Dismissed, Lieutenant," said Read.

Jack walked out of the tent with an uncomfortable energy buzzing through his head. None of his concern, and so he was dismissed.

The Phantom's enigma unravelled. Jack hated himself for it. He dignified the words of a murderer.

In the two weeks since that day, he thought about it more than anything else. Every day he would walk the dusty, deserted roads of Afghanistan, letting injustice question everything he believed in. Landscapes of flat, empty deserts and barren mountains brought about revelations, such as the manipulation he succumbed to. The one that now had him wandering the streets outside Ghazni, chasing a man he trusted over his own superiors for only a split second. A man who could not be trusted but did not lie.

Jack had never questioned his own integrity nor that of the men he worked for. They painted a clear picture of good and bad. His sudden distrust was purely speculation. But despite his madness, the Phantom knew something. Jack simply wanted to know if he had put his faith in the wrong people. Especially after the years he had dedicated to service. Perhaps it was time to seek a life elsewhere. After the Phantom is killed and the operation over, he could leave the armed forces for a life he believed in.

It may be a distant future considering their recent attempts. But first, Jack would have to reach the end of the road he was currently on. One step at a time. He surveyed the empty ruins while following Gillian's path in the merciful shade.

All six of them slowed to a halt in their line. They looked around and at each other for something amiss, but it couldn't be seen. A flicker of sound travelled with the breeze, coming from nowhere. They could only stare into space as they concentrated silently and listened out. It was both a high and a low pitch at the same time. Almost loud enough to be real. Soon enough it grew until they could hear it phasing in and out of earshot on their left. Jack couldn't see anything past the derelict houses.

A kind of squeaking and squealing, yet at the same time, a deep rumbling. Realization sunk in. The ground beneath them vibrated lightly as the rumbling grew into growling. Above all, the unsteady squealing was unmistakable.

"Off the road!" Gillian stressed, suppressing his volume. No one hesitated. They bolted to a wide alley on the other side of the street. Their footsteps echoed until they reached an open yard enclosed by the surrounding buildings. There were alleys to the left and to the right but nothing straight ahead. The crumbling of brick and stone echoed down the alley behind them. Jack ducked for cover on the right side with Kelly. Gillian was peeking anxiously around his corner. Jack did the same. Low rumbling filled the yard. Each of them pressed up against the shuddering floor and walls. The portion of the road Jack could see was still vacant. He grabbed Kelly's shoulder, ready to pull himself out of the way at the first sign of movement.

First was the barrel - moving left to right. Thick, hollow, and dark grey. It extended a few metres ahead. A row of long, sharp, ploughing teeth protruded from the front. Then the rectangular hull came slowly into view, fitted with an extra frame of bars. Seven-wheel treads squealed beneath a roaring V12 twin-turbo diesel engine. The turret was flatter than most but unbreachable, nonetheless.

Jack had never seen a tank like it. She was a monster. He and Gillian whipped back when her turret came into view. Jack could see their pale, sun-kissed faces on the other side. Gillian looked straight ahead. The treads slowed with a metallic screeching before coming to a stop at the other end of the alley. Jack wanted to look but kept his head leaning away. Beside him, Kelly had her eyes shut. She was shaking when a deep electric whirring told them the turret was rotating.

Jack wondered what reason the beast could have for stopping unless she knew where they were. Then he remembered Kandahar when they were so sure they were hidden only to be compromised all the same.

A concussive force blew out of the alley, deafening them with a dizzying boom. They just had time to cover their ears when the wall of the opposite building exploded in front of them. Clouds of dust expanded over the yard. Chunks of stone were sent flying in every direction.

Null sound had filled their ears. She started moving again. They could feel her in the ground, exciting it, resonating in their bones. Panic filled Jack's veins. He couldn't hear where she was moving, then her barrel broke through the wall above Gillian. He and the other two leapt out of the way, the last man narrowly missing her plough of teeth. The two men on the other side escaped out the left alleyway.

Jack felt anchored to the ground. When the turret turned to look around the yard, he jerked up with a hand on Kelly and followed Gillian back into the alley between them and the monster tank.

The beast surveyed the scene. She spotted the last man after Kelly. The walls of the alley cracked and shook as she reversed. Gillian skidded to a halt, looking frantically at the wall. It was impossible to tell where she was moving. There was no sound, only feeling. All Jack could hear was her low growling vibrating his skull. She was hungry.

A surge in vibration shook the foundations as she broke through the wall beside them, across the alley, and into the neighbouring house. Jack's legs were shaken out from underneath him. He backed up against the wall and shuffled sideways. Debris cascaded off her armour and deflected off his helmet and shoulders.

The tank – nearly ten metres end to end - disappeared into the dust of the building. She had a shorter row of teeth at the back, covered in what looked like dry blood.

They watched cautiously through the dust. She broke out into the road on the other side and turned right. Gillian pushed Kelly into the yard with him. Taking hold of Jack's head, he spoke loudly into his ear.

"THAT'S A LEOPARD."

Jack had heard of them. Unstoppable beasts. German engineering.

The squeak of her stalking was coming back. She made a pass by the alley behind them and looped around the block. Jack and Gillian hid behind the corners of the left alley as she went by. They could see the other two across the road, peering at them. 'WHAT THE FUCK?!' mouthed the one.

Jack moved into the alley to watch the Leopard. She was crawling down the road, searching alleys and openings. The men on the other side signalled for them to run across.

Gillian pulled the other man forward. His label read L. Miller.

Jack heard a faint whirring and spun around to look. She was searching the right side. His side.

Miller had as good a chance as he ever would. He sprung out into the road and bolted to the other side where the others pulled him to cover.

Jack was ready to run when the Leopard stopped. Everyone backed against the walls. All was silent except for her distant juddering. When the whirring started again, Jack realized they had left their rifles in the first alley. He dismissed the unnecessary concern and peeked past the wall.

She had her eye on them. Her wide, round, black eye was aimed right at him. Jack's diaphragm plummeted, forcing his lungs to fill with air before he jerked himself backwards. He could barely get the words out, but Gillian and Kelly got the message. They ran back to the yard with the sound of accelerated revving closing in behind them. There was an alley ahead on the left leading to the other side.

The Leopard skidded to a stop where she had seen them and obliterated a house on the other side of the yard. The force of the blast buckled Jack's knees once more. He turned to help Kelly up just in time to see the previous alley break out with an avalanche of stone and dust. She was in the yard with them.

They couldn't feel the heat anymore. Adrenaline carried them across the road. Tight spaces and alleys were her weakness. She couldn't manoeuver well with the long barrel. Their best chance was to slow her down with more obstacles.

Everything they passed was a blur. Jack's spatial awareness was heightened. He seemed to flow through without taking in what he was seeing. Pushed by prey-fear. They ran from her. From the sound of her hungry growling. And she followed.

They sprinted on shaking ground. Her treads screamed behind the buildings to their right. Jack heard the blast of a tank cannon. Not from her, but from somewhere in the distance. It boomed over the valley accompanied by gunshots and crackling. Before Jack could tell where it was coming from, the building on their right blew across the path in front of them. They collided at top speed with some of the dust and rock. They skidded on the sandy road and darted into the building on their left.

Jack's ears were numb again. Out the other side, Gillian collapsed in the road. He was coughing blood into the dusty air. Jack attempted to hoist him up when vibrations in the road electrified him with apprehension.

She broke through the building and stopped in the middle of the road, shaking Jack and Kelly to the ground. Jack pressed his palms against his ears and forced his head against the earth. His vest restricted his breathing. He expected to die at any moment. Final thoughts raced through his mind without sticking. Each of them overtaken by the next. But the end never came. There was no blast.

Jack lifted his head from between his shaking fingers. She remained dormant. She hadn't even turned to look at them. His body relaxed. Dust irritated his eyes, but he continued to stare. She seemed to be waiting... considering something. Jack's mind scrambled for an explanation until the answer snapped into place simultaneously for both of them.

The monster rotated on the spot and went back on the hunt. Jack grabbed Kelly's leg and scuffled into a run. The three of them slipped into the nearest building and ran to the back. Jack couldn't hear it but somewhere out there was a firefight with another tank. It had to be with the other units, which also happened to be their only way out.

They backed against a wall and fell to the floor, each of them gasping for air with Gillian coughing most of it back out. The dull sound of cannon blasts passed through them.

Jack considered staying there to peacefully wait it out. But that was not what they were trained to do. When the distant sound of gunfire came back, he pushed himself up, his legs shaking but holding strong.

They started their journey through the empty town - dizzy and covered with sweat and dust. The sounds of fighting grew louder and clearer with each turn. Finally, they saw smoke coming from across an open yard. Pure white and grey - from a friendly's smoke grenade. Their familiar smell filled Jack's nostrils. It was hard enough to breathe, but if he coughed, they could be compromised. He buried his face in the middle of his arm and strained to see ahead. A wall on their left guided them forward.

Gillian couldn't hold it, he coughed and spluttered with watery eyes. Jack and Kelly managed to dive around the corner. Gillian gave up on stealth and stumbled past them.

Foreign voices of the local militia began shouting on

their right. Random and aimless gunfire sprayed the smoke. Jack was pinned to the ground against the building. He reached for the doorway when a hand came out and pulled him in. The door slammed behind him as he slid across the ground on his belly. Although the voice seemed distant and muffled, he could understand well enough.

"*You muppet!*"

Jack flipped over. The room was filled with soldiers. Kelly and Gillian had been pulled in through the wide windows which he could see had no glass. There was no smoke inside. It was creeping along the road outside from the right.

"What's happening?" Jack mumbled.

"Taliban ambush! Where's your weapon soldier!?" The man looked Jack up and down. His dusty, wrecked appearance said it all.

"Where are the tanks?" Jack moaned.

"We can 'ear 'em but we 'aven't seen 'em yet! On your feet!" The captain and another soldier helped Jack up. Men at the windows opened fire at the opposing rooftops.

Jack couldn't put his thoughts together. His head lolled with a pounding headache. Luckily the captain did all the thinking for him.

"WE HAVE TO RETREAT TO THE VEHICLE LINE FOR SUPPORT AND EXTRACTION!" He yelled over the gunfire.

Without much thought, Jack went with it. He readied himself beside Kelly and Gillian. There was still a row of assailants on the opposing rooftops. They scanned systematically to see where the shots were coming from. Across the two roads was another open yard. Hostiles occupied a rooftop on the right overlooking the yard and the street.

They held fire for a minute. Smoke continued to ooze

along the road in a wave as high as three metres. Jack surveyed the rooftops when a familiar revving sent a shock down his spine. A blast obliterated the rooftop, exploding it across the yard. Chunks of stone and meat bounced everywhere beneath a rain of blood-red dust. The smoke in the street shifted and rolled. It began crawling across the ground and arching over in an expanding wave.

"*Hit the deck!*" Hissed a soldier at the window. Jack dropped in time to feel it. She was stalking again. In the street somewhere. Everyone took cover and watched the windows.

It started with the barrel again, slowly out of the smoke wave. Then came her teeth, sharp and scratched.

A ringing in Jack's ears synchronized with the squealing of her treads. The full metal might of her body emerged, dragging the smoke along. The breath of her exhaust sent the cloud whirling into chaos. The building around them shuddered and vibrated. Many of the soldiers were gripping their rifles and helmets.

'We can't stay here,' mouthed the one.

Jack could see the captain's eye twitch as he watched the great grey beast crawl past.

Seeing her rotate to look away, the captain motioned for them to move through the buildings.

The vehicle line followed the ground units for backup and extraction. They couldn't have been far behind. The sudden hostile presence complicated their options.

Jack fell in line and followed them out the back. They moved parallel to the road she was on. Gunshots coming from near and far indicated worrying conditions of the vehicle line.

Their knees ached. The sun was setting, taking all visibility with it. One of the radios made scratching noises. They stopped and knelt down while the captain tried to make contact with the others.

"This is Captain Samson, come in – over."

More scratching came from the radio. Jack could still hear the gunshots in the distance.

"Anyone there!? Do you copy!? – over."

Another loud tank blast came from far away. At that moment they could hear voices over the scratching, and an echo of the tank blast, only much louder.

"Switch it off," said Samson, "Proceed on foot *with caution!*"

A couple of the soldiers gave Jack and Kelly their pistols. Jack moved with the squad and checked his gun. A 9mm - it was something. He thought about the Phantom's massive silver pistol. He always seemed to have the bigger guns.

Then it clicked. The beasts were *his*. Unmarked and unidentified Leopard tanks. They had caught up with the Syndicate at last.

The block came to an end at a T-junction. Scouting an opening, they prepared to make a break across the road towards the firefight when a chugging engine came noisily from left of the junction. Naturally, every soldier took cover and waited. They did not have to wait long. A white pickup truck skidded along the road in front of them with a manned .50 calibre machine gun mounted on the back. The gunman swivelled to look at them when an intense wave of hot air came blasting down the road. The manned gun was disintegrated. Shreds of metal and shrapnel were blown at high speed behind it. The broken chassis and charred remains rolled backwards, burning and glowing orange.

The force of the blast hit them before the sound in a quick double-punch. Their heads rang in their helmets like clappers in bells. It happened so quickly that no one was quite sure what to make of it. Jack's vision was scarred with the image of a thousand metal pieces being ejected from the truck.

One of the soldiers surveyed the road. To everyone's surprise, he gave the signal to run across. Jack hesitated but followed the others. He scanned from right to left as he crossed.

She was backing up over a hundred metres down the road, deflecting shots from the militia. Her mini-gun whirred in the distant smoke, shredding them and the walls they hid behind.

The truck had almost been split down the middle. The metal warped inward and backwards. Still red-hot and flaming. There was no sign of the occupants other than a sizzling red streak.

Once across the road, they didn't stop. Jack, Kelly, and Gillian had to be pushed every so often to keep up. They gripped their pistols and stayed close to the others, following their lead, shaken and dazed. The firefights were all around them now. The first vehicle they found was a wrecked and smoking Humvee.

No other soldiers were in sight, so they passed by without stopping, only to hear the quick, mono-rhythmic shots of a .50 Cal as it gunned down the last two men in the squad. Multiple shots whizzed past or rapped against the broken Humvee.

Jack hit the ground with his pistol raised. Blood filled the road beneath the two soldiers. Large bullet holes in the Humvee shimmered in the setting sun. The light was fading, but they could see that the men weren't getting up again. The truck came after them, scaring Jack to his feet and sending adrenaline down into his thighs and calves. There was nowhere to go. The Squad scattered but the truck, flatter than the last, came firing around the corner.

It managed to hit one man before the wall behind it

broke open. A monstrous Leopard came crashing down with all its weight, swallowing the truck and flattening it beneath her belly.

Somehow Jack found himself lying face-down with his hands on his head again. The men around him looked shocked but re-motivated to escape. They were looking at her. She was different than the last. Desert-coloured but equally bulky. The edges of the truck could be seen under her treads. She couldn't see through the settling dust, so Jack made his move with everyone else. They scrambled away again, putting as many walls between them and the Leopard as they could.

There was no shortage of serendipity. They ran up to the vehicle line which was pushing hard against local militia. Jack's doubt soured his appreciation of 'good luck'. It was the second time he should have died by the Syndicate's hand.

He and Kelly helped Gillian into a Humvee and sat on either side. A medic arrived and forced Kelly out so he could check Gillian. They were in the last of three Humvees. Jack's head fell back into the headrest. His comprehension spun to the sound of gunshots and shouting. He didn't care how close it was anymore.

The sudden motion of the Humvee made him jolt awake. They began accelerating through the streets. Jack became anxiously aware of his bearings. Gillian was half-conscious on his left, still in need of medical attention, but they weren't retreating. In his disorientation, Jack didn't notice it was darker outside, or that the medic was gone.

"Where are we going!?" He yelled through numb lips. The soldier in the passenger seat didn't answer, so Jack yelled louder.

"WHY ARE WE GOING BACK IN!?"

"We have to follow the Syndicate!" He yelled back.

Jack's anger grew but he had no energy to protest. He imagined Brigadier Read safe in his tent surrounded by high-ranking officials, ordering dying men to stay on mission.

Jack wanted to check on Gillian when the Humvee was almost sideswiped by one of the Leopards breaking out into the road. Her dark grey teeth clipped the back of the Humvee causing it to swerve violently.

"DRIVE FASTER OR WE WON'T MAKE IT!" Shouted the soldier.

Jack looked over his shoulder, the Leopard turned her turret. There was only shade left across the town, but he could sense she was preparing to execute them. All they needed was a turn, a curve, to break her line of sight. What he did not expect was the second monster tank to break into the road from the other side, narrowly missing them. Her dented desert body filled the road and blocked her sister's shot. Jack managed to see her barrel get stuck in a wall before he was shaken sideways by a sudden turn.

It was the fastest he had ever ridden in a Humvee. All subsequent events happened within a matter of seconds. Individual moments flashed by in frames, unprocessed in his delirium. They charged with full attack into the militia-heavy streets. Jack ducked and pulled Gillian with him. Metallic thuds against the sides told him they were under fire.

The next few moments happened all at once. He was looking up. The Humvee was blown aside and filled with smoke. Then Jack felt weightless as his vision went black. The last thing he could remember was an odd feeling of spinning. Turning over. Rolling.

Ghazni, Afghanistan
??:?? AFT, July 2016

For the first few moments, Jack didn't know if he really was awake. There were thoughts, but they were more like dreams, flashes of images and ideas. Gradually he gained consciousness and self-awareness. His memory was static; he couldn't remember where he was or why. It was an odd sensation of confusion. He tried to open his eyes, but nothing happened. He could feel his eyelids moving but no light was getting in. The thudding in his chest grew with mild panic. He turned his head trying to find a source of light but it only hurt his neck.

He had to make sure he wasn't blind.

All was silent. All was black.

Then a sharp pain in his back reminded him where he was. And a throbbing headache brought about the memory of why. He let himself slide across the roof of the Humvee. His legs fell from the chair above him. Pins and needles in his feet made him tense up but a sudden hazy light put his mind at ease. His vision was blurry but there was a dim glow.

Despite the pain, he was euphoric to have some vision back. He pushed his foot against the door of the Humvee to slide towards the light. His head reached the other side and tilted up at the window. Multiple lights shrunk into sharp little stars. The night sky was sparkling down at him. He stargazed in appreciation for all of an eternal second.

Tapping the Humvee tested his hearing. It was there… mostly. Turning his eyes, he spotted the handle of the door and reached over with a weak hand. He pulled the handle and pushed with his other elbow. The door opened slightly before getting stuck in the ground outside.

Silence was golden, he didn't want to disturb it. Little by

little, he pushed the door against the dirt until there was a big enough gap. The street outside was dead. He didn't recognise it at all.

Every one of his joints was sore, but with combined effort, he pulled and pushed his way out of the Humvee. Cool air washed over his face and filled his lungs, fresh and rejuvenating.

Since he likely had all the time he wanted, he took it slow and steady, first leaning against the Humvee, then lifting himself to his feet. Finally extending his legs made him dizzy but he held on. Sharp pains and aching bruises wracked his body, sinking into his muscles. A line of blood had dried on his cheek. The river of blood that had flowed from his nose and over his lips had mostly dried.

The area was a large fork in the road. They had come from behind and chosen to go right before overturning. The Humvee had rolled off the road and over a barrier.

Jack leaned against the wrecked Humvee and made his way around. Its windows were cracked and shattered. There were bullet holes everywhere. Dust had settled on everything, and there was a man. A dark silhouette. Jack nearly buckled against the Humvee before realizing it was a soldier. He was tending to someone propped against a wall.

"I'm surprised you can stand," he said in a hushed voice.

"Me too," Jack choked. He coughed up some blood with a little spit and cleared his throat. Every question he wanted to ask was pointless. The man probably knew as much as he did.

Jack stumbled over to the wall and leaned a shoulder against it. It was Gillian against the wall. Even in the dim moonlight he looked pale.

"Died about half an hour ago," the man said without looking up. He was sitting with one leg stretched out and the other bent.

Jack wasn't surprised but felt disappointed all the same. He slid down the wall next to Gillian's body.

"What's your name?" Asked the man. He had a husky voice and some type of American accent.

"Thawn, Jack Thawn. His name was Gillian," Jack said, looking over at the lifeless body.

"Yeah, I saw. I'm Eddie," said the soldier.

There were no more ranks. No more borders. No more missions. There were only allies and enemies. Everything had been stripped down to the most basic categories. They didn't need to shake hands or share interests. They didn't need to debate or discuss the next move. They were as good as brothers now, and there was only one thing left to do: Leave.

"Leslie's dead as well. We can't take them with us, I don't know where we are," Eddie said, looking around.

"What time is it?" Jack asked through a painful yawn.

"Almost ten," Eddie replied. His watch was cracked but must have been working well enough.

With tears washing the blood off his face, Jack took hold of Gillian. "Help me put him in the Humvee."

Eddie said nothing. Together they lifted the body and set it down gently in the back of the vehicle. They couldn't wait around and they knew it. It had been hours since the crash, and if no one had appeared yet then no one was coming. Search and rescue parties likely knew as little of where they were as they did.

The tracks of the crash led back the way they came, but the tracks of the other Humvees led deeper into the town. The two of them stood there for a while, looking at both sets of tracks, each disappearing in different directions.

"If we go back," said Eddie, "they probably retreated

already."

"Where were *they* going? Jack asked with a nod to the other tracks.

"Following the Syndicate. They could be long gone," Eddie sighed.

Even if the Humvee could power the radio, it was still busted like everything else, so they left a message by carving into the wall with a knife:

2 DEAD 2 ALIVE
GONE TO EX POINT D

"We need to figure out where we are, then the extraction point shouldn't be hard to find," said Eddie.

There was a three-story building two blocks into the town. Probably not the right direction, but they would have to go forward before they could go back. Jack had a rifle now. They salvaged ammo, mags, helmets, and vests from the Humvee. The walk was quiet. Cold, cooling air drifted through the town.

The building was a mess. Paint peeled from the walls and scraps of debris covered the floor. The stairs had been worn away. Dampness had damaged the walls near the windows. Clicking and tapping from their rifles echoed up and down the staircase. Once on the top floor, they had to take a ladder to the roof, holding their rifles over their upper arms and under their chins. The weight of the rifle nearly choked Jack, but he hoisted himself up for a breath after every step.

The view was adequate. They could see the rise of the town as it got closer to the city. Ghazni was bright with dazzling lights. Further out it got darker with fewer houses on the edge of the town. Their more immediate surroundings were nearly pitch black. A few lights scattered the town but left much to the imagination.

"If that's the way to the edge, Delta should be back the way we came. It's a play park at the corner of the town, easiest to find," said Eddie.

"But that..." Jack pointed.

"I know," said Eddie, "I see it too."

There were moving lights deep in the town. Hostile territory. They watched the lights waiting for some form of identification. Militia weren't known for their use of torches. Especially powerful ones.

"Change of plan," Jack said, mesmerized by the professional motion of the torches. They were at least three blocks away, so they set off making special note of the surrounding areas and everything between them and the lights. Jack had the path mapped out in his head. They would use the buildings as landmarks for navigation. One building with strange archways. One with unique windows. One taller than the rest.

Jack had a sudden thought and relaxed the rifle in his hands. If they did find another squad, he didn't want to look antagonizing.

First they saw the lights again, then the sounds of hushed voices grew as they approached. Jack leaned against the wall and listened to be sure. He had never been so happy to hear the English language being spoken.

"Friendlies coming in!" Eddie called in a half whisper.

The chatting stopped instantly.

"Identify yourselves!" Came a stern reply.

'Fuckit' Jack thought and walked out with his rifle in hand. The unit backed up but relaxed at the sight of him.

"Jack Thawn, English," he announced. They could see

the rips in his clothes. The holes and stains. The blood on his face and neck.

"Medic," said the sergeant.

Jack and Eddie stood next to each other as the medic jogged over to look at them.

"Where'd you two come from?" The sergeant asked in a thick Texan accent.

"Hunter-killer, sweeping units," Eddie answered.

"They left hours ago. Looks like they left you behind, boys," the sergeant replied sympathetically.

"No shit," said one of the others.

"You had better come with us," said the sergeant. "Can you fight?"

"Not very well." Jack stretched his arms out to loosen his shoulders.

"Stay at the back then, don't engage unless you have to. We're tracking the Syndicate through the town. They could be anywhere so stay vigilant," the sergeant ordered.

"Kill the lights," said Jack.

The sergeant turned to face him again. "What's that, boy?" He leaned in.

"Kill the lights. If we can see you from three blocks away – so can they."

The sergeant nodded, considering the information. Then after he called for them to be switched off, the squad started moving out.

Once again Jack found himself moving with an unfamiliar squad, following from the rear, forced back into the mission again. His gun shook as he shivered. Loss of blood in the cold night was making him numb and weak. They walked for fifteen minutes before reaching an incline. The town became denser as it got higher ahead.

"Nothing yet – over," one of the soldiers said into the radio.

The break in silence gave Jack pins and needles in his arms.

"Eye in the sky says the tanks are two blocks ahead – over."

"The tanks?" Jack asked shakily.

"You seen 'em? I heard they're quite big," said one of the soldiers.

"Bigger," Eddie spoke without a shred of exaggeration.

The squad shifted uncomfortably as Eddie maintained his serious expression. Jack could almost laugh. The poor blokes had no idea what they were getting into.

They probably didn't enjoy the next few minutes much either, edging closer to the monsters of Ghazni. They could be heard growling somewhere in the night, Hunting.

The squad tensed up. Commotion further ahead. Movement and mobilization. Whether or not it was militia or the Syndicate made all the difference to Jack.

A deep revving echoed over the town and in the streets. It died away quickly letting silence settle in again.

"Off the street. Let's get a view from above now," said the sergeant.

It was a welcome idea with near unanimous agreement. Jack thought back to the militia on the rooftop earlier that day… how the Leopard had arrived… how that rooftop no longer existed.

Breaching the door made one of the soldiers hesitate and hold up. "There was someone in there," he whispered back.

The squad entered with their rifles raised at eye level. Jack stayed against the wall. It was dark but there was an orange light coming from outside somewhere. A couple of men could be heard running away.

"If they tell the rest of the militia we're here we're fucked," whispered one of the soldiers.

The sergeant shook his head and lowered his weapon. There was motion upstairs. They could hear shuffling and light footsteps on a dusty wooden floor. The sergeant marched up the stairs quickly and quietly. Jack watched with wide eyes and a tight grip of his gun, but the shooting never came. The rest of the squad followed their leader the same way.

Either the militia had taken to a new camouflage tactic or something was horribly wrong. Three women draped in cloth, four kids clinging to their mothers, and two teens holding onto furniture. All frozen at the sight of them.

"Civilians, hold your fire." The sergeant lowered his weapon and raised his hands in a friendly gesture. The kids relaxed a little, but the mothers looked sceptical.

"Civilians!?" Asked one of the soldiers.

"This area is supposed to be uninhabited," said another.

The sergeant was thinking hard.

"So what?" Eddie whispered, "Just watch your fire."

"That's not what we're here for," replied the soldier.

Jack felt the numbness spreading throughout his body. There were complications. Eddie felt it too.

Sergeant tried the radio, but the connection was poor. "Rooftop. Now," he demanded.

On their way out, Eddie and Jack ran alongside the last few soldiers up the stairs.

"What *are* you here for?" Jack asked sharply.

"The Syndicate. But we can't follow them with the tanks fucking us over, so they need to be destroyed." The soldier huffed up the stairs.

At the top, Eddie barged through the squad. "Their

armour is too thick! There's no way you can destroy those tanks."

"We can't," said the Sergeant, "But the A-10's can."

"Warthogs?" Jack said with dry breath. Everything was becoming clear at last. Warthogs were jets, armed with every hell-grade weapon in existence. One of the few competitors of the Leopard tanks. But one thing stood in the way.

"-There are civilians in the town – I repeat – there are unarmed civilians in the strike zone – over," Sergeant said into the radio, evidently frustrated.

"Now what?" Asked one of the soldiers.

"Now we wait," Sergeant's voice was elevating.

"We can't leave until the tanks are dead."

"I know! But things have changed!" Sergeant said forcefully. Only a moment passed before the air around them was filled with bullets snapping and whizzing past them from nowhere.

Jack's weak legs let him fall faster than the others. The shots missed horribly. The metallic shots of AK-47 rifles were distant but higher up. They could barely hear the radio.

"*How copy-Say agai- o-ver*" It was quickly silenced so that they could return fire.

Eddie stayed low and Jack did the same. Gunshots poisoned the peace of the night. Smoke from the rifles clouded the starry sky. Stress gripped at Jack's nerves. Everything was happening as once. Shots coming in from the rooftops forced them into cover. There was yelling on the ground. Fearful yelling and retreat. The firing died away quickly. Jack's many questions were answered as the quiet of the night was allowed to settle back in.

Deep growling was approaching fast. She had heard the commotion. She could smell the scent of gunpowder. Jack looked over as the revving amplified. Below them, the family was escaping into the neighbouring building. It was lower and more fragile.

The dark grey Leopard was charging up the inclined road. With a long burst from its mini-gun, militia in the street were chewed up by hot lead.

Now or never. The sergeant frantically switched on the radio. "We have eyes on one of the tanks! Be advised, civilians in the area! – over."

"*Air support on standby, awaiting laser targeting – over.*"

"Did they not hear what I just said!?" Sergeant yelled.

A theory sparked into Jack's mind. The minor issue preventing them from getting to the Syndicate was suspiciously inconvenient. The Leopard's weakness was scratching the sky somewhere above - but the Warthog's weakness surrounded the Leopards.

"It's a play," Jack said as one of the soldiers switched on his laser. "The Syndicate is hiding in a populated area so we can't airstrike!" He said desperately.

"We have our mission, son! We aren't letting them get away this time." Sergeant said harshly. "Target that Leopard; it's in the open!"

And so she was, sitting comfortably in the open. The best place for them to attempt a strike. Jack remembered the last time their target was in the open, so he wasn't surprised when everything started going to shit.

Two men had their lasers on the Leopard. Distant echoing revs told them its sister was closing in.

"We have target in sights – over," said the Sergeant.

"*Please confirm target – over.*"

"We're aiming at target – over."

"Cannot lock onto that many targets – over."

"There is only one target! Over!"

Jack felt it coming again. The panic. The fear. Flowing cold through his veins and deep into his bones.

"Aerial surveillance can see at least forty lasers-"

"There are only two!"

The surveillance drone high above could see a complex web of green lasers all pointed in random directions across the town, sometimes moving, sometimes two or three pointed at the same place, but all of them indistinguishable from one another.

"Too many lasers. Advise switching to thermal flares – over."

Jack's head swivelled around looking for the other lasers but there was only darkness with scattered lights. In the lighter areas, he could see motion. Laundry swayed in the wind. Rooftops had sheets and clothing hanging to dry. Beneath which, families likely laid terrified and helpless. Then the squad turned to listen to the new sound on the radio. A sound that made the sergeant recoil from the radio like it was a violent animal.

"Copy that. Switching to thermal flares – over," said a voice. A British voice, one they had never heard before.

"Who is this!? Come in!?" The sergeant yelled in an offended tone. There was no reply, not even from command.

Then there was a fizzle. First one, then another, then another. Soon there were multiple, all firing up and lighting the area in red. Several rooftops had flares generating a lethal glow.

Then another much closer. Behind them. The rooftop entrance sparked into life with red light as a flare on top began spitting fire. Jack scanned the surrounding red rooftops. On the road ahead – She was gone.

His legs felt numb and incapable of taking his weight.

He let his gun slide off and held onto the brick wall he was leaning against. The squad clambered at the doorframe of the entrance trying to put out the flare. The sergeant's commanding voice yelled pleas to call off the strike until finally, he got his answer.

"Roger, *targets confirmed. Strike inbound – over.*"

Eddie hoisted Jack to his feet. The squad was jumping down the stairs. All sounds seemed dim and muffled. Jack's ears were hot with a light ringing. His head pounded with high pressure. He was on the brink of passing out when a column of red smoke injected adrenaline straight to his head and heart. The neighbouring building had a flare as well - housing an innocent yet oblivious family.

Jack pulled from Eddie's grip and charged with all his strength to the edge of the building. Without much thought, he put his remaining energy into the leap, leaving none for his landing. The fall felt like hours. Air rushed past him and filled his lungs.

The full force of his landing was taken by his ankles, cracking something in each of them. Then it travelled up his shins, testing their strength before delivering a crushing punch to his knees.

In a matter of seconds, he was rolling on his side, letting out a soundless scream in agony. His teeth clenched while he grasped his bursting ankles. There was shouting coming from the rooftop behind him, but he blocked it out. The flare was atop a wooden pole that connected several damaged cables. He crawled over, the cracks in his legs prostrating him. The flare was secured into the pole, but a hard pull tore it from the cables. Jack pounded it furiously against the floor, killing the flame little by little until it died away completely.

Darkness swept over the town as a predator cut through

the sky above. Some of the flares burnt out and died. In the distance, lights were going out, leaving night-black to accompany the silence.

Jack bore witness to the growing void. Defeat befell his face with tears picking up the blood and streaking red down his neck. The squad was gone. His energy was gone. All that remained was the wall he could lean against and the final lights.

A rooftop doorway two blocks away was glowing dreamy white, outlining the hooded figure that stood inside. Jack knew there were two bright green eyes in the hood, penetrating the darkness and watching him draw desperate breaths. Then all lights around him went out in sequence, plunging him into darkness. Starlight illuminated his vision with silhouettes and outlines of the town. His heart beat harder and faster against his ribs, his lungs tired from the speed of his breathing. He awaited what came next.

The game is Hunt and kill. Hunt or be hunted. Kill or be killed.

A shadow glided across the sky, switching the stars off and on as it passed below them. The familiar streaking sound followed it after a delay. It ever so lightly tore at the tranquil sky, teasing the town with its hissing engines, flowing higher and lower with every pitch and turn, lining up the strike.

The silence was the worst part. Jack could hear his own panicked breaths. Seconds felt like minutes, crawling by painfully slow. He gripped the collar of his vest with both hands.

Minor flashes above the town made him flinch but he continued to stare. They were followed instantly by a chain of deep thuds pounding at the stone houses. A line of dust clouds formed at his ten o'clock. Vibrations from the impacts resonated in concrete beneath him. The last few thuds echoed through the town for almost a second before a crackling, metallic whirr came from behind him. The A-10 glided high over the dust clouds, followed by a Doppler-tail of screeching fury, like a banshee screaming overhead.

Another few seconds passed before the raining started. Little rocks, then bigger ones, falling around the strike zone, raining heavier and harder, then dying away. As the dust clouds lifted, Jack could see the devastation in the starlight. A line of pure destruction. Shattered buildings shaken off their foundations.

His head lolled about from dizzying fear. Each aching muscle was taught with apprehension. Still, he gripped the collar of his vest, drawing dry air into his tight chest. The jet engines screamed into a higher pitch and trailed off. Jack felt the sound stabbing at his ear drums. He shut his eyes. Flashes lit up his eyelids before another sequence of thuds shook him and the wall he was leaning on, quickly approaching louder and harder. His face tensed up and contorted with terror, but the pounding shots ended a block away. Another second and the lethal metallic whirring followed. Jack pressed his palms into his ears when the banshee scream came carving through the sky overhead. He could feel the wind of the Warthog, hot and quick. Then he closed his forearms over his head to shield himself from the raining stone. It punched at him from above like a hail storm, bruising him further.

Minutes passed by the second. Distant wavering banshee screams carved the night sky with terror. Pitching, repositioning, and lining up. Jack let a shaking hand slide off his ear. He couldn't track the Warthog because of the delay. It was faster than its own sound, faster than its own perceptible presence. He could only hear where it had been by the high-pitched screech and silence that followed.

He let an eye open to scan the stars. Darting from shadow to shadow, he caught no sight of it. It had been silent for too long now. He thought of the family below, wondering if they were still there. Wondering where they could go, or what they thought was happening.

The ground shook like the Leopards were on top of him. Impacts from the strike like a two-ton jackhammer obliterated the buildings on Jack's left and filled his ears with pounding bass. He keeled over, hands over his ears and forearms closed over his face. His grip was almost shaken loose by the vibration. Then the metallic whir echoed through the streets and let the town know the beast was away.

The shadow passed beside him. No matter how hard he pressed his ears, the screaming still managed to pierce deep into his head. Blood and dust soaked into the distant drying bedsheets. It pooled beneath piles of ash and rubble. Stacks of stone and brick lay as unmarked graves. Walls cracked and collapsed under the concussive force. Crying and wailing was lost beneath the unforgiving scream of the jet's propulsion. Hot and undeterred, it thrust the Warthog weightlessly in its soaring arc over the beleaguered town.

Buildings were obliterated like glass under the mighty force of a thousand hammers per second. There was no real protection. A roof over your head brought peace to your mind. Thoughts of a mother's protection, a shielding enclosure of unbreakable walls, invincibility, would be the last some children would ever have. They would see nothing. They would hear the muffled approach of a thousand heavy thuds. They would feel their mothers' arms constrict around them, shaking violently, then nothing more.

It wasn't over. Jack could tell. There was still one more run in the bird. Lightning didn't strike the same place twice, there was no point in taking another run over Jack's block. And yet, this comforting thought could still be his last.

He heard the turn. The high-pitched scream of the jet as it made its wide arc. It would be lining up behind him now. The pain in his legs prevented him from turning to look over his shoulder. There would be no telling where it was. At any next moment, it would commit to its line. The throbbing ache in Jack's head mimicked a ticking clock as though he was counting down to his own demise.

The family was still below him - so close they could likely hear his beating heart. Every muscle in Jack's body was shaking and twitching with the rhythm of the seconds. Within those seconds, he could be destroyed at the order of his own league.

Anger had just begun to swell inside him when it finally started; flashes and pounding impacts approaching from behind. So loud and yet so slowly it left a series of craters and cracks in the ground. He could feel it just as much as he could hear it. His hands clasped over his ears and muffled everything but the bass. The ground around him shook violently until he thought it would break apart.

So near that it felt like it was on top of him already, yet got closer all the same. The stone cracked around him. The air pressure reverberated around him, forcing the breath into and out of his lungs. Dust and stone flew sideways overhead. His sense of gravity was unhinged. Delirium took over in the moment, under a second, shouting as loudly as his diaphragm would allow, unable to hear it, unable to feel it, his soul shaken from him, detached from reality.

Chapter XI
The Challenger
Chengdu, Sichuan, China
20:55 CST, Tuesday, 6th September 2016
(55 days later)

"I'd rather not wait for the Phantom to escape so you can use a Marine death squad. I'll authorize sufficient air support for the open assault and if that doesn't work, then you may call in your unit..."

Secretary Miles' embarrassment was immeasurable. He was lucky not to have been fired. It was hard to tell which was worse; claiming they killed over thirty civilians and two of their own soldiers (by accident because of some communication error) or admitting that the Phantom and his Syndicate had bested them for a second time. Insult to injury, they lost the Syndicate heading east as a result.

Multiple formal apologies from the Department of Defence weren't holding back the shit-storm of bad publicity. National embarrassment was escalating. Desperation had Miles on a thin thread of hope. His career was in the balance and only a single lead was holding it up.

Ambiguously named unit Zero. Marines like those didn't get listed with the others. Covert to the point where their name was gibberish to all except those in the need-to-know. It only made them more suitable for the mission: A search and destroy task that had them carrying the fragile weight of political instability.

The Chinese president, Ji Zhang, wasn't stupid. If the Syndicate was lost heading east in Afghanistan then they would almost certainly be on their way. Zhang had dropped a great red curtain all around his borders. Immigration had a tight grip on anything getting in. Unit Zero had no trouble; Miles had authorized a great deal of investment into the Phantom's capture, so getting into China with all the toys and provisions they could want went appreciated without question.

Calibre, or Caliber, refers to the diameter of a gun's barrel, being the same as the diameter of the round it fires. Higher calibre means larger rounds, means harder punch. Big or small, it only took one bullet to kill a man. So why use higher calibre? Ask anyone from Unit Zero and they will tell you "In case you need to kill something across the street, on the other side of town, from the border."

Bigger weapons demanded equal counter-measures, so equal firepower. Like trees attempting to outgrow each other for more sunlight, it's unnecessary, but your opponent won't care, so neither should you.

Despite the free nature of kill-on-sight lethal force authorization, the mission required a somewhat delicate approach. China's government was getting jumpy with the notorious Syndicate closing in, calling them another rogue militia. The scar left from the Beijing massacre was dangerously close to reopening, and for that reason, Unit Zero had been keeping their heads down as they roughed up the local gangs.

In some twisted fortune, they didn't need the firepower in the search. They would sure as hell need it for the 'destroy', but thus far it had been an uneventful endeavour. The gangs and crews didn't put up a fight. They didn't have the numbers.

The Phantom was cutting through the criminal underworld leaving a path for Unit Zero to follow. If that wasn't easy enough, the trail of breadcrumbs just made it all the simpler. With each depredation and slaughter, the Syndicate would leave one man alive to warn the other gangs and spread a message of fear.

Lieutenant Alex J. Cole led Unit Zero. As far as he was concerned, every survivor left behind was another foot deeper in the Syndicate's grave they dug themselves. Not as much of a challenge as he was hoping for but the Syndicate's belligerent reputation didn't come from running away. Six restless trigger fingers yearned for the much-anticipated collision of US Marines and the Phantom himself. It was only a matter of time. The bodies they found were getting fresher. The blood left behind was getting warmer. The scent was getting stronger.

"You smell that?" Asked Deck, second-in-command. He squinted at the windows and sniffed at the cold air.

"*Smoke, fresh powder, and death,*" Charles said on their linked-channel earpieces.

Cole took in a slow but deep breath. There was indeed a hint of freshly burnt gunpowder in the cold night's air, accompanied by a sour smell more commonly associated with corpses.

"We're definitely in the right place." Cole's gravelly voice muttered. "Any movement?" He asked.

"*Nah.*"

"*Nothing.*"

Three teams of two. Three angles of the building. Three perspectives. Eight guards in visual range, all of which had yet to take even a single step.

"Seriously Cole," Deck said, looking through his binoculars, "They haven't moved at all, they're sleeping on the job or something. How do you sleep standing up?"

They hadn't been there long, but everything was off. Out of synch. The pattern had finally changed into something they couldn't predict.

"We can't wait around for long, let's make this quick. Move in." Cole demanded. Side by side with a few meters spacing, he and Deck closed the gap between them and the two guards standing outside the entrance. Neighbouring houses weren't able to see them but were close enough to hear them, so suppressors were mandatory.

They counted down to synchronized neutralization with practised precision. Two shots to their chests and the guards swayed backwards. Cole and Deck moved forward with their rifles aimed at the entrance in case anyone came out, yet they stopped anyway, frozen with perplexed apprehension.

The guards had swayed but not fallen. Their bodies remained limply erect with their rifles in hand. Cole and Deck lingered for a moment before it became apparent there was no threat. For the first time ever, they walked casually toward the enemy with their weapons lowered.

"Guys be advised: The guards at the main entrance were already dead. Their bodies are propped up by poles and their guns are tied in their hands," Cole said in a hushed but urgent tone.

The other two teams reported the same. If anything, they needed more caution now than before. They weren't just too late, they were expected.

"*Watch for booby-traps,*" said Bentley.

"*Syndicate specialty,*" Charles commented.

The smell of powder wasn't dissipating. Deck assessed the corpses. Their bodies were flexible but rather cool, so rigor mortis had already passed, placing their time of death somewhere between twelve and twenty-four hours ago.

"Find that survivor," Cole demanded. He made his advance quick despite some new premonitions.

The inside of the building looked like it was still in use.

Lights on and devices playing. All contributed to the illusion. Besides the many tricks and artifices, it was very much hollow and devoid of all life. All except for one.

Checking corners and scanning surroundings didn't slow them down. After grouping up, the last push went by quickly. Six pairs of eyes unified in cautious exploration. At one far side of the building, there was a long room lined with pillars a few metres from the windows. Below the chipped, cracked, and bloodstained walls was a pair of legs sticking out from behind a pillar, writhing and twitching.

"Hold," Cole said firmly. He couldn't see the rest of the body yet, so he took slow steps forward, thinking over the dubious simplicity of it. Only the left side of the room had lights on. Ropes hanging between the tops of the pillars cast web-like shadows on the ceiling. Some of the glow reached the survivor, illuminating his bloody figure, and the aged, grey ropes that tied his hands to the ceiling.

That could have been it, nice and simple like every time before, if it wasn't for the pulley attached to the ceiling, leading the rope from the survivor's hands into the depths of shadow where Cole lost sight of it.

"Hey, *Nǐ hǎo!*" Cole called. His deep tone resonated through the room.

The survivor's eye's opened bringing his face to life. He moaned out of exhaustion, unable to properly form his words.

"Tell him not to move," said Cole.

Hayden called out to the man in imperfect Mandarin.

Cole looked around with his weapon lowered. "Search the room, find the other end of that rope."

It was a riddle. The rope that tied the survivor's hands spread over the room like a web, twisting and turning around pulleys and poles. They would often lose sight of it behind a wall or pillar, and sometimes in the dark corners of the room. Yet, they continued to trace it, looking for an end.

"Here!" Bentley called from nearer the front of the room where they came in. Hidden underneath itself was the end of the rope, tied to a metal loop at the top of a pillar. "There's nothing on the end," he said.

Meach walked over to confirm and shook his head at Deck.

Cole followed the roped furiously.

"Another trick?" Meach asked.

"I don't see why they would. The police would just cut him down," Bentley replied.

Cole dragged a metal barrel across the room to the survivor. "It's not for the police. Deck, pull the rope down," he said. Deck freed the survivor and held the rope in place. Cole managed to fit the end around a rod he found and insert it into the hole of the barrel. "Perfect," Cole whispered to himself, noticing a chair by the window behind the survivor. He dragged it into the light for the survivor to sit on while the barrel held the rope down nicely.

"Doesn't look like it does anything," Charles said as he hoisted the survivor onto the chair.

"Can't tell, can't afford to chance it," said Bentley.

"Hayden, front and centre," Cole demanded.

Hayden stood beside him as he looked the survivor in the eye. They knew the drill: Cole interrogated – Hayden translated. Another working day.

"What happened here?" Cole started lightly.

The survivor's wounds were reasonably fresh. He was catching his breath when Cole kicked his chair to get his attention. After asking again, the survivor finally croaked a response.

"'Attack', he says." Hayden rolled his eyes.

"Yeah! We know!" Cole suppressed his voice again, "The Phantom was here. Tell me everything."

The survivor shook his head, mumbling a plea.

"He's saying they will kill him." Hayden looked confused.

Cole stared at the man suspiciously. Past survivors had never been threatened. The Phantom knew he was being followed, and he knew how.

"Let me make this perfectly clear," Cole said gruffly, "He's not here right now. I'm here. I'm the one you have to worry about." He took the .44 magnum out of his thigh holster and held it for the man to see.

He watched Cole rotate the cylinder of the revolver with his thumb. It made six distinct clicks, one for each round. The man grimaced harder with each click.

"What did he say to you? What do you know?" Cole asked with his thumb over the hammer. The survivor begged and pleaded even harder.

"Phantom's really done a number on him," said Charles.

"He must have something good," Deck added.

"I'm not going to be patient," Cole said darkly.

Hayden only translated Cole.

"Here's what we're going to do." Cole pushed the cylinder out the side of the magnum and showed it to the survivor. Holding one round in with his finger, he let the other five slide out onto his palm and showed the survivor the one remaining round. With practised sleight of hand, Cole secretly let the last round slide out as he stood up straight. Then he pushed the cylinder back in and aimed at the survivor. "I'm sure you know how this game is played," he said.

The survivor writhed in the chair, his face twitching and

quivering.

"Tell me what you know. You have between zero and five chances." Cole spun the cylinder. It clicked rapidly then slowed to a stop. The survivor mumbled indiscernibly. Cole cocked the hammer and pulled the trigger. An empty click echoed around the room. The survivor jumped in his seat then burst out, pleading faster.

"Again," said Hayden.

Cole pulled the trigger to let out another empty click.

The survivor jumped again, crying as he pleaded and spoke fast.

Cole looked between him and Hayden, who looked like he had forgotten the language. Hayden said something in Mandarin which everyone could tell was some variation of 'slow down'.

The survivor then started over. "Um, They- They send him to take a side in a rivalry. Even if he has to start the rivalry. They send him to be hired by the weaker side, so that he may eliminate the opposition." Hayden tried desperately to catch up.

Somewhat perplexed but transfixed with interest, the Unit stared at them both. "Him?" Deck asked, pointing at the weary man.

"The Phantom." Hayden corrected. "He builds them up and climbs the ranks until the opposition is eliminated, then overthrows the one who hired him."

"What rivalries?" Cole asked with his brow furrowed.

"Gangs, mafias, just-" Hayden paused to listen to the survivor, then turned back to try and explain. "He builds their strength but takes control. Until only he remains. He 'replaces all the evil in the world with his own'."

"Is that what happened here? Is that what we've been following?" Deck asked, but Hayden was still trying to understand the survivor.

"Who is *they*? You said *they* sent him, who is *they*!?" Cole demanded.

The survivor stuttered with his explanation when his face suddenly blossomed like a meaty red flower, spraying blood over Cole and Hayden. The wall behind the survivor had burst with a new hole. Dust shook from every surface. Moments after the bullet became embedded in the wall behind them, a metallic boom from the .50 calibre round's origin bombed the silence, leaving a thunderous echo pulsating in and around the buildings.

Every member of the Unit hit the ground. Yells of 'SNIPER' were lost in the echoes. The body fell forward off the chair and landed in front of Cole with a meaty splat. Familiar adrenaline rushed to his head. He saw the door and crawled to it at top speed. Behind him, the Unit followed.

"Split up! Don't let him get away!" Cole yelled as he launched himself to his feet. He ran with everything he had, leaving his rifle behind and shedding unnecessary gear to make himself lighter. Cold air streamed past his face. He slid around corners and pushed off the walls to keep his momentum up until semi-cautiously bolting out of the building. There was only one building the shot could have come from. The rest of the Unit jumped over the fences and instinctively took different routes into the building, surrounding it as much as they could.

With his only remaining handgun raised, Cole jogged up the stairs towards the higher windows. The number of possible escape routes increased with every hallway and corner he passed.

"Guard the exits! Let him come to you!" Cole pressed in his earpiece.

It was a different kind of roulette. Any one of the six of them could encounter the shooter at any moment.

The game is a chase. Don't lose sight of your opponent.

Covering the exits was a smart move, but unnecessary. The Phantom watched as Cole found his nest. He left nothing for Cole except an empty, smoking cartridge standing where he once knelt.

Cole picked up on the taunt immediately. If he had only realized the chair behind the survivor was left specifically for them to put him on. The barrel, however, was a good move. Cole was clearly an intuitive improviser. The Phantom was eager to see what he was made of. First, his unit would have to be dealt with. They had split up to cover ground. Their first mistake was giving up the strength of unity. The Phantom could exploit their weakness best if he remained unseen, drew them out, divided them, and then picked them off.

Rather than split them up manually, he could get the one in charge to do it for him. Which would mean pissing him off. Desperation always drives the push.

Cole was searching the hallways of each floor with minimal hesitation. He ran down a path with broken lights and up to a dark open doorway ahead. A great black boot appeared from the void, hitting Cole's chest like a battering ram and lifting him off his feet. He flew backwards, winded by the impact of both the boot and the ground. Shock suppressed his limbs for just a few seconds. Glints of silver, a purple-hue pattern, and remnants of Vantablack decorated a jet-black figure. The Phantom looked down at him dominantly before swinging the door shut and locking it.

Cole pulled himself up forcefully and ran shoulder first against it. "The Phantom is on the third floor! He's heading to the north-east side!" He yelled into his earpiece.

Just as expected, the others scurried to the north-east exit. Phantom waited until they would be able to see him before leaping out the window and zip-lining over the property's boundary wall. Atop a building at the other end, he looked back to watch them come after him. They were out in the wild now. The favela-like neighbourhood offered a maze of paths and escapes. With Cole left behind, the Unit dispersed without proper leadership. Thus, blindly entering the slums. Phantom watched from high above as Unit Zero isolated themselves in foreign territory. Fools driven by the illusion of control.

Meach worked his way up the stairs to find the end of the zip-line. He was a big guy. They all were. But exhaustion from the pursuit meant their breathing was weakening. Phantom swung himself over the bannister of the stairs and landed a kick to Meach's midriff. Meach flew down the stairs and collided with the wall at the bottom. Leaving no time for him to recover, the Phantom leapt from the stairs to deliver a knee into his diaphragm. With Meach unable to breathe, the Phantom needed only hold back his fighting attempts and let him pass out from a little pressure to his throat.

Deck searched slowly between the houses. He was sensible having his gun raised to look up and around frequently. The window for attack was short. Up ahead, Phantom could see a lamppost. He waited until Deck was almost next to it, where his eyes would be forced to adjust to the bright light, before shooting it out. A moment of impaired vision panicked Deck but allowed the Phantom to blend into the darkness of the night sky for an aerial attack.

Hayden was easy. He found himself cornered beside a house after seeking the source of the shot. In such close quarters, it only took a few consecutive hits to his head and up his ribs to incapacitate him. Then a vice-grip around his neck finished the job.

Charles and Bentley were close together converging on the same position. Charles didn't look around as much as he should have. Time was running out; Cole would soon catch up. Since there were only two left, Phantom pulled the pin from a stun grenade on Charles' belt. Charles reacted at the same time the Phantom turned away.

The flash was loud and blinding. The Phantom didn't waste time or risk the chance for Charles to use his weapon. He gave no opportunity for counter-attack. The sound of the flash would attract Bentley, so Charles would have to be down by then.

By the time Bentley found Charles' unconscious body, the Phantom had repositioned. Bentley's alert was only heard by Cole, as he was the only other conscious member.

Cole sped up through the narrow slums. He stopped around a corner seeing bodies ahead. Bentley lay beside Charles. Cole raised his pistol and moved around instead of forward. His frustration peaked when there came no reply on their comms.

He scanned the area, searching furiously before moving in to assess their conditions. His fear was lifted seeing that they were only unconscious, but concern had distracted him for too long, so he ducked out the way of the incoming attack. The Phantom had dropped soundlessly, narrowly missing Cole's head. He let his momentum carry him forward while Cole rolled backwards.

Cole locked eyes with the Phantom. It wasn't how either of them had imagined. Cole was furious but sensibly cautious. The Phantom's green eyes beamed with excitement. The prospect of a formidable opponent was invigorating. It had to be one-on-one. As Cole reached for his gun, the Phantom slinked backwards into an open house. Cole kept the gun close to his chest so it wouldn't be vulnerable in close combat.

The faded deep-black of the Phantom's overcoat blended in well with the darkness. Swirls of old purple patterns blended with the fabric. Cole lost sight of him but tailed confidently. His heart pounded beneath his Kevlar vest. Breathing felt uncomfortably loud. He could see everything dimly but the doorways offered no light.

The kitchen was empty. A silver blur spun in front of him and hit the wall, making him turn briefly to see that it was a knife. At that moment, the Phantom kicked at his hand. Cole tried to recover and take a shot, but the gun seemed stuck to the Phantom's left leg. In another moment of hesitation, the Phantom landed three hard hits to Cole's face, shaking him up with surprising strength. Then he grabbed the knife and whipped it around. Cole let go of the gun to break free and ducked aside.

The two of them took a moment to appreciate each other's tactical improvisation. Cole had nothing left. The Phantom had his gun stuck to his leg and the kitchen knife. With a press of his ankle, he took the gun and threw it – with the knife - out the kitchen window.

Cole understood. "Fair fight," he said, nodding with a mean stare as he controlled his breath.

"**More fun**," the Phantom said calmly. His voice filled the whole room at once. It was deeper and crisper than Cole's.

To keep the advantage, Cole engaged first, trapping the Phantom in the kitchen. Although the Phantom could block his first few strikes, his defence was odd. He took the hits. Cole could attack as much as he wanted without counter, but with good reason. The Phantom was able to deflect and block almost every single hit and used this to reposition himself on the other side of the room.

Cole tried new ways of engaging that forced the Phantom down the hallway, each as useless as the last. They continued down until they ended up outside again. The Phantom had led him to the opposite side, away from Charles and Bentley, so Cole had no immediate reinforcements.

Cole's muscles strained with fleeting speed. His attempts bore no fruit. He had been wasting energy, and the Phantom was still as calm as before, breathing easily.

Cole changed his initiative and reached for the Phantom's hood as soon as it was vulnerable. In response, the Phantom punched hard into Cole's armpit, nearly dislocating his shoulder. Phantom kept the advantage and head-butted Cole to arm's length for a sequence of quick punches that impacted well. Cole lifted his arms in front of his face leaving his midriff open for a spin kick that almost winded him.

There was a strange spring sound as the Phantom retracted his left leg. Slightly out of breath and with a numb shoulder, Cole thought about going for the Phantom's mask, but he could see it was a polymer and wouldn't be worth the effort. His left leg, however, seemed abnormal. Irregular, even.

Cole engaged in Tai-Chi. The Phantom countered accordingly. As soon as his left leg was open, Cole swiped a kick at it, which came to a crunching stop. It felt like kicking a signpost. Pain gripped at his foot and ankle.

The Phantom let him fall to the ground and circled him like a predator.

It had to be a prosthetic. Cole could hear the springs inside working as the Phantom walked. He lifted himself to spin a kick but the Phantom tossed it aside and countered with a jab to Cole's diaphragm. He had to take the hit to pull the Phantom's arm and throw him over. Landing with grace, the Phantom immediately re-engaged with an unnecessary mixture of Mui-Tai and Kung-Fu.

Cole tried desperately to counter but the Phantom's expeditious attacks intensified. Each engage reinitiated apparently of its own volition as though each of his limbs had a mind of their own. His unrelenting strikes found new angles and gaps within his defence.

All Cole needed was time. The rest of the unit could help, but they had to wake first. All he needed to do was buy them time. The Phantom slowed down but engaged precisely. Cole's blocks were useless. He could feel himself bruising and tiring. As much as he hated to admit it, the physical battle would not last much longer. Victory, if at all, would only come from fortitude. The Phantom was right in the palm of their hand. He just needed to buy time.

Cole let himself stagger back and fall against a wall. "Not bad for a terrorist," he spat. Blood drooled from his mouth and nose.

The Phantom towered above him, approaching passively. **"Is that what you think I am?"** He looked inquisitively at their surroundings.

"That's what you are," Cole countered aggressively.

Phantom stopped to look him in the eyes. **"By definition, perhaps. Only because I operate on a larger scale."** His voice filled the night with depth and articulation.

"Operate?" Cole acted intrigued, "Under whose command?"

"Don't bother, Alex."

Cole tensed up. A weight hit the bottom of his stomach. There was a glint in the Phantom's eye. Confidence within an intelligent mind. As though he were unravelling the secrets behind Cole's eyes, making him feel vulnerable.

"You only know… what I want you to know." The

Phantom didn't blink, nor did he waver.

"I know you're hired into criminal rivalries." Cole refused to show weakness or fear. He kept his voice steady.

"**How do you think he knew about that? I wanted to see if you could get it out of him. Our methods differ, Cole, but the outcome is the same.**" The Phantom's head tilted slightly. His bright green eyes gleamed under the starlight.

"You 'replace' evil."

"**Your unit is a covert death squad. How 'legal' are *your* operations.**" The Phantom spoke quietly yet with strength. He dropped to one knee, leaning on the other and returning Cole's mean glare.

"Doesn't justify what you do," Cole shot back.

"**To fight the dark, you have to be in the shadows. I figured you would understand that…**"

"And the strike in Afghanistan!? Those were innocent pe-"

"**It wasn't supposed to happen like that!**" The Phantom's firm tone overpowered Cole's weak voice. "**They weren't supposed to go through with the airstrike. Their negligence killed innocent people. Their incompetence is infuriating.**"

"You set it up!" Cole yelled indignantly.

Phantom thrust a hand against Cole's chest and pushed hard, forcing the air out of his lungs. "**I created unfavourable conditions that would force them to give up the assault. At this point, they have killed more civilians than I have.**" The Phantom spoke slowly but harshly.

As soon as the Phantom withdrew his hand, Cole drew in a breath and pressed his earpiece. "The Phantom is on my position! In the open south of the apartments!"

The Phantom simply glared at him, undeterred. Then he

reached into his jacket pocket, and removed the other five earpieces, dropping them in front of Cole.

"HERE!" Cole yelled with the last of his breath. With all his fury, Cole kicked him in the chest. The Phantom staggered back then leaned in to re-engage while Cole got to his feet.

Cole lifted his arms promptly enough to block the flurry of concussive punches to his head and chest. He thrust his knee up following with a right hook to counter, but the Phantom simply swiped them both aside and continued to pound at his sides, forcing Cole against the wall.

Losing breath, Cole ducked and kicked off the wall, pushing them both away. It took more breath than he had. The Phantom capitalized on his moment of weakness by kicking his knee down, back-handing his defences aside, and punching hard up into his stomach. Cole spat a mouthful of blood as the air evacuated his lungs. He saw growing spots and felt a nauseous bruise under his diaphragm.

There was quiet in the night again. He lifted his arms to block but nothing came. Through hazy vision, he saw the black figure of the Phantom whip out of sight. The voices of Charles and Deck echoed from higher up in the favela.

The Phantom ducked down and sprinted into the alleys. He put as many walls between him and Unit Zero as he could. They were awake again. He did not kill Cole but looked forward to round two.

Born of the dark, the Phantom approached the garage at a brisk pace. It opened ahead of him, letting white light expand out into the black street.

Garrick was sitting on the hood of a car ready to hear the report. "Is it done?" He asked. An intense glare from the Phantom made him lift off the car and let him pass.

"**Not this time.**" The Phantom strode through the garage

and into the building. Mercenaries in mechanic's jumpsuits worked on cars and weapons. Cleaning, fixing, and modifying.

"Why not? Something go wrong?" Garrick asked as he jogged to catch up with the Phantom's strides.

"We still need them. Keep leaving survivors, make sure they follow you," Phantom demanded calmly.

"That's going to make things difficult for us," Garrick said, glancing at his men working out below the stairs before following the Phantom up.

"That's your mission, lieutenant," Phantom said flatly.

"And if they catch up?" Garrick asked, "What's the counter?"

"Scatter. Dissolve your men in the city to regroup later. Do not underestimate Cole and his unit, Remember: Kill before capture."

"But my men don't know enough, they have no valuable information."

"Leave nothing to chance." The Phantom walked over to his M82 rifle, which lay under its leather cover as requested. **"Have you heard from the lady?"** He asked lightly, gathering tools to dismantle the sniper.

"She says the agents are looking into something."

The Phantom's head turned slightly to one side expectantly.

"That's all she would tell me," Garrick exclaimed defensively. "I asked for more but you know the Lady Danger - she only listens to you."

The Phantom stood soundless and motionless. **"Prepare to leave."**

Garrick turned away. He had to navigate past a few workers carrying large crates of ammo. The Phantom marched into the corner room and sat on a bench next to his toolbox. He lifted his left trouser leg to reveal the scratched steal underneath; a smooth, leg-shaped frame with rods holding it together on the inside. There was no dent in the shin piece or the long, main spring that ran behind it. The two springs that ran inside the calf frame were squeaking again. Calibration of their cogs and the axis at his ankle let the mechanism work smoothly again.

Once he finished, he could put the knife back into the holster attached to the outside of the prosthetic and pull his trousers over the bearings on either side of his knee. The magnet in the lower part of the leg functioned perfectly but felt too heavy. It diminished his agility but put a lot more force into his kicks.

Next time he would have to be faster. Cole was an intelligent and formidable opponent. He lasted longer than most despite falling for the Phantom's plays. It would be a far more even match next time. Cole would not underestimate him next time.

Chapter XII
Dominion

Brooklyn, New York, United States of America
18:30 EST, Thursday, 15th September 2016
(9 days later)

Margarete took in the salty, smoky air and sighed. It felt like the end of times. Like being forced into old age. The organization was past its prime but still had a few good years left. The time for greed had passed. Retirement was all that remained. Peaceful, stress-free retirement.

She would have to leave it all behind. But the old saying held true for all, including her. It was not a life you left behind. It always caught up with you again. It finds you. It's relentless.

She knew the risks. They never mattered. But times were changing, and a new king was taking power. The Phantom had done her the favour of eliminating competition. Yet the empty market felt more unsettling than profitable. Like it was dying away. Rusting and falling apart. The end drew ever closer for all.

"We're no exception," said Margarete, "He will come for us as well."

Joe could say nothing. Margarete took another puff from her cigarette and let the smoke blow over the desk.

"What should we do?" Joe asked.

Margarete stared into space, hiding her defeated expression. "Stop the imports. Next month's shipment will be the last," she said gravely.

"That's it? Just like that?" Joe asked.

"You don't have kids, Joe, so I wouldn't expect you to understand."

"I understand, boss, but you don't need to retire the organization as well." Joe stepped forward. He was a big man. With broad shoulders and large gut that had matured over the years.

"I would let you take over but it's not that simple." Margarete sighed again. "You can't stop him. Too many of ours have quit out of fear and more are sure to follow." She took another puff of her cigarette.

"A smaller crew is easier to hide," Joe suggested.

"It's only a matter time before he traces the drugs to us and we become a target. This organization's days are numbered. If I am going to give my kids a good future then what they need now is safety and security." Her wrinkled face tensed with desperate concern.

"It's almost time to start thinking of college. They don't just need my money they need *me*," she said wholeheartedly.

Joe remained silent.

"Have any of the others stopped their operations?" She asked.

"Not that I know of." Joe said confidently. A loud bang came from somewhere in the warehouse below. Joe drew his weapon. Margarete's trembling fingers held her cigarette as she listened closely to the shouting. She was significantly more relieved than frustrated. Pursing her lips, she put out the cigarette and waited.

"FBI! GET DOWN ON THE GROUND!" Came yelling as the door was breached. Joe had put his gun on the table and stood with his hands partially up. Margarete calmly turned to address the agents.

"What is all this?" She asked politely. A man pushed past the yelling agents and stood in front of her.

"Margarete Joules?" Owen asked with a serious

expression.

"Yes?"

"If you would come with us, we'd like to ask you a few questions."

"As long as I have my lawyers you can ask me anything." Margarete stood up and made her way out with the officers surrounding her. "I can find my own way, thank you! I'm old, not elderly," she said bitterly.

"We got Joules at the Brooklyn docks." Owen said into his comms.

"*I know. I told you.*" Caitlin replied.

"What if you were wrong?" He shot back.

"*I'm not.*" Caitlin said confidently.

"*So Brooklyn is New York, who had New York?*" Asked Dennis.

"*I did.*" Joel boasted.

"*No way,*" said Henry, "*Cait has to be conspiring with them or something. Mercer?*"

"*No she's right, the ports in Brooklyn.*" Sophie admitted.

"*I don't buy it. He cheated, he got help from Chris.*"

"*How is that Cheating? Mine is just the better guess.*" Christian exclaimed.

"They definitely cheated." said Owen.

"I've got him right here in front of me." Caitlin paced past the man with Sophie watching him from the side. He was handcuffed to a metal chair and keeping his mouth shut. Sophie was getting sick of the smell. Hot sweat on a humid Brazilian night gave a foul odour. She just wanted to be outside in the breeze.

"You want to ask him yourself?" Caitlin asked

sarcastically.

"*Suck it up, Busher, that's two–one to the English.*" Dennis said finally.

"Where did you say?" Caitlin asked as she released the cuffs from the chair and stood the man up.

"Jersey," said Sophie.

"I had Maryland." Caitlin rolled her eyes. Together, they took the man away to turn him in.

"Here." Stanley Martin handed the folder to Dennis.

"Thanks, Stan."

"Where was it?" Stanley asked.

"New York, Brooklyn area." Christian replied.

"Nice," Stanley smiled, "Keep it up, lads." His bright face and vivid blue eyes beamed down at Christian.

"Anything more on the rogue militia?" Christian asked hopefully, pushing up his glasses.

"Nothing yet," Stanley shrugged. Once he left, Dennis followed soon after.

"It's not going to stick." Said Christian.

"It doesn't have to." Joel said simply. He was looking down a list with his reading glasses on the end of his nose.

"They should be prosecuted, it's safer for them." said Christian.

"That's the FBI's job, or the DEA or whoever. All we're after is information." Joel concentrated half on the list and half on Christian.

"So far no ties to the Syndicate, which can only mean the Phantom is yet to get to them."

"And we will be waiting."

"Only once they strike. I bet the others wouldn't

appreciate using living people as bait." Christian raised his eyebrows at Jocl.

"We don't have much choice." Joel said, looking up at Chris. "There are only a handful of organizations left and each one gets us a step closer to the Syndicate-"

"A lot of people are going to die before that happens. The Syndicate may be in China now but if we keep making the world around them smaller then they're going to lash out." Christian got quieter as he spoke.

"It's the best plan we've got. We tried going to them and people died, innocent people. Now we're going to let them come to us. And these-" Joel pointed to the profiles on the desk, "-are not innocent people."

Christian understood it more than he would have liked. Potentially letting people die felt cruel. Like something the Phantom would do. As though MI6 was taking inspiration from his psychosis. The *Art of War* book spoke of the necessity of sacrifice for victory. A strategy adopted by the Syndicate, no doubt. By the end, reflecting the Syndicate felt like a Mephistophelian moral strategy. Nevertheless, an internecine sacrifice was the best chance they had in an already shrinking time limit. Joel knew it, and the weight of responsibility pressured him into acceptance.

Dawson wouldn't hear the end of it from Dennis but he didn't care. Whether or not the English were winning some silly competition, they were getting somewhere. Not just anywhere, but closer.

"Miss Joules my name is Special agent Nathan Dawson." He closed the door of the interrogation room.

"Your name is special agent?" Margarete raised her

eyebrows sarcastically.

"I know this isn't your first rodeo but I'm from the CIA, not the FBI." Dawson said intensely.

"CIA? We're in America aren't we?" Margarete asked, undeterred.

"Yes. You know what else is in America? Brazil." Dawson replied.

"As much as I appreciate the geography lesson I won't be answering questions until my lawyer arrives." Margarete crossed her arms and pursued her lips.

"My questions aren't about you." Dawson dropped a single picture on the table in front of her. An image of the Phantom, clear as night.

"Who's that?" She asked convincingly.

"You can drop the shit. I'm not after you, I don't give a shit about you. I want what you know. And you want to go home." Dawson said suggestively.

"What I want is my lawyer." said Margarete.

"He's on his way, but you should know that a lawyer won't stop me from searching your grounds for something to keep you on. Days, maybe weeks of court trials that won't amount to anything but will sure as hell waste a lot of your time. Or you could just answer my questions alone, and leave here tonight." Dawson raised his eyebrows and took his seat opposite her. She could see in the surly wrinkles of his face that he wasn't the negotiating type.

"You sound desperate," she said, mildly astonished, "You won't find anything on my grounds."

"Choice is yours." Dawson spoke darkly, "If we could find you in a few weeks how long do you think it will take him."

The photo pulled at Margarete's gaze. A man in a suit entered with Henry. Margarete's eyes glazed and blurred as her lawyer spoke. Dawson stared her down.

"Wait outside," she said to the lawyer. He protested, but she insisted. Henry escorted him out into the hallway. A few seconds of silence passed while Dawson watched her and waited.

Lucy twirled left and right on her office chair. Her head nodded to the tune of a song that was still stuck in her head from that morning. The opening and closing of a door in the background announced Christian's return before he did. Lucy was watching her inbox while listening to Christian on the call.

Owen's appearance startled her slightly. She recovered from the little scream and put Christian on speaker.

"Stop sneaking up on me!" She said with an embarrassed giggle.

"*Hey Owen.*" Christian chuckled.

"Hey Chris. It was Margarete Joules in Brooklyn. Good work, Lucy." said Owen.

"Thanks." She smiled.

"*When are the girls getting back?*" Christian asked.

"Tomorrow I reckon, but you know them, will probably spend the morning at the beach trying to get a tan or some shit." Owen pulled a chair to sit beside Lucy who opened a message on her computer.

"Henry says Dawson is speaking to her alone," she read.

"Let's watch, I'll give you the password." Owen said hurriedly. Lucy pulled up the feed from the interrogation room and Owen unlocked the viewing privileges. Christian couldn't hear so worked quietly in the background.

They watched from the beginning. Once the lawyer left,

it took a while for Margarete to start talking.

"*What do you want from me?*" She asked.

"*Everything. You see him before?*" Dawson asked.

Lucy payed close attention to Margarete's body language.

"*No.*" She replied sternly, crossing her arms.

"*What do you know?*" Dawson sat back in his chair.

Margarete remained upright, tapping her fingers on her arms. "*I see what he's done on the news,*" she said.

"*He's also made the underworld a lot smaller, it's getting harder for people like you to hide.*" Dawson knew he had the upper hand.

"*You must be so proud.*" Margarete said, "*He's doing your job for you. You should be thanking him.*"

"*You can do it for me, you'll likely see him first.*" Dawson didn't hold back the impact of his statement. Margarete's care-free persona was collapsing under the weight of his truth.

"*If he gives you the chance.*" Dawson cut her off with another hard nail in her coffin.

"*What's your point?*" She hissed.

"*The FBI's case against you is the least of your worries right now. We share a common enemy and I think you need our help more than we need yours.*"

"*What do you have in mind?*" Margarete asked hesitantly. She tried weakly to hold back a chesty cough.

"*Cooperate, and when your case finally goes to court, they might just take it into consideration when it comes to your sentencing.*" Dawson's vague suggestion had Margarete on edge. She considered it with her lips pursed.

"*I have daughters, they have to be protected,*" she said finally.

"They will be."

"*What do you need me to do?*" Margarete asked. Owen sat back in his chair smiling.

"That was quick." Lucy said in gleeful awe.

"*Did we get her?*" Christian asked.

"Hook, line, and sinker." Owen said proudly.

Unknown, Unknown, Russia
22:12 MSK, Thursday, 27th October 2016
(42 days later)

A light sprinkling of snow glided in the cold night's air. A few millimetres had built up on the ground. The wired fences dripped with icicles. Lamps and floodlights revealed the gentle flow between the parking and the building. Multiple SUV's were parked under aluminium roofing, surrounded by armed men. All remained still and patient.

Leaning against the side of an armoured car, which hosted an armed .50 Cal on top, Mahkahr Stepanov held his cigarette with crossed arms. Scratches and stitched tears gave his thick leather jacket an old and worn quality. Fur lining underneath was patched with washed blood stains, up to the collar where the ends of his hair rested. His square jaw, broken to the point of near disfiguration, was coated with a greying beard.

They had been waiting outside for him, and would have to come to him where he stood. He waited with a passive expression and a loaded pistol in his thigh holster. So long ago the roles were reversed. Mahkahr could remember how the commander stood his ground in hostile sights. He wondered if even back then the commander knew what would happen. They call him the *Phantom* now, but back then Mahkahr only knew him as the commander…

The mafia made them wait. Outside in the cold, surrounded by armed men all sporting mean looks. The two of them went alone as per request. Mahkahr stood idly behind the commander, who stood upright with his chin up and chest out. They weren't allowed guns, they weren't allowed inside. When the doors of the garage opened, the Mafia made them stand outside for the duration of the meeting. Yet the commander did not complain, nor did he look bothered. It gave Mahkahr the confidence to stand close and keep his mouth shut.

They had little reputation and practically no value on their word. Yet the commander spoke as though they were on equal ground. They looked down at him, laughed at him. Yet what he supposedly had to offer was something of great value. They heard him, and took their own time. What they did not see, was fear. The commander did not hesitate. He did not negotiate. He laid out the terms and set the stage. The mafia would not engage in such a high investment without proof, and that is what they would get.

That was their first job. The agreement would be a task of unheard impossibility in exchange for something so simple; the commander's word. Once they shook hands, the commander turned away and left without another word. Leaving the Mafia and a dozen machine guns in silence akin to awe. The brass balls he had to leave them on his terms bought him respect. But not nearly as much as his arrival the following month.

The commander left a line of blood in their snow. He desecrated their land with dominance of his own. Bringing back what he promised. The Mafia, wherever they were, always battled against competition. This, one of the most powerful organizations, naturally accumulated opposition across Western

Europe.

The heads of these opposing Mafias had to eat sometime. They would visit restaurants, their favourites for the most part. Private bars, sport centres, gentlemen's clubs. That is where the commander's agents would serve them. When the time came for rich men to use their credit cards, agents of the 'Syndicate' would provide card machines modified to record the pin. A simple trick. One they would not look out for. That was all the commander needed.

In one fell swoop, the commander struck mercilessly and took what he needed. The credit cards, the fingerprints, and the heads. All very literally.

Upon his return that same evening over a month since the deal was set, he handed over a case and bloody sack. Heads of the heads. Fingers on keychains. Credit cards and pins. A handful of items valued at something in the billions. As well as something worth more than Rubles: Power.

All at once the commander gained their respect, their investment, and the highest value to his word. The start of an insidious climb to power.

So long ago it was. Now Mahkahr stood surrounded by his own weaponized forces, looking down at the very same men he met with all those years ago. Once titans in their empire, now servants to the Syndicate. Since that first meeting, the Phantom made the Mafia meet them outside in the cold. A show of dominance like a boot that never stopped pressing on their genitals. A cold reminder.

Petrak and Kiel approached Mahkahr impatiently. Mahkahr did not react nor did he acknowledge them at all. He simply stared down at his cigarette, letting his misty breath out slowly.

"We have done everything as the commander

instructed." Kiel said through shivering lips.

Mahkahr didn't move.

"There is nothing more to report, everything is in place." Kiel began to sound frustrated.

Mahkahr nodded slightly, still not looking at either of them. He threw his cigarette to the snow and pressed his boot over it.

"Where is your boss!?" Kiel yelled. The man on the .50 Cal tightened the grip of his leather gloves around the handles. Kiel retreated a step back to Petrak. "We want to speak with the grandmasters." He demanded.

Mahkahr appeared as though he didn't hear him, until he suddenly spoke out in his strong husky voice. "Why?" He asked simply.

Petrak stepped forward. "Our influence in the government has become unsettled. Something broke out between them and the Chinese. The government went silent before we could find out what. But now they want nothing to do with you." Petrak's old voice was crisp in the cold breeze.

Mahkahr glared at them expectantly. "What are they doing now?" He asked.

"They are cutting ties with us," Petrak said gravely.

"They've been burning evidence, covering up every trace of their connection to you or us," Kiel added strongly. Mahkahr stroked his beard and looked out into the night. Kiel was shivering. His cheeks were bright red. Petrak was still, his aged face bitter beneath his hood.

"Why are all those officials afraid of you!?" Kiel called.

"Keep your eyes on them. Have your men monitor the situation as it develops. I want to know what evidence they're disposing of, and how." Mahkahr responded calmly. He span his forearm above his head to signal his men to mobilize.

"Remember, we will be watching closely." Mahkahr warned. He thought of the Syndicate agents hidden amongst the ranks of the Mafia. The Phantom always had agents 'babysitting' his projects or investments.

"Where is the commander!?" Kiel yelled.

Mahkahr ignored him. His team was ready to leave within seconds. They left in an orderly fashion with Mahkahr in the middle of the convoy.

"Is he back from the operation yet?" Mahkahr asked the man in the passenger seat.

"No, Lieutenant," he reported.

"Let Tadao know the Mafia this side are ready, and that our suspicions were right." Mahkahr said gruffly.

Beijing, China
08:48 CST, Friday, 28th October 2016
(The next day)

A world once vibrant in colour had decayed into grey. Stained red then irradiated by loss. Something stirred the once dormant past. Pain rose again as it once did and breached the surface in need of confrontation. It could not be left unchecked, and it could not be left unfinished. A shiver travelled up the spine of the nation. A Phantom approaches.

Ji Zhang, President of China, was not about to let his streets need to be as clean as they once were. Washed and polished looking new and unused, so that no amount of blood remained.

They could not see it anymore. They could not smell it. They could only feel it. No number of political stitches can heal the 'Beijing massacre' scar that cursed his presidency. That cursed his family.

His eyes focused on something in front of him that didn't exist. The weight of his chest suffocated him through a heavy sigh. Terrorism could not be given any amount of freedom in the world. He offered his support and investigative programs to aid the west in their struggle. Where they failed, he would have to succeed, or stand down as an incapable leader.

The picture of the boy on his desk was one of many. Countless pictures in the homes of all citizens living across China. All different. All loved. All under threat. That picture in particular once served as a reminder but now only left him perturbed.

Flipping the broken record in his mind, he pushed out all thoughts of the past. The Russian's had been pulling away with their heads down like burglars caught before the act. Just like they did three years ago when the terrorists slipped through his fingers. This time he would be careful. He would trap them slowly and elegantly within a shrinking cage. Whatever secrets the Russians were hiding would be forced out between the bars leaving only the guilty for persecution. After the events in Afghanistan, Ji knew what was coming, and a new security detail held china with a firm grip. Militant forces had been spreading from the north. As soon as the great red curtain fell upon the border, the Russian government flinched and their forces retracted. Ji had severed a limb which still remained in China. It would lead him to the beating heart of the beast. A serendipitous opportunity he did not take for granted.

Ending the rampant militancy and bringing the devastation to a close would not stem the tears in his wife's eyes, but it could ease the fire in his own. The boy in the picture could finally be just a memory, and rest easy, letting Ji retire having fulfilled his duty as a leader and a father.

Ji didn't acknowledge the door of his office opening. The woman that entered had her hair tied up so tight it almost looked fake. With immaculate posture she addressed him urgently yet politely. She spoke faster than usual when she would come to him with news of outlying criminal activities. Outlying from the norm because they matched the descriptions provided by MI6.

"The blackout?" He asked in a low, monotone voice.

"Yes. Early this morning," she confirmed.

"Tell me," he said, equally as monotone.

"Sixteen injured but none killed. They broke into the Azure Power facility at two thirty this morning and stole high-end machine parts. Removing the parts caused the system to crash, hence the blackout. The station is back online and functioning normally."

"Where are the thieves now?" Ji asked.

"We lost them in the blackout. Two matte black vans with no license plates and 'a supercar darker than night'" she said with some confusion.

"Hand me that file," he demanded. She did so without hesitation and stepped back to let him skim through it.

"Dark as night!" He spat. The Phantom had made it all the way to the capital before being identified. How he had passed the great red curtain was an infuriating mystery. Ji felt powerless. He understood how they must have been feeling in the west.

That's when a glossy gleam of brass caught his eye. Photos of cartridge shells taken from the scene of the crime.

"No alarms were triggered until the end," said the woman.

Shells that were unique to very few instances in past years.

"A lot of security footage was corrupted but some survived," she continued.

The style, the make, was identical to those recovered from the Beijing massacre. There were side by side comparisons of size and shape. Haunting images of old evidence.

The old cartridges were not, however, recovered from the terrorists. They were recovered from the victims; a rogue militant group that was supposedly the central target of the massacre.

The last instance of the unique cartridges appeared near the northern border between China and Russia right before the trail died away. Now they had appeared again - and the Russian government had locked down - Again.

Ji finally had a path to follow. Grey sky's bred thunder in his heart. A second chance was often more crucial than the first. Because of this, it would take his utmost patience and self-control to execute the capture of the Phantom. An enemy with such a profound reputation for meticulous strategy could not go underestimated.

Time pulled away at his opportunity like searching for small fish in an ocean current. A current that almost certainly travelled north.

Last time they pulled on a lead the Russians cut themselves away claiming ignorance to militant exploits. This time he would not pull, but rather follow, so whatever was on the other end could not cut them off the same way. Ji would have to claim some ignorance of his own.

The game is cunning. Don't chase a white rabbit in the snow.

The city was always so beautiful at night. Grand structures and buildings beamed with lights of life even at that early hour. And New York thought it was the only city that never slept.

Phantom looked out of the wide window at the splendid scene beyond. Streets with next to no cars and rare civilian walkers. The mysteries tied to such people at that hour would have him contemplating their stories.

His hands were together behind his back, his feet shoulder-length apart, his back straight. He could see them, but they could not see him up on the fifth floor, looking down as the superior night dweller. A hidden mystery to the mysteries of the hidden.

His men worked behind him. Their tools sometimes loud, but no worry, no-one in the building was awake to hear them anymore. They would wake up later with no more than bruises and disorientation.

A little sound proofing meant the drilling and sawing barely reached the street outside. Not enough for a noise complaint but enough to gain a curious eye from passers-by. They dared not enter. A single pane of glass was all that separated them from the Phantom's mercy. A box of steel, glass, and stone hosted dark forces unbeknownst to the common citizen. They knew not how close they were, they never did. Forever surrounded by all types of evil reaching out in the hope they stray too far from safety. A criminal scourge that preyed on the weak and vulnerable. A virus that plagued the planet.

Nature must be allowed to restore balance, but they were victims to an unnatural system. Excrement of a man-made hierarchy trying to claw their way up using hard working people as shortcuts. Nature played no part, in fact, its selection called to them endlessly.

Phantom elevated from the depth of his thought when

footsteps approached from behind. He remained still and patient, waiting for the man to speak out.

"We've detached the mechanism, it's coming out now." said the Captain. The Phantom took in a slow breath, letting his chest expand against the straps of his armour.

"Take your time, Captain. Slow and steady."

The captain turned back to relay the command. Fortunately the station had more than one of the machines, so losing one wouldn't drastically inhibit its functionality. Once the men access the building's server, and the system recognizes that a part is missing, it would shut down so as not to harm the rest of the station. The selection of machines operated in parallel circuits and were programmed to redistribute power to each other if they overheated. By manually heating one of the temperature sensors, the system diverted power to the other lines, allowing them to remove the mechanism without risk of getting shocked or alerting the system. All server access was disconnected so the system couldn't run diagnostics on the overheating part and raise the alarm when it was removed. In order to access the server for the additional information he needed, Phantom would have to allow full server access. Without the temperature sensor being heated, the system would soon give power to the missing part, recognize its missing, and shut down while activating a password protected emergency protocol. They could prevent the shut down if they had the password. Without it, they would be letting the alarm trigger, and making a hasty escape with the machine.

Complicated enough that no one could argue or contest. The Phantom turned and marched towards his technician. They had retrieved a login password at least. The dramatic irony was giving Phantom a thrilling sensation of enjoyment. His men would never know the reality behind his fiction. He could simply disconnect server access from the machines and accessed the server without setting off the emergency protocol. Plus, he had the emergency password to prevent shutdown as a contingency.

The machine was a significant by-product of the mission. The server held critical information for the future. A bright dark future.

Officials would discover the break-in and stolen mechanism once the syndicate left. With their attention on the damage, the server login would go overlooked. President Zhang would be too busy wondering how they got past the red curtain to pay attention to the details.

"The payload is ready to go, sir." Said the captain. They knew what came next so the Phantom simply nodded in approval. With that, his men packed up and cleaned every trace of their presence. The technician left the computer ready and open for Phantom to login and access the server.

The vans were ready. Phantom allowed server access and waited calmly as the system booted. The alarms screamed a perilous warning while the Phantom searched the server's files. Tires screeched outside indicating the escape of the vans.

Phantom initiated the wireless transfer of data to a safe-house which would be abandoned soon after. In addition, he left a malicious program on countdown before striding to the emergency exit and jumping the rails two staircases at a time.

Police response made it half way from the municipality building before the Phantom reached the outside parking. Technicians and security from the opposing wing of the station ran to the alarm and found the break in. With the monitor off, they did not see the active computer.

Phantom waited in his car, gripping the luxurious Italian leather. Sirens got louder from the left. His internal clock ticked away. He turned the key, listening to the vicious Italian engine come to life in seconds, then waited some more. The sirens got louder still, just about reaching that point. It was time.

The Phantom accelerated out into the road as the police turned into the parking. Firefighters bypassed him heading directly to the facility. The Phantom revved his engine provocatively with each shift in gear, eliciting every police car to spin back into the road and chase after him. He reached the main road knowing that dispatch would already be sending more cars.

Phantom kept his turns slow to give them time to keep up. He had to keep the police responses chasing him to buy freedom for the vans.

Block by block, street after street, he took them through a city sprint like a maze. Every few turns they would think they have him boxed in only to lose him to yet another turn. During which the Phantom mapped his path carefully. Every new car that entered the ring would be swept up in the current of the chase and left behind in the Phantom's wake. A vehicular vortex was taking shape throughout the streets.

An unexpected stop had the police screeching either side of the Phantom's deep-black Lamborghini. Their flashing lights reflected off of his tinted windows. Gripping tension had the police anticipating his next move, yet the Phantom cruised forward leisurely. They followed, some cars advancing ahead to cut him off.

Phantom accelerated with only seconds remaining. His speed left them in futile pursuit. The weight of their cars leaned out as they made a strong right turn. Bright police lights overwhelmed the view of the Phantom's car ahead. He had made a complete circle in the city that was now closing. Two ends of the police chase closing like a pincer.

The program at the facility reached its inevitable end and removed itself, taking some of the facility with it. All lights in the station switched off. Streetlights and neighbouring buildings followed suit in the subsequent seconds. A wave of darkness spread over the city leaving everyone in blind fear and confusion.

The Phantom flipped a custom switch installed where the radio had been. As the wave passed, the lights of the Lamborghini went out with it, letting the Phantom melt into the wave. Police sirens and bright blue lights filled the length of the street between the closing police. Neither side could see the distance in-between, nor could they hear anything as the Phantom turned away. Within seconds they were looking upon an empty street flashing blue.

The entire underground vibrated with the arrival of the Phantom. His supercar put the life back into the men with its roaring vigour. He parked up and left it to be managed by his mechanics. Areas of the black coat had been scratched off by walls and police cars. A distraction presented itself as reward. His men had removed the payload and were loading it safely into the transport truck.

It was time to leave again before they were found. Tadao watched the men struggle with the weight of the machine. Phantom passed him and scaled the stairs two steps at a time.

Tadao followed confidently. "Mahkahr's meeting with Petrak is over. He's waiting to hear from you." He said as he walked beside the Phantom.

"Let him know I've returned." Phantom's voice boomed. Tadao gestured for one of the nearby men to do so.

They reached the main office with a table in the centre and benches on either side. The Phantom's tools were packed for transportation. Tadao passed him the little box of tools for his leg and sat opposite him. A finished game of chess lay on the empty table between them.

"What's that strange engine for?" Tadao asked.

Phantom had his prosthetic on the bench and was checking its calibration. "**It's not an engine. It's for something far more powerful.**" Before Tadao could ask more about it, Phantom continued with a calm yet urgent tone. "**Are the transports ready?**"

"Yes. And I'm taking my chess board back, I want a rematch." Tadao collected the pieces and folded the board into a case to hold them.

"**As long as you get that truck where it needs to go.**" Phantom slid his duffel bag out from beneath the bench and packed the toolkit away. "**Will you be ready for** *the game*?" He asked deeply.

Tadao felt hesitant on the topic. "All preparations have been made. Mahkahr said the mafia that side are ready." He said.

Phantom turned to him inquisitively.

"I've never opposed your plans before, but this one feels excessive." He confessed.

"**There is no such thing as overkill. If I do not teach them how will they learn? It's necessary to knock out key players before we get to the** *bigger* **plans, and what is necessary is always what is right.**" Phantom spoke strongly with firm eye contact.

Tadao could see raw malice behind his green eyes. They had come far. The Phantom never failed to deliver. "I'll let you know when I make the drop in Japan." said Tadao. He stood up from the bench to take his leave.

"**Tadao.**" Phantom said darkly. He was staring into space with a fiendish expression beneath his mask. Belligerent thoughts were crafting cruelties beyond Tadao's own comprehension. "**Where is Garrick?**"

"I'll have to check." Tadao said after a moment of thought.

"**Contact him.**" Phantom said suddenly, "**I have a message for Unit Zero.**"

Tadao recognized a maniacal smile growing beneath the Phantom's mask. It was the kind of look a predator would have after a kill. The smile Phantom would get when playing with his prey.

Cole's fury burned into his cheeks and ears. He felt sick and aimless. It was a hard pill to swallow but it would have to be done before he could leave. Grade-A humiliation. The Phantom had promoted himself from something of a *bête noire* to the bane of Cole's existence.

They stood amidst defeat. No death, no blood, just a great big practical joke. Confetti showered them from all sides. LEDs of multiple colours lit up their snarling faces. A clear, provocative, humiliating message.

Cole knew he should have seen it from the start. The red smiles gave it away from the very beginning. Multiple assailants with plastic guns in their hands shook at the sound of their entry. The building was messy but reasonably new. In the entrance, and on the balcony overlooking it, they stood in place gripping their plastic guns tightly. All of them wearing their own white masks with red X's over the eyes and wide red smiles spray-painted on.

The nature of the situation was yet to make itself clear. Taking off one of the hostage's masks, Cole saw the fear in his eyes and the sweat running over his duct-taped mouth. The hostage wailed when Cole ripped it off. His gravelly voice breathed fire into the hostage. He let his frustration out and demanded answers. The hostage gave them willingly, an answer they would not like. Cole ran to the nearest open door and into the darkness of the hallway. Calling after him, Deck and the team followed with their weapons raised.

As told, red arrows led them through the building. Cole often slowed down seeing pictures in silly frames hung up on the walls. In the dim light he could just make out what they were; photos of his unit. One photo of them interrogating the first survivor labelled 'popping your cherry'. Another taken of them as they drove through the streets of a city labelled 'road trip'. Even one of them figuring out the rope puzzle labelled 'memories'. Charles cursed at the line of almost twenty pictures hanging along the final hallway. A sick feeling grew in the pit of Cole's stomach until they reached a single door dripping with red paint. A face had been wiped into the wet paint creating a distorted smile. Carved above it were the words "Welcome, Unit-0".

The door was already ajar. Cole pushed it slowly. It was not fear that drove him, but a great anger. He spurned the idea that once again the Phantom had played them. He knew full well the Phantom would not kill him. When last they met, it was a test of skill. There had to be a reason the Phantom let him live. Such mercy was out of his character.

Cole knew the answer as soon as he opened the door all the way. He received answers to all the questions he had been asking since the Phantom got away.

The entire room lit up with colourful party decorations. Unit-0 kicked aside the balloons covering the floor as they entered. Small party cannons blew confetti everywhere with party blowers whistled simultaneously. Colourful ribbons and wallpapers decorated the walls in a messy collage.

Cole's eyes were glued to the opposing wall. A world map had been stuck there with the word "SURPRISE" hanging above it. He walked forward to inspect further. A bloodstain line crossed the map. Then he saw the message, written in the country of China:

THE GAME WILL BE STARTING SOON!
DON'T BE LATE!

Cole followed the line of blood from their exact location on the map in Northern China to the East Coast of the United States. Washington DC.

Chapter XIII
Eye of a Hurricane
Virginia, United States of America
06:13 EST, Monday, 31st October 2016
(2 days later)

Clouds overhead the city were changing. They darkened into shades of grey, stretching with the wind. The breeze was volatile. It changed direction and speed so suddenly. People in the streets zipped up their coats and braced against the cold. Newspapers were being blown in erratic gusts. A gust whistled through the slit in a window. The pitch undulated eerily from high to low and back again, until it became so loud and distracting that Joel forced the window closed. Then he watched as the clouds overhead sped by.

His temporary apartment was on the third floor. He had been there only a few weeks and felt rather comfortable. It may have been small but it was close to the CIA. He rubbed the morning scruff that was growing on his jaw. "Looks like home out there," he said.

Caitlin was sitting on the other side of his bed behind him. They had been sharing the cost of renting a car and travelled to and from HQ together. She looked over her shoulder at the growing gloom outside and let out a heavy sigh. "It's been getting colder every day," she said.

Joel nodded. "Perfect day for a run with Sophie eh," he said as he put on his shoes.

"I miss my gym." Caitlin fell back on the bed. Her hair was curling less and was now only halfway down her back.

"I wish I could tell you we aren't going to be here long. I told them you don't need to be here, I even asked Stanley if he could switch with you but he's too busy," Joel explained. It was standard that agents collaborating from overseas had to have backup. MI6 wanted at least two agents together when working on the case internationally.

"Its fine, Joel, thanks," said Caitlin, "It should be Chris here with you anyway."

"No, he needs to be there with Dennis, and he isn't as intimidating as you," said Joel.

"Not much use when there's no-one to interrogate," she said agitatedly.

"The Syndicate has been restless all along the coast, something has to happen eventually. I just hope it's worth us being here all this time." Joel stopped in thought. "Something is happening… they're closing ranks maybe. We must be getting close in some way…" He stared into space, lost in thought. He didn't have much waiting for him back home. At that point, he was detached from his past like his memory had been erased. He was soaring higher than he ever had before. Higher than MI5. Higher than friends or family.

It was Caitlin's time being wasted. She was there in the event of big 'if's that would likely never come to pass. Christian had seriously recommended that there be a team of two in the US even though it could not be him.

A sudden gust of wind passing the window drew Joel's attention.

"Something's going on," said Caitlin.

"That's what I've been saying, for like the past two weeks-"

"No right now, Joel, they're calling us in," Caitlin said firmly. Joel looked to see her sitting up-right transfixed by the notification on her phone. She read it over again and strode out. Joel grabbed his blazer and went after her.

Lucy scrolled through her emails with her chin resting on her hand. She would have rather been playing chess with Christian again but he was greatly preoccupied. A wide yawn made her eyes water. Her hair was tied in a ponytail but some of it was sticking out the sides. The collective hum of the computers was loud but she was able to tune it out. She fought back against weighted eyelids. After another long yawn, she sat up, lifted her foot onto the chair, and swivelled to keep herself awake.

The door at the corner of the room opened with Sophie storming in, her face tight with concern.

Lucy dropped her leg and cleared her throat. "Hey," she said lightly.

"Hey, where's Dawson?" Sophie asked quickly.

"I don't know, maybe he's on his way?" Lucy shrugged.

"What about Cait and Joel?" Sophie asked.

"Also on their way," said Lucy.

"What could be so important? No-one's even here." Sophie paced behind her.

"I don't know," Lucy exclaimed, "I didn't even have time to get coffee this morning."

The door burst open and Dawson marched in, followed closely by Owen. "Where are the Brits?" Dawson asked strongly.

"Coming," replied Sophie.

"Chris is waiting to call you guys," Lucy said timidly.

"Get him on," said Owen.

Lucy sprang into action while Sophie enquired to Dawson about the situation.

"Some new development he wants to talk to us about,"

Dawson explained.

"We should wait for the others," said Owen.

"Just get Chris and Knight on call and worry about them later. You - out." Dawson pointed at Lucy and then pointed his thumb to the door. She left hurriedly without a sound.

The bags under Christian's eyes were dissipating. He typed furiously, trying to get a hold of Lucy, but no answer came. He fell back in his chair with a sigh while tapping his fingers. The notification he'd been waiting for sounded on his computer.

"Finally!" He exclaimed, and read a message that claimed to be from Sophie. Shrugging it off, he started the call anyway. It took a moment before they answered and Sophie's voice came through his speakers.

"*Hello?*" She answered.

"Sophie, where is everyone? Where's Dawson?" Christian asked harshly.

"*I'm here, what do you want?*" Dawson asked from the back.

"You have to pull the kill order on the Phantom," Christian said strongly.

"*Why?*" Dawson protested.

"I'll explain now, is everyone there?" Christian asked firmly.

"*Cait and Joel are on their way here,*" said Owen. The door behind Christian swung open and Dennis came marching in with his tie swinging.

"There you are," Christian breathed. He turned back to his computer and searched through his inboxes.

"Chris, slow down alright. They're working on a location now," Dennis said while catching his breath.

"*Knight? What's going on?*" Dawson asked.
"We're gonna explain, we're just busy trying to uhhm…" Dennis trailed off reading over Christians shoulder.

The three of them expected it to be Cait and Joel when the door opened. Dawson straightened up and let go of Sophie's chair.
"Grace…" he said with some confusion.
"Hello Nathan, Bradford, Mercer," said Grace. She walked up beside them normally. "What's the word?" She asked.
"How did you know we were here? I didn't call you did I?" Dawson asked, rubbing his temple.
"I told you to keep me posted on everything going on," said Grace. She watched the monitor as Sophie navigated her way through the unfamiliar program.
"Well," said Dawson, "Chris here wants us to remove the kill-order on the Phantom."
"*Yes! Please!*" Christian demanded. "*We need him alive!*"
"Whoa, alive? Why alive?" Owen asked.
"*Since your tip-off we've been going back and looking for organisations under the Syndicate-*" Everyone's attention was redirected to the door where Caitlin and Joel were coming in.
"Morning, what's going on?" Joel asked.
"*You're late!*" Christian yelled.
"We're five hours behind you!" Joel replied indignantly.
"*Listen! Organisations under the Syndicate's wing ARE the Syndicate, they just don't all know it themselves. The missing links on the timeline aren't eradicated - they're merged.*"

Christian finally released the pent-up frustration inside him.

Joel processed the idea through every angle and finished in seconds with a fresh clarity. He traced back memories opening the flood-gates of the past. He wondered if his old team at MI5, and even Elizabeth, were involved in retrieving the information. Everyone else considered the information in a collective pensive pause.

"Every link on our timeline?" Joel asked.

"So... we should be able to go to any one of them and follow the chain of command up," Dawson said simply.

"*We did,*" Dennis interjected, "*They work under the high command of a board called 'the Grandmasters', they don't even know they're in a syndicate let alone* the Syndicate."

"And these Grandmasters work for the Phantom?" Sophie asked.

"*No he works for them!*" Christian said quickly and clearly, "*That's why we need him; to get to them. They date back further than he does.*"

"*And there's one other thing...*" Dennis added.

"*We measured the models for accumulation of the Syndicate's manpower according to all the fucking data mining we did-*" Joel was taken aback by Christian's seething mood and leaned closer to pay better attention. "*-and managed to get an* approximate *estimation of their numbers. Good news is they're only as big as a first-world fucking military-*"

Dawson's face tightened up as he put his hands behind his head and shut his eyes. Caitlin rubbed the burning sensation in her cheeks and pulled her hair back even tighter. Joel pulled up a chair and fell into it with a miffed expression. Owen tightened his grip on Sophie's shoulder, who stared blankly at the screen with her arms crossed and her shoulders drooping. The overall mood in the room equalized into a general discouragement. Christian's rant continued with incandescent tenacity. "*-bad news is there's a void in their finances so big they're either printing their own cash or they're in more debt than the government.*"

"What exactly is a 'void in their finances'?" Grace asked with a concerned glare. Joel's head was leaning on his fists like he was praying.

"*Even by estimation, there's no way they would be able to fund their operations just from what they've been doing. Despite all the income they could have possibly gained over the last two to three years there's no way they could afford to sustain their current forces. Cost of manpower, specialized and custom high-grade equipment and arms, transportation with no trace or record. It's waaay out of league for supposedly 'non-profit' vigilantes. There is a significant amount of money coming from somewhere.*"

"How much?" Owen asked reluctantly.

"*Our growth models have a few estimates all with large margins of error. It's too much to be capital or investment, it has to be a systematic income,*" said Christian.

"But we don't know through what or whom to where. Tracing it is out of the question," Joel added.

"However," Christian said with a sanguine pause, "*If these 'Grandmasters' control the Syndicate then the distribution of funds must be going through them as well. Given the theoretical size of their private organisation as a placeholder to fill the big blank space of power in the Syndicate, they do hold a large income-gap themselves, but they should still be the financial hub of the entire Syndicate.*"

"If so, all we need to do is shut down that hub and the entire Syndicate will lose funding," said Dawson. He looked to see Grace's reaction, who was nodding along.

"*No-one has had contact with the Grandmasters, I'm guessing the Phantom is a middle-man, a General,*" Christian suggested.

"That's why you want him alive," said Joel.

"*I don't see any other way. No matter what happens from now on, we at least need the Phantom alive.*"

"And we're back where we started," Sophie sighed.

"While we have everyone here. Margarete Joules gave us an important tip late last night," Dawson interjected. He gave Owen the 'tell them' glare which prompted him to clear his throat and step closer.

"The Phantom's employers, the 'Grandmasters' I assume, reached out to her yesterday. There's going to be a meeting here on our side. Supposedly involving several other high ranking crime families," Owen reported.

"*How soon?*" Dennis asked.

"They didn't say when or where yet, but Joules will let us know once they do." Owen finished.

Grace took out her phone and walked to the corner of the room.

Dawson rushed after her and put his hand over her mobile. "What are you doing?" He whispered.

"I could ask you the same," Grace replied, a little shocked.

"You can't call this in," said Dawson.

"You were supposed to keep me informed. We're not going to do nothing," Grace pressed.

"He's right," Caitlin said from behind them, "The more people we tell the more we risk the Syndicate finding out what we know."

"And if it's a deceit? Or a trap? We need to be careful how we deal with this information," Joel said from behind

Caitlin. The group looked at Grace as she considered it.

"We can't rush into this, we need to do it right," Dawson whispered.

Grace relaxed, conceding to their strategy. "I still need to stop the kill-order." She started a call and wondered away for privacy.

"Chris you still there?" Caitlin asked.

"*We're here, don't worry we heard the whole thing, we'll keep it need-to-know,*" said Dennis.

"*Your line is secure right?*" Christian asked.

Caitlin raised her eyebrows at Sophie who responded by rolling her eyes.

"If the meeting is happening here then maybe the Grandmasters reside here," Owen theorized.

"Or England, given their presence there as well," Joel added, "Could be either/or."

"*Makes sense since they would be familiar with the currency values,*" said Christian.

"And the home language," Caitlin added.

"*Still just theory,*" Dennis said finally.

"Exactly," Dawson agreed, "So let's get to work."

He clapped his hands and gestured for everyone to leave. That's when they heard Grace snapping her fingers. They stopped and glared at her. She had a horrified look growing on her face while snapping for their attention. She tried to get a word in but whoever she was on the phone with didn't grant her the chance. A new thought seemed to spark behind her eyes. She spoke strongly and barged her way to the computer in front of Sophie. Everyone backed up around her.

"Show me! No, just tell them!" She yelled. After putting her phone on the desk she logged into her own email and waited. "The meeting is going to have to wait, there's been a string of murders along the coast featuring the Syndicate's symbol."

"How many?" Owen asked, taken aback like everyone else.

"They're still counting," Grace said gravely.

"*What's going on?*" Dennis asked. No reply came. Their eyes locked onto the images Grace had opened, their jaws limp with shock. The scenes were identical to past aftermaths of the Syndicate's work; Slaughtered victims and flesh mosaics. Intentionally disturbing. Nightmares brought into the world by sorcerers of a psychotic imagination. Artists of inhumane talent for bloody atrocities.

"Don't engage on the Phantom alone," Grace said in a shaky voice, "If he comes for you… just run." The screen was glowing red onto their faces. "They're recent, and the trail leads to us. Go, all of you," Grace said urgently.

"Miss Credette?" Dennis said into the mic, "Are you there?"

"Somethings going on over there. What do we do?" Christian asked. Dennis adjusted his reading glasses and thought for a moment. Christian was about to speak up when a high pitched squeal pierced his ears. He scanned the roads outside but nothing drew attention. Behind him, people passed the office hurriedly. Forceful premonitions took no note of his denial. The process flooded his body with an anxiety, starting in his chest. He rushed to see what was drawing so much attention.

There were a few people looking out the windows. Another high pitched screech came from the side with the most onlookers. Several cars were hooting as Christian reached the windows and stared down at the street. A delivery truck was swerving on both sides of the road causing other drivers to take evasive action. The final near miss accelerated the truck toward the pavement. It hit two parked cars and a lamppost before coming to a crashing stop against the wall of the opposite building. Dennis walked up to the windows in time to see Christian running for the elevator.

Once inside, Christian clenched his fists and tapped his foot in anticipation. By the time he reached the lobby entrance, there was a crowd of people watching MI6's security approach the truck. Christian got as close as he could. A member of the security yelled something and they all backed away with their hands ready to draw their pistols. Christian forced his way through the throng and around the circle of onlookers.

There was no one driving the truck. The front compartment was empty. Dennis entered the lobby to see a bomb disposal unit making their way out. Christian was among many being forced back to a safe distance. One man in a bomb disposal suit walked over to the truck gripping a stick with a mirror on the end. He used it to search the undercarriage, then when he got to the compartment, he looked over to see a complex mechanism of pistons and electronics attached to the steering wheel and pedals.

The two back doors of the truck blew open with smoke and paper. Dennis barged past the security to get a look. Hundreds of pieces of A4-paper were scattered in the street and showering down through the leftover smoke. Christian could see something printed on the pages. He stepped past the security who moved in with him and sped up to a run. They yelled for him to stop but he reached the van before Dennis who called them off. The back of the truck was empty apart from the contraption that launched the paper.

Blood drained from Christian's face, turning it white like

the pages he stood upon. He and Dennis shakily collected a few of the still warm pages. On them were two words beneath a photograph. Christian's breathing got uncontrollably quicker. A heavy feeling grew in his diaphragm. He felt dizzy looking down at the photo of Sophie. Beneath it, the text said 'PLAYER 6'. The other two pages in his hand had pictures of Joel, saying 'PLAYER 1'.

"Chris…" Dennis said worriedly. He was holding a few pages; a photo of himself as 'PLAYER 2', a photo of Christian as 'PLAYER 7', and a photo of an unknown man as 'PLAYER 11'. Looking around, Christian could see photos of Caitlin, Lucy, Owen, Dawson, Henry, Grace Credette, and several men he did not recognise. They were not official pictures like passport photos, nor were they public photos from social media. They were more like paparazzi photos, taken unbeknownst to the subject. In his own, Christian recognised where the photo was taken. For lunch one day he had walked from the SIS to a park a few streets away. There were a lot of dogs out that day, which he figured he must have been looking at when the Syndicate took the photo of him. Dennis' photo was taken outside of his kid's school one day when he was waiting for them. He inspected it with his mouth agape. Christian looked up and down the street frantically, unsure of what he was looking for.

"Oh no," Dennis managed through lost breath, "No. No."

Christian pulled out his phone and tried to make a call. The tightness in his chest restricted him into near hyperventilation.

A bell rang in the kitchen. No-one else in the café seemed to care. The machines behind the counter switched off, bringing silence to the gentle atmosphere.

Henry's phone buzzed in his jacket pocket. He put down his coffee and twisted to reach it. He could feel it somewhere at the corner when he heard an unusual set of metallic clicks come from beyond the staff door. Paused and still, he watched the door with no expectations, but as if in a dream, two men in civilian attire came out with suppressed Uzis and looked him dead in the eye.

"GET DOWN!" He yelled with the remaining breath he had while flipping his table for cover. His cup shattered across the floor. Densely muffled shots filled the café. Henry curled up as tight as he could against the table. He struggled to keep his eyes open. Glass and plaster sprayed from the walls. None of the shots hit his table, which wouldn't have been able to stop them anyway. After the final shots and clinking of empty cartridges, Henry waited for a moment, his heart beating rapidly. He could hear scuffing footsteps beyond the staff door and peeked around his table. The shooters were gone, but it was little comfort next to the scene they had left behind; the walls were decorated with bullet holes. The floor was covered with plaster and glass. Not one of the customers had moved.

Henry stared wide-eyed at them all. He scanned the room for a reaction but it was as if the shooting never occurred. Like an elaborate hallucination. The customers sipped their drinks, read their books, and carried on as normal.

Henry grabbed a knife from the front counter and shuffled carefully between the chairs and tables. His disdain for every one of them made his body stiffen up. Their unnatural mystique asked questions he refused to acknowledge the answers to. Once outside, he scanned his surroundings and jogged away from the café. People in the street were still going about their daily lives without delay or hesitation.

The missed call on Henry's phone was from Owen. He called back with the knife still in his other hand.

"*Henry where are you!?*" Owen asked urgently.

"I just got shot at in Tina's café and nobody seemed to give a shit, what the fuck is going on!?" Henry asked desperately.

"*WHAT!?*" Owen exclaimed.

"These guys just shot up the café and left!" Henry checked over his shoulder every few seconds.

"*Where are you now!?*" Owen asked.

"I'm coming to you," said Henry.

"*WAIT, DON'T GET IN YOUR CAR, we're coming to get you! Stay put!*" Owen stressed.

Henry stopped in his tracks and stepped back. He could see his car parked across the road a few meters away. He thought of how long he had been in the café, and how long it would take to plant a car bomb.

Gripping the knife behind his back, he continued to scan his surroundings, watching the 'civilians'.

"Henry's in trouble! We're going to get him, stay here!" Owen said firmly. Joel and Caitlin leapt up instinctively. They watched Owen and Sophie rush out before calling Dennis and Christian.

Owen rushed through the lobby exit and did a quick scan of the area. He considered his car for a second before breaking into a run. Sophie followed him easily. Their steps sounded heavy against the pavement. Passers-by watched curiously as they raced along the curb.

"OWEN!" Sophie called. She grabbed the back of his white shirt and pulled him out the way of the oncoming car, which had mounted the curb and accelerated over a grass corner towards them. Owen backed away in shock and watched the car continue straight over the road next to them and onto the opposite curb. Onlookers screamed and yelled for people to get out the way. The car scraped against a wall and slowed to a stop, its bonnet smoking.

Owen watched it for a few more moments, fuming and shaking slightly. Sophie scanned desperately for threats until he grabbed her arm and continued running. Everyone they passed looked at them. Owen couldn't tell if they were curious… or if they were watching.

They made it a couple of blocks from the café when an oncoming car broke from the traffic ahead of them and began picking up speed. Owen skidded to a stop and jumped aside between two parked cars, pulling Sophie with him. The attacking car tracked them and crashed into the line of parked cars forcing them to roll into traffic to avoid being crushed. Regular oncoming cars hooted and swerved to avoid them.

They recovered briskly and passed the smoking wreck of crumpled cars as fast as they could.

A hooting from down the road caught Christian's full attention. He peaked cautiously down the street. A convoy of SUV's was struggling past security. The entire street had been sealed off, so Christian stepped outside for a better angle. There were at least three plain black SUV's with a polished black sedan in between. On the front corners of the sedan, Christian could see diplomatic flags. Members of security were still talking with the driver of the first car as others checked the undercarriages with more mirrors. Christian went back to the lobby where Dennis was on call with Caitlin and Joel.

"Are we expecting a visit from a foreign diplomat?" Christian asked. Dennis thought from a moment and nodded. Christian felt his face go cold as the blood was drained from it again. He shook his head, which conveyed the message to Dennis, who gripped his phone and bolted outside.

"SEARCH THEM!" Dennis waved his arms and yelled at the security once he saw the convoy. "DON'T LET THEM THROUGH."

Christian followed him out in time to hear screeching tires. The sedan broke out from the convoy and charged at Dennis, who managed to throw himself out of the way in time. Christian launched himself back into the lobby. The car crashed into the steel doorframe and broke chunks off the concrete wall. He turned onto his back, shocked and horrified, glaring at the devastation.

Dennis picked himself up with heavy breaths. The front of the car was warped around the corner of the entrance. He let security move in closer around him. His phone in one hand and his gun in the other, Dennis searched for Arthur Euwin's contact details.

Sophie scanned the entire street for Henry, hearing her own breath above everything. She and Owen would check the road for charging cars every few seconds. Each driver looked as innocent as each pedestrian.

Henry appeared a few meters ahead of them. He was hiding in a small alley entrance, watching and waiting. Sophie jogged to him with Owen beside her.

"What the hell is going on?" Henry asked in a low voice.

"I don't know, we were just attacked on our way here," Owen replied as he caught his breath. Henry checked him up and down.

"Two cars charged at us, separately," said Sophie. Henry rubbed the back of his head. Sophie could see a cutlery knife in his other hand.

"How are we gonna get back?" Henry asked.

"As fast as we fucking can," Owen replied. He looked up and down the street before breaking into a run again.

Sophie followed with a keen eye on the road ahead. Cars pulling away would spark her reflexes to sidestep mid-run. The three of them passed the crash site of the parked cars. There was a crowd of people around it, but they could see the empty driver's seat through the gaps. Henry looked over his shoulder more often after that. Then there was the first crash. Another crowd surrounded the car, which hadn't moved. There were still fresh tire tracks over the grass and the sidewalk. Owen didn't hesitate over the last road. He dodged the cars making them skid and hoot loudly. Henry and Sophie took advantage of the path and followed.

Sophie looked back to see the all the attention they had drawn. They crossed the park directly to the CIA lobby. Just before crossing a path, Sophie caught sight of a grey sedan between some trees. It was cruising toward them on the right, further down the civilian path. "Guys hold up," she said seriously. She watched the car between the trees with her hand unclipping the pistol on her thigh. Henry and Owen stopped just before the path and followed her line of sight. A loud revving filled the air as the car accelerated onto the grass towards them. Sophie drew her pistol and opened fire on the driver's side window whilst moving sideways out of the way. Henry ran across the path but Owen remained stationary while opening fire at the bonnet. Their shots connected but the car charged relentlessly. Sophie saw Owen too late. She was too far to pull him out of the way. When his mag ran out he promptly backed up and stopped on the other side of a nearby tree. Sophie's mag was empty. She searched frantically for another while watching the car charge at Owen. He saw it coming and ducked down a couple of meters from the tree in a single calculated move. The car crashed and bent around the tree, knocking it back at a slight angle. It rebounded with its rear tires bouncing on the ground.

Sophie sprinted to the car with a new magazine in her pistol. But there was no driver. She looked aside at Owen whose head was less than half a meter from the dented trunk of the tree. He twisted on his knee, looking around at the crash furiously.

The two of them, joined by Henry, walked stiffly to the lobby. Several security members passed them, some asking if they needed medical attention. They waved them off limply.

"A truck in England crashed outside MI6 headquarters," Owen said once they got inside. They were walking down the path to the open area of desks on the right side of the building. "It released hundreds of photos of each of us."

"What does that mean?" Henry asked.

Joel and Caitlin caught sight of them from ahead. "Are you guys ok? What happened?" Caitlin asked, inspecting their dishevelled appearances.

"We heard gunshots," Joel added.

"We're all targets," Sophie said gravely. Joel and Caitlin glared at her nervously.

"We just got charged by three separate cars out in public," said Owen. He had his hands on his hips and continued to pace beside them.

"And the drivers?" Joel asked.

"There were none," said Sophie.

Joel stared down at the floor, nodding.

"The same thing just happened to Chris and Dennis,"

said Caitlin.

"What just happened out there!?" Dawson came shouting around the corner. Grace Credette was following close behind but couldn't keep up with his long, furious strides.

"Rogue cars have been charging at us with no drivers, and in the UK as well," Owen said strongly.

"Yeah and a couple of guys with submachine guns shot up the café I was in. And no fucker even flinched," Henry added angrily.

They could see Dawson taking it in but struggling to comprehend it. "And all our photos came out of that truck?" He asked. Caitlin and Joel nodded. Dawson's gruff demeanour turned to helpless anger in one swift motion.

"Your picture was there as well, Grace," said Joel.

"Wait," Caitlin said suddenly, "Where's Lucy?"

Lucy felt a vibration in her bag and stopped to let it fall from her shoulder to her hand. There was no one else on the sidewalk so she put her coffee down and took her phone out to answer.

"Hello?" She said sweetly.

"*LUCY WHERE ARE YOU?*" Joel blurted.

"Um, I'm just walking back now," Lucy said timidly.

"*We're all being targeted by the Syndicate! Watch out for rogue cars, they will charge at you!*" Joel said rapidly.

"Uh… wait…" Lucy was taking it in but couldn't grasp the full weight of it. For a few seconds she felt no concern, only a slight dizziness. She didn't notice how light-headed she was getting until the reality of Joel's panic actually began to ground in her mind.

"*What street are you in!?*" Joel asked.

"I… I don't know…" Lucy looked up and down the road

for signs. Two cars drove past her normally giving her goosebumps.

"*Get back here now! Stay calm and watch out for cars!*" Joel demanded.

"Ok," Lucy said breathlessly. She hung up and started walking briskly back to the CIA. The uncomfortably present thumping of her heart sped up every time she looked over her shoulder. She thought about what to expect from rogue cars; what they would look like, how they would behave. But every car she saw drove as normally as the next.

Ten yards from the end of the street, a man came around the corner wearing cargo-pants and a black jacket. He walked casually towards her staring into her eyes. Lucy slowed to a stop, wide eyed and pale, watching him approach. There was no point in pretending she didn't know, but doing so gave her the smallest feeling that maybe she had the wrong idea. She crossed the road hastily and turned left at the end.

She barely made it twenty meters when she saw a woman up ahead, leaning against a tree, watching her the same way. Lucy swallowed and averted her gaze. She stopped and waited until there were no cars at all before crossing. As she reached the other side she saw another pair of eyes watching her. A man sitting on the steps of a house on her right smiled at her, so she turned away from him, half-jogging away. Over her shoulder she could see him getting up. The man in cargo-pants passed him, sipping from the coffee she had left on the ground.

Lucy sped up to a half-run when she saw a man and a women were walking towards her, grinning. Lucy surveyed the area desperately. The women across the street was skipping along parallel to her. Lucy stopped. Her chest ached around her pounding heart. Panic began to vocalize in her rapid breaths. She was stepping back and forth as the men approached, when she saw the bright yellow gleam of an oncoming cab.

"YES! TAXI!" She yelled as she ran out into the street in front of it. The driver was taken aback and had to break hard but stopped to let her in.

"Go. Just go," Lucy stressed as she got in. They pulled away, letting Lucy watch the men and women disperse from out the back window.

"You ok, Miss?" Said a heavenly feminine voice. Lucy whipped around to see the female driver. Her straight, dark-blonde hair stopped at the right side of her head, which was clean shaven.

The doors of the taxi suddenly locked, making Lucy jump. She considered grabbing the right handle but sat frozen in the middle of the backseat. The car slowed to a halt at a stop street.

Lucy watched the driver's head turn to face her. There was a collection of small scars along the right side of her head and down her neck. Now that she was looking properly, Lucy noticed the metal frame that went up the back of the woman's right arm and over her shoulder. She looked at Lucy with pretty blue eyes and a kind smile. The scar across her face unhinged Lucy's resolve.

"What's wrong, Miss? You look like you've seen a ghost," the woman smiled. Lucy gripped the seat on either side of her thighs, whimpering as tears began to fall down her shaking face.

"I'm the Lady Danger," said the Lady. She offered a handshake but Lucy remained paralyzed. "It's a strange name. I know. I'm known as a dangerous lady and it just… stuck," the Lady said calmly, "I know who you are, Miss Rei. Or would you prefer 'Lucy'?"

Lucy's bottom lip trembled. She had no intention of

speaking, only staring wide eyed at the Lady Danger.

"Give me your phone," said the Lady. Lucy's muscles tightened in protest, but under the sadistic gaze of the Lady Danger, they obeyed. The Lady took it and began trying to guess the password.

"I'm going to lock you out of your phone, just for a little while," the Lady said lightly. "You see…" she turned back to Lucy with a lethal gaze, "I want you to deliver a message for me… from the Phantom."

Dawson skimmed helplessly through the work on his desk. There was nothing that could help them now. There was no answer hiding somewhere in the data farm. Grace was in his chair, trying to get ahold of some contact, but the phone just kept ringing.

Dawson stormed out and went to look over the catwalk for the others. They were gathered around Henry's desk talking to Christian in the UK.

Henry looked up and saw him. "Dawson!" He called, waving for him to join them.

Dawson jogged over to them and looked over their shoulders.

"There's something going on in London as well," Caitlin said gravely. She nodded at news reports of civil unrest throughout the city not unlike their own.

"Any killings?" Dawson breathed.

"Not yet," Joel said flatly. Two security guards jogged past them from upstairs. Owen and Joel watched them head towards the lobby, which they now realised was generating a lot more noise than usual.

"There are no coincidences anymore," Joel said to

Owen.

Owen glanced at Dawson before making his way after the security guards.

Dawson had his hands on his hips and was frowning angrily. "Fuck it," he said, finally caving.

Owen stopped in view of the lobby and waited. As they reached the end of the hall they were met by a litany of arguments and pleas.

"Ok, what the fuck is going on here!?" Dawson yelled. They could see gangsters and other civilians desperately and sycophantically begging the officers at the lobby entrance. One of the security members heard him and met them half-way.

"They just showed up and started asking for refuge," said the man.

"Refuge from what? Hey!" Dawson pushed past him and pulled one of the gangsters aside, "Refuge from what? What's going on?" He asked forcefully.

"He's out there, man, him and his cat, it 'aint safe out there." He fidgeted uncomfortably.

"He's out there…" Dawson held him still and looked into his eyes, "The Phantom."

"Yeah," the man nodded nervously.

"You've been arrested before, haven't you?" Owen asked. The man avoided eye contact with them and continued to move uncomfortably.

"Don't dodge the question, moron," Dawson growled.

"Yeah, man, but I been four months clean, I promise, I 'aint been in no trouble or nothin."

"They're criminals, all of them," said Owen.

"And I bet you all those victims were as well." Dawson crossed his arms, "He's hunting them, and he thinks he can scare us out of the way."

"Dawson we're getting calls of Phantom sightings!" Sophie came up behind them holding out a page with a list of details.

"This is from this morning?" Dawson asked.

"Yes, sir," Sophie nodded.

"Why wasn't I informed!?" Dawson gripped the paper tightly.

"The Phantom is still in China," Sophie said defensively.

"Not anymore!" Dawson pointed to the criminals being held at the door. Over Sophie's shoulder, he could see Joel leading Grace towards them.

"What's all this?" She asked.

"These criminals want refuge from the Phantom," said Dawson.

Joel looked at each one curiously. "Send them away," he said.

"Why?" Dawson asked.

"Any one of them could be a trap or a setup," Joel said seriously.

"He's right, get rid of them," said Grace.

"They're human beings, you could be sending to their death," Sophie protested.

"They can take care of themselves," Grace said finally.

"We have the locations," Joel said to Owen, who was now holding the list, "The frequency of sightings gets denser towards us, we're at the epicentre-"

"GUYS!" Caitlin shouted as she ran over to them, "Lucy's in trouble! She says the Phantom's men are following her!"

"Where is she?" Joel asked.

"She's close, let's go!" Caitlin pushed her way out of the lobby, followed by Joel, Owen, and Sophie.

"There's too many to send units to every-one, we have to wait for something more substantial," said Euwin.

"We've already sent officers to some of the nearer sightings," said Dennis. He glimpsed around to see Christian looking out the window at the street below. "Chris, get away from the windows…" he said. Christian looked confused, then backed away from the window like it was diseased. He was suddenly over-aware of how many windows and rooftops there were overlooking the building.

"They're so close…" Christian breathed.

"Check in with your officers, leave the rest to me for now," Euwin said to Dennis.

"Which sightings did you respond to?" Christian asked. Dennis turned the monitor and pointed at three places within 250m of their position. Christian looked at them with a new thought gleaming behind his eyes.

"What is it?" Dennis asked.

"I know that place, I'm going to check it out," said Christian.

"No, Chris, wait!"

Christian was already rushing out before Dennis could stop him.

"Go with him," said Euwin, "I'll manage things here."

Dennis grabbed his blazer and went after Christian. The two of them exited the elevator together and walked out into the cold, crepuscular darkness.

"I'm going with you," said Henry.

"You're a target as well, Busher." Dawson checked his

side-arm and slid a mag into his belt.

"We all are, I can help." Henry took his old pistol out from his desk drawer.

Dawson looked displeased with where he hid it but disregarded it for time. "Fine-" He conceded.

"Come on, let's go," Grace said from behind them.

"You as well? You don't need to come with us," said Dawson.

"I know now come on we're wasting time." She led the two of them and the SWAT team out of the lobby. They drove in an armoured van to where Lucy claimed to be. It was a large, modern, stone courtyard with a few trees and a stone sculpture in the middle. The SWAT team got out and followed Dawson.

The modern building had load-bearing diagonal beams behind two-story glass walls. The four agents were waiting at the foot of the steps by the entrance with their pistols out.

"She's inside, coming to us," said Caitlin. Dawson advanced cautiously. The SWAT team did the same, spreading out into the lobby of the building.

Lucy came running down the stairs at the right corner of the lobby towards the exits. She saw the SWAT team's black attire in her peripherals, then screamed and jumped upon site of them.

"Lucy, are you alright?" Dawson asked.

She nodded, breathing rapidly. "They're still here."

Every pair of eyes scanned the top of the stairs with their firearms following exact.

"Search the building!" Dawson yelled. Most of the SWAT did so, leaving two to escort the agents. "Come on, let's go-"

"No wait!" Lucy yelped. "They told me... to deliver a message," she said timidly. Each of them stared with anticipation, making her lip tremble. "The Phantom is here. He says you must all get ready to play." The memory of their player numbers from the photos in England jumped to the front of their minds. "I sent everyone a link to a broadcast that we must listen to now," she took a small bag out of her handbag and offered it to them with shaking hands. Dawson put his hand in hesitantly and pulled out an earpiece. One-by-one, they each took an earpiece from the bag, except for the SWAT. Henry saw people walking by outside in the street and courtyard, apparently oblivious to their presence. "And there's a hint: Its bad luck to cross paths with a black cat."

"Black cat?" Dawson murmured.

"The ex-con," Owen spoke up, "He said the Phantom is here with his cat."

Joel walked to the exit by the corner of the glass walls. No black cat had been mentioned in the sightings. He surveyed outside and found exactly what he was looking for; down the road, a man in a hoodie was standing still and looking right at him. Joel pushed the door for a better look. The man pivoted around the corner of the building out of sight.

Joel knew the man may want to be followed, but the Syndicate was too close to ignore. He slinked out while the others were distracted and went after him.

"Who told you all this?" Grace asked.

Lucy's lips went white. Her breath was slower but still shaky.

"Lucy," Sophie said gently.

Lucy was close to tears. "She did…" she said, pointing behind them. Outside the entrance, walking toward them in the afternoon sun, was the Lady Danger. The two SWAT members aimed at her, moving either side of her as she approached. Everyone else had their guns raised in seconds.

"Hello…" the lady said kindly. She stopped at the foot of the steps and backed away to keep the SWAT on her sides. She wore a tight red dress with a slit down the side from her hip. Her stilettos had glistening knives for heels. The Exo-suit frame up her right arm was polished black.

"That's far enough, boys." She held her palms out to the SWAT to stop. "Everybody *freeze*," she hissed with a wide smile. Everyone stopped moving, ready to tackle her down.

"Why should we?" Dawson spat back.

The Lady smiled again. "Failure to follow any and all instructions will incur a *lethal* penalty," she said softly, "And I said… *freeze*."

One of the SWAT members kept his aim while moving behind her. He barely made it two steps when three shots from three angles shook his body like a ragdoll. Everyone but the Lady Danger flinched, watching helplessly. The man gargled and choked on his own blood, clutching his chest until his body went limp.

"Lower your weapons," the Lady said strictly. After a moment of hesitation, they acquiesced the Lady's command and lowered their weapons, seething with impotence. "Good," she said kindly. All around them, people continued to walk and drive by undeterred. "I see Lucy passed on the message," the Lady walked around them provocatively, the knife-heels of her stilettos scratching the ground. "You should put those earpieces in once you've connected them to your phones… and listen carefully… like your lives depend on it."

"Listen to what?" Caitlin asked angrily.

The Lady passed behind her gracefully. "The broadcast, Miss Harper," she said gently, "It will be starting soon. And don't bother asking for help, no-one will come to your aid. Not Stuart Gilmore, nor Leanne Wesley, not even Haden Philips."

"Never heard of them," Dawson said gruffly.

"One of you has." The Lady stopped in front of Grace, meeting her gaze. Dawson and the others waited expectantly.

"They're... Agents. Tasked with going undercover... to infiltrate the Syndicate," Grace said darkly.

"Didn't work out so well, we know plenty of names," the Lady smiled. She stepped back to address them all. "The game is starting soon, you better get the link from little Miss Lucy before she runs out of air."

Each of them looked over their shoulders slightly, moving as little as they could. Lucy was tied up inside the lobby with duct-tape over her mouth. They turned back to the Lady who was watching with a sadistic grin.

"Don't leave the lobby until we tell you to. *Go.*"

They span and sprinted to Lucy's aid. The Lady strolled away leaving the SWAT member over his teammate's corpse.

"Are you ok?" Owen asked after removing the duct-tape. Lucy nodded while catching her breath.

"The link," Dawson said reluctantly, "Where's the link, Lucy?"

"E-mail," she squealed between breaths. They took out their phones to find the link she sent. It was under the subject 'The Game'. "Once your earpiece is in – don't move," Lucy stressed. They stood around her, fingers hovering over their links. Owen went first, then Caitlin, then everyone. They put their earpieces in and clicked the link. It took them to a site with a message that said 'Starting Soon!'

"Where the fuck is Joel?" Dawson asked wrathfully. The group looked at each other in collective panic.

"I saw him over here last." Grace walked over to the exit and looked outside. Dawson followed and opened the door next to hers.

"NO DON'T GO OUT THERE!" Lucy shouted. But Dawson and Grace had already stepped over the line. Suddenly, the pedestrians in the street stopped and turned to face them. Grace and Dawson froze and tensed up. All perfectly normal looking civilians were staring them down. Above them were more men and women in the windows of the opposite building, staring down at Dawson and Grace. At least fifty pairs of eyes watched them with blank disapproval.

Dawson stepped back inside, pulling Grace with him, and froze in place again.

"Hey!" Christian called at the officers. Their reflective vests stuck out in the growing evening darkness. The officers saw the two of them running and stopped.

"Dennis Knight, SIS, and Detective Christian Taylor," Dennis said, holding up his badge and ID.

One of the officers inspected the badge, and nodded acceptingly. "We got a call the Phantom was 'ere," he said simply.

"Find him," Dennis said strongly. The officers went back to searching the grounds. Christian looked around at the park. There weren't many people out, it was too late for an afternoon walk. Surveying the area, he recognised the one park bench immediately. He had sat there once before for lunch. The photo of him released from the Syndicate truck was taken there. He followed the direction the photo was taken from. Dennis watched him from behind. The angle led him to bush with a bench behind it at the edge of the park.

Christian didn't need a lot of time to search the spot. Already on the bench was an old flip phone. He was ready to take a cloth out and pick it up as potential evidence when the street lamps all over the park came on. The once shadowy dark-green grass became illuminated with a raw, red glow. Christian, Dennis, and the officers looked up in horror at the blood-soaked street lamps that cast an unnerving bloody gloom over the entire park.

Christian grabbed the phone in a cloth and almost dropped it when it rang.

"Answer it," Dennis said anxiously. Christian let it ring a little longer and used the cloth to flip open the phone and put it close to his ear.

"You can lose the cloth, you won't find any prints there, Detective," said a low voice. It was a typical, local, London accent. Christian capitulated and let the cloth fall.

"You're early, pretty clever. Now listen close, I will not repeat myself."

Joel was four streets away from the others now. The man in the hoodie was leading him further away from his backup. Joel kept to the one side of the path furthest from the road. He looked for rogue cars often enough with his focus on the man.

They were on a quiet street with few people and almost no cars. Joel was alongside a large office building when the man turned left at the end of the path. Joel sped up after him but slowed down when he heard yelling coming from beyond the corner. He proceeded cautiously with a tight grip on his sidearm. Civilians came running from beyond the corner on both sides of the street. Some looked back or checked over their shoulders. Joel watched them with curious premonitions. He considered stopping one of them to ask what they were running from, but he knew he would soon find out.

The flow of fleeing pedestrians died off as he reached

the corner. He peaked around with his pistol ready. The street was empty. There was no sign of the Syndicate member. Joel hugged the wall as he kept going. A couple more people ran desperately on the other side of the road. He kept his focus forward and raised his gun to shoulder level. After a few metres, he saw motion ahead. The office building on his left gave way to a tall brick building that extended half-way onto the path. Joel backed against the office building, using the extending brick wall for cover.

The street was devoid of wind and sound. Joel struggled to keep his noise, and by extension his presence, to a minimum. He leaned to look around the corner, gradually revealing more of what lay beyond. Metre by metre the street was barren. There were no cars or civilians at the end of the road either. Lastly, he looked parallel to the brick wall in time to see a large, jet-black head appear from the other side. Joel's reflexes pulled him back. The head was low to the ground. He peeked again for another look. A Panther walked to the middle of the road and stopped. It was bigger than Joel thought them to be. One of its paws could easily cover his face. The Black Panther's large yellow eyes surveyed the street. It turned to look the other way, its ears twitching to the sounds of distant traffic. Joel felt the air get colder and denser. It was bad luck to cross paths with a black cat.

The Phantom was near. The Panther's smooth sloping back arched as it lowered slightly, sniffing at the ground and air. It sensed something. Its tail flickered. Just as it turned back around, Joel pulled himself back again. His silence was futile, the Panther could smell him. He became uncomfortably aware of the sweat under his pits and down his back. His scent was emanating from him.

Cats loved to chase, as did the Phantom. Joel couldn't go

back the way he came without being seen. The Panther's prowess at hunting loomed closer with its owner not far behind. Joel leaned forward slightly to look again. The Panther was watching him with dilating pupils. Its tail stopped at the same time as his heartbeat. The Phantom would soon find his pet and its prize. Every hour that a second passed drew the predator closer to its prey.

Joel pushed off the wall and tried to run at a less inviting speed, all the while keeping his body against the wall of the office building. Before he rounded the corner, he looked back to see the Panther walking after him slowly yet confidently. He didn't wait for the Phantom to follow. He broke into his fastest run as soon as he was out of the Panther's sight. Every so often he would look over his shoulder to check. But the Panther didn't appear again.

Joel slowed down as he reached the building where he left the others. There was an entrance on his side which he figured must lead to the lobby somehow. Anxious to get off the street, he gambled with it. Up a flight of stairs and down a couple of corridors. He found himself at the top of the lobby. He could see the others at the bottom and ran down the stairs to join them.

"JOEL STOP!" Caitlin shouted. Joel slowed in confusion but continued down the last few steps.

"STOP, JOEL, STOP!" Everyone yelled. They held their hands out to gesture him to halt. Joel's panic rose again. They glared at him with fear expanding in their eyes. For a split second, Joel thought he saw the people outside standing still and looking at them, and people in the windows of the opposite building doing the same. But they were all moving normally, like an illusion or trick of the light.

"If we move we die!" Caitlin said sternly.

Joel remained still. His chest undulated with his heavy breaths.

"Go to the link Lucy e-mailed you and put in your earpiece, do it now," Dawson demanded. Joel took both items and did as he was told. The link led him to a site with a countdown at seven seconds. He connected the earpiece to his phone and heard the countdown beeping. When it finished, the broadcast began, and the voice of a little girl came through the earpieces.

"It's time to play the game!"

Chapter XIV
The Game
Everywhere

The game is fear. The whole world is playing.

The city was swimming in a grey gloom. Clouds overhead had filled every corner of the sky. The breeze was cold and calm. But it was not the reason for the chill down their spines. The storm had arrived. They stood in the epicentre of ubiquitous peril. Omnipresent eyes followed their every move. The adrenal gland is what produces adrenaline, and as the voice teased them, taunted them, cursed them, their adrenal glands throbbed. Anxious energy filled their veins letting uncertainty infect them further. The voice, which therapists would later come to know as "the little girl", assaulted them with playful glee akin to sadism.

"Let's go through the rules shall we? If you run – you die! If you try to contact anyone – THEY die! If anyone tries to help you – they die a horrible death! If you don't do as you're told – you die a horribler death! The game consists of six rounds. The aim of the game is simple: Survive. Each round has a unspecified time limit, fail to finish in the given time and everyone playing will die. The only way to win is to survive, the only way to survive is to win! Lose a round... lose your life. Are you ready?"

All they could do was stare down at the ground and wait, ready to comply. Their minds searched for the rhyme or reason of any of it, desperate for escape. There was no prison cell or cage. No walls or boundaries. They were trapped in their own heads, scratching at the walls looking for loopholes or cheats that did not exist.

In London, Christian and Dennis were listening to a little English girl's voice on a different broadcast. They had done as the man on the phone instructed and found the earpieces along with the link to a site. They stood in a circle with the officers, looking down at a corpse. They were told to stand still, and he did not. They watched the officer bleed with helplessness gripping their hearts into guilty submission.

Lucy shook as she stood up slowly. She had her hands up in surrender and waited for the Syndicate's decree. Her shoulders relaxed when mercy came in the form of stillness.

"Round one! Philosphy is very complicated. Over the course of your careers you are forced to solve many difficult ethical conun-drums. If anything were to feel wrong, you could always fall back on your systems and laws to maintain the moral high-ground - even at the expense of innocent lives. You will have no such safety net today! You're going to have to choose once and for all the weight of a given moral soul. On your phones is a map to two separate events in the city; one-hundred convic-ted f-felons, and ten innocent civ-il-ians with no criminal records. When you hear the starting cannon, you must choose which one to let die, and find them! If you don't choose by the end of the round, all will die, so you better hurry, you don't have all day!"

The air had gone thin and meagre. Sophie felt light headed. She tried clasping any one of the a thousand twirling thoughts but remained unable to focus any one of them. The gravity of what was happening swayed ethereally between dream and reality. Everyone around her listened in dismay. She could see they were struggling to put it all together as well. She wanted to speak but the words could not form.

"And just in case you don't think we mean it..."

The SWAT van outside exploded in a brief ball of flames. It was blasted a couple of feet in the air. The windows shattered instantly. The sound of the blast made them flinch and duck. A SWAT Officer rolled out the back of the van in a cylinder of flames. His body writhed for what felt like minutes before finally resting.

A second sound distracted them from the burning van. The bodies of the other SWAT Officers came tumbling down the stairs of the lobby, leaving trails and splatters of blood. They watched the top of the stairs with vengeful anticipation. The black figure that appeared made them cower for a full second before they realized what it was. A large Black Panther came out and stopped to take a look at them. It had wide yellow eyes and silky fur that blended well into the shade of the building.

"Don't move. Don't move." Dawson whispered. Sophie's knees and shoulders instinctively pointed toward the exit. She watched the Panther apprehensively, as did everyone else.

"It's his," Joel whispered, "It's *his* cat."

The Panther sniffed at the blood on the floor and began to lick up the trail. Sophie turned her attention to the top of the stairs again. Every second she expected to see the shadow give birth to a dark silhouette.

A deep, reverberating growl sent a new feeling up Sophie's spine. The Panther bore its fangs and hissed violently. Grace broke first. She pushed the glass exit and held it ajar. The Panther slinked down two of the steps toward her. Dawson followed her lead, then everyone else.

Sophie helped Caitlin shut the exit after Joel passed through. The Panther followed the trail of blood down the steps to the bodies. Joel took his belt off and tied it around the handles of the doors. Caitlin wondered aimlessly through the courtyard.

Dawson came marching from around the corner with Grace, Henry, and Lucy.

It was still again. The breeze had gone. Sophie then felt a hot flash in her cheeks when she saw it; there was a thin red arc in the sky. High up about five blocks away. The others turned to see what she saw.

The rocket travelled up with a slight curve. Then without a sound, it burst into a flaring red cloud. The sound hit them just over a second later. A pop-like explosion.

Light pollution from the city made the stars over London dimmer. But the great red arc that soared overhead was as bright and clear as the matching street lamps that surrounded them. The explosion sparkled red like a dense firework, crackling in the cold air. Silence took over again. Christian's eyes glazed over with a fresh perspective filling in his blank mind. He started walking aimlessly with the little girl's rules repeating in his head.

"Your mistakes will hang over you for eternity. If one who fa-ci-li-tates illegal action is considered an accessory, then the cracks in your justice system should be trialled along-side the princi-pals for their in-com-petence. If you will not see justice done... then we will do it ourselves."

There was shrieking in the distance. Women screamed and called out. Christian let his instincts take over. He and Dennis ran from the park to the source of the commotion. The high street two roads away was bright with a relieving white glow from the streetlamps. They could see crowds of people gathering on either side of the road. Cars were driving slowly and even stopping. All eyes aimed skyward.

Christian and Dennis followed their collective gaze up the tall buildings as soon as they reached the road.

"*You had your chance...*" the little girl whispered. Every third building had a burning flare on top and a rope hanging over the edge. Twenty metres below, bodies hung by their necks, swaying in the icy breeze, their faces pale and blank.

Euwin watched the news reports on a grid of four televisions. Hangings were being sighted all over London. Some from high buildings, some from the bridges. Men calling out from beyond his door drew his attention to the other side of the building where officers amassed around a window. He figured there would be a body hanging from the neighbouring building, but instead, there were two lines of blood streaking down their own.

Joel fumbled with his phone. Sophie's breathing quickened uncontrollably. The Panther was gone but the bodies remained.

"I have the locations," said Joel, "They're both about half an hour away."

"We don't know how long we've got," said Henry. He and Owen looked to Dawson who was quietly collecting himself.

"Let's go," he growled.

"Which one?" Caitlin asked.

Dawson glared at her. The gears were grinding in his head.

"It said choose which to let die. The convicts, right?" Joel asked strongly.

"Yes." Dawson's defeated expression tensed with

frustration.

"Wait let's talk about this-" said Henry.

"We're not going to do as they say!" Caitlin burst out.

Dawson was already marching off.

"What choice do we have!?" Joel countered.

Caitlin turned to him with silent disdain.

"Nathan, please," Henry pleaded, "we can't…"

"What would you have us do!?" Dawson yelled as he span to face Henry.

"We have to find some other way!" Sophie yelled desperately. She caught up with them and stood by Caitlin.

"WHAT OTHER WAY!?" The vein on Dawson's forehead was bulging through his wrinkles.

"You're being awfully quiet, Grace," Owen said darkly.

Grace held her chin up. "Do as they say," she said without a second thought.

"Come on Dawson we're wasting time," Joel said furiously.

"We can't let you do that!" Caitlin's temper was rising.

"YOU WILL GET US ALL KILLED! *THEY CLEARLY AREN'T AFRAID TO FOLLOW THROUGH!*" Dawson pointed aggressively at her and then to the bodies in the lobby. Caitlin reached for her gun, Joel did the same. His sudden opposition shook her out of focus. She watched him, eyes wide and mouth agape, as he backed away with Dawson and Grace.

"Find the civilians and stay out of our way!" Dawson demanded. Sophie wanted to stay with Caitlin, but a new light was burning in Dawson's eyes. She went with him to see if she could stop it going too far. Caitlin stormed off with Owen right behind her. Henry and Lucy jogged to catch up with them.

Back in the world, Dawson walked into a busy road. He approached an oncoming car and pulled out his side-arm. "Out of the car! Get the fuck out now!" He demanded. The woman in the car stiffly obeyed. Dawson pulled her out and got in her seat. Joel got in the passenger seat at the same time. Grace and Sophie reluctantly ignored the woman and got in the back.

Joel navigated while Dawson ignored every traffic law they had. Sophie had to grip the handle in the back as the car swung around traffic. It was only a matter of time before the worst came to pass. A cop car hidden by a turn caught them speeding in the last mile. Dawson and Joel ignored the sirens. Meanwhile, Sophie formed a plan. They broke through a security beam at the entrance to a marina and skidded to a halt in front of two large, double-decker coaches. Sophie could see the orange jumpsuits in the tinted windows as she got out.

"Hold them off." Dawson pointed Grace to the cops who were stopping a few meters behind them. Grace reached for her badge and walked to the police car with Sophie close behind.

"Did I say let die? I meant kill! Kill while you still can!" Said the little girl. Sophie and Grace stopped and span around. Dawson disbelievingly watched Joel find a detonator between two sailing boats. His petrified expression sank the fear deeper into all of them.

"Please!" Sophie called to the cops, "Help us! Get them out of the coaches!"

"Sophie! DON'T!" Grace pulled her back. The two cops were sideswiped by multiple shots from the sides, spraying blood over their white car. To Sophie's horror, they collapsed on the floor in front of her.

"Do it!" Dawson stressed, ducking and looking around wildly for any sign of the shooters. "DO IT NOW, JOEL!"

Joel's hands shook wildly as he gripped the detonator. His face contorted with fear and guilt. In desperation he looked around for something. Another way, or a way out. His muscles were paralyzed for an eternity of indecision. The men in the coaches were yelling something he couldn't quite hear, but there was fear in them as well. Every excruciating moment brought him no options or escape. Fear took over him and enclosed his mind. The reality became clear.

He pressed the trigger in. The subsequent explosions came from inside the coaches. Suppressed but loud. Blood and fire hit the windows right before they shattered outward. The flames continued to rise up and char the sides of the coaches. A screaming choir of agony made them cringe uncontrollably. Sophie stumbled between two rows of boats to vomit. Joel shook harder until he threw the detonator into one of the flaming coaches. By the time they were back in the car, the screaming had stopped. Dawson gripped the wheel furiously. Joel had his hands on the dashboard and was trying to shake away the smell of burning flesh.

"*Yaaaaay! Well done! Get ready for the next round!*" Said the little girl. Sophie shut her eyes as they passed the dead cops on their way out.

"*Come find me...*" The little girl whispered. Screaming from afar had Christian and Dennis running as fast as they could. The dark street echoed with the sound of their heavy shoes hitting the cobblestone. One scream turned into two, turned into four. They split and multiplied in random directions.

The two of them slowed and spun around in search of the distress. The street was empty. The wailing voices drifted around them in and out of existence. Christian recognised the taunt of ghostly cries and tried to block them out. He walked to the origin of the first voice and ignored the rest. A sudden high pitch of shattering glass brought them back into the world. It came from a rectangular courtyard of stone within a three story apartment block. Christian looked up at the cracks in the mossy brick archway entrance. Glints of glass pieces in the courtyard drew his line of sight down to the broken window on the first floor.

The fragments cracked beneath Dennis' feet. He covered his eyes from the moonlight and looked inside. In the shade of the room was a shivering woman standing on her toes with a rope looped around her neck. "Hey! Are you ok, Miss?" Dennis asked. As his eyes adjusted to the level of darkness, he saw more complicating details of her situation. Her hands were tied behind her back and she was gagged. "Chris…" Dennis pointed above her.

Christian followed the rope up. It was one of three thicker ropes that hung loosely across the second floor room. "It's rigged," Christian breathed. Beyond the broken floorboards, he could see the thicker ropes coming out of the wall on the left and into the wall on the right. He backed away and tried to see into the neighbouring windows.

"Just hang on, we're going to get you out of there, ok?" Dennis said to the muffled woman.

Christian walked along the courtyard following the ropes in the second floor windows. They spread to the first and third floors, continuing all the way around the apartments.

"Hello? I need backup on my position-"

"*I thought we told you not to contact anyone…*"

Dennis froze, lost for words. The voice was the same as the man who called them at the park.

Christian grabbed the phone from his hand and threw it through the archway. "What are you doing!?" He hissed.

"They hacked my phone," Dennis said. A heavy metallic

thud broke off the conversation. The two of them looked to the far corner where it came from. Then followed a sequence of deep clicks, another thud, and the sound of chains rattling. The same sounds came from behind them shortly after. The rest of the building began to creak. There was more thudding, but consistent, like gears turning. The deep clicking increased with each second. The creaking got harder. Something began to wind in several parts of the building.

Christian heard the cracking and aching of wood behind them. The woman was shuffling frantically and rising into the air. "DENNIS!" He yelled.

Dennis kicked the rest of the glass out of the window frame and leapt in. With his hands under her feet, he lifted her with all his strength. The woman gasped for a modicum of air but ropes above her were being pulled into the walls, lifting her higher. "Cut the rope!" Dennis demanded.

Christian watched the silhouettes of the rope system through the windows. They pulled on each other slowly. The heavy gears and deep ticking got gradually louder. "I don't think we can…" he said as he followed the system all the way around with unblinking eyes.

"What!?" Dennis yelled. The woman's feet were rising above his knees.

"It's all rigged, I don't know…" The ticking started up at two other locations in the building. They clicked and thudded at different rates, increasing the creaking and cracking with each passing second. Christian found a rock and smashed one of the first floor windows. Inside was another rope leading in and back out through the walls. He grabbed the rope and pulled toward the room with the woman. It barely moved a few centimetres when the creaking spiked and the thudding sped up. The tension in the rope forced it out of his hands. All around the building, the system tightened up and wound harder.

"CHRIS!" Dennis shouted from the next room.

Christian returned to find him holding the woman's feet up above his head. He climbed the broken ceiling to the second floor and grabbed the rope she was looped in. Then he planted his feet against the wall and pulled with all his strength. The woman got lower, but the rest of the system contracted. The gears grinded and clanged. Chains rattled with the cracking of stone and wood. The winding tightened and creaked under the strain. With it, several new voices cried out into the night.

Christian jumped down and ran out into the courtyard. There were at least five other people locked into the system. He tracked their voices to find two that were on the first floor; a man with ropes wrapped around his limbs, and another with chains wrapped around his mid-section, pulling him into a wall.

"WAIT!" The man called out as Christian was returning to Dennis. Christian tried to ignore his pain and kept walking.

"I KNOW ABOUT THE ROGUE MILITIA!"

Christian stopped dead in his tracks. He ran back to the man and broke the window open with his elbow. "What did you say!?" He asked, rubbing his new bruise.

"I know! I have information…" The man struggled for breath against the tightening chains. "About the rogue militia!"

"What!? WHAT DO YOU KNOW!?" Christian yelled.

"Help me get out of here!" The man cried out through gritted teeth.

Christian stepped back and re-evaluated the system. It was pulling in on itself with equal force. Pulling on the rope in one place tightened it everywhere else. Which meant that conversely, cutting the rope would imbalance the neighbouring systems, causing them to tighten on the other sides. The Phantom had given him a puzzle.

"What's happening!?" Dennis asked, seeing Christian return.

"It's a puzzle. One of the people trapped here says he has information about the rogue militia, I need to get him out." He panted.

"We need to get them all out, how many are there?" Dennis asked, gripping the woman's feet above his head.

"I don't know," Chris admitted. "I need to loosen his chains, but…" Christian saw the loop around the woman's neck. It wasn't a knot, only a slack loop, so that she could not be cut free. "Spin her over the rope. If I pull on it you can spin her free."

Dennis twirled to evaluate the loop as Christian freed the woman's hands and pulled off her gag. He then climbed back up and pulled hard on the rope. Dennis lifted her as high as he could, shouting for her to spin and release her neck. A hard clashing came from several sections of the building. The gears clanged harder and faster. The woman balanced with her legs and arms on the rope while spinning backward. Dennis pulled on the other side to loosen the rope and set her free. She dropped to the floor, twisting her ankle. Christian and Dennis released the rope in unison, which pulled with increasing force. All at once, the cogs all around the system spun back, tensing everything and cracking the walls around them.

"Get out!" Christian yelled shakily. He dived out behind them and ran across the courtyard to the other man. The walls around the courtyard were cracking inward. Several windows shattered one after another. Screaming from the rooms rose with the deep clicking that ticked faster and harder. The winding got uncomfortably high in pitch, nearing a break point. The walls and floors of the apartments broke and collapsed, releasing more of the ropes and chains, which contracted even harder. The tighter the system became, the stronger it pulled.

Christian scratched his arm climbing through the window. The chains were constricting the man, who cried out in agony with the last of his breath. Christian passed him and kicked down the door to follow the network of chains and cables. Heavy humming and thudding was coming from directly above. The ceiling and walls cracked in around them both. Christian ran back to the window, then charged shoulder first at the man. The wall behind him broke apart but not completely. Christian backed away and tried again. He and the man fell through the wall, which loosened his chains slightly.

"CHRIS!" Dennis called from outside. The system was pulling in on the brick walls. The corners caved under the tension of the chains and cables, filling the courtyard with debris.

The man could breathe again but his chains were still getting tighter. The ceiling in the room behind them broke down as a large machine fell through. Multiple chains were coming out of it and stretching out into the building like a web.

Christian crawled over and grabbed a piece of glass from the floor. He ran under the collapsing hallways and passed by cracking walls until he found a rope high above his head.

The largest cogs clanged with the weight of tension pulling in. Dennis tried to look for a way to get in and save the screaming civilians but the walls were breaking apart, collapsing all three stories in toward the courtyard. The cold air in the courtyard was filled with chilling shrieks and cries for help. Weak spots in the brick threatened to break at any moment. Dennis couldn't even approach the volatile windows.

Christian kicked off from a section of broken bricks and grabbed the rope. Wood and debris fell past him from the third floor. He gripped the piece of glass with the blood soaked sleeve of his suit and cut at the rope. Just as he was being lifted and pressed against a caving wall, tension pulled in the last strands of the rope and snapped it. Christian fell to the floor and covered his face from the avalanche of stone and wood that fell around him. Dennis leapt back and kicked away from the walls of the apartment as the mechanism of cogs and chains broke through. Several ropes snapped around the system, letting the chains and cables collect enough tension to break free of the building. Chunks of stone and brick were scattered violently across the courtyard. The metallic clicking turned to snapping. Each floor collapsed and broke away with the walls. The winding snapped causing the taut cables to vibrate and wobble loudly. Remaining gears clashed and slowed until the system finally stopped. Dust settled on bloodied chains with Dennis watching in horror.

The others arrived twenty-five minutes later. Owen saw them coming and walked over to meet them. Dawson looked blank. Gruff, as usual, but blank. There were rosy circles around Joel's eyes that made his pale face look even more ill. Grace had composed herself, but Sophie was in tears when she got out of the car.

"What happened?" Owen asked in a hoarse voice. They didn't respond. They didn't even look at him as they passed by. Owen secretly agreed with their choice, but looking at their faces, their shaking hands, he didn't feel so sure anymore. Caitlin and Henry were talking to the ten civilians who had been chained together on a set of barrels. The gasoline in the barrels was connected to an active switch they found to one side. The Phantom was not bluffing.

Caitlin and Henry heard them enter. Caitlin took one look at them and closed her eyes in repentance. Lucy sat to one side, ignoring what she knew to be true.

"*Round two: Abusing law, manipulation, rogue militias... your system of justice comes with no shortage of ironic self-contra-vening. You may trust yourselves, but how well do you trust the people in your ranks? A series of checkpoints are hidden around the city. Each checkpoint will reveal the next as well as details of corruption or injustice within your very own system! Starting low and getting higher up the ranks. For every checkpoint you fail to reach, a member of your team dies! However, you can reclaim a checkpoint by killing someone named at one of the other checkpoints.*"

Lucy already had her phone out. She and Grace waited for the first checkpoint to show.

"*Ready? Set? GO!*"

"We got it," Grace said urgently. She pulled Lucy behind her and jogged to the car.

"Owen, go with them," said Dawson. He looked around the room; Joel was still pale and looked like he might be sick. Sophie had dropped against a wall and buried her face in her arms. "Henry, you too," Dawson added quietly.

"I'll drive!" Owen called as he ran after Grace and Lucy. "You tell me where to go."

Lucy rushed to the passenger seat. Grace and Henry got in the back. Within seconds, they had left tire-smoke and black streaks on the road. The first checkpoint was fifteen minutes away. Its convenient proximity satisfied only the Phantom's expectations of them. Their predictability simply trapped them within his linear demands. Owen stopped to let Grace and Henry get out and look. After a few minutes, Henry found the Triskelion symbol spray-painted on the side of a garbage bin. He reached in cautiously and pulled out a regular paper file.

"Let me see," Grace demanded, she took the file from

Henry after they both got back in the car. "Allen McFonder: City cop... assaulted and raped at least 5 young adult women..." Grace's disgust grew as she discovered evidence of the crimes underneath the reports.

"It has his location," Henry said, pulling a sheet from the folder. "How has he not been arrested? There's a code here for the next checkpoint." He showed the code to Lucy who entered it into the website and revealed the next location. "Owen. My ex-wife is here," He said, reading through the rest of the document. "Sharon is in here... Child neglect! There was never any evidence!"

"Henry! Deal with it later." Owen said as kindly as he could. The next three checkpoints went the same way; a Triskelion symbol marking a hidden file with incriminating evidence against law enforcers, as well as their current location. Checkpoint two: A Special-agent, that Henry and Owen knew, bribed into abuse of discretion. And who sold information on other agents, including Owen, Sophie, Henry, and Dawson. Checkpoint three: Forgery, blackmail, and extortion in the department of defence. Checkpoint four: High ranking members of the FBI and the CIA, some merely yards away from Owen's office, selling classified information and tampering with evidence. The final checkpoint was outside the CIA. Moments later, Grace got a call from Dawson.

"Grace? We're close to the checkpoint, we're on our way now," he said.

"Wait for us," said Grace.

Owen glanced at her in his rear-view mirror.

"We'll meet you there." Dawson hung up and Grace told Owen to drive faster. They arrived back at the CIA a few minutes later. The others were waiting for them with forensic investigators dusting a case in the middle of the walkway.

Dawson ran over to Owen once he parked on the grass.

"We've got a problem," he said.

"What is it?" Owen asked with furrowed brows.

"They've taken it," said Dawson.

"The website said this is the last checkpoint, we need the final code!" Owen said.

"Who took it?" Henry asked restlessly.

"One of ours-" Dawson broke off when the little girl's voice came back.

"*Times up! Did you get them all? You better have, the next round is starting soon.*"

"Fuck…" Dawson said under his breath. Owen had his hands on his hips.

"Guys there's a countdown until the next round, forty-five minutes" Lucy called out.

"I'll get the file from whichever idiot took it," Grace said through gritted teeth.

"There's no point, there's just a timer on here now," said Lucy.

"So that's it? We missed one?" Henry asked, subtly checking the rooftops for snipers. Tears fell down Lucy's trembling lips.

"Nathan," Owen said in a low voice, "We can get it back."

Dawson locked eyes with him, then looked at the ground again.

"Show me the files." Dawson took them from Grace.

"No… seriously? They could be bluffing!" Sophie interjected.

"WHAT PART OF ANY OF THIS MAKES YOU THINK THEY COULD BE BLUFFING!?" Joel's thundering voice had everyone glaring wide-eyed at him. "We are running out of time," he said forcefully.

"This one; Allen McFonder, this shitbag should be rotting in a cell anyway," Dawson said scornfully.

Owen watched Caitlin come to accept it. The defeated expression on her face, and fear deep in her eyes, brought about a primal anger he knew too well. He took it all in - the sight of her helplessness. The fire within came bursting back to light, and with it, rage.

Owen took the file from Dawson without a word. They watched him get in the car and shift into reverse. No-one moved except Henry, who walked over to the window of the car.

"You have forty minutes, the file has his patrol route." Henry stepped back to let Owen drive away. After he was gone, Henry pulled Dawson aside. "There's something you gotta see," said Henry. He opened the fourth file and pointed to the bottom of the one page.

"What's this?" Dawson asked in a hushed tone.

"Two agents at the FBI tampered with the evidence of two cases, one of which we know well…" Henry whispered.

Dawson skimmed through the details on the paper. "Did he see this?" He asked quietly.

"No," Henry replied.

Dawson closed the file with a sigh of relief. "Don't tell him until this is over, we need him to stay focused," he said firmly.

"Yes, sir." Said Henry.

Owen raced through the streets. High speed kept his adrenaline up. He knew what he was looking for, and where to find it. He sped through a red light before finding the patrol route, then began circling it like a track. If he didn't find them, they would certainly find him.

He saw a line of square, red and blue lights over the top of a car on the other side of a four-way stop. The car pulled away and Owen took his chance. He accelerated across and came to a skidding halt in front of the cop car, forcing them to do the same. Both cops got out, watching him with confusion. The driver had balding grey hair and a pot-belly, the other had a young face and was neatly shaven. Owen got out slowly with his gun behind his back.

"Allen McFonder?" Owen asked with monotony.

"Yeah?" The larger man answered. Owen's heart pulsed uncomfortably. He stared at Allen, thinking about Caitlin. Time was sweating down his temple. He pulled the gun up and aimed at Allen. Both cops froze with shock and fumbled for their side-arms.

Christian's eyes fazed in and out of focus on the man. He sat on the back of the ambulance with a nurse checking his injuries. "I need to know what he knows," Christian said hoarsely.

"There are more important things to take care of right now," Dennis said austerely. The noise had attracted some civilians to watch from their windows. A pure-black car came from the high street and parked a few metres from the ambulance. Once the headlights switched off, Stanley Martin got out, with Elliot Spencer on the other side. Christian then saw the police van park directly behind them.

"What happened here?" Stanley asked.

"You're too late," said Christian.

"Some... puzzle trap," Dennis sighed. "Only two survivors."

"We need to get their statements-" Elliot spoke up.

"That one-" Christian pointed at the man in the ambulance. "He's coming back with me. He has information and I need to know how." Christian dropped his voice.

"We'll get him back securely," said Stanley. He took out his phone and stepped away to make a call. The CTFSOs (Counter terrorism specialist firearms officers) stood by passively with their guns lowered.

"What's going on? What's this *game*?" Elliot asked quietly.

"I'm not really sure," Christian admitted.

"Let's get back." Elliot surveyed the street warily. Together they walked back to the car. Christian went to grab the man when a shock from several explosively loud shots shook him off balance. The nurse screamed and stumbled away. The back of the ambulance was sprayed with the man's blood and wrecked with bullets.

"CEASE FIRE! FRIENDLIES!" Dennis' voice was lost in the gunfire.

Christian couldn't lower his shaking arms from his face. He glared wide eyed and mouth agape at the disfigured body. Blood ran off the edge of the ambulance and pooled onto the floor.

"WHAT ARE YOU DOING!?" Dennis shouted. He grabbed one of the CTFSOs members by the collar and pushed him into the others. The unit looked at him with confusion, their expressions hidden behind their goggles.

Christian could not stop staring. Elliot helped him to his feet. His knees wobbled under his weight. "Who gave the order?" He asked with a broken voice. The blank goggles of the CTFSOs glared back at him.

"WHY!?" He yelled indignantly. Elliot pulled him to the

car. Stanley was standing by it with his hands behind his head, watching it unfold with wide, unblinking eyes.

A siren at the end of the road drew them to watch the pair of bright headlights coming around the corner. The entire street was lit up by the cruising police vehicle. Christian eyed it while opening the back door of Stanley's car.

Dennis squinted against their beams while waving them down. Christian stopped with a hand on the top of the car and the other grabbing Elliot's back. "Dennis! Move!" He called desperately.

For a split second, Dennis was going to turn around, but the acceleration of the police car locked him in place. Stanley pulled him all the way back from the road. Christian kicked away from the car pulling Elliot with him.

The police car scratched against the police van and rear-ended Stanley's car into the ambulance. After trying the locked doors, the CTSFOs smashed the windows of the police car revealing it to be empty.

"What now!?" Stanley asked.

"Back the way we came." Christian swayed around the crash with his dizzy focus on the path they took before. He checked every corner before proceeding and kept the left walls within arm's reach. The others followed with their side-arms at hand.

"Head to the following location before the sands of time run out!"

Shooting from outside drew their attention to the entrance of the lobby. A dumpster-truck came crashing into the glass doors, bending and warping everything with its momentum. When it finally stopped, scattering glass fragments across the lobby floor, the group circled it cautiously. Security members moved in with their rifles raised. Desert-red sand poured from the bullet holes and spilled over the glass-covered floor.

"Cease fire!" Caitlin yelled. Joel picked up a handful of sand to feel and let it run smoothly between his fingers. Caitlin grabbed his shoulder and pulled him with her.

"Where's that location, Lucy?" Dawson asked in more of a statement.

Lucy took out her phone while running. "I've got it," she announced nervously. They followed Dawson to the parking bays before Henry suddenly spoke up.

"Wait, NO," he yelled. The others slowed to a stop in front of him. "We can't use our own cars, remember?" He said.

"Why not?" Dawson asked impatiently.

"We don't know what they could have done," Henry said darkly. Dawson's wrinkles contorted with anger. He took out his pistol and headed to the road again. Within seconds he ran in front of a maroon, four-door family car and scared the driver out. Joel did the same with the car behind. Lucy began navigating once everyone was in.

"Second right at-" Two metallic crunches jerked the cars forward whiplashing everyone. A black SUV had rear-ended Joel's car into the back of Dawson's and kept pushing. Joel and Dawson accelerated away with their tires screeching. Shaken but back in focus, Lucy continued to navigate.

They drove into oncoming traffic ready to take a hard left when a white van came speeding from the other side of the four-way-stop, aiming for Dawson, who stopped so hard the seatbelts winded them all. The van only hit their front pumper but shook them like ragdolls. Joel came squealing around them from behind, which distracted them from the sedan that T-boned them into the side of Joel's car as he passed. Joel wasted no time and restarted the stalled car. Lucy and Owen were still recovering from the first hit, letting them avoid most of the damage from the second. Joel and Dawson sped away with a keen eye on surrounding vehicles.

Once at the location, they stopped suddenly and bolted from their dented, smoking vehicles. The location was an open entrance to a mall, not dissimilar from the lobby where they saw the panther. Minutes after their arrival, their previous car came rolling past the entrance. Its windows were shattered and most of the side was dented and crushed inward.

The door was jammed so Owen pulled himself out the window. He had a little blood running down his sunken face. Caitlin and Sophie helped him inside.

"This way," said Lucy. She led them to a large, square, marble walkway with benches and a popcorn stand. Several people were walking in and out, some of which slowed to stare at their dishevelled appearances.

"*Round three: The un-con-ditional love of family is ch-cherished by all. You don't choose your family, and according to old traditions, you don't get to choose if you love them. In reality, this is a prison. Regardless of how much you like them, or how well you get along, you are tied to them with res-sponsi-bi-li-ty. When really, they are a weakness. They hold you back to the past. To be strong, you must sacrifice your weakness.*" The little girl's voice became more and more glitchy, sometimes dropping in pitch.

"*This is where it gets deadly. I'm going to offer you a way out. We still have a few rounds to go and a lot more people have to die before this game ends. You can vote to end the game right now, but then one of your families will lose a couple of members at random. If your hands aren't up by the end of the round, it will count as a vote to agree to this deal. There are no ties."*

Caitlin, Sophie, Henry, and Dawson raised their hands above their heads. Joel, Owen, Grace, and Lucy raised their hands to shoulder level. Caitlin saw a darkness growing in Joel's eyes. Pain like pressure rose from within until it became too much to ignore.

"She said more people are going to die," Joel said in a low voice, "and they'll make us do it."

"Joel…" Caitlin watched him without blinking.

"It will only get worse," he said more loudly.

"Don't!" Caitlin's heart pounded harder against her ribs.

Owen dropped his hands, leaving everyone in breathless shock. Then Joel did the same.

"What are you doing!?" Henry shouted, drawing the nervous attention of people nearby.

"We can end this now," Joel said strongly, "no one else has to die by our hands."

"One of our families will!" Caitlin yelled indignantly.

"A small sacrifice, this has already gone too far," Grace said firmly, lowering her hands.

"You can't be serious!" Dawson shouted.

Sophie saw tears begin to fall from Lucy's eyes. "Lucy…" She attempted a consoling voice that wobbled with anxiety. Lucy sobbed. Her hands wavered below her shoulders. Sophie leapt forward and grabbed Lucy's forearms to hold them up.

"Don't," Sophie said strongly. Lucy cried harder, mumbling incomprehensibly. Owen stepped forward and tried to come between them gently. He struggled with her until they became forceful with each other.

"I just want this to be over," Lucy cried.

"*Ten.*"

"Owen stop!" Sophie growled, locking eyes with him.

"*Eight.*"

"Owen!" Henry stepped in to assist Sophie.

"*Seven.*"

Lucy broke free, falling to her knees and letting her hands fall.

"*Six.*"

Owen suddenly gripped Sophie's arms and forced them down, struggling against Henry's strength.

"*Five.*"

Caitlin grabbed at Joel before he could reach Henry and held his arms up and away.

"*Four.*"

Dawson pushed Grace aside before she could help Owen.

"*Three.*"

"Get 'em." Dawson pulled Owen back with a headlock.

"*Two.*"

Henry forced Owen's hands up. Owen kicked furiously in protest. Sophie grabbed one of Joel's arms to help Caitlin.

"*One.*"

Owen's face went red as he choked. Dawson felt him go weak and kicked behind his knee before letting go to raise his own hands. Owen fell to one knee, unable to pull his hands down. Sophie twisted Joel's arm. She tried to ignore his cries, but for an eternal moment, she felt her brother's strength in her arms from when they were younger. She rejected the strength of a bully like it was an insult but it was too late.

"*Zero! The Game shall resume shortly.*"

Caitlin let go before Joel's arm approached breaking point. Joel dropped to the floor, gripping his arm in agony.

Dawson let his arms fall and caught his breath. Henry let go and backed away from Owen, whose arms fell limply to clutch his aching throat. Caitlin turned away so as not to look at Joel. Lucy crawled backward to let herself cry safely.

"WHAT?" Dawson yelled at the people watching them. They continued to stare curiously but walked away nervously.

Owen watched the man at the popcorn stand look down and get back to work. He was expressionless, seemingly disinterested in the scene. Owen rubbed his throat and observed him filling another large bag of popcorn to hang alongside the others. There were no smaller bags of popcorn, only clear garbage bags filled to the top. The vat of popcorn the man worked behind went all the way to the floor with nothing keeping it warm.

"Round four: Head to the marked locations in teams of two."

Owen swayed but stood up and marched toward the popcorn stand. The man inside paused and watched him approach without a hint of fear. Owen took out his gun and aimed at the man, who raised his hands in surrender.

"Owen!" Dawson yelled.

"Get out! NOW!" Owen yelled hoarsely. The man stepped back calmly with his hands still up. Everyone ran to Owen, but picking up on the hint, Joel grabbed one of the large bags and tore it open. Cold, flavourless popcorn poured out along with a desert-coloured sub-machine gun. Joel picked it up and aimed at the Syndicate member.

"Put it down, Joel!" Caitlin hissed.

Joel saw a crowd of people gathering in his peripherals. There was a growing circle of onlookers watching them threaten an unarmed and surrendering man. He couldn't tell which of them were civilians and which were Syndicate members standing by, so he pointed the gun upward and opened fire. The circle broke. They screamed and ran with little concern for each other. Joel fired half the mag before stopping to see the effect he wanted; about five or six civilians left alongside the rest more reluctantly than fearfully. They walked quickly or jogged and were the only ones to look back.

Owen gestured just as reluctantly for the Syndicate member to follow the rest of his team, and so he did. The group left without a word and went to find undamaged cars to take. Owen gravitated towards Caitlin who avoided Joel. Grace followed Dawson, and Lucy kept with Henry, leaving Sophie to go with Joel who was first to find a car and leave.

"You're all liars," the little girl whispered harshly, *"You handle information so delicately. You want only the truth but give only lies, or sometimes nothing at all."* Her voice dipped in pitch and glitched eerily. *"That greed is heavy and the ice beneath your feet will only get thinner. How can you expect to beat us if you can't even be honest with each other? When were you going to tell the British officers that you never had any valuable information to provide, and lied to gain their Intel in a false exchange?"*

"What does she mean?" Joel asked, looking back and forth between Sophie and the road. She shook her head, the words 'I don't know' could barely pass her lips.

"You said you had encountered them in the past, you and Owen!"

"We had!" Sophie countered.

"But you never gave any details about it! Is that why Chris and I had to sort through *your* data!? Because you hadn't!?" Joel interrogated.

"And you two were using our intelligence and resources for your own investigation! You knew the CIA was using you and you used them in return!" Sophie countered.

"It was supposed to be *our* investigation but you were leeching off us from the start!" Joel steered aggressively.

"You did the same! You knew what you were doing!" Sophie grabbed a handle but kept the GPS open in her other hand.

"We used what your government gave us, which they used to distract us from the intelligence you offered and never had to begin with!"

"Why does it matter!?"

"*When were you going to tell them about the rogue militia?*"

Joel's focus was redirected. "What about the rogue militia? What do you know!?" He yelled.

"I don't know anything!" Sophie said with genuine confusion.

"*When were you going to tell him about the tampered evidence in his fiancé's case?*"

"No…" Sophie breathed.

The park was still alight from the blood-soaked lamps. There were several more police on the scene where the one had been shot earlier. Christian avoided them and circled the park back to headquarters.

"He was shot by a sniper when it started," Dennis said, seeing Stanley and Elliot observe the scene.

"Did you search the rooftops?" Elliot asked, looking up and around.

"It's not that simple… let's go." Christian ushered them to follow him.

"Are- are you Officer Knight?" One of the police

officers asked timidly. They were frozen in motion, fixed on the sight of Dennis and Christian.

"Yes," Dennis nodded. The police looked at one another nervously.

"What's wrong?" Stanley asked. One of the officers took out a pistol and held it tightly, then the rest of them did the same.

Elliot, Stanley, and Dennis gripped their pistols with both hands.

"Easy now… talk to me…" Dennis said cautiously.

Christian tried to leave but the officers aimed up at him, demanding him to stop.

"Lower your weapons!" Dennis yelled, raising his own.

"So you all work for him!?" Christian asked sarcastically.

"He's making us do it…" One of officers said uneasily.

"You don't have to do anything they say," Dennis said strongly.

The officer shook his head. "We have to-" They narrowed their aim but Stanley was the first to shoot. Dennis ducked away and ran towards Christian. The officers backed away whilst shooting in Dennis' direction.

"Go! We'll cover you!" Elliot shouted over the gunfire. He took cover with Stanley and shot at the ground beneath the officers.

Dennis grabbed Christian by the shoulders and pushed him down and out of the line of fire. Once near enough to a corner, he threw Christian behind it and ducked away behind him. Bullets whizzed past and clipped the corner of the wall. "We have to keep moving," Dennis said through rapid breaths.

"When the boys are away… the girls will play!" The little girl sang.

"HQ!" Christian said, crippled with panic. Dennis pulled him to his feet and started running back. The sounds of gunshots died away behind them. Christian struggled to keep up with Dennis' full sprint. Adrenaline electrified him but his lungs ached with the strain of his breathing.

Owen kicked the breaks. "Is she talking about me..." he asked strongly.

Caitlin kept her quickening breaths inaudible. She felt her cheeks burning but forced herself to look at him anyway.

"Is she talking about the death of my wife?" Owen asked more forcefully. He stared directly ahead, ignoring the angry drivers that passed them.

"Yes." Caitlin said simply.

"What tampered evidence?" Owen asked sternly.

"I don't know-"

"DON'T LIE TO ME!" He shouted.

"I don't know! Dawson had it in the files." Caitlin said desperately.

"What files?" Owen's mouth twitched restlessly.

"From the checkpoints, Henry hid it so you wouldn't see..." The silence hurt enough without Owen gripping the steering wheel so tightly. "We're running out of time." Caitlin said more confidently.

Before she could finish, Owen had accelerated with such force that Caitlin almost got whiplash again. His driving was even more reckless. Caitlin remained quiet and gripped the handle above her window. When they finally arrived, they proceeded to the marked location in agonizing silence.

"You have no right to be mad at me for holding back

information." Caitlin said as she followed him into a factory where the marker led.

"The map says it's just in front of us," said Grace.

Dawson drove through the construction site slowly, searching for threats. It was late afternoon now and the site was empty. The location was in the middle of a dirt opening where trucks and building materials had been left for the next day. The building was still skeletal with nothing more than steel beams and concrete floors surrounded by scaffolding.

"One of you has been more dishonest than most." The little girl only whispered. *"There lies a traitor among you. A double-agent, embar-rassed by their mistakes. Trying desperately to fix what has already been done. Kill the traitor, or everyone dies. Time is already running out."*

Owen and Caitlin had stopped half way down some stairs when they exchanged disbelieving looks.

Henry and Lucy had entered a large room with glass walls built on a terrace. It was hidden on the second floor amongst multi-story apartment buildings. They watched each other, unsure of what to do or say, but apprehensive of each passing moment.

Joel and Sophie were looking around a set of small garages hidden behind a Chinese restaurant. Although they were confident they were both innocent, they kept their distance. Joel went over it in his head but nothing stuck out about any of them. He reconsidered the Syndicate's potential aptitude to bluff, but they had not lied, and there wouldn't be an entire round dedicated to a traitor if there wasn't one. Yet from how much they were being played with, it wasn't unlikely.

Dawson stood up straight after checking beneath the

trucks for explosives. He turned to grace who was standing with her hands on her hips.

"They have to be bluffing," she said.

"They don't bluff," Dawson said darkly.

Grace thought hard for a moment and shook her head. "Could it be one of ours?" She asked nervously.

"Slide your gun over to me," Owen said with his hand by his hip.

"It's not me!" Caitlin said defensively.

"You're military like them, and that woman in the red dress, she knew your name-"

"They know all our names!"

"You and Joel were there at the interrogation in South Africa and then they were waiting for us in Afghanistan." Owen lifted his pistol.

"You and Sophie were there as well!" Caitlin turned her hip, threatening to reach for her own.

"I know Sophie, and it couldn't be Joel, he's the reason there's a case against them." Owen had to keep his hands from shaking.

"You were pretty desperate to keep the game going," said Joel.

"Because I actually have a family," Sophie shot back.

"It doesn't make sense, did anyone actively joined the investigation?"

"Chris-"

"Chris isn't here, he doesn't count. You were the only other person to choose to be a part of this."

"Stay calm," said Henry.

Lucy felt sick. "I'm just an analyst I'm not even supposed to be here."

"I don't think it's you, Lucy, I don't think it's either of us," Henry said lightly.

"Just, stay away from me," Lucy said as she backed away.

"Alright." He raised his hands and stayed put. "It's okay."

"Yes, Grace." Said Dawson. "It could be."

"W- Any ideas?" She asked.

"Something wrong, Grace?" Dawson asked. "Something you want to tell me?"

Grace shook her head and scanned the site once more. "I'm just trying to figure out who could have been a double-agent all this time. You can't possibly think it could be me!"

"Calm down, Grace. You've been nothing but supportive of this investigation," Dawson said thankfully.

"That's right," Grace said matter-of-factly.

"Since the beginning you've helped me put this all together even when it was just a theory. You didn't even question it. You took great interest in it."

Grace watched him with her arms crossed.

"You watched over us, maybe a little too much. You personally took part… even when I didn't ask you too."

"Because this is a very serious case," Grace added.

"Very out of character for you. I reported everything back to you and still you would periodically check on us for anything new. You're not even on this investigative team but here you are with us anyway." Dawson watched her reaction as he spoke. Monitored her body language, details large and small.

Grace's trembling lips couldn't get a word in.

"Owen said you were acting strange when looking for the checkpoints. You asked me to wait for you before reaching the last one. You wanted to see what was in it because you thought it might reveal you."

"Nathan, you don't understand-"

"No I understand perfectly now, Grace, why you took such a sudden and great interest in this case the moment you heard about it. You already knew who they were."

"No, Nathan please-"

"Have you been reporting to them this entire time?" Dawson growled.

"No I swear, listen to me-"

"What have you done for them, Grace?" Dawson interrupted again.

"I didn't know it was them, it was a long time ago-"

"Don't bullshit me! TELL ME WHAT YOU DID!"

"They helped us, they worked for us, ok? It was all legitimate."

"What was legitimate!?"

"It was all part of a deal..." Grace's voice shook. She stepped back from Dawson as he drew his weapon. "It was a covert operation against the insurgency in Afghanistan, its classified information-"

"I DON'T CARE!"

"I didn't know, ok!? None of us did, that rogue militia was never our fault-"

"You're the one who knows about the rogue militia!? TELL ME!"

"It wasn't my fault!" Grace cried. Her unintelligible pleas were lost beneath desperate wailing. "Just listen to me, it wasn't supposed to happen the way it did, they were hired but requested equipment. We had to give it to them. They took it for themselves but it doesn't matter now! There is no more rogue militia! Please, Nathan, you have to listen to me!"

Dawson shot her just above her heart puncturing her aortic arch. She fell backward and twitched in shock. Blood poured from her chest and over the rest of her body. Her crying turned to a desperate gasping until finally she went still.

"Congratulations! Continue to the marked locations for the next round."

Joel backed up against a wall and slid down. One of them had been killed. Possibly Lucy, or even Caitlin. He and Sophie were in the marked location but he didn't feel like searching any more. The Syndicate would reveal their next torment soon enough. Meanwhile, the two of them ignored each other in a fearful yet vengeful mourning.

Lucy began to relax a little more. She walked closer to Henry who welcomed her with open arms.

"It's okay," he sighed. His mind was racing uncomfortably.

Lucy embraced him in a hug of relief. Together, they stood and waited, saying nothing.

Owen lowered his gun. The furious look in Caitlin's eyes amplified his remorse. An apology was worthless. He couldn't look at her, so he sat on the steps and stared down at the floor, hiding his contrite expression. After a few moments of collecting themselves, Owen's phone rang in his pocket. A sharp sensation in his hand wanted desperately not to take it out in case it was the Syndicate. "Dawson..." He answered.

"*It was Grace. She was the double-agent.*" Dawson said in a low voice.

Owen rubbed the back of his neck. He had nothing to say but had to say something. "What now?" He asked.

"*Do as they say. Let's get this over with quickly.*"

Dawson hung up and leaned back in his car seat. The day was getting colder so he closed the door. Then, he surveyed the construction site whilst dialling the next number.

"Hello?" Sophie answered.

Joel looked up and climbed to his feet. "Who is it?" He asked cautiously.

Sophie ignored him and listened to the caller with a blank expression. "Yes, sir," she said, then put her phone away again. "Dawson says it was Grace," she said after a pause.

Joel didn't know her well enough which he realised should have been a partial giveaway. He hadn't enough time to think before one of the garage doors behind them opened by itself. Sophie had her gun out almost immediately. Joel followed her with his own at the ready. They approached the garage as the light from outside revealed that which lay within. There was a desk against the back wall with a long bar across it. Thick electrical cables were attached to either end of the bar leading through holes in the back wall.

To Joel's immense stress, Sophie switched on the light in the middle of the garage. The motor next to it then closed the door behind them. Joel put his gun away and inspected the bench. The cables were also connected to a small monitor behind the bar. "I think these are handles," he said, spotting roughened patches on the bar.

"Joel look," Sophie said suddenly. On the back of the garage door was a message written in yellow paint: '*Hold on tight!*'

"*Now that everyone is ready...*" said the little girl, "*We can begin round five! Do not attempt to leave wherever you are. Whether you're in a car or room, you will have to remain there for the rest of the round. You should be able to see one or more exits available. Do not attempt to open them.*"

A machine behind the wall hummed into life. There was buzzing coming from the wall. The small monitor booted up and showed a reading of 0.1mA.

Dawson struggled to see out the windows of the car. A powerful engine had started up and began moving with sounds of heavy machinery. A vehicle approached from the rear. He had to duck his head to see out the back. His view of a yellow beam was obstructed by the roof of the car when it suddenly caved in. Dawson leaned toward the centre of the car and away from the edges that were now closing in. Five large, yellow pincers were grabbing and crushing the car around him. He pulled his legs as far in as he could and held onto the wheel. The pincers stopped crushing but the car began to rise from the platform. Dawson could hardly see through the cracking glass. Out the back left window, he could just make out the crane that was lifting him, and the Lady Danger behind the controls.

Caitlin had found arrows on the walls that led them further downstairs. She and Owen eventually found the end at the bottom of a single stairwell that led to the basement level of the building. That's where the little girl told them to stay. Their exits were a heavy door at the bottom of the stairs and a lighter one at the top. They did as they were told and didn't go through. Instead, they investigated the loud crashing at the top door. A large grey frame locked into the doorframe. Secured into the frame were twenty large pipes.

A sudden clanging from behind made them both jump and spin around. A vent cover had fallen from the ceiling, revealing another large pipe half a metre in diameter.

Although they were all closed, Henry could see plenty of exits. He could break any one of the glass windows to escape.

Lucy screamed when the sprinklers burst open, spraying fire for a few seconds instead of water. She dropped to the floor so as not to be burnt. Henry dived down and covered her as best he could, watching the sprinklers apprehensively.

The light inside the entrance was dim. Dennis barged through the door with his gun raised. Christian slipped inside as the door was about to close. There was no one inside. A hissing of high pressure drew Christian's attention back to the door. It shut firmly with air seeping through.

Dennis rammed into the door at the other end of the security room. He hit it with his shoulder while pulling down hard on the handle. Christian turned back to the exit and tried to open it. The handle broke off effortlessly. Sickening panic began to rise exponentially. His breathing got uncontrollably quicker. He could feel a weight in his diaphragm. His skin burnt neither hot nor cold. The muscles up his arms and legs switched between limp and taught faster than he could control.

"HEY!" Dennis banged on the door and shouted loudly

to see if anyone was on the other side. His ears felt blocked with an odd sensation of forceful warmth. The same feeling pressed all over his face. "You feel that?" He asked, looking at his red hands.

"The pressure," said Christian, "It's going up." Christian looked around the security room, his head lolling weakly.

Dennis kicked above the handle of the door but it only pushed him back.

"By now you have realised what's happening. Each team faces their own life threat-en-ing situation. The truth is, only one of these situations is going to be lethal. However, if a team in a non-lethal situation attempts to escape, all other teams will be killed instantly!" The little girl's voice dropped in pitch towards the end.

The pincers began crushing again forcing Dawson to the middle of the car. The light metal warped easily under their strength such that one pincer went straight through the back of the car. Dawson kicked the shattered window on his right, revealing a handle on one of the pincers; his way out.

Caitlin and Owen jerked out of the way of the water as it came gushing from two of the pipes. The bottom of the stairwell began flooding at a perilous rate. A column of sand then came channelling from the pipe above them, forming a pile at the bottom that merged with the water. The conduit frame was locked in, leaving the bottom door as their only exit, which was quickly disappearing beneath a rising pool of sand and water.

Once again, Joel found himself refusing to accept what he already knew. They had to hold the bar, but there were no cameras watching. He wouldn't tell Sophie what he saw, but he grabbed the bar and told her to do the same. By the time she did, feeling the current run through her arms, the message on the monitor had gone: '*Do you want your friends to die?*'

Henry let go of Lucy and circled around the room toward the main exit. The sprinklers weren't active but he avoided them still. Lucy followed closely. A low hissing around the room turned to whistling. The threat quickly became apparent. It wasn't long until all they could smell was the gas being released from the sprinklers. Propane wasn't an entirely unpleasant smell, but the quantity became revolting with no sign of relenting.

Christian dropped to his knees. The pressure plummeted, pulling the air from his lungs and making his ears pop. He could hear the air being sucked from the room but the more he swivelled his head to look for it, the dizzier he became.

Dennis swayed and grabbed onto the handle of the door. He shook his head, sending spots flying across his vision. "Chris…"

Christian struggled to form the words. His heart beat against his ribs but he felt like he was getting colder.

Blocking the pipes was futile in itself. The flow was too strong. Caitlin and Owen tried anyway in the absence of another option. The Syndicate responded by opening flow from another one of the pipes. Caitlin backed away and fell against the wall. Not from the force of the water, but from the weakness in her legs. The Syndicate, the Phantom, had intrigued the Game airtight. She was contesting with something she could neither see not touch. Something that waited all the time it wanted for a head start. Something with the resources and means to do exactly what it wanted without restriction. She felt an odd relief as a weight left her body taking everything positive with it. Her subconscious mind capitulated to the Game, fatiguing her will. Owen struggled to measure the rising water level and sand. It had passed half way up the door.

      Dawson positioned himself for a leap of faith. He knelt uncomfortably in the middle of the two front seats. The handle on the pincer outside the window was easily reachable, but he dared not grab it prematurely. Remaining space in the car closed around him. His neck was arching over painfully but he kept his posture ready to climb out the window.

      The reading on the monitor rose by 0.1mA every few seconds. It started as a tingling sensation in their hands and up their arms. At 4mA the tingling became uncomfortably strong, yet they were still easily able to hold on. Joel could see that Sophie wasn't doing as well. Her arms were twitching and her eyes were shut tight. He tried to keep talking, to console her and cheer her on, but the current only got more intense. He knew they were just getting started. A galvanic pain was stirring in their arms.

      Henry and Lucy had their shirts over their noses and mouths. Lucy was up against the door with Henry covering her as much as he could. Once the coughing started it didn't stop. Lucy shut her eyes but Henry could see they were watering. It wasn't until he began to feel light headed that his panic rose higher than any other point that day. He pressed harder against the door with only Lucy's dry gasping to indicate her vitals. The rest of the group's condition was a mystery, but he had to give them a chance, no matter how much it hurt to breathe.

      Dennis' muscles were aching painfully, but he continued to pound at the door for help. He couldn't stand by himself so resorted to leaning against it.

Christian was lying with his back against the opposite door. He struggled with each breath while staring through Dennis with dazed vision. When Dennis finally fell to the floor, Christian could feel tingling at the tips of his fingers and toes. He lay limply, his head falling under its own weight.

"We need to be able to get out." Owen was watching the sand and water touch the handle of the door below. Caitlin saw it as well, but didn't move. Owen jumped to the door. He sank slowly as soon as he landed but managed to grab the handle before it went under. "Come on Cait!" He called. Caitlin glared at him with a blank, pale expression while he sank beneath the rising tide. He continued to call her down, apologizing for joint catharsis, but she could only think about how much sand and water the Syndicate had. Whether they could fill the room or not. She remembered Joel's agonizing words. The Syndicate did not bluff. She pulled herself up and managed to leap around the column of sand next to Owen. He held her tight and pulled her against the door. The cold water seeped into her shoes as the sand scratched her legs.

The crane could only crush the car so much, so Dawson knew he stood a good chance. Although they were slow, the pincers were closing in consistently. Parts of the car were stabbing at Dawson's sides. There was no more wiggle room. He writhed with amplified distress, failing to keep his limbs from becoming trapped. The window bent in on itself and shrank. A dizzying desperation was taking over. He had to wait as long as he could, regardless of how much the Lady hurt him. He knew he could recover but only if someone found him before he bled out.

"*Feel it...*" the little girl whispered. "*You think you know this feeling.*" Her pitched dropped suddenly, then rose and sank with every syllable. "*Breath it in... feel it closing in around you...*" The little girl's voice wavered between her own and that of another, deeper, crisp and dark. "*Feel it crawl up your nerves. You think you know what that is.* ***You don't.***" The little girl's voice faded away, and the Phantom's took over. "***That's fear. Real fear. Feel it take over. You are not in control. They cannot help you. You cannot help yourselves. You live… only as I allow it. Your souls balance at the edge of my will.***"

Joel couldn't find the energy to speak. The reading passed 10mA. He was gripping as hard as he could, fighting the pain that was now stretching up his neck and down his legs. Sophie cried out every few moments. Her whole body shook uncontrollably. She could still let go, but with the pain sizzling through her body, and his voice in her head, she held tighter than ever before. Time stretched further into infinity. Their minds begged it to stop. Begged them to let go. An internal battle for control of their bodies was raging chaotically.

Dawson pulled himself as close to the window as he could. His legs were struggling to move against the sharp obstructions. He kicked desperately and cried out in pain. A piece of the ceiling was stabbing down on one of his calfs. Blood flowed from his tightly gripping hands and down the broken glass around the frame of the shrinking window.

A small part of Christian's mind woke from his fleeting consciousness. The sound of the Phantom's voice echoed into his numbing ears. His remaining cognition focused on the deep, crisp voice. Every word, every inflection, recording in the black-box of his mind while the rest phased out of recognition.

The voice was all that could get inside Dennis' head. His vision was blurring out of perception. He felt like his energy was being drained from him with every numb gasp for air. He lay on the floor covering his ears so that he could listen to that dark voice.

"*This is not a game you can win. You will lose… or you will die.*"

Henry felt like he could vomit at any moment. Lucy already had. They were gasping and heaving on the floor. He could see spots in his vision but kept his hand on the handle of the door with its weight barely able to pull it down.

"***I will break you.***" The Phantom's words boomed wrathfully, sinking deeper into their unhinging minds.

The rest of the pipes burst with more water flooding the stairwell. The peak of the sand sloped down to their chins. Caitlin and Owen raised their faces at the top of the doorframe. The weight of the wet sand pressed them harder against the door and locked their limbs into place.

Joel gritted his teeth and dropped to one knee. At 15mA the current began spiking randomly. It jabbed sharply at Sophie's nervous system, making her muscles spasm rapidly. She screamed and cried out, unable to control any part of herself. Joel looked up just enough to see the reading on the monitor spike between 18mA and 22mA. His arms tensed and pulled him against the desk. He could no longer let go.

Dawson grabbed the handle on the pincer and tried to pull himself. The blood on his hands weakened his grip. His legs and shoulders were pinned in the warping metal. He shouted for help but could no longer breathe in enough air to vocalize it.

Lucy went limp under Henry's arm. He was choking and

spluttering involuntarily. He tried to pull the handle of the door but could barely feel his arms. Spots filled his vision. His mind floated into a void.

Caitlin took a deep breath and shut her mouth as tight as she could. She writhed against the weight of the sand. Owen's hand gripped hers tighter. She kicked and twisted but only sank deeper. The weight of the wet sand pressed heavily against her chest, forcing some of the air out her nose.

Christian felt like his lungs were being pulled upward. His eyes felt swollen. The tingling around his body turned to numbness. Images of what was in front of his swayed around his mind, but he could not make sense of it.

Dennis couldn't feel the floor against his body. There was only the throbbing headache that broke his thoughts up into fragments, and the pain in his chest that pressed deeper with each passing moment.

Joel was yelling at the top of his voice. He tried to kick away but his legs only spasmed. His arms were pulling him against the desk. Every nerve in his body felt like it was on fire. The remaining control in his body tried to pull away. He let his legs contract until they were off the floor. A new pain grew where his arms bent over the edge of the desk. He stressed every muscle in his body to spasm harder, bending his arm harder until something cracked and his hands broke free one after the other. Then he launched himself sideways without hesitation. Sophie's grip was strong. He tackled her with all his weight and pulled her wrists. She screamed louder than ever before. Joel kept his weight on her and swung his left arm against hers. With an assist from his knee, he managed to break Sophie's grip of the bar and use her own weight to pull away her other hand. The two of them fell back and rolled apart, twitching between spasms while taking deep gasping breaths and clutching their arms.

Henry felt an odd sensation of weightlessness followed by a cold surface against his face. His aching chest forced him to cough hard. He could feel drool down his chin. The numbness in his fingers gripped at a soft material and pulled at it whilst kicking against nothing. He dragged Lucy out as far as he could with his remaining energy.

Dawson felt his own weight lifted from him. He braced for a crash but simply bounced against the inside of the car. The handle slipped out of his hand. The pincers pulled away from the car and floated upward. Dawson caught his breath and rested for a moment. A familiar sensation of wet warmth trickled down his legs and hands.

Owen held the handle down. A few seconds felt like hours that the door didn't open. When it did, the avalanche of sand and water launched him out and planted him on the floor. He kicked and clawed at the stone surface until he broke free and pulled in a full breath. Feeling returned to his hand that was being pulled by Caitlin's. He pulled back to draw her out. She slid out heaving and debilitated. Together, they crawled away shakily from the mountain of sand and lay on their backs, letting the water flow around them.

One by one, Dennis' senses came back, like he was waking from a long nap. He could feel cold blowing against his face, and a hard flat surface beneath his knees, hip, and shoulder. His taste buds stung with the same repulsive taste that he could smell. Muffled voices spoke quickly in the distance. He tried to open his eyes only to realise that they were already blinking. Over his small streak of vomit, he could see Stanley Martin pulling a body out of the room, then running past it towards him.

"*Round six:*" The little girl was back. With the Agents and Officers incapacitated, the only ones listening were back at the CIA. "*Find the red case.*"

The explosions were distant but undeniable. Bentley instinctively ran for the closest window. Even with miles of buildings in the way he could see the flames rising in the darkening twilight.

"Cole's not responding, neither is Deck," said Meach. Together, they returned to the analyst's room.

"Can we get ahold of anyone?" Bentley asked urgently.

"Wait... you hear that?" Meach was pressing in his earpiece. Everyone stopped to listen carefully.

"Turn up the volume on that broadcast," Bentley ordered one of the analysts. Hiding quietly like background noise was a ticking. Like an analogue stopwatch.

"What's going on in the city!?" Secretary Miles yelled over the shoulder of another analyst. The analyst typed furiously, managing to bring up satellite feed over the city. A perfect circle of glowing red flames encircled almost ten blocks.

"What's in the middle?" Bentley asked quickly.

"Uuhm... An apartment building I think." The Analyst answered timidly.

"Feed us the location," Meach said to Secretary Miles, then he and Bentley bolted out with surprising speed. Another burst of explosions sent them running back inside before they even reached the lobby.

"The circle is closing in! Go now!" Secretary Miles commanded.

Bentley and Meach sprinted to the parking lot outside. They screeched away using one of the CIA's standard SUV's. Bentley dodged the traffic with ease. Meach had the directions from the analysts in seconds. The circle was enclosing in Washington.

They could hear a great deal of hooting as they passed over a bridge into the city. Bentley squinted at the intersection ahead and switched on the bright headlights. Several cars at the stop were reversing frantically seconds before a dumpster truck came rampaging through the intersection, charging in and out of the light in the blink of an eye.

Bentley switched back to the normal headlights. He kept his speed, dodging at least five broken and dented cars over the intersection. Some were badly crushed and smoking from their bonnets. The next set of explosions were much louder, and indicated to Bentley where he needed to go.

He mounted the curb to pass an area sectioned off by the fire department. There were ladders high up for the firefighters to put out the fires on the rooftops. The rest of the building appeared unscathed.

"They're not attacks, they're markers," said Meach.

"Anything from the rest the rest of the team?" Bentley asked. He passed a crowd of people at the second fire-circle with a visual on the third further ahead.

"Nothing, but Miles says there's a conference centre in the middle of the circles." Meach memorized the directions and put the phone away.

"Come in. Meach..."

"I'm here, over," Meach said into his radio.

"The building is empty, we have backup units on the

way," said Secretary Miles.

"We're arriving now," Meach replied. They skidded to a halt in front of the conference building. Provocative revving grew behind them just as they started running. An unknown car mounted the curb and accelerated. They couldn't see past its headlights so they shot slightly above them. The shots broke through the windscreen and into the void beyond.

Bentley and Meach barged into the lobby of the building with a few seconds to spare before the car came scratching past at high speed.

"I'll go up you go down!" Bentley called. Wasting no time, he leapt up the stairs three at a time and slowed to a fast walk with his handgun at the ready.

"*Remember, they said find the red case,*" Meach said over the radio.

"Copy that," Bentley replied. The building was dim and vacant. Every door that Bentley kicked down would fill the quiet with sudden crashing. The further in he ventured, the dimmer it became. He switched on his flashlight and held it under his gun so they aimed in synch.

The building shook with the next set of explosions closing in. An orange glow came to life at the other end of the hallway. Bentley jogged over. The flames were still a few blocks away but grew taller than the surrounding buildings. He remembered what Meach said in the car about markers and paused with an epiphany. The conference building was taller than its neighbours, and the fires were all on rooftops. Within a minute he had bolted to the stairwell and climbed them three steps at a time. He used his shoulder to break out the emergency exit at the top and started surveying the rooftop.

"*I've got something-*" Meach said urgently. "*Miles we need a bomb squad on the first floor!*"

"Copy that. On its way." Miles replied.

Bentley checked around the vents that covered the rooftop. This time the Syndicate made it easy enough to find. In one corner, on top of a desk, was a red briefcase.

"I have eyes on the red case," Bentley said into his radio. He approached it with his gun raised and his torch aimed right at it.

"What else do you see?" Miles asked urgently.

"There's a note on top that says 'open me'" Bentley replied.

"I... I don't really know what I'm looking at here..." said Meach.

The moment Bentley laid a finger on the case, the ticking from the podcast got louder and faster. He held the torch in his mouth and knelt down to unclip the case. There were no cables, no detonators, only a single rectangle inside. Bentley opened the case all the way and picked up the device. "There's a tablet inside, it's on," he reported. The screen came on to show a grid of four by five. A few of the squares were green while the rest were plain blue. "There are some green squares and some blue ones."

"Anything else?" Miles asked.

One after another, the blue squares turned green at random. "They're turning green, there's three left." After five minutes there were two left. A few more minutes and there was one. Then after the last square turned green, the little girl spoke again.

"Now that all twenty of you are ready, let's play the final round! Each square represents a nation that is currently taking part in the Game. As much as you all support each other, and build mutually ben-ef-icial relation-ships, you secretly only look out for one: Yourselves. No-one is really on the same side. You

wear masks of positive polit-ical symbiosis yet spy on each other all the same. Because you know you're lying. You know there are secrets."

The twenty squares turned into flags, displaying the nations currently listening to their own versions of the little girl. Bentley stared down at the tablet in his hands, trying to remember which flag was which.

"Bomb squad is here, but the explosives are not in this room," Meach said over the little girl.

"What do you mean?" Miles asked.

Bentley struggled to pay attention to both the radio and the little girl.

"What harm have you done to one another?" She whispered.

"This room is filled with different clocks connected by a network of red and blue cables. Too many to count... It's covering the walls." Meach explained. *"Wait... It's the conduit! The wires feed into the buildings electrical conduits! It's running along all the walls!"*

"There are never any winners... only losers. Time for a demonstration-" the little girl said harshly. *"You get one vote... For which nation should lose the Game... For which nation to be detonated."*

"There's explosives in all the routers and switches!" Meach said, partially out of breath.

"Can they defuse it?" Miles asked urgently.

"No. There's too many clocks and wires. They're all counting down but at different times," said Meach. *"Some of the timers have ended already, but most are still going."*

"Bentley, do you copy?" Miles stressed.

"I copy. They want me to vote-"

"We know, stand by."

"*Isn't it strange that acts of terrorism often never come from the country's own people? Your diversity breeds conflict, so this is going to be a team effort. Time is running out for you all... Every time a nation votes, everyone else's time goes down. Not voting will be considered a vote for yourself. Any nation that ties for first place will suffer the same fate.*"

The ticking immediately sped up, and kept doing so randomly.

"*Evacuate that building and get everyone to a safe distance!*" Miles ordered.

Another set of explosions circled Bentley by three blocks. The flames rose up to fifteen metres of bright red and orange against the night sky. "I'm running out of time here, please advise!" Bentley said shakily. He paced the rooftop with the tablet in his hands.

"*Which nations do you see?*" Miles asked quickly.

"Uhh, I see England, France, Germany, Italy, China, North Korea, Japan, Russia… Greece, Iran, India… Ukraine, Brazil-" Another set of explosions cut him off. The radius was merely two blocks away.

"*What are the smallest nations!?*" Miles yelled.

"I don't know them all!" Bentley's hands were shaking. The rooftops of the neighbouring buildings burst into flames that rose above his head and up into the stars.

"*Sir these clocks are going haywire!*" Meach added.

"Please advise!" Bentley yelled over Meach.

"*Alright!*" Miles burst out, "*Listen to me very carefully…*"

Chapter XV
The Grandmaster's Meeting
Unknown, Unknown, United States of America
23:36 EST, Monday, 31st October 2016
(*That evening*)

The game is power. Your opponent will never reveal how much they truly have.

Tall flames looked like candles in the city. Something raging so far away appeared only as a flicker. Sirens echoed from a great distance, amplifying each other. Orange lights danced in the reflections of the black cars. Men and women gathered with secretive silence under the apocalyptic glow.

The biggest of the men, the bodyguards, escorted their bosses in close groups. Motion in the shadows sent a pulse of skipped heartbeats through the arriving parties. Syndicate guards were watching them from the second floor balcony. Their soulless, skull-like masks offered no emotion. They simply watched, almost motionless, with large rifles ready in their hands.

The double doors at the entrance creaked open, revealing a stunning woman with straight red hair flowing down her shoulders. Her tight, snow-white dress shined brighter than the distant flames. "Please follow me." She said with a weak Italian accent.

The guests looked at each other unconfidently. The lady in the white dress disappeared into the lobby. Each group followed her cautiously one after another, keeping some distance between them. Torches and oil lamps lit up the old oak wood that decorated the lobby. Clean red carpet led left, right, and up the stairs directly ahead. A crystal vase of freshly picked roses sat atop a circular mahogany table in the middle. They had bloomed into a luscious bouquet with their thorny stems interlocking. More of the Syndicate's men were standing either side of the doorways.

"Right this way." The lady in the white dress looked down at them with her hand on the dark oak banister. The guests kept a couple of metres between their groups and made their way up the staircase. She led them through a short, candle-lit corridor with mature oak walls. At the end, she opened a pair of double-doors by their golden handles, and stepped inside to let everyone through. The large rectangular room offered just enough space for them all, with more space on the two levels of balconies looking down on them. The ceiling three floors above was carved elegantly with old stylings. In the middle of the room was a long, polished mahogany table with matching hand-carved wooden chairs all the way around.

"You may take your seats, the meeting will begin shortly." The lady said once they were all inside, then she closed the doors on her way out. Syndicate guards were sequenced on the two balconies and ground floor. Many of the guests had some of their men go up to the balconies to prevent the room from being too crowded. They then shed their coats, and took their seats around the table.

For a while, nobody spoke. They did not know nor recognise anyone else sitting around them. There was only a single shared topic of interest.

"Has anyone met them before?" Asked a man with a crooked nose and a full beard.

They all wore similarly semi-formal suits, with the exception of the one older woman. "Well don't everybody answer at once," she said after a pause. The men around the table shook their heads.

"Has anyone even spoken to them before?" The man asked. Once again, everyone shook their heads.

"I'm sorry, I didn't catch your name," said the woman.

"Why do you want to know?" The man relaxed in his chair, meeting her gaze.

"Oh don't be so childish," she snapped, "If we're going to have a discussion I need something to call you by. I imagine you have a preference?"

The man thought for a moment. "Shartley," he said.

"Shartley. And you mutes?" The woman took out a cigarette. She jumped slightly when one of the Syndicate guards stepped forward.

"No smoking." He said with a strong but muffled voice. The woman rolled her eyes and put it away.

"They're very strict," said a man in a silky suit.

"Is that supposed to be funny," said a middle-aged man with balding dark-grey hair. "You know who they are? I can't be the only one who did my research."

"Obviously we know who they are," The woman spoke up, "We're all here under the same terms aren't we?"

"And what are your terms, lady?" Shartley asked.

"Margarete is fine," she shot back.

"The invitation said 'to discuss terms of surrender and mutual alliance'. And you can call me Olive," said the man in the silky suit.

"So…" A man near the end of the table cleared his throat and leaned forward in his chair. "Nine businessmen, and one woman, come to surrender to the Grandmasters." His voice was old and gravelly, and left the room in shameful silence.

"I don't think it's the Grandmasters any of us are worried about, am I right?" said Olive.

"Don't beat around the bush, son," A thick Irish accent came from a skinny man with short hair sitting opposite Margarete. "I came half way around the world to keep that Phantom from coming to find me."

"*Da*," said a Russian with medium-length wavy hair.

"Their pet has killed a lot of guys like us," chimed the old and gravelly voice. "Only a fool would make an enemy of them. Hell, I owe them my thanks for what they've done. Ill kiss their bloody shoes for it."

Margarete chuckled. The relaxing of her shoulders was quickly undone by the sound of a door closing somewhere in the building. At the end of the room were two sets of double doors with only one guard in the middle. The doors on the left opened, drawing every pair of eyes to watch the two Syndicate officials that came through. They were dressed in all military-grade gear with side-arms in thigh holsters, but no masks. They leaned against the walls on either side of the doorway and waited without expression. Beyond the doorway was too dark to see. To avoid waiting so anxiously, the guests stiffly attempted to show strength, even though their hearts now beat a little harder.

A silhouette emerged from the shadow. The Black Panther strolled in and stopped at the sight of the guests. Disconcerted mumbling throughout the room was quickly silenced by the arrival of the Phantom. His smooth hood sloped down to his collar bones and met seamlessly with the rest of his overcoat. A blank, black material covered his nose and mouth and tucked into his shirt. The purple patterns all over his coat were gone, leaving only their indentation. He stepped to the chair on the end of the table, his bright eyes paying them no attention. Without a sound, he gestured for the Panther to get up onto the table, and gracefully took his seat. The Panther leapt up and stood for a moment, eyeing each of the guests before laying down to the left of the Phantom. The guests nearest to the Panther shuffled away, causing everyone to move further down the table away from the Phantom.

To avoid staring at him for too long, they looked to each other with apprehensive disorientation. They watched him, unblinking, as he reached under his coat to his inside pocket. Blood ran over his fingerless gloves. He pulled out a thick piece of raw meat and threw it just in front of the Panther, who immediately started chewing on it. The Phantom then wiped his hand with a rag and stroked the Panther's back as it enjoyed its treat.

The room was deathly quiet apart from the Panther's chewing and panting. Then to everyone's relief, someone spoke up.

"I thought we were meeting Grandmasters," the Russian enquired quietly. The Phantom looked directly at him, making him unconsciously lean back. There was a long pause before the Phantom released him from his gaze and continued to admire the Panther.

"**You think only what I want you to think.**" His voice filled the room with its strength. "**You may think this is a Jaguar, but in reality, he's a Leopard**"

The guests watched the Panther chew on the meat and swallow it whole. He was much bigger than a Jaguar, in fact, much bigger than each of them.

"**In Africa, he was loved for his unique colour. For his lethality. He played an important role in keeping balance in his territory. But humans... refusing to acknowledge the natural order, claimed his territory and the animals who called it home. Alpha predators do not share.**" He turned his gaze to his fear-stricken guests. "**He had to hunt. But the locals hoarded his source of food. In his aggression, he**

fought them for his right to survive." He leaned forward and stroked at the fur from the Panther's shoulder to its head, revealing old and hidden scars. "**They were going to hunt and kill him for posing a threat to their livelihoods... Hypocrites.**" His brows furrowed slightly. He gripped the Panther, making it growl deeply. The guests felt it in their chairs. The table shuddered under the force of the Panther's vocal power. "**As a species, we have to do better... or we must perish.**"

"What would you have us do?" Asked the balding man.

The Phantom's eyes darted to him. "**You know why you're here... but you do not understand.**"

"To discuss terms of surrender," said Shartley.

"We're here to speak with your employers; the Grandmasters. Under the condition that you stay out of our business?" Margarete said as sweetly as she could.

"**Do you feel like I have invaded your territory? You should be thankful. You've all thrived with the removal of your competition. Alphas of your territories. The blood I've shed has provided a near limitless foundation, but the authorities have followed those murders and assassinations to each of you. They're following you.**"

"So they follow all us here!" The Russian's voice elevated. The rest of the guests murmured in agreed vicissitude.

"**I have taken care of it. We will not be interrupted.**"

"Why are you doing this for us?" Olive asked politely.

"**For you?**" The Phantom asked deeply. "**I agreed not to go anywhere near your organisations.**"

In several locations around the globe, occurring almost simultaneously, men and women broke from their ranks. Their friends and colleagues watched them leave hurriedly. They made their way to the entrances. Some in compounds, some in buildings, and some in enclosed estates. Together, they unlocked the doors and gates, letting in a cold breeze.

"Glad to hear it," Margarete breathed.

"**But you do not own any…**" Phantom said plainly.

The guests' perplexed looks twitched with agitation. The Panther's right ear turned slightly. The Phantom observed it twitch and listen out. His eyes looked for the source; a couple of the guests were subtly pushing away from the table. "**They belong to me.**" He said finally.

Once the entrances were unlocked, the hosts stepped aside. Multiple units lined up and stormed past. They wore full military-grade gear and advanced quickly with their high-powered rifles raised at eye level.

In Washington, the Lady Danger led her squads into the coastal warehouse to take rightful ownership. Smoke and stun grenades discombobulated the tenants. She let them writhe and bleed under her boot as an army of men flooded to every corner of the property.

In Russia, Mahkahr Stepanov led his company through the houses of the remaining mafias. Bloodlines with decades of power and influence wiped out of existence. He carried a baby boy away from the carnage, passing the swarms of men rushing into the mansion. Behind them, the Mafia's assets were seized over the bodies of dazed and choking men.

Tadao's men on the coasts of China and Japan subjugated their masters, then left them bleeding over the floors of the properties they fought so hard for. Years of work and invaluable gain were stripped from the walls. The bare architecture burned and crumbled around the bodies of those who remained loyal to the end.

Garrick gripped his cigar and looked down at the courtyard of the complex. His men dragged the last of the bosses to the middle and kicked them to their knees in a line. He turned away with a smile as their throats were cut. On his way out, he pressed his cigar into the petrol on the wall. Flames spread over the blood-soaked walls and engulfed the hallways. Blood in the courtyard seeped into the hot cartridges that had rolled between the stone tiles.

The collective besiegement outnumbered the guests' men by nearly four to one.

"What do you mean?" Asked Olive.

"Your reign has come to an end." The Phantom stated.

The men kicked over the tables and shattered the glasses. Some shot at the walls and decorations on their way out. Strippers climbed down from their stages and ran into the back with the bartenders. The club's music had been replaced with classical. The Lady danced a graceful ballet on the centre stage. Her men marched out, paying her no attention. Foreign blood was splattered across her face, almost matching her rose-red lipstick that stretched with her gleeful smile.

"That isn't part of the agreement!" The balding man spoke out.

"I've had enough, I want to speak with the Grandmasters!" Margarete called over the increasing volume of complaints.

"We will not tolerate-"

The Phantom slammed his fist on the table with such sudden speed and force that everyone, including the Panther, flinched and froze. They stared at him with wide remorseful eyes. Every muscle in his body was tensing. He took in a deep pacifying breath, then laid his hand on the Panther's back to calm it. The candle flames flickered in the glassy reflections of the Panther's bright, round eyes. Behind the calm of the Phantom's eyes raged a storm of raw fluctuating ferocity. A half tamed fury waiting to lash out like a lion surrounded by overconfident housecats. The room remained inhumanly still for many eternal moments.

"I have waited years… to look you all in the eyes and tell you… I *hate* you. You, your practice, disgusts me. I used to believe that the nature of humanity as a whole was responsible for the decline of the planet and its inhabitants, like a virus that had grown stronger than its host. But that's not a fair assessment. Its people like you that are responsible. People who don't care… who feed off the good in this world, leaving it sick and decaying." He surveyed the table, basking in each of their petrified faces, savouring them. "Some of you deal in drugs, some of you in arms. Because of you, the streets are filled with violence and poison. You will notice no one at this table deals in flesh. Those people deserve only a slow, *agonizing* death… which I granted to every one of them… personally."

The Panther rose to a seating position and licked its front legs. The guests dared not make even a fraction of a sound, nor look at the Phantom directly.

"This is the end of your era… This world will not miss you. Your children will get your money, and be spared of your insidious influence."

Two of the men near the other end of the table stood up and prepared to leave, averting their eyes. Margarete and three others signalled for their men to come down to them.

The Phantom waited with them. Their hearts pounded against their heaving chests. They could feel the weight of apprehension in their diaphragms, making their breathing more desperate. The bodyguards on each level remained in place and stared blankly at the guests, evoking a rise in their panic.

"**Take your seats.**" The Phantom demanded.

Bodyguards around the table forced the guests back into their seats and pushed their chairs in. Those on the balconies above stepped forward to look down at them. The guests gripped the table, looking incredulously around the room.

"**I want you to know… that I was never going to let you live. This is inevitable for all those who reap the rewards of profitable epicaricacy.**" The Phantom said with vehement disdain.

Syndicate members stepped past the bodyguards and stood directly behind the guests.

"**LOOK AT ME. I want to see it in your eyes when you feel the cold harsh reality pressing against your skulls.**" The Phantom growled sadistically.

The Syndicate members took out their pistols and pressed the barrels against the backs of the guests' heads. The guests tensed and recoiled inside themselves. They forced themselves to look sideways at the Phantom, trembling yet paralytic.

"**This… your reckoning.**" The Phantom's bright green eyes dilated with fiendish and wrathful pleasure.

Chapter XVI
Fallen From Grace
London, England
10:26 GMT, Tuesday, 1st November 2016
(The next day)

Christian was sitting on the floor with his back against the wall. He stared into space, his arms resting on his knees. The window above him overlooked the now empty street that once featured hundreds of photos of him and his friends. Gentle sunlight filled the empty offices from his right. The only thing he could hear was the decaying ringing in his ears.

Arthur Euwin came in with a quiet, fatherly demeanour. Christian expected him to pull up a chair, but instead, he sat on the floor against the wall at a respectable distance.

"How are you feeling?" Euwin asked genuinely.

Christian had to think for a moment. "I'm not even sure," he said. His breathing sounded controlled like he had to do it manually.

"Let's start with physical." Euwin said after a kind pause.

"They cleared me," said Christian.

"I'm not asking them." Euwin looked sideways at him. "Decompression sickness is no joke, you can't just shrug it off."

"I'm fine," Christian said drearily.

"No. You're not." Euwin's voice easily overshadowed Christian's. "Every available officer is out there cleaning up. We haven't stopped rounding-up suspects in the past four hours. Local hospitals are assisting police with the number of dead appearing all over the city."

"Then why are you here? Why let me stay?" Christian

lolled his head to meet Euwin's eyes. The bags under his own quivered and twitched.

"Because the Phantom attacked *your team* personally. He's been busy, and I need you back now more than ever."

"*He* knew you would. Where's Dennis?" Christian asked exhaustedly.

"He went home to his family. My guess is we won't hear from him until he's ready." Euwin sighed.

"And the others?"

"I'm not entirely sure but I can tell you it's not good. They're shaken, same as you, and I believe that was the Phantom's intention."

Christian grinded his teeth at the sound of his name.

"He could have killed you two, in our own bloody headquarters, but he didn't. Why?" Euwin asked firmly.

"I don't know," Christian said disgruntledly.

"There's a lot we don't know, but we need to understand. We traced the broadcast of that little girl-"

A childish giggle echoed through Christian's head like a ghostly bell.

"-to the network that hosted them all."

Christian snapped back into focus. "What do you mean?"

"We weren't the only ones playing his Game. There are nineteen other countries suffering just like us. We believe he's following up on the threat he made in South Africa, he marked all twenty with his symbol. Our broadcast was a dead end but the US traced theirs to one location."

"Because that's where he was-"

"That's where he *is*. He's still there." Said Euwin.

Christian met Euwin's gaze equally. "It's not a lead…" he said.

"No. It's not." Euwin agreed.

"He'll be expecting us. We'll have to change our approach." Christian raised his eyebrows.

"Yes. We will." Euwin agreed identically.

Christian's mind began to wake up. It started processing the incomprehensible turn of events, evoking fractions of pain and humiliation that boiled into rage.

"That's why I need you to take the lead. It's a battle of wits, and it's not going to be clean." Euwin said in a low voice.

"I need Joel… and Dennis and Cait. I need the team." Christian was trembling with indignation.

"They're in pieces. It's going to take time for them to put themselves back together. But I need to act now, Chris. The window is closing. What do you need me to do?"

Christian's lips quivered with a thousand words a minute. "Buy me some time, ill deal with the others," he said finally.

"How much?" Euwin asked. He got up slowly and helped Christian do the same.

Christian's knees trembled but held. "Freeze everything. Preserve everything and everyone you can get your hands on. Don't let anything slip between the cracks."

"US border control has already begun the strictest military intervention the world has ever seen. He's not going anywhere."

"It's not enough." Christian's breathing quickened. "Help them, send the Navy-"

"They're big enough to handle it themselves, we have our own island to worry about." Euwin countered.

"So were the Chinese! He made it through the red curtain *twice* and they hadn't an inkling of when, or where, or how. Send ships to their coasts, tremor sensors at the north and south borders, submarines with sonar at the oceans-"

"Alright," Euwin said strongly. "I'll see what I can do, but I can't promise all of that."

Christian held onto the windowsill as he caught his breath. "Don't pull on any of his threads."

"I can only stall for so long, so you had better hurry."

"Get me a flight to DC," said Christian.

"I'll send Martin with you-"

"No. It has to be Dennis." Christian could breathe normally at last. "Euwin…"

"Yes?" Euwin stopped.

"There was a man last night," Christian said softly, "He said he knew about the rogue militia. The police killed him-"

"I know." Euwin confirmed.

Christian had to calm himself for a moment. "Who gave the order?"

"I don't know," Euwin admitted.

"How could you not know!?"

"The order came from British command but I have yet to find out who. They're hiding."

Christian calmed himself once more. "Are… are the British involved in the rogue militia?"

"I believe so. But you have more immediate concerns, let me deal with our own." Euwin spoke earnestly with his hand on Christian's shoulder.

Christian recalled all he could about Euwin. There was no logical or beneficial reasoning for his actions if he was an agent of the Syndicate. With trust in full question, having Euwin on their side meant everything.

Virginia, United States of America
11:12 EST, Wednesday, 16ᵗʰ November 2016
(15 days later)

Everything had gone still in the two weeks since the Game. Euwin couldn't get any support sent over. Their Navy was already being stretched thin over various hotspots around the world. It mattered not, the US had more than enough to seal the country.

The agencies were working overtime almost daily to keep up with the aftermath. MI6 strictly prohibited actively going out to pursue the Syndicate. They could not afford to fall prey to the Phantom's play in a time of such weakness and chaos. With Dawson's help, Christian tore through weeks of red tape in days and forced the US department of defence into submission with relentless diatribes. It almost took too long for them to understand; protocol was predictable.

The only leads that followed through were those unrelated. Open and shut cases, some forcibly reopened, possible only with the information provided by the Syndicate. By the end, there were so many chairs and offices vacated that nearly two percent of the law and intelligence workforce was arrested or under suspicion. Fear replaced the faith of many, reducing their numbers further.

"In the UK as well?" The agent asked.

Joel nodded limply.

"When did this start, Joel?" The agent asked sternly.

Joel was still feeling a little shaky. He didn't have the energy to lift his head all the way. "What do you mean?" He asked groggily.

"Everyone else is saying it started with you. Now, when did it start?"

Joel thought for a moment. A particular day stood out in his mind. "I started to investigate them myself, early this year," he said, pinching from his temples to the ridge of his nose. "I guess it started the day I called MI6. The interview that day gave me what I needed to... set things in motion."

"Were they watching you back then?" The agent asked.

"No," Joel shook his head weakly, "I don't think so. There's no way..."

"How long ago was this?" The agent wrote something on his notepad.

"What do you want from me?" Joel spat.

"We just want to understand." The agent smiled kindly.

"So do we. I don't know why you're asking us, we're at the forefront of the investigation..." Joel stuttered.

"Calm down. Why don't you-"

"No why don't you do us a favour and stop wasting our fucking time! You can go and ask the Phantom yourself!" Joel held the sling around his arm and stormed out.

"Hello."
"Lucy, how are you?"
"Why are you calling, Chris?"
"We need you back here... and I wanted to know how you were doing."
"I don't want to come back."
"I know. I know, ok? But we still need to talk. We need your side of the story."
"I told them everything already-"
"I need it from you, Lucy. Where are you?"
"I'm staying with my sister."
"Just... Please come and talk to us."

"I'm not going to stay."
"I know. I'm not asking you to."

Sophie drifted past to answer the door. Caitlin was fiddling with her phone, itching for it to vibrate with a new message. Ben must have been busy the last couple of days. Talking to him and her brothers was as close as she could get to home. With that, her phone had become something of an obsession.

Sophie had taken to exercising religiously. They would do it together sometimes, rarely talking. Sophie refused to go see her niece and nephew but her brothers would visit every so often. It seemed they were also too busy to talk the last couple of days. Caitlin dared not consider the coincidence but as Joel had put it, there were no more coincidences.

The more time went on without seeing her own family, the more Caitlin inadvertently thought of Sophie's brothers as a sort of extended family. It felt all the better when they treated her the same. Thanks to them it didn't take long until Sophie was recharged with a peaking vengeance. Something about their past reminded Sophie of her ability to overcome and fight. Caitlin just admired their support quietly. She had yet to pick herself up from the dirt. Their attempts at motivation did nothing for her. All it was worth would amount to nothing. They were ignorant to what foes she and Sophie faced. If Sophie were to reveal the burn marks on her palms, maybe then they would understand better. But their hearts were in the right place, and that's all it took for Sophie to gain strength. The Phantom thought of family as a weakness holding them back, but watching Sophie exercise, watching her bench weights like she had a feud with gravity, was watching the growth of redemption that could only be possible from her brothers' influence.

However, something grotesque had attached itself to Caitlin. Not the words of the Phantom's message, but the intent, an idea, infected her. Maybe the others didn't understand because they were taught and trained to think themselves above the threats of criminals or terrorists. But the Phantom was right with one thing; they leaned too heavily on the agency's ability to justify them. Caitlin was trained to take every threat seriously. If the enemy pointed a gun you had to assume it was loaded, and that they had every intention of firing with immaculate aim. In the military she learnt to see the difference between a feint and a threat. Most threats are feints disguised for the illusion of power. The Phantom had made one single threat. He crushed them between his hands, threatening to finish them off. He chose not kill them though it could have been so easy. It was more than a display, it was a demonstration. Something Caitlin couldn't help but take more seriously. How the others did not see what they were truly up against she could not understand, but one thing they learnt universally was finishing the mission. Her greatest fear above all was the fate of their decisions. Playing into the Phantom's game would be the end of them. Her friends, all they had done, and all they stood for would mean nothing. Ash and dirt over which the Phantom's empire would rise. Graves sinking under the concrete of his foundations, pushed deeper into insignificance by the weight of his victory. When, if at all, would the cause worth fighting for become something worth dying for?

"Cait..." Sophie called from down the hall.

Caitlin got up and looked around with her phone still in hand. Sophie was holding the door open and leaning aside. Owen was standing up straight in the middle of the doorway. He made eye contact with Caitlin but didn't avert his gaze. He stood at the ready, saying nothing, returning her bitter expression.

Dennis and Henry stood apart with their arms crossed, watching James play outside through the glass doors. He kicked his soccer ball against the wall and fumbled with fancy tricks.

"He'll be safe." Dennis nodded more to himself.

"Do you believe that? Honestly?" Henry asked.

"I have to. I don't know what I'd do if I didn't." Said Dennis.

"I don't think you do believe it. Makes me wonder why you're here." Henry didn't take his eyes off his son.

"I chose this over my family." Dennis said through gritted teeth. "I don't even know where they are, the only comfort I have is knowing they're as safe as they can be. *We* have a mission. A duty that is *our* responsibility, I can't just pass it on to some other poor bloke with a family of his own. I helped start this. I have to see it through."

"We also have a duty as fathers!"

"We're not just doing this for our kids!"

"The Phantom knew about James' mother. He's not safe with her." Henry said, watching James again.

"Not while the Phantom roams free. But we can do something about that." Dennis countered.

Henry's eyes wondered as he considered it. "How are we supposed to do that?" He asked despairingly.

"Things have changed," said Henry, "The rules have changed."

They formed a crooked circle around the room. Joel was slumped in a chair beside a desk. He leaned on his good arm to make space for his other. Sophie was standing against the desk on the other end with her arms crossed. To her left, Caitlin was leaning back against the wall, her hand gripping the phone in her pocket. Lucy was sitting on a chair in front of Caitlin. She held her knees against her chest and leaned her head on them. Henry was sitting on the floor near the corner beside her, with Owen standing up straight on his left. Then to Owen's left, Dennis stood opposite Joel with his hands on hips. Between them, Dawson pulled up a regular wooden chair and wedged it up against the handle of the door. He groaned as he stood up straight and leaned on his crutch to face everyone. Christian watched from the corner behind Dennis.

"Thank you all for coming," Dawson said strongly. "It's been a while since we were all in the same room. But don't worry, while you were all taking time off, Chris and I were getting some work done. Vacations over, now it's time to talk."

"What is there to say," Sophie mumbled.

Dawson raised his hand to stop her and shook his head. "Let me tell you what's going to happen. Each of you is going to stop moping. You're not going to bitch or whine. You're going to stop feeling sorry for yourselves and you're going to talk. Like adults."

"How inspiring," said Henry.

Christian put his hand on Dawson's shoulder before he could respond. "You're going to do it, or we've already lost. We *should* talk about what happened and forgive each other but we're out of time and quite frankly I don't want to give... *him*... the satisfaction."

"That means put a fuckin pin in it and let's get back to work. We're here to talk about our next move." Dawson said gruffly. "A lot has happened that you don't even know about and Chris and I have managed to keep it under control... just."

"You mean by sealing off the country?" Caitlin asked

vindictively.

"Oh trust me that's going to get a whole lot worse soon." Said Dawson.

"Why!?" Caitlin shot.

"Because I told them to." Christian stepped forward. Caitlin towered over him but he stood confidently in front of her. "We're isolating the Phantom as best we can. Ben won't be answering because he's been placed in protective custody per my instruction."

"Who gave you the right to do that!?" Caitlin let go of her phone, seething.

"Common fucking sense, Caitlin!" Christian didn't flinch.

"Why wasn't I informed!?" She asked indignantly.

"The same reason no one else was informed when their families were taken in: Because it wasn't done officially." Christian said in a hushed tone. "The UK is just as strict with everything getting in and out, it had to be done off record and untraceably."

"If they're so strict why did they let you two leave and not us?" Joel asked hoarsely.

"They didn't." Dennis said plainly.

"We're confined to British soil under paid work leave." Christian added.

"But you're here… working…" said Owen.

"The word you're looking for is treason." Christian said cheerfully.

"Only about half the work we've been doing is legal." Dawson shrugged.

"And that's how things are going to be." Christian said finally. "The reason we're all here, even though we don't want to be, is because we are the only people we know we can trust…

and rely on. The point of the Phantom's Game was to tear us apart. Specifically us. I didn't realise it until I heard you weren't on speaking terms. The details of what happened has surely circled through every agency involved. Why else would so many people be tapping out, Quitting, unless they're afraid."

"Why didn't he just kill us?" Henry asked.

"Kill us and others will take our place, then he must start over. Fear is his greatest weapon. Everything in the Game was designed to torment us and turn us against one another, then people will begin to lose hope, and the fear will subdue them." Christian walked around the room as he explained.

"I knew this girl," Joel said suddenly, "I got in contact with my old team at MI5. They've never been so busy. There was this girl, still in training, but she was a natural. She was determined to prove herself. So I helped her, guided her. She had a promising future." Joel looked down, a shadow of defeat covering his face. "She left them a week ago. Probably the most hopeful of them. It's already too late."

Everyone shared a moment of silence. A kind of guilt rose from the grave of hope. A feeling that they let it die.

"Everything we do from this point must stay off paper. We don't tell anybody more than they need to know." Dennis said sternly.

"What happened during the Game was not your fault," Christian directed it to everyone at once. "Don't hold it against each other. It was all the Phantom. He's the one we need."

"Remember: Trust no one outside this room." Everyone looked to Dawson as he pulled the wooden chair out from the door. "Let's get to work."

"So what's your plan?" Sophie asked, striding alongside

Dawson as he limped with his crutch.

"Not my plan. I'm just doing as he says." Dawson pointed to Christian who was leading the group toward the analyst's room.

"If you're letting Chris take the lead there's something you should know." Sophie said with a keen eye on him.

Christian stopped in his tracks and span to face her directly. "No. Here's something you should know." He pressed a finger against her shoulder. "Everything before - does not matter now. We don't work for the government. There are no politics here! We are on only one side! OURS! You understand me?"

Sophie looked deep into his eyes. Behind the anger that bore his aggression was pain. She knew that he knew what she was referring to. But she hid the same suffering that he did. It connected them by an apologetic sympathy. She wasn't mad. She was scared, same as him. She didn't want things to be the way they were, and she saw now that he didn't either. It equalized them, unifying them the way they wish they were from the beginning.

Christian lowered his hand and backed away, somewhat surprised by himself. Sophie nodded.

"What happened to him?" Caitlin asked Dennis as they started moving again.

"The Game happened." Dennis said simply.

"He's tired of losing," said Joel.

"There's a lot of that going around," said Owen.

When they reached the analyst's room, Dawson scared off the people inside and locked the door behind them.

"First thing's first," Dennis began, "While everyone was dying and the police were scattered after us, the final round was a bomb threat in the city that connected to the other countries playing the Game. As you know, Iran was the chosen to be attacked. Fortunately, only eight people died."

"What you didn't know was that while that was all happening, the Syndicate was culling criminal organisations in every city that was busy with their own bomb threat." Christian said as he brought out a hard drive and connected it to one of the computers.

"Lucy," Dawson gestured to the computer.

Lucy looked down with her arms crossed.

"What's the matter?" Dawson asked.

"I don't want to be a part of this anymore. I Quit. I'm sorry." Said Lucy.

"Look I know you're scared, but we need you. You're one of the few people we can really trust." Dawson said softly.

Lucy shook her head without looking up.

"Look at me, Lucy." Dawson held her arms gently. "We know what we're up against, we can protect you now. You're going to be here at your desk, safe and sound, I promise."

"I'm too scared to go to my own apartment," said Lucy.

"You don't need to leave," said Owen, "You can stay in the building under our protection. There's nowhere safer."

"Owen will even stay with you." Dawson said quickly.

"I-"

Dawson gave him a quick but reprimanding look.

"I'll stay with you." Owen smiled.

Lucy looked at them both. "Would they even allow that?"

"Lucy," Christian said from behind Dawson, "What part of any of this makes you think we care what we're allowed to do."

Lucy giggled nervously, filling everyone with sanguine contentment. Even if for a moment, propitious hope had come back to life for the first time since before the Game. Lucy then took her seat in front of the computer and brought up the data about the final round.

"The broadcast was traced to a club on the outskirts of Washington, which just so happens to be the only club with a shady background that wasn't hit by the Syndicate's purge." Dennis pointed to its approximate location on the map.

"So it's a trap," said Joel.

"It's a trap." Christian confirmed. "And since we have to assume that we're always being watched and bugged, we cannot be seen going anywhere near it."

"If we're always bugged then why are we talking in a room full of computers?" Caitlin asked.

"We already had it wiped," said Dawson.

"Thoroughly," Christian added.

"What do you plan to do with the place?" Henry asked.

"A witness from one of the other clubs is going to serve time for possession. With a little luck, we might be able to approach her without the Syndicate knowing." Said Christian.

"And do what, exactly?" Joel asked. "You put a wire on her and you will be sending her to her death."

"The club is still open, all she will need to do is apply for a job and be herself." Said Dennis.

Joel rubbed the back of his head uncomfortably.

"This would take some time to get approved so I'm guessing we're skipping that part?" Sophie asked.

"What part?" Dawson asked rhetorically. He and Christian led the group out again.

"The goal of this is the Grandmaster's meeting. Since the Syndicate's purge multiple 'persons of interest', some of which we've spoken to, have gone missing." Said Dennis.

"The club in question is tied to Michael Shartley, who

was last seen the night of the Game." Said Dawson. "He's likely either dead or captured. All we need to know is where he went."

"Either way it means the meeting has already happened. But we're going to keep the Phantom under the idea that don't know that. Dawson, its time." Christian stopped and gave him the nod.

"I'll get the stripper. Owen, come." Dawson left alongside Owen.

"Henry, Cait, we're going to need a way to set up surveillance of the club without being seen anywhere near it. Assume you're always being followed but don't let them know that you know. Sophie, take Lucy, make sure she has her things and a place to stay. Dennis, let Euwin know we're not going to be available for a while. See if there are any updates from his side." Christian was about to turn away when he remembered one last thing. "And take your time. We need to look busy but not too busy."

Christian left with Joel. Nobody moved. They looked confusedly from Christian to Dennis.

"Do as he says." Dennis said plainly. He left at a casual walking pace. Sophie turned back the way they came with Lucy. Henry led Caitlin the same way Dawson left.

Joel walked alongside Christian in uncomfortable silence. "Where are we going?" He asked, looking ahead.

"I need your help looking through something." Said Christian.

Joel held back until they reached an old storage room full of cabinets and shelves. He closed the door behind them and finally spoke out. "So you have no issue sending this woman to her death?"

"You once used criminals as bait to draw out the Syndicate-"

"That was before he made me kill them myself." Joel said harshly.

Without looking at Joel, Christian put down the box he was holding. "I'm sorry you had to do that. But you had to do it."

"And I'm not going to do it again if we have any other choice," said Joel.

"There's no other way inside that club. It's the only active link to the Syndicate that we know of. Help me look through these and maybe we can find another." Christian poured the box of documents onto the table.

"Why can't we just raid the club?"

"You know why!" Christian said forcefully.

"They could just as easily be expecting an infiltrator!" Joel yelled equally as loud.

"She's not even going to wear a wire! She will gain their trust and report back to us indirectly." Christian said finally.

Joel rubbed the back of his head. "With units on standby."

"There was going to be anyway." Christian shrugged.

"I still don't like it," said Joel.

"I know, but it's happening with or without your help."

"Whatever's on your mind you may as well speak up now." Dawson said in a low voice.

"You think it's about what happened during the Game," said Owen.

"The men who stalled your fiancé's case are being investigated. We'll find out the truth soon enough. I need you to stay focused." Dawson gave him a stern look.

"I bet you do." Owen said bitterly.

"You can interrogate them all you want when we're done. Believe it or not there are more important things to think about right now." Dawson tried hard to control his temper.

"When we were in South Africa I looked down on them. I was disappointed by how dirty their government was. How corrupt they were. It made me feel proud of what we have here." Owen dropped his voice, "we're just as bad… we're just better at hiding it. I want nothing to do with them."

"There are still good people on our side," said Dawson, "And they're going to help us do whatever we need to do."

"You trust them? How did the Phantom know but not us?" Owen asked.

"We can talk about this later." Dawson whispered aggressively. He pacified his anger seeing the prison guards escorting the stripper towards them. Per his request, the visiting room was empty. The woman sat opposite them. The guards then removed her handcuffs and left the room.

"Stacey Warner, is it?" Said Dawson.

"Yes." She nodded.

"You were working as an exotic dancer at the Pink Dolphin when it was attacked?" Dawson asked.

"Yes." She said again.

"Alright listen very carefully, Stacey, we don't have a lot of time. You're meant to be transferred to a state prison for possession, but we can change that. Do some work for us and we can get you off with community service instead of prison time." Dawson said simply.

"What do you want me to do?" She asked, taken aback.

"We want you to become a confidential informant. We have reason to believe the organisation who attacked the Pink Dolphin are residing in another club on the west side of the city. We want you to go in and work for them, then report back to us." Dawson said in a hushed tone.

"What if they attack again?" She asked. Her wide eyes and closed body language indicated hesitance.

"It's their property. They won't attack themselves." Dawson assured her.

"You won't be wearing a wire, all you will need to do is work as normal and try to hang around the men in charge, listen in on their conversations." Owen explained.

"How dangerous is it?" She asked.

"There will be a SWAT team on standby in case there's any trouble." Said Dawson.

Stacey rubbed her wrists where the cuffs had pulled at her skin. "I don't know how," she confessed.

"Don't worry," said Dawson, "You will be sent home with instructions hidden among your community service papers. Everything you need to know will be on there."

"Being a confidential informant also means that all of this remains confidential." Owen said quietly.

"That means you don't tell anyone about this. If anyone asks, this meeting was to ask about the attack and give you a reduced sentence in exchange for your cooperation. Your community service will be near the club and so that is why you will be moving to that area. The reason you don't talk as much is because of your trauma. Is that understood?" Dawson asked kindly.

Stacey nodded. She still had a concerned expression but no signs of changing her mind.

"For your safety you won't be reporting to anyone in person, so follow your instructions carefully." Dawson gestured for the guards to collect her. "Remember, don't talk to anyone about this. Everything will be taken care of for you. Good luck."

Virginia, United States of America
22:29 EST, Friday, 25th November 2016
(9 days later)

On Wednesday the twenty-third of November, US president Thomas Cameron gave a speech regarding the recent bombing in Iran. It would go down in history as the most heart-felt load of bullshit ever to be said by a US president. It had nothing to do with the bombing (that occurred almost a month prior) and everything to do with a recent surge in political discord that no one was aware of.

Meanwhile, the operation was up and running. Over the week it had become easier to work in secret. Stacey was working as often as she could to pay for her new apartment. From her eavesdropping and planted bugs, she had the entire building under audio surveillance. Thus there were two agents and a couple of officers in the opposite building at any given time.

The Syndicate was careful. Chatter rarely turned toward the Syndicate itself. There had been mention of the purge that left theirs as the only good club to remain. The way they spoke as they came and went suggested they moved in shifts. Like being there was a responsibility they could enjoy. They did not argue, nor did they complain. They were content with their situation. Up until the first Friday night.

Stacey had said that Fridays were always the busiest in the service industry. The club manager had told her to prepare for a busy night, and to expect a lot more people to come.

Owen and Joel were shifted to listen in from across the street. Christian, Lucy, and Dawson were back at the CIA while everyone else was home to avoid suspicion on the Syndicate's part. There were no calls or direct messages since their phones were almost certainly tapped. From the Syndicate's perspective, it was just another evening.

The night got busier at around eight o'clock. The street was packed with cars. The club was buzzing. Owen and Joel could hear it from across the street even without the equipment.

Stacey was something of a favourite in the club. A noise complaint earlier that week led city cops to investigate. Stacey held them at the door and apologised on behalf of the owners, promising to keep their volume reasonable. Given the nature of the club and what happened inside, turning the cops away at the door went greatly appreciated. Only Stacey knew the complaint was faked and the cops were sent by Christian to help her gain her boss's trust. It got her exactly where she needed to be; anywhere she wanted. And since she kept the volume down to avoid the cops coming again, she remained trustworthy whilst ensuring it was easier to listen in on their conversations through the bugs. Even so, it was difficult to hear with the number of people there. Close to midnight they settled into quieter groups.

"*What's this news you wanted to tell us?*" One man slurred.

"*There's an update. But we don't discuss business around others.*" A second said clearly.

Joel tugged Owen's arm to get him to listen as well.

"*Come oooon, it's not business. And she doesn't care, do you, sweetheart?*" Said the first man.

There was a pause before the sober man spoke again. "*The arrangements been changed, but we do not talk about it around others.*" He said more strongly.

"*It's not like we have anywhere else to go!*" A third man said loudly.

"*Yeah this is the last good place we have!*" The first man

agreed. "*I'm sure he won't mind, ay?*" He breathed.

Joel could almost smell the alcohol on his breath through the headphones.

"*He's not the forgiving type, so you shouldn't be talking about him.*" The sober man's tone changed.

"*Oh I know haha! You seen what he's done? And I thought I was fucked up!*" The second man chuckled.

"*You need to stop talking. Now. You two – get out of here.*" The Sober man instructed.

"*Hey! No! Come on! Girls!*" The first man called out.

"*Why such an asshole, huh?*" The second man's words were stretched out and slurring slightly.

"*You're compromising this place.*" The sober man said plainly.

"*Fuck off.*"

"*This is our night off. Phantom has us working clean-up at the docks. I'm fuckin' sick of it!*"

"*Yeah the fucking smell! Aghk!*" There was a pause leaving only the distance thumping music. "*Where you going!?*" The first man yelled lazily.

No more than a few seconds later, the sound of suppressed weapons made Joel's stomach jump up through his throat. His mind synchronized the shots with the beat of the music like an illusion of disbelief. He flicked off the headphones and leapt up to his feet. "GO! THERES SHOTS FIRED!" He yelled.

"No! Hold that order!" Owen called out from behind him. The officers paused indecisively.

"What are you doing!?" Joel asked, face-to-face with Owen.

"Shhh! Look… it's too late. We can't stop them now, but we can-" A couple of high pitched screams were partially audible over the music across the street.

"Stacey is still in there!" Joel made a move but Owen grabbed and held him.

"She's already dead! There's no point giving ourselves away!" He struggled against Joel's surprising strength.

"They didn't kill her last time!" Joel tried desperately to pull away but couldn't get to the stairs.

"Listen! She didn't press her panic-button. She's dead." Owen said sympathetically. The SWAT team watched them apprehensively. "Don't engage," he said to them. "If we go in now they will know we were listening."

Joel was still pushing, but his struggling lessened.

"Targets leaving the building." Said one of the officers.

Joel and Owen rushed to either side of the window and looked out. "We can at least followed them." Said Joel.

"Call nine-one-one." Owen rushed for the stairs.

"Anonymously." Joel said as he followed.

Owen waited until the Syndicate car was far enough away before running to their own. Joel had his eye on the club as he got in. They pulled away and followed the Syndicate indirectly until they caught up. Owen's history of tailing let him blend in well enough. He would let cars come between them when he could. Joel sat uncomfortably, staring out the window but watching the Syndicate out the corner of his eye. They were headed north in no rush.

Owen began to slow as they approached the outskirts of the city. "We can't keep following them up there, that area is too isolated." They watched the Syndicate vehicle drive out of sight before heading back to a safe point close to headquarters.

"What happened? There was a nine-one-one call to the

club." Said Dawson.

"A couple of drunks said too much and the Syndicate shot up the place… then we followed them." Owen said discreetly.

"Were there any survivors?" Joel blurted.

"No." Dawson shook his head and continued talking with Owen.

Joel slowed with a cursed feeling in the pit of his stomach. He let the others walk ahead and diverged to find Christian. The numb rush he felt let him skip the stairs two at a time. There was a dizzying clarity, like something of a devil's prophet. To finally understand some nature of the Game; isolation. It was between them and the Syndicate. He shoved the door of the analyst's room and marched in.

Christian looked away as soon as he saw him. "Don't pin this on us!"

"No, you're right. Her death is on you! Only you!" Joel was shaking.

"Like every other innocent person in there? They were in the wrong place at the wrong time! It would have happened regardless of our minor intervention." Christian retorted.

"That 'minor intervention' was a living person, Chris! Stop thinking like *him*!" Joel rubbed the back of his head.

"There was no way we could know what was going to happen! He's trying to divide us! Stop giving him what he wants!" Christian yelled.

Joel took the recording out of his blazer pocket. "You got what you wanted." He threw the tape across the desks in front of Christian. "The hills and the docks. Start searching."

Virginia, United States of America
20:01 EST, Saturday, 26th November 2016
(The next day)

In the light of recent developments, new points of interest began to shine with possibility. Enigmas once hidden were outlined under a new filter. In the hills, an estate glowed with a dark and unmistakable mystique. No apparent owner. No apparent use. But the bills were paid in full and on time. Practically a trademark of the hidden Syndicate. That's the name they gave to the lesser known side of the Grandmaster's organization. The docks were a simple puzzle. The only remaining notorious owner of property by the coast was Margarete Joules, one of the many missing persons of interest. Owen was already familiar with her primary warehouse where he had picked her up once before. It had since ceased operation, until the Game. Too long later, a great deal of overdue investigation revealed an antithesis causality.

Since Margarete's disappearance, her warehouse had been at maximum capacity. A fleet of trucks had been transporting from the docks on a daily basis. Yet, there had been nothing coming in by sea. As if production was coming from the thin and salty air itself. And what more, the delivery points were exclusive to the darkest corners of the East coast. That was, at least, until recently.

Since the club shooting, nothing came or went from the estate in the hills nor the warehouse at the docks. Thus, the shift in the timeline accelerated investigative schedule. Mounting simultaneous raids (To prevent one side from getting spooked and vanishing as they so often do) meant taking their investigation to a more official level. To inevitable detriment, where there is official intervention, there is political agenda.

"Fucking bullshit-" Caitlin mumbled something under her breath.

"It doesn't matter." Said Dawson.

"They obviously want the credit." Joel leaned back in his chair.

"Yeah so what?" Dennis interjected. "They're embarrassed. They want to make up for their losses."

"What about our losses?" Caitlin asked indignantly.

"I don't care!" Dennis yelled. "I really don't. Because it doesn't matter who makes the finishing move, as long as it gets finished. So do as Secretary Miles has asked and take a backseat with me and Chris. We still have eyes in the operation."

"Something tells me this order doesn't come straight from Secretary Miles," Dawson suggested.

"You think someone higher? Like the president?" Christian asked.

"Miles never had a problem with your involvement. Cameron is way more likely to see this politically." Dawson scratched his chin which was sprouting a short and scruffy beard.

"Doesn't matter who it was. They don't want us to take part then fine. Owen and Sophie are still on the inside." Dennis shrugged.

"They said you can't take part." Dawson said loudly as he moved to the operations room. "They didn't say you can't watch. Move aside!" He yelled at the security members by the entrance. Dennis, Caitlin, Joel, and Christian followed him inside. Henry was speaking on the comms at a desk on the left.

Christian fiddled with the note in his hand. It span and twirled in synchronicity with the idea in his mind: It needed to be done all at once. Every end tied. They had to do it now. All at once. Every end tied. By whom? He gripped the note and walked up beside Dawson. "Doesn't matter who does the job as long as it gets done. Right?"

Dawson's eyes narrowed. "Spit it out, Taylor."

"The club has a twin. A sister." Christian said under his breath.

"Why are you only telling me now?" Dawson growled.

"It's been closed for almost a year but the bills are still being payed to this day."

"That doesn't answer my question, Chris." Dawson pacified his tone.

"All three locations need to be taken at the same time, these two are already going to be on record. It may not be a terrible idea keeping at least one to ourselves…" Christian whispered.

Dawson watched the feed from the SWAT teams head-cams come up on the monitors.

"We also happen to have a couple of off-record officers…" said Christian. The two of them looked back at Caitlin and Joel, who returned bewildered glares.

"Go." Dawson commanded.

"Here's the location." Christian handed him the note, then left with Caitlin, Joel, and Dennis in his wake.

"Sophie's ready, so is Owen. Who's unit zero?" Henry asked.

"Don't worry about them, they're only here for the Phantom." Dawson said, watching the head-cam feeds.

"Where are they going?" Henry asked.

Dawson saw him watching the others leave and knelt down to explain quietly. "-Be ready to dispatch backup to them if necessary." He said, leaving the note on Henry's desk.

"Yes, sir." Said Henry.

Sophie watched the windows through her binoculars. The lights around the estate came on shortly after the sun had set. The lights inside had been on since before she arrived.

"*ETA: five minutes.*" Said Henry.

Sophie kept watch of the estate. There had been little to no activity throughout the day. The element of surprise carried far more weight against the Syndicate. No sirens this time.

"*Two minutes, Sophie.*"

She did one last scan of the estate before putting the binoculars down. Then she picked up her gun and torch carefully. The temporary aluminium office she was in belonged to a plumbing company doing maintenance checks on the city's highland sewage infrastructure. By coming in from the hill behind, she could use the cover of trees to sneak in. Yet she still had an uneasy feeling. A paranoia that, just maybe, they knew she was there. There were no cameras. No witnesses. But the uneasy feeling remained, and somewhat supernatural in nature.

Owen was hiding behind two towers of wooden crates at the docks. He could see parts of the warehouse through the slits. The outside was lit up but there was no way to see inside.

"*ETA: sixty seconds.*" Said Henry.

Owen gripped his gun and torch. He kept looking between the warehouse doors and entrance gate down the road.

Squad cars and SWAT vans came racing up the hill on Sophie's right. She opened the door of the office slowly with her gun at the ready. With the sun set, everything had been reduced to shadows and silhouettes. She leaned the door open but stopped herself switching on the flashlight. It felt safer not knowing what lurked in the hollows of the dark, for until she revealed herself, they would know not that she hid among them. The vans parked outside the estate. She kicked away from the office and ran towards them.

As Owen approached them, he used his hand to give the flashing signal with his torch. He joined the SWAT units and prepared to breach the first door of the warehouse. Thus far no response to their arrival.

Sophie stood beside the SWAT members with her gun and torch aimed at the ground. They brought out a hand-held battering ram and prepared to breach the first door.

They rammed the door just beside the handle and pulled back. Then instead of a second swing, the SWAT members threw the ram aside. The door was ajar. The force of the hit had caused the already open door to bounce and swing open slightly. Taken aback, they opened it all the way with every sight and scope locked onto the inside.

Owen saw nothing. There was just blackness beyond. He knew the way around from last time and directed the units accordingly.

Sophie was welcomed by the gentle orange glow of oil lamps and candles. The smell of smoke and mature wood greeted them as they entered. One unit left, one right, then two in the middle. They advanced around the circular table in the middle. On it was a bouquet of dead and decaying roses inside a crystal vase. Sophie followed the maroon carpets down dark oak corridors deeper into the estate.

The original salty smell of the warehouse was thick with decay. This time, the only sound was that of their heavy boots on the damp concrete floor. Every room they breached on the way was as deserted as the next. Owen stepped to one side for a moment. The rooms seemed less than vacant, like they weren't even used. They were full of old junk from around the property. The perturbing realisation presented itself much too late; whatever they were exporting came from the main warehouse.

Deliveries may not have been made above the surface of the water that they monitored so closely.

"Sir," said a man from behind.

Dawson's mesmerized focus broke off. "What!?" He spat.

"A girl just came in saying she was being held by the Syndicate," said the man.

Dawson and Henry looked uneasily at each other. "Go deal with her." Dawson commanded.

"Why me?" Henry asked.

"You know why! Go take her to Christian or something." Dawson went back to watching the cam feed on the monitors.

Every unit reported vacancy throughout the estate. The SWAT team in front of Sophie was about to enter a set of double doors when she noticed a mess on the carpet. After a point, the maroon melted into a bright and splendid red like a reverse stain. The red was the carpet's original colour, not a blood stain as Sophie first thought. The rest of the carpet was stained maroon. It had been darkened by something. There was no smell of faeces, but a grave realism brought Sophie back to her original assumption; the red of the carpet could be darkened by a darker red, like that of blood. Except, the maroon was much darker, similar to how blood stains darken and even turn brown over time.

Something at the foot of the door caught Owen's attention. The damp on the floor thickened and seemed to almost clot. He had dismissed the damp as water, only seeing it at the edges of his torchlight. When he pointed his torch directly at the ground, the true underlying colour of brownish-maroon was revealed. Mostly in the centre of the hallways. It led under the door they were preparing to breach, behind which awaited the main warehouse.

"WAIT! CALL THEM OFF!" Henry came running through the security.

"Why? What happened!?" Dawson turned to ask.

"The girl said she was being held by the Syndicate," Henry said, slightly out of breath. "Says she knows where they are-"

"Where!?"

"THERE." Henry pointed at the monitors of both operations.

Dawson looked between them all. "Hold position!" He commanded loudly. The command was relayed but too late.

One of the SWAT members had pushed the double doors open. They swung and bounced back on their hinges. The unit was moving in quickly, but Sophie hesitated with her speed. The large room was lit by the same glow of gentle flickering flames. There were units coming in on the balconies above. They filled every corner of the room in seconds and stopped outside another two pairs of double doors on the right. Sophie turned left to get a better look at the men around the great oval table. Their heads rested on the gleaming polished wood. Their backs arched away from beautifully carven chairs. In front of each head, just a few inches away, was a thin but deep hole. The varnish was singed around the outsides. On the inside it gave way to the natural colour of the mahogany wood. Old and drying pools of blood soaked into the flattened faces of the men. Sophie noticed one woman at the table, and one empty chair on the end. From where she stood, she could see the angle of clean entry and the fragments of brain and skull that had sprayed over the immaculate sheen. Some of the holes had filled with blood. Once bubbling from the heat of the bullet beneath, now soaked into the wood. The SWAT units flooded in from all sides and left through the double doors at the other end of the table. As Sophie began to follow them, she noticed paw prints in the last puddle of blood. They trailed onto the ground, through the doorway, and around the corner into the unknown.

Owen opened the door himself, breaking the old and crusted blood underneath. The warehouse was darker than the previous rooms. There wasn't a single source of light coming in. It stank in a way he could not quite describe. A hard metal thudding came from somewhere on the other side. As the rest of the squads entered behind Owen, a dozen flashlights lit up the entire floor. More damp stained the concrete but outlined footprints in all directions. Owen walked toward the centre. "There's nothing here." He said, shining his torch at every empty corner of the warehouse. The thudding turned to pounding at the large ocean-side entrance gate. A couple of men went over to break the locks from the inside and let in the squad on the other side. They slid the large gate aside and came in, letting in a cold, harsh breeze that shook the tall, jagged ceiling exactly like chains. They stopped pushing it half way, just enough to let a little light show them what they already knew. Owen and a couple of others ordered them to open it all the way for more light and access. As the gate squealed on its track, more of the wind from outside rattled the ceiling. Owen Stopped. He was surrounded by a gentle cacophony of rattling chains. The sound bounced around overhead in light waves that decayed but never died. With each gust of wind, a new wave would be sent bouncing through thousands of chains to all corners of the warehouse. Owen looked up with repugnance at the jagged and lumpy ceiling. He raised his flashlight tentatively. First were the outlines of a thousand crowded feet swaying in waves. Then shins, legs, waists, pale and dirty. Limp and motionless hands on the ends of limp and motionless arms.

All hanging from taut chains wrapped around bruised necks. Pale, bloated faces stared blankly down at him and the others. Their bodies swayed, constantly rubbing against one another. Bullet holes and knife wounds had gone black and rotten with old blood stains trailing down to their feet. Every torch was now lighting up the throng of dead hanging above them. Owen let his arms fall to his sides. He looked down at the floor and closed his eyes with a grave expression. The decaying genocide loomed above, sending a cold tingle down the back of his neck.

"Every raid across the city has found nothing, because they've all been taken to the docks." Dawson said in a defeated tone.

"The trucks…" Henry said under his breath. Regretfully distinguishing exporting from importing with an equally defeated expression. "The trucks. The girl, Dawson, she described the same truck that took her."

"Where?" Dawson asked gruffly.

"An old run-down bar. That's all she said." Henry shrugged with his hands on his hips.

"Bar or club!?" Dawson asked aggressively.

"Uhh…" Henry concentrated hard. The image of a thousand corpses was engraved into his every thought.

"What street!?" Dawson pulled something off Henry's desk.

"It was F-something road-" Henry stuttered.

Dawson opened the paper Christian had given them and showed the address to Henry, whose eyes widened as his face went cold and pale.

"Caitlin and Joel…" Dawson said remorsefully.

The main entrance to the building wasn't locked. Caitlin and

Joel entered with their guns and torches half raised. The shapes of what used to be a club had decayed it into something of an old storeroom. Worn into the layer of dust and unkempt furniture was a single path that led directly to the back corner. The air was thick with the smell of the aging carpets. But it was quiet, peaceful even.

Caitlin followed the many footprints of the path step-by-step. Filth and cobwebs covered everything. Nothing in the room appeared to have been used in months. The path rounded a corner to the left into a smaller room. There were circular tables spaced out with chairs around them. Against the right wall was a bar with empty shelves. The path split and weaved in-between the tables towards doors at the back corners. Various marks and scratches on some of the dusty tables indicated more recent use than the rest of the building.

"Here," Joel said in a half whisper.

Caitlin followed his line of site. The Syndicate's triskelion symbol had been marked in the tablecloth of dust on one of the tables. Caitlin evaluated it as Joel walked cautiously to the door on the other side of the bar.

"We're in the right place." Joel whispered.

Unlike the rest of the scratches and marks, the triskelion symbol didn't have a new layer of dust settling in. It was the single cleanest thing in the building.

"Caitlin-" Joel said slightly louder. He had his gun raised and his torch aimed through the doorway.

"This is a fresh mark-"

"There's something in there." Joel whispered. "I heard it."

Caitlin instinctively checked her corners and surroundings with military prowess.

Joel had lowered his torchlight in front of the doorway to

make his way forward, with the rest of the glow letting him see inside. At that same moment, the motion of the circular centre cast by his torch attracted a curiosity from the other side. With the two steps Joel took to round the bar, two steps brought a pair of bright yellow eyes into the light of his torch. A void of silky black fur absorbed the light, while the large round eyes reflected it right back at Joel. His breath staggered. He flicked his torch to shine in the panther's face. The panther's eyes squinted. Its pupils constricted.

"Caitlin." Joel whispered breathlessly.

Caitlin saw the reflection of the panther's eyes for a second but comprehended them in a fraction of a moment. A piece of the otherwise motionless shadow broke away from above the door behind them. The figure hit the ground with a heavy metallic thud that sent a paralyzing jolt throughout their nervous systems, leaving them tense. The static tickled their spines and necks making the hair stand up. Caitlin had to force her diaphragm to draw air into her lungs. Joel's heart beat with a force that could almost be seen through his shirt.

The Phantom straightened up to full height, just about equal to Caitlin. The springs in his prosthetic leg creaked as the ankle-joint rotated. Caitlin's own muscles battled against one another in a frightful stalemate. Joel wanted to turn around but the panther's eyes had locked with his and kept them so. Another creak of taut springs released the tension in Caitlin's body. She bent her knees and span on the spot but the Phantom already had a hand ready to grab her gun and hold the hammer back. Joel span and aimed for the Phantom's head which hid behind Caitlin's.

Phantom drove his knee into her wrist, pulled the gun from her hands, and held her arms up. Before she could pull free he twisted her arms and gripped her in a unique headlock. Her reactions granted her only a moment of panic behind a blurred sight of Joel's anxious expression. Then she used the Phantom's grip to lift herself and kick her weight down. The headlock tightened against her jugular but granted her to chance to kick against the floor and head-butt backward at the Phantom's face. He didn't release, so she quickly dropped again low enough to untangle from his python grip.

Joel moved away from the growling panther. The Phantom head-butted Caitlin and repositioned to keep her between himself and Joel. A speedy jab up at her diaphragm made her stagger back and wheeze. The panther strolled in and howled at the sight of her. Joel's reflexes redirected his aim at the panther.

"**Don't.**" The Phantom said forcefully. He held his hand out to try order the panther to back away but its dilating pupils were transfixed by Joel's gun.

Caitlin recovered hastily and kept herself at a distance from them both. Joel kept his gun aimed at the panther, looking between it and the Phantom.

"**He has no stake in this. He doesn't like guns.**" The Phantom's eyes met with Joel's.

"Why should I care!?" Joel seethed through quivering lips.

"**You of all people should know not to let innocent creatures get involved.**" The mask around the Phantom's face hardly moved as he spoke.

"*You* don't care about that! Why should I!?" Joel yelled, breathing heavily.

"**Your families were never in any danger. They still aren't. Christian had them moved but I didn't follow… because they have no stake in this either.**" Phantom said earnestly.

Caitlin managed to calm slightly, but Joel was still tensing every muscle in his arm to aim at the panther.

"I KILLED ALL THOSE CONVICTS TO STOP YOU FROM KILLING INNOCENT PEOPLE!" Joel shouted indignantly.

"I was never going to kill them, Joel, but I still had to prove the point."

Joel was on the brink of hyperventilating. His hands shook. "Fuck you." He said wrathfully.

"DON'T. This is between you and me." Phantom said more desperately.

Joel glanced at the panther and fired, hitting the top of its head. Caitlin jumped from the shot but the Phantom simply watched as the panther collapsed. His face twitched with fury.

Caitlin saw him begin to shake and lock onto Joel like a predator with growing omnipotent rage. She bent her knees a little, ready to come between them.

Joel was still shaking but returned the Phantom's wrathful glare with a fleeting fraction of the energy. His anger filtered through regret into the same intense fear he felt during the game. He felt his body weaken slightly as he aimed at the Phantom's head.

Phantom bolted forward. Caitlin grabbed a chair and swung but he caught it and used its momentum to pull her into his shoulder, cracking her chest plate and knocking her off her feet.

Joel fell victim to his reflexes and reached out to catch her with his dominant and armed hand. The Phantom took full advantage of his lowered gun by grabbing and twisting it painfully out of his hand, only to throw it over the bar. He thrust a hard punch up against Joel's ribs, another between his eyes, then grabbed and threw him effortlessly across the nearest table.

Caitlin reengaged with practiced blows, but instead of blocking or dodging, the Phantom hit them aside, bruising her knuckles. He quickly returned by rapping the side of her head and spinning the opposite way to lock her throat between his thigh and calf. His weight forced her to bend backward uncomfortably, but she could still breathe. He grabbed her hands before they could reach his leg and twisted her wrists. The more she struggled, the tighter his leg got around her neck. She could breathe a little but her head was getting light and numb. Her panic rose, and with it, her struggling attempts, which led the Phantom to tighten his leg, and cause her to panic all the more. Her vision was soon gone followed closely by her consciousness.

  When he was sure she was out, the Phantom released his leg and let her fall limply to the dirty floor. Joel was still on the floor, dazed and barely moving. He saw Caitlin fall and looked up dizzily at the Phantom. There were two bright-green, flaming eyes watching him furiously. The Phantom marched toward him pushing tables and chairs out the way with his impetus. Joel felt a burst of tingling energy through his numb body but only managed to lift his torso and raise a hand in defence. The Phantom's large fist and metallic knuckles passed around his hand and boxed his head to the floor where it bounced and left a print in the carpet. Joel's cracked cheekbone began to bleed. His glassy, half-closed eyes stared at nothing. The Phantom pushed his boot down on Joel's chest whilst his own heaved with rage-filled breaths.

Chapter XVII
The Dragon's Den
Bethesda, Maryland, United States of America
7:09 EST, Sunday, 27th November 2016
(The next day)

Everything had changed, and everything had not. They had strayed from the predictable path and found themselves at the same end. The Phantom didn't see them coming, but expected them all the same. A girl came in with the exact information they had been working for. He had become impatient. His traps were ready and he was tired of waiting.

Christian stared down at the dusty, blood soaked carpet. He thought he had learned his lesson, but the Phantom had Caitlin and Joel. The game continued.

Dennis was facilitating the crime scene investigators. He was already working towards finding them. Christian was contemplating the largest of the bloodstains. It was a large and humiliating pill to swallow, but if he wanted his friends back then he would have to play the game they were trapped within.

Back at HQ, Sophie heard crashing from behind a corner. She looked shyly around at Owen's office. He was throwing his things at his walls. A few people were staring from their desks. Sophie thought of interrupting, maybe trying to stop him. He grabbed at anything he could and launched it randomly, pausing restlessly for a moment before starting again. Sophie backed up behind the corner and kept walking until she couldn't hear it anymore.

Henry stood helplessly as Dawson tore through Christian and Joel's work. He was looking for something. Anything that could have helped them foresee the events of the previous night.

Anything that they missed. Anything that he might have missed. He eventually crushed up everything he was holding and slammed it back on the table before storming out. Lucy didn't move at all. She was still in her chair, looking without seeing. Henry put his hand on her shoulder. After they sent backup to Caitlin and Joel the previous night, Henry saw Dawson make a call in private. He didn't yell, nor did he show frustration. Henry figured it must have been personal in nature. The only personal call he had ever seen Dawson make.

Henry remembered why he came back. The promise that Dennis made that things would be different. They didn't feel different. Henry sighed and left the analyst's room. Nothing about the Phantom's scheme to have them close ranks gave the impression that Caitlin or Joel were dead. Christian emphasized that. Yet it left a lot to consider about Henry's own mortality. Final priorities were under highest consideration. Surely there was a way to find his son and bring him home. To get him away from his mother at least. Whatever it could be would have to wait until Caitlin and Joel were safe again. Now was not the time to retire.

Cole watched a middle-aged man storm away two floors below. "The Phantom has you exactly where he wants you. Do you understand that?" He asked.

"We were close. Now we need you to finish the job." Secretary Miles stood beside him also looking at the floors below.

"You expect me to do any better than your investigations team-"

"They're not as good as you think. They abandoned their protocol and stepped outside the law multiple times," said Miles.

"Did it work?" Cole asked.

"It's going to get them in serious trouble-"

"Did it work?" Cole asked more firmly, his gravelly voice getting deeper.

"Right up until they lost two agents," Miles sighed.

"Interesting." Cole nodded unconsciously.

"No. I need to know everything you do. You can't get away with your *usual* methods here. You work for us." Miles said strongly.

"Whatever you say, *Sir*," Cole said as he turned and marched away.

"Don't fuck with me, Cole!" Miles yelled after him.

Cole kept his pace without looking back. Everyone in the hallways evaded him and stayed out of the way discretely.

Unknown, Unknown, United States of America
10:24 EST, Sunday, 27th November 2016
(The same day)

Caitlin woke up smoothly. Despite the aching in her neck, she felt unusually comfortable. The cushions on her chair were thick and plump. Her hands were tied behind with a silky rope. She tried lazily to push herself upright but her ankles were tied to the legs of the chair. She swayed and struggled with her balance, finding the chair to be bolted to the ground. Joel was unconscious in his chair over a metre on her right. His face was bruised and bleeding down his dirty white shirt. She noticed his chest was still undulating slightly. There was damp beneath his pits and below his neck where his shirt was torn and ripped.

"Joel…" Caitlin whispered. She tried to kick the chair from the ground but only caused her ankles to ache.

"Hey…" said a voice.

Caitlin stopped and looked around the dark room. The window was blocked and the door was shut. "Hello?"

"You ok?" The voice of a man came from the neighbouring room.

"Who are you?" Caitlin asked. She could feel increasing pain in her chest.

"Major Hugo Bennett," said the man.

"Army?" Caitlin asked, struggling with her breath.

"Correct. British armed forces deployed in Afghanistan," said Bennett.

"How did you get here?" Caitlin asked. She was pulling at the ropes around her wrists to no avail.

"We were sent to find the 'man in black'. Whole thing went tits-up, firefights broke out all over the place. I was taken while my unit escaped." Bennett explained.

Caitlin stopped struggling against her restraints. "You were captured at the trade site?"

"Yup. They patched me up, been here ever since," said Bennett.

"There were no reports of captures, everyone who didn't make it out is presumed dead." Caitlin said sympathetically.

"Oh I know," said Bennett, "He told me everything."

"Who?" Caitlin asked redundantly.

"You call him the Phantom don't you?" Bennett asked.

"What has he done to you?" Caitlin tremored.

"Don't worry, he's a good host. Saved my life. Told me I'd done my part, and there was no need for me to die. They've been good to me, even saying I'll be released when it's time." Bennett spoke cheerfully, mixing Caitlin's mind with a perplexing concoction of emotions. A door opened on the other side of the thin wall. "Just do as they say and you'll be fine."

"Come on." Said a new voice.

"And don't piss him off!" Bennett called as he left his room.

Caitlin's knuckles throbbed. She gave up on wriggling free given the extent to which she had been tied. She could feel uneven bruising on the side of her head which spread like a migraine to her frontal lobe. The door on her left opened. After a moment, the Phantom stepped in and closed the door behind himself. Caitlin's eyes were better adjusted to the dark. She could see sown cuts and tears all over his coat, and the remaining patches of Vantablack that had not worn off like the rest. His thigh-holsters were empty but there was a bulge in his chest pocket.

The Phantom grabbed a regular wooden chair from the corner and swung it so the back faced Caitlin. "**How are you feeling?**" He asked, facing her and resting his arms on the backrest.

Caitlin could almost feel his voice. She sank into the depths of his eyes. They no longer showed malice, but instead seemed to offer neutrality. "Is he ok?" She asked, glancing at Joel's motionless body. The pain in her chest rose with each vocal vibration.

"**For now.**" The Phantom pulled down the collar of her shirt to reveal a purple bruise between her breasts. "**You have a hairline sternal fracture. Try not to move your chest so much.**" He said, checking on its condition.

"What do you want with us?" Caitlin asked more confidently.

"**I've been looking forward to meeting you... after all this time. I don't want to hurt you, I just want to talk.**" He said calmly.

"About what?" Caitlin spat.

"**I was surprised when you came to find me. I wasn't**

expecting you until the following day. You've been busy, and hiding it from me..." The Phantom said with admiration.

"How did you know we would come?" Caitlin asked.

"**Because I made it so. I didn't know who would come... I'm glad it was you two. You've both come a long way.**" The Phantom spoke deeply yet softly. His eyes darted to Joel who was waking up.

"Where are we?" He groaned.

"**You're safe for now, Joel**" The Phantom growled.

Joel's breathing quickened. He looked up and met the Phantom's gaze.

"**You have done an awfully good job of upsetting me.**" The Phantom said darkly. He took out a needle and injected it into Joel's thigh. "**That's all the morphine you're going to get. I've been wanting to talk to you.**"

Joel lifted his head, relaxing his body as the drugs took effect. "Me too..." He husked.

The Phantom smiled beneath his mask. "**You were the first. The one who started it all.**" There was a faint air of pride behind his booming voice.

"You made it obvious..." Joel mocked, "You let the witnesses see you-"

"**I couldn't help myself,**" Phantom grinned. "**I like to deal with traffickers personally. I knew the victim's descriptions of something... exaggerated... would typically go overlooked. Someone was bound to put it together eventually.**"

"Why the charade? All the black... and the hood?" Joel asked.

"**So that my enemies cannot see me in the dark. Worked on you...**"

"You're ex-military?" Caitlin asked in a half-question.

In the blink of an eye, the Phantom's gaze locked onto her without his head moving. **"Still trying to find out who I am... does it really matter?"** His head tilted slightly.

"If it doesn't matter then you can just tell us," she shot back.

"I want you to focus on what's *really* important." The Phantom paused, watching them expectantly.

"What do you want?" Joel managed to keep his head up straight.

"Now you're asking the right questions..." Phantom said more quietly.

"Why are you doing all this?" Joel asked intently.

The Phantom's grin stretched above his mask. **"There it is."** He leaned toward Joel. **"Come on, Joel, you put the pieces together even when I distorted the puzzle. You could figure this out, that's why I had to have you killed."**

"You failed." Joel scoffed.

"I was impressed when you broke your arm. Saved Sophie as well... Admirable." The Phantom nodded gently. **"For that I let you live a little longer. You earned it."**

"Is that your attempt - at being moral?" Joel coughed and spluttered.

"There are no defining lines between us. We are all points on a moral scale trying to achieve the same goal. Or did you learn nothing from the Game..."

"Killing criminals isn't moral!" Joel gritted his teeth.

"Then neither is saving innocent people." Phantom said strongly. **"Either both are moral or both are not. That's the truth I was trying to teach you. The relativity of ethics. Billions of perspectives on the moral scale, no two alike, all believe they are right. The only constant is the choice that has to be made."**

"You said you weren't going to kill the civilians! You made me kill those men for nothing!" Joel yelled indignantly.

"**It was a demonstration of the choices that have to be made. The hard choices you refuse to face.**" Phantom gripped the backrest of his chair.

"When do *you* have to make these choices?" Caitlin interrupted.

"**There is only one way to learn - the way I learnt - the way I forced you to learn…**"

"I never had to do anything like that in the military." Caitlin countered.

"**You can't learn moral consequence working for the government. I encounter far more criminals than you because I am not so limited.**"

"And you're no better than any of them." Caitlin retorted.

"**I kill people far worse than myself; abusers, killers of the innocent, rapists. The difference is that I do it so the bad does not live with the good, but instead, dies with me.**"

"Doesn't make you good." Caitlin said flatly.

"**We are good versus evil, not good versus bad, because not all evil is bad. We condemn murder to try and prevent it… yet it still happens… primarily to innocent people. The world is dangerously overpopulated, it's no longer a question; we *need* to cull those who don't deserve to stay.**"

"It's not fair for anyone to decide who deserves to live." Caitlin countered.

"**You have killed people. Was it *fair* for you to decide they should die? Is it fair to let good people get hurt or killed because you want to maintain the moral high ground?**"

"We never let people get hurt," said Joel.

"**You don't know that you do because you haven't had to make the choice directly... until I made you.**"

"We never had to until you came along. You forced us to do it to prove that we do it-"

"**To prove it is necessary-**"

"Necessary for your twisted philosophy-"

"**Necessary for the greater good on a scale you refuse to understand-**"

"People do bad things it doesn't mean they deserve to die!" Caitlin spoke up.

"**Those people I killed, the ones I hung for all of London to see, were some of the worst people. They were selfish and sadistic at the expense of the good. If you have to take from others to better what you have then you don't deserve anything at all.**"

"They didn't deserve to die! They can still redeem themselves." Caitlin pressed.

"**You optimists are as bad as pessimists. You believe all factors in this world amount to ideal conditions in one way or another. A perfect world of fiction.**" Phantom said strongly.

"There are many like you trying to create a 'perfect' world," said Joel.

"**A 'perfect' world cannot and does not exist.**" The Phantom said, standing up straight.

"No... 'cus in a perfect world men like you would not exist."

"**In a perfect world... men like me, like *us*, would not have to.**" The Phantom made his way over to the door. Two guards came in with a third just outside the door. "**Make sure this room is guarded at all times. Check on them frequently. And do not go anywhere near her.**"

"Yes, sir. She won't be much trouble." Said one of the guards.

The Phantom stopped next to them. "**Do not underestimate her.**"

"What can she do tied to that chair?" The second guard asked confidently.

The Phantom paused for two full seconds before grabbing the guard's arms, twisting them, and holding him in the same position he had Caitlin. "**She could escape this headlock... can you?**" He said without difficulty. Moments later he let the unconscious guard fall to the floor at his feet for the other to drag out.

"What's the rogue militia?" Joel called out suddenly.

Phantom stopped outside the room. He stood with an unnatural stillness before looking back with a glint of shame in his eyes. "**What *was* the rogue militia, Mr Masier.**"

Virginia, United States of America
15:15 EST, Wednesday, 30th November 2016
(3 days later)

Fresh layers of snow had been replenished every night since the weekend. Christmas decorations all over the city were finally beginning to make sense. They distracted the public from everything that had happened. The coming of a white Christmas brought a change of scenery which helped them forget, as though the blood across the east coast was now covered by the innocence of fluffy white powder. Henry could not revel in such ignorance. Everyone else at the park was running around in thick coats, woollen mittens, and matching woollen hats. They threw snowballs and destroyed their poorly constructed snowmen. James fit in with the blissful and merry scene. For him, it was still a season of jolly fun and celebration. It reminded Henry of his own childhood Christmases with his parents. The jolly smiles they had as they let the fabrication of festivity bring him excitement. What cynicism they had hid behind masks of uplifting grins and laughter.

Henry replicated his father's smile from every memory he could still recollect. He felt the warmth of James' ecstasy and encouraged him to revel in the season's promises. Henry stood as a pillar of influence smiling down at him with gleeful reassurance, hiding the weight that bruised his shoulders. He did not care for labels like 'coward'. James overshadowed the inconsequential opinions and views of those who didn't know better. Henry was not critical to the investigations team like Christian or Joel. Yet, the Phantom attacked him personally all the same, and won. Henry lost without a single point or favour to his name. It was unorthodox for him to even survive. Accepting his defeat for James was a priceless luxury.

Despite the power and lethality of the Phantom he let Henry live. Even understanding the case against his ex-wife as evident from the Game. A sliver of possibility, Henry thought, that underneath the darkness and evil... the Phantom was sympathetic, offering him escape.

"I want to ask you something." Henry said as he crouched down.

James was shovelling snow into a tower and protecting it from one of the many dogs enjoying the snowy park. The owner called the dog's name, 'Mindy', but James' petting and stroking won her attention over.

"If we were to move away together, where would you want to go?" Henry asked.

The dog ran back to the owners calls. "I dunno," James

shrugged.

"Would you want to move away? With me?" Henry asked.

"What about my friends?" James looked up at him.

"They would miss you, but you will make more friends, maybe better friends." Henry said sanguinely.

"Mom won't let me go anywhere." James went back to shovelling snow.

"What if it wasn't up to her... what if it was our choice? Just you and me, wherever we want to go." Henry adjusted James' hat to better cover his ears. "We could go somewhere new. A nice place with a nice school, lots of friends, maybe a dog." Henry said suggestively, looking out at the other families across the park.

"Really?" James said through an uncontrollable grin.

"Whatever we want," Henry smiled back.

"What about mom?" James' grin faded.

"Leave that to me, I'm going to see what I can do." Henry rubbed James' back to keep it warm.

"After you help your friends?" Asked James.

Henry's eyes glazed over. "Yeah," he sighed.

"Are they okay?"

"They're fine, don't you worry." Henry pretended to watch the happy families and their dogs while searching for the eyes of the hidden Syndicate.

James held his fist out for their handshake but Henry's focus removed it from his vision. "My feet are cold," James said, lowering his hand dejectedly.

"Yeah, mine too," said Henry.

"Are you serious?" Sophie asked. She couldn't help but

sound a little disappointed.

"If I had gone with them the Phantom would've taken me as well, then there'd be no-one to take care of James." Henry held his coffee with both hands to warm them up.

"He was taken care of. You're just going to abandon us?" Sophie asked a little louder.

"His mother doesn't take proper care of him, only I do. I'm going to help get them back... but them I'm gone." Henry said shamelessly.

"Owen said you took your son out of protection two days ago." Sophie narrowed her eyes.

"I took him to the park yesterday. He should be spending Christmas in the snow not locked up in some apartment." Henry exclaimed.

"He should be safe-"

"You have all the resources you could want," Henry said indignantly. "All he has is me."

"I know," Sophie conceded. "But we need people we can trust more than resources. We can't afford to lose anyone else." She stood in a contemplative silence in front of Henry's desk before finally leaving.

Every few seconds during her twenty minute drive were spent watching every other car on the road. Ahead were threats, behind were tails. She was so focused she didn't realise her radio was off, and even slid a couple of times forgetting about the icy roads. The fright of losing control made her anxiety rise. Through it, whirling emotions streamed with thought equally as uncontrollable. Her guilt of opposing Henry was not from disappointment, but in fact her own empathy. What he said about the consequences of his death resonated with the only other men she knew that well. Her brothers, and father, and what they would do in Henry's position. They do not have the privilege of her solitude. She could not accept Duncan risking himself when there would be no gain. Sophie would have to explain to her niece and nephew, Jenny and Franklin that their father died trying to beat a psychotic mastermind at his own game. A statistic of their immutable losses. No benefit to a cause or step towards an end. Driven purely by hubris atop underestimation. Could Sophie live with that explanation about her father? Caitlin was right. She knew to be worried about facing the Phantom. Sophie's presumptuous self-confidence had brought her only pain and defeat. If she did not make a change, like Henry, her corpse would be one of ten-thousand steps to the Phantom's throne.

She parked in front of witnesses and fast-walked to the doctor's office. Dawson was sitting in the reception with an eye on his watch.

"Sir," said Sophie.

"Mercer, here for your appointment?" Dawson asked gruffly.

"Yeah, you?" She rubbed her hands together and walked over to the front desk.

"Owen should be coming out now," said Dawson.

Sophie bumped into him after making her way to the psychologist's office. "Hey," she said cheerfully.

"Hey," Owen responded robotically. He gave her a friendly nod but only glanced in her direction. Then he stared down at the floor the same way he had done throughout most of his session. He couldn't get away with his indifference the same way he could in his old group therapy sessions. They allowed him develop a sort of immunity. The doctor's words simply passed around him like air around a bullet, leaving his mind free to churn through his own thoughts in private. For fifty minutes his mind turned in on itself trying desperately to discern between his fiancé and the figure of her resemblance, captured by the man who knew as much about the men behind his fiancé's case as the men knew about her murder, which was more than they led him to believe. Throughout so many years, he had never once considered that one could see more from the dark side than from the light.

Dawson stood up and left with him. "Don't worry, I'm not going to ask. I ignore the fucker anyway." They began walking back to the car, planting their steps carefully on the slippery sidewalk.

"Now we find out how quickly your car warms up," Owen said darkly.

"Car bombs - fucking hilarious." Dawson said flatly.

"We're forced to park in view of the public knowing full well *they're* among them." Owen put his hands in his pockets. His dark blonde hair moved stiffly with the icy breeze.

"We don't know that for sure, they could be making fools of us." Said Dawson.

"Chris doesn't think so, he wants us to assume we're always being followed. Which would mean one of these cars is parked here waiting to tail us once we leave." Owen tried to look inside the parked cars up and down the street.

"It would mean they're watching us right now," Dawson added.

"Probably somewhere around your car." Owen became overly aware of his walking speed and tried to keep it consistent.

"Like you said, we parked in public view. There's too many to pick out from." Dawson scanned their surrounding casually.

"Not if we force them out." Owen pretended to watch where he was stepping. They walked in silence until they reached the car.

"Keep going. Keep going, look ahead." Dawson spoke without moving his lips.

"We have to get out of view of the street," Owen said quietly. They followed the side-streets until they were sure they were out of visual range.

"Slow down, give them time to catch up," said Dawson.

Owen slowed and pressed his feet into the untouched snow to leave prints.

"We can force 'em inside over by that railway tunnel." Dawson kept his pace heading for the stairs that led down to the tunnel.

"Make sure they see us go down." Owen counted six people waiting at the train station above the tunnel. Once they reached the stairs, they held onto the railing and stepping down slowly and carefully as if on ice, when really the stairs were just wet from frequent use. In the tunnel they quickly hid behind the corners where more stairs led up to the station.

"How do we know who it is?" Owen whispered.

"I didn't see anyone coming." Dawson kept himself a couple feet from the corner and flattened against the wall.

Owen did the same on his side. They watched the space and the floor between them, counting the seconds and listening out. Wet footsteps came from behind and echoed through the tunnel at the same time as a pair from ahead. An older gentleman was coming from the other side. Owen and Dawson kept their positions nonchalantly to avoid his gaze giving them away.

A man in a dark green jacket and black jeans came past before the old man reached them. Owen jumped forward to kick behind his knee while Dawson grabbed his other hand and covered his mouth. The older man stopped and stumbled back, watching them hold the man down and drag him aside.

"CIA. Go." Owen nodded for the old man to pass.

Dawson flashed his ID with his other hand on the struggling man. They pinned him against a wall and let go of his mouth.

"What the hell are you doing!?" He yelled.

"Don't bother, asshole." Dawson growled.

"Draw any attention and you'll be explaining this to the police." Owen pulled a handgun from the man's jeans and held it up before tucking it in his own.

"You been ordered to follow us, right?" Dawson asked, spitting a little in his face. The man continued to struggle but didn't answer, so Owen punched hard into his abdomen.

"Look at me." Dawson said a little more quietly as the man recovered, coughing and spluttering. "The Syndicate has you following us, correct?"

The Syndicate member nodded. He shook stiffly in their grip.

"Where is the Phantom now?" Owen asked, grinding his teeth. He punched the man again and thrust him against the wall before he had a chance to think.

"I don't know! I don't know." He confessed hoarsely.

"Mhm?" Dawson pushed him harder.

"Nobody ever knows!" The man husked.

"That I believe," said Owen.

"Well who do you report to?" Dawson asked.

"No-one," said the man.

Owen held his head against the wall and punched him in the nose.

"You think we're stupid!?" Dawson yelled, holding the man's head up by his short brown hair.

"Ugh, my captain," he choked. There was blood trickling from his nose.

"Your captain? Who's your captain? What's his name?" Owen asked firmly.

"No name! Just Captain!" The man coughed.

"What do you call him?" Dawson asked impatiently. A couple of pedestrians were watching timidly from the top of the stairs.

"Captain!" The man insisted.

"Where is he? Where do you go to find him?" Dawson asked.

The man's head lolled but his eyes focused on Dawson's flaming resolve.

A click somewhere in the room lit up his eyelids. He kept them closed and remained limp and relaxed.

"Wake the fuck up you're not fooling anyone," said a gruff voice.

He felt a kick knock his feet aside forcing him upright in his chair for balance. Nathan Dawson was standing beside him with his hands on his hips. His agent, Owen Bradford was leaning against a concrete wall directly ahead. A single fluorescent light lit up the dank, dusty room they had taken him to. He could just make out Dennis Knight standing upright by the door with his arms crossed.

"So you're the captain," said Owen Bradford.

They were smart enough to take him away and hide in their headquarters which minimalized his chances of rescue. The Phantom would be very upset, but he would want his men back. He needed only buy his time.

"Are you or are you not the captain?" Nathan Dawson asked aggressively.

"Depends which captain," he said plainly. He felt his jaw

click when Nathan Dawson punched him. A bruise rose on his cheek. The shock tingled. Pain throbbed below his ear as he moved his jaw back around.

"Don't play games with us." Nathan Dawson growled in his ear.

"Listen up. Hey!" Dennis Knight's voice approached from the corner. "Look at me... who is your superior?"

He looked up at Dennis Knight who bore a vengeance in his eyes as neither an agent nor a man of the law. "Is this how you treat a man in custody?" He asked mirthfully.

Dennis Knight put one foot forward and swung a dazing right hook. This time, the shock manifested as butterflies in his stomach. He felt the warmth of his blood flowing from his nose. His head rung with fearful disorientation. "Where am I?" He asked with an uncontrollable quiver. No answer came. Someone walked from left to right behind him.

"Let us put this simply," Nathan Dawson whispered. "The only people who know you're here are here with you."

"You think so, huh?" He scoffed.

"You have a lot of faith in the Phantom," said Dennis Knight.

"I know what he can do." He quivered.

"Well if he's on his way we can wait," Nathan Dawson raised his eyebrows sarcastically. "I'd love to negotiate." Nathan, Dennis, and Owen got comfortable leaning against the walls.

"Your funeral."

Dennis Knight stepped up casually and wrapped the side of his head. The ringing in his ear resonated with throbbing pain and sang above a voice:

"We lost our patience a long time ago. I'm going to make living very difficult for you..." Dennis Knight spoke gently but seethed with frustration.

"*He* will do worse-"

"Are you sure you want to test that?" Owen Bradford piped up.

"Have you met him before?" Asked a passive British voice from behind.

Nathan Dawson held his hand up to stop the speaker and knelt down. "You answer to someone. You know where we can find them. You either tell us or things get worse for you." He said. There was no hint of disguise or masking of tone. They knew what cards they had and were now laying them on the table. Plain and simple.

"I don't know anything. I follow their orders but they don't tell more than I need to know. That's how the Phantom likes it." His swelling face ached with the motion from his jaw.

"Now… lying like that really pisses me off." Nathan Dawson said gruffly. "We were told you communicate directly with the Syndicate."

He flinched when Dawson got up so quickly. "That's not true."

"He's lying," said the Brit behind him.

"I'm not lying! They don't tell me anything!" He yelled.

"We didn't ask what they told you." Owen Bradford moved clockwise around him.

"I'm in charge of keeping an eye on you. That's it!" His desperation grew until it became audible.

"And then?" Owen Bradford asked.

"And then I have you followed-"

"No. Then that information goes to the Phantom-"

"Not in person." He responded within a second.

"Then how?" Nathan Dawson asked, getting a little closer.

417

"I don't know-"

"Lie." The Brit spoke above him.

"We don't have time for this…" Dennis Knight said under his breath.

Nathan Dawson rolled up his sleeves. "We're going to have to be more hands-on."

"What do you mean?" A female voice asked from next to the Brit.

"Get out… leave this to us." There was a clanking of iron tools when Owen Bradford spoke.

"That's all I know! I swear it's the truth!" He pleaded.

"Owen…" the woman said under her breath.

"Just go." Said Owen.

"Get out of here Mercer, go back to HQ." Dawson commanded.

"Take him with you." Dennis nodded to the Brit. Dawson then whispered something to Dennis. "No I can stay," Dennis replied in a hushed tone.

"Dennis… its ok. We've got this. You go get your agents." Dawson spoke kindly but with some form of grave remorse.

Sophie Mercer held the door for Christian Taylor and Dennis Knight. Once they left, Owen brought out a rusted toolbox and emptied it onto the floor. Rusty screwdrivers, spanners, and a hammer clanged against the one another. Dawson pulled a hunting knife from his belt and locked the door behind the others.

The Captain tried to jump in his chair, shaking and quivering. His pleas encountered nothing but cold concrete walls. Impotence had finally come back to reap a vengeance cold like the sweat that mixed with his blood. Fair was not a preceding characteristic of the sweet release he desired, especially not in the face of a looming, unequivocally fair revenge.

Christian and Dennis had likely gone to find Lucy. Sophie wasn't sure where she was going or why. She was running from a thought. Dawson and Owen in that room with the Syndicate captain. It wasn't the crime, heinous as it was, that was stuck in her mind like a hateful melody. Nor was it how swiftly the guys had resorted to it. It was her own reaction that shocked her. She walked out, saying nothing and bringing no reasonability to anyone. She herself synchronized with them in something of an out of body experience. Once there were no witnesses, no outsiders, she turned into a something spiteful.

Her head span slightly. Nausea swirled so violently in her stomach she thought she might vomit right there in the hallway. She could feel her cheeks and her palms getting warm. Veins of wicked and malicious intent had spread though her own pumping thick, dark blood. The Phantom's sadistic sickness had spread to her through a medium of pain and anger. Dawson, Dennis, and Owen were far more susceptible to it. Their aggressive and competitive nature drove them so easily into the chronic pain of aching desperation such that they now stood into the shade of the Phantom's game. Sophie had it as well. She could feel it manifesting as fear. She strode down familiar hallways toward the exit for fresh air. A cancer cell in an otherwise functioning organ.

A light breeze from outside already began to replenish her dizziness when a young girl caught her attention. She stood like a lost puppy next to indifferent men in suits and ties. Her eyes and interest wondered around the large, monochromatic entrance hall and the front doors still under reconstruction.

Sophie doubled her pace towards the men. "Hi." She smiled sweetly at the girl who responded with a thin, gratifying smile. "What's your name?" Sophie asked as she knelt down to the girl's height.

"Sabrina," the girl responded timidly.

"Sabrina," Sophie smiled again, "I'm Sophie." She stood up and forced her way between the men. "Hello. Who's taking care of this girl?"

"We are." One of the men said officially.

"Clearly not, where is she supposed to be going?" Sophie asked.

"I don't know yet," said the man.

"What do you mean you don't know?" Sophie hissed.

"It's part of the Syndicate case-"

"I'm on the Syndicate case." Sophie said officially.

The men turned their full attention to her. "Her father went missing aboa-"

Sophie held her hand up to stop him. "Sabrina, would you go take a seat over there please, sweetie?" She asked kindly.

"Her babysitter filed a missing person's report after the father didn't come back. He's missing abroad, something to do with your investigation."

"And the mother?" Sophie asked. The men shook their heads. "I'll take care of her. Sabrina!" She called across the hall. Sabrina looked up and slid off her seat.

Sophie held her hand out as she walked so that Sabrina could hold it and follow. "Let's find you somewhere warm to stay, hm?" She led Sabrina past offices and occupied rooms until they reached a vending machine near the far corner of the building.

"You hungry?" Sophie asked as she looked around for somewhere to sit.

"Yeah," Sabrina said lightly.

"Here," Sophie led her to an empty break room further down. "Take a seat and wait for me here, ok? Do you want something to drink as well?" She asked.

"No," Sabrina lifted herself onto one of the chairs.

"Ok, wait right here I'll be back in just a moment." Sophie fast walked back out.

Sabrina stared at the black and white pictures on the walls. They had men in suits standing and doing nothing. Most weren't even smiling. Her focus on them blurred out as the lights in the room switched off with a click. She watched them lose their glow above her head when a deep but friendly voice spoke from the other side of the room.

"Hello there."

She watched him nervously. He sat still in a chair by the door, wearing black clothes and a hood. Above his silver mask were a pair of kind green eyes that looked upon her own with gentle vulnerability.

"Hi," she responded uncertainly. The man smiled delightfully at her until she couldn't help but do the same.

Sophie fumbled with her ringing phone as she marched toward the vending machine. "Hello?" She answered.

"Dawson has a location. We're moving in tonight." Dennis spoke with finality.

"Already?" Sophie said breathlessly. Her cardiac rhythm skipped uncomfortably with the rise in her debauched moral fidelity.

"Come to the operations centre," said Dennis.

"I-I can't. There's this umm… this girl here whose father is missing and… I don't know what to do with her." Sophie struggled between breaths.

"*Let someone else deal with her.*" Dennis hung up the call. Sophie leaned against the vending machine with both hands and caught her breath. She then took out her purse with shaking fingers and anxiously selected something.

"**You must be Sabrina, am I right?**" The man asked.

"Mhmm," Sabrina nodded.

"**I'm a friend of your dad's. He misses you very much. He's been caught up with work so I promised him id check up on you.**"

"When's he coming back?" Sabrina asked.

"**I'll get him back as soon as I can.**" The man smiled reassuringly. "**He'll be back before Christmas. But those men were supposed to take you to child protective services until then.**"

"Ok," Sabrina agreed to hide her confusion.

"**Sophie is a nice girl. She will make sure you are well looked after until your dad comes to fetch you.**" He stood up gracefully. "**Make sure to have her call child protective services, ok Sabrina?**"

"Ok." She nodded with more confidence.

The man's soft eyes beamed at her proudly. "**Here,**" he offered her a little red sweet.

"Thank you," she said lightly, taking the sweet from his long, rough fingers.

"**You're welcome.**" He opened the door without a sound and switched the light back on as he slinked out backwards.

Sabrina unwrapped the sweet and started to suck on it. The tantalizing strawberry flavour filled her mouth making her feel far more content.

Sophie returned a couple of minutes later with juice and a bag of chips. "Sorry that took so long, I couldn't find the one with drinks." She put them both on the table and pulled out a seat for herself.

"Thank you," Sabrina said awkwardly.

Sophie noticed something in her mouth and the wrapper on the table. "What have you got there?" She asked.

"Sweet. Someone gave it to me." Sabrina said, looking at the juice flavour.

"Oh that's nice, who was it?" Sophie opened the juice for her.

"My dad's friend. He said you must tell child services." Sabrina sipped her juice with the sweet still in her mouth.

"Oh." Sophie went blank as she thought for a moment. "How does he know your dad?"

Sabrina shrugged.

An epiphany came to the forefront of Sophie's mind. "Child services is a good idea though. Did he tell you his name?" Sophie looked up the number on her phone.

"No. He was wearing a mask." Said Sabrina.

Sophie lost her breath again. "What kind of mask?" She asked.

"I dunno-"

"Did he have a hood on? Like a black hood?" Sophie stressed.

"Yeah," Sabrina said happily.

Sophie held her nauseas stomach and stood up. "Which way did he go?" She asked with kind panic. Sabrina pointed at the door on the other side. One of the chairs had been moved to face their table. Sophie approached the door stretching to look down the passageways. Both sides were vacant. Even when she walked out there was no sign of activity. She wanted to keep going but stood in the doorway looking up and down, unable to bring herself to step any further. Her hands gripped the doorframe to hold her up, otherwise she felt she might slide down to the floor. Adrenaline filled her tightening muscles with anxious energy like shots of caffeine running through her chest and arms. She tried despairingly to pacify her thumping heart with controlled breaths but it only weakened her joints until they caved. Her fingers slid from the frame. She shook to the floor, heaving out of control.

Sabrina watched curiously with panic rising in her own chest. She sat, too afraid to move or speak, watching Sophie shiver and desperately draw in each breath.

Unknown, Unknown, United States of America
00:00 EST, Friday, 2nd December 2016
(The next day)

"Joel. Wake up, someone's coming." Caitlin pressed her ear against the door. There were men talking over clustered stepping. Their discussion died out once they stopped outside the door. Caitlin stepped back next to Joel and awaited their instructions.

If it was food they were bringing, they would first tell them both to kneel with their hands behind their heads. Their protocol was fastidious but loose enough to grant them more freedom and comfort than the average prison inmate. They were allowed to use the bathroom every morning, every night, and anytime they requested. Fresh clothes and towels were provided for showers as well as shampoo and conditioner. They were given newspapers, magazines, books of their choice. Their food was the same as their guard's and indistinguishable from a home cooked meal. Under care from the Phantom's doctors, their wounds healed quickly and painlessly. They could even make shopping requests. Anything (As long as the Phantom approved it) from chocolate to coffee to maxi pads. Something Caitlin couldn't get used to above all were the guards. Syndicate members, well trained and always armed, were respectful and quiet. They showed no hostility nor aggression towards either of them. One morning Joel enquired about it to the guard outside their bathroom. "Phantom says 'just because you're prisoners doesn't mean we can't treat you like guests'" The guard responded simply.

This time the door was unlocked and swung open without a word of warning. Caitlin and Joel stood in front of their chairs facing the figure in the doorway. The Phantom stepped inside calmly and met their gazes. "**Sit.**" He said, circling to his left.

The Lady Danger strode in after him, cat-walking right up to them as they sat down. The corner of her mouth curled up into a slight smirk.

Caitlin caught a glimpse of the silky rope in her hands when she stood beside the chair. She tried to look up at the Lady discretely but she was already eyeing her with psychotic lust. Caitlin kept her eyes forward like a soldier at attention while the Lady tied her hands and feet to the chair.

"Are you ever not dressed like an emo teenager?" Joel mocked as he too was tied.

"**I'm afraid your speaking privileges are revoked today.**" The Phantom gripped Joel's mouth with a piece of duct-tape in his palm. "**I'm only here to speak to Cait.**"

Caitlin felt the Lady's hands run over her shoulder and down her back. The Lady breathed lovingly in her ear as she tightened the ropes one more time.

"What do you want?" Caitlin asked irately.

The Phantom leaned forward on his stool, saying nothing

for a long while. He rested his forearms on his knees and ran his fingers over the metal that protruded from the knuckles of his fingerless gloves. They were old and worn like the rest of his outfit, with one exception: His mask was smooth and polished. Its new shape was flat and angular and pressed right up against his face up to his eyes and over his nose. There were still tears lined vertically with black grids inside for breathing.

"**I want you to know that none of this is personal. Someone had to be in your position... I know how that feels...**"

Caitlin had no response. She felt an honest empathy from him, an understanding between them that offered more humanity than she ever thought to receive.

"**That was until Joel stepped over the line.**" He growled, meeting Joel's gaze. "**I trusted you to understand the innocence of the panther but I guess you're too *broken.*** "

Joel's breathing got heavier, forcing some air out from behind the duct-tape.

"**I thank you though,**" Phantom nodded, "**You taught me something I needed to know. Something very fascinating about breaking a mind. You see, you are no longer yourself... are you? I have corrupted your conscious and unconscious beyond repair. You are... finished.**" He pulled his stool to the middle of the floor, facing them both equally. "**It was painful, but pain teaches the most important lessons. If you don't learn then all you will do is suffer.**"

Caitlin couldn't pull her eyes away from his. They held her mesmerized with their entrancing shade of green.

"**I gave you every opportunity to back away and still you persist. You're grown adults, trained and tested. You know you're responsible for whatever happens to you. You have no-one to blame but yourselves. Your resistance causes** a friction that breeds a lethal heat. I thought I taught you that. I don't know if you're stubborn or stupid, either way, I have a schedule to keep so now it's time to learn through pain."

The Lady pulled Caitlin's hair back forcing her to watch the Phantom. Caitlin felt her panic start to rise uncontrollably again. All sense of safety and security was pulled out from underneath her by the reality the Phantom had concealed. His fictitious hospitality had run its course, leaving her scared and ripe for his consumption.

"You have spent a lot of time with the Americans. By now you must know how to access their network, yes?" The Phantom asked passively.

"No." Caitlin responded honestly.

The Phantom slammed his fist on Joel's knee as fast as a reflex. Joel's muffled cries grounded her deeper into their dirty reality.

"We don't have access to their computers!" Caitlin stressed.

"You have had access for months. At some point you must have been given access to their network and their servers." He asked more tensely.

The Lady released Caitlin's hair and glided around her.

"No they would never let us do that!" Caitlin stated firmly.

The Phantom's hand shot up to Joel's throat and contracted.

"Letting foreign operatives access their network would be a serious security risk!" Caitlin explained.

"I know," Phantom said without blinking. **"I need this to sink in. You're a smart woman, Caitlin."** Joel choked under the Phantom's tightening grip.

"I don't understand what you want from me!" She said indignantly.

"**A username and password to access the CIA network and servers.**"

"You know I don't have that!"

"**Do I?**" Phantom released Joel's throat and reached for the lump in his dark coat. "**I don't think you understand yet...**"

Caitlin's chest constricted against her lungs. The Phantom pulled his Desert Eagle out and held it on his knee. She could see down the barrel that he aimed at her abdomen. No answer came to her to buy more time. There was nothing to understand. "What do you want me to understand?" She asked.

"**A lesson you should already know. Give me the password... or Joel will die.**" Phantom lifted the gun and aimed at the centre of Joel's chest without looking his way.

"I don't have a password. I swear they never gave us access they did it all themselves they would not let us-"

The Phantom stood up to his full height kicking his stool to the other end of the room. He then leaned toward her, keeping the gun aimed at Joel. "**All fear comes down to two things; pain, and death. Accept those and you will know no fear. Making someone realise their worst fears can set them free. Tell me – Or be free.**"

Caitlin tensed her body to control the shaking. The Phantom would still hear it in her shivering breaths. Looking away from him, empty words trailed off her quivering lips. "P-Please. Just tell me what you want. Don't kill him."

"**You know what I want.**"

"I don't have a password-"

"**My Patience is deathly thin-**"

"You know I don't! What else do you want!?"

"I don't have time for excuses."
"I don't have it!"
"Seconds remaining, miss Harper-"
"I DON'T FUCKING HAVE IT!"
"I'm going to count to four…"
"NO! PLEASE, please, I'll get you a password."
"One." The loudness of the shot masked all sound besides splattering. Every one of Caitlin's muscle fibres jerked into maximum contraction causing her to jump in her seat. Her jaw locked with her mouth widely agape. There were warm drops all over the right side of her face. She could not turn her head against the taught tendons in her neck.
"Two."
She could only hear him faintly over the numb ring of her eardrums. Her diaphragm only allowed her lungs to pull in rapid breaths that made her head dizzy.
"Three." The Phantom hadn't moved since the recoil. He watched her shakily comprehend it as her involuntary nervous system began to relax. **"Four."**
Ethereal silence distorted the passage of time. Caitlin's eyes were wide and unseeing. Her mind burnt with a backlog of emotions that awaited nothing. Unrelenting denial surpassed bargaining and anger, leaving her with only a hollow sadness.
"The agents are on their way," Lady said in a hush voice.
"They're early… again. Time to go dark." The Phantom turned and opened the door.
The Lady Danger stood in front of Caitlin and bent over to give her an affectionate kiss on the lips. Caitlin's wide eyes filled with tears that fell to their connected lips. The Lady finished by licking them up from Caitlin's lips and cheek. She then walked backward, caressing Caitlin's cheek and sealing her mouth with duct-tape. With a malevolent wink, she strode out

behind the Phantom.

Their timeline was out of synch. They had shifted it once before. Just a little, not out of Phantom's way. Now they had done it again. This time too close for comfort. Had he not prepared everything well in advance it could have had permanent effects on the small scale of his plans. Long ago the alignment of timing in Afghanistan was beyond satisfying. He had baited them to the trade site in parallel with the insurgent's arrangement. Then they took risks. They followed him up to China just as intended but got a little warm on his tail. It hurt him to do it, but his emergency disruption of the Hunter-Killers outside Ghazni was necessary. He would not take risks like they did. Leave nothing to chance.

Cole was easy to manipulate. He saw what was shown to him without a second glance. His tunnel-vision needed only a road on which to travel. Though in the time to come, he would know better. He would become a much greater threat in need of addressing.

The investigations team rallied. The game broke their spirits but something held them together still. Even in defeat they stood against Phantom as players in his game turning the rules to their advantage. This time it was his men that were missing. Whatever held up the team could not last. It was parasitic, feeding on their souls so that they might confront him in his own underworld. They would destroy themselves at the breaking point of a fate he could not foresee. They could not be allowed to win, but they could not be allowed to die. They were people. Broken, yes, but alive. They needed not suffer further. They would have to be displaced before their darkness eroded their souls beyond repair. He would not let them suffer his same fate. They would not survive it like he did. No good soul deserved it.

One stood above the rest in Phantom's mind. Christian was on a separate path. The darkness did not affect him as it did the others. He was an intelligent man, but perhaps in his pursuit of understanding the criminal mind he would find himself lost. The deeper he looked the further he strayed from himself. When he finds himself more on one side than the other, it could be too far for him to find his way back, especially in the grey, paradoxical maze of moral philosophies. Phantom thrived there, but it was a lonely existence. Christian had the potential to understand the 'Phantom'. To understand everything that happened, the rogue militia he chased so desperately, and maybe even all he did not yet know. So much to come he could not see. So much more for him to learn. While a great curiosity, no doubt equally the Phantom's greatest threat to come.

North Bethesda, Maryland, United States of America
01:11 EST, Friday, 2nd December 2016
(*One hour later*)

Once the ground began to shake it didn't stop. City cops established a wide perimeter around the old factory. Onlookers watched two tanks escorting six wheeler trucks that carried squads of soldiers. Surrounding buildings were evacuated. Snipers on the rooftops. Three helicopters shined spotlights on the factory building and grounds. SWAT teams prepared their breaching equipment while the National Guard lay walls of sandbags. Dozens of heavy boots scuffed the gravelly ground lifting dust into a misty cloud around their ankles. Every window around the factory had been boarded up. No light came in or out. The front entrance was just under ninety metres from the main gate. Two mobile barriers were placed in the gate with walking space in between. Three soldiers knelt on either side with their weapons aimed at the front door, surveying all they could see.

One of the tanks slowed to a squealing stop and took aim at the building. Henry followed its line of sight. He looked sideways at Owen who caught him in the corner of his eye but looked back at the spotlights coming from the helicopters.

Cole stormed past the idle infantry to get a look at the factory. Deck followed, looking over his shoulder. They turned back with most of the infantrymen watching them. "When you engage on the Phantom make it count! His counter-attack is faster than his attack!" Cole yelled as he passed them.

Dawson heard the shouting coming from beyond the trucks. "Anything on thermal?" He asked on radio with the main helicopter.

"Three spiral shapes on the rooftops, over."

"That's their symbol," Dawson sighed.

Sophie listened intently to the conversation between Dawson and the pilots when the sound of Dennis' commanding voice swept over her. He had the blueprints for the factory on the bonnet of a cop car and was deep in discussion with the assisting colonels.

Christian sat in the passenger seat of Dennis' car admiring everything coming together. The sounds of marching, yelling, and powerful engines were muffled, allowing him a more peaceful place to clean his glasses. He could see the tip of the factory and the helicopters circling ahead. Their ability to summon such a force quickly enough to minimize the Phantom's response, knowing full well he already had one prepared, left him with contentment akin to foolish hope. Whatever the Phantom's game may be, this would be the last of them.

The game is resilience. It's not over until it's over.

When the time came it started slow. First the SWAT, then the National Guard. They approached with a controlled pace from every side, crossing the dusty gravel grounds towards the entrances. Nothing came between them and the building.

Owen and Henry knelt down along with the rest of the soldiers while the SWAT team prepared to breach a loading door.

Sophie kept her eyes on Dennis' back. They followed the SWAT unit gathering around the main entrance.

Cole and Deck hoisted Bentley up the side of a back wall for him to reach Meach's hand and get pulled up.

All at once, the doors were blown open to let the squads flood into the darkness of the factory one after another. Cole shined his torch directly across the first room. His light reflected off baron walls and an empty floor. Nothing was left, not even from the factory's original tenants. As he proceeded, rifle raised to eye level, his steps barely left a single print. The floors had been mopped and swept clean. Through the next door, an even darker abyss awaited. Their torches showed three different directions and multiple rooms each way. They could hear echoes coming from the breaches on the other sides. The soldiers would wash through every corner of the building, so Cole led his unit straight down the middle toward the centre. As soon as Charles brought the rear passed a certain point, looking back as he went, a large round object fell into his torchlight. Hollow, metal clanging had them all spinning to see barrels falling from an opening in the ceiling and blocking their way back. Cole turned back around to advance, his face tense with resolute focus.

The soldiers at the front entrance cracked a couple of glow sticks and threw them to the other end of the reception. Each side, corner, and crevice was as bare as aged bone. Some men entered keeping to the walls. Some marched straight down the middle. Dozens of torches lit up every corner of the reception, revealing a word painted in black on the wall behind the front desk.

APOCALYPSE CO.

Dennis skimmed over it and matched the pace of the squad. Sophie forced herself to stay close behind him, letting the soldiers lead the way.

Coming in from the north side, Owen led Henry their own way, disregarding the squads. Although there were many directions to go, he was determined to go deeper, to the heart of madness. A few torches jerked around drawing his attention. The soldiers had ducked from squeaking bats flying out of a vent on their right. Even as they advanced, they could hear squeaking and flapping behind them. The lead man kicked open a door and marched in with his rifle up. Two more men followed while the rest waiting outside, shining their torches down both ends of the hallway. Owen and Henry looked in as they passed. The room seemed to be filled with nothing but tall gas canisters, all connected by pipes. "Find out where that leads," Henry called to the lead man.

"There's a room here with gas canisters." Owen said quietly into his comms.

"*Copy that.*" Dawson responded. "*Be on the lookout for gas canisters.*"

"Copy," said Dennis. "We've got some here as well, stand by." Dennis lowered his rifle and took Sophie's torch to shine on the canisters. Although scratched and faded, the 'flammable' warning still remained. "There's flame warnings," Dennis reported.

"*It's hydrogen.*" Owen's voice was scratchy over the comms. "*Leads to th- vents, and the valves open.*"

"Open?" Dawson asked. He clicked his fingers in Christian's direction.

"*Yeah, there must be dozens of canisters in most of these rooms all bol-ted into- the vent-ela-tion.*" Owen's voice lagged.

"Hydrogen being pumped through the building. The whole thing is a bomb." Dawson said to Christian.

Christian considered it and surveyed the outside of the building. He doubted the Syndicate's capability to make the entire factory air-tight, when in fact they didn't need to. "You can't shoot," he sighed with a daunting realisation. "It will light the whole place up. He wanted us to find the hydrogen so he put it first."

Dawson wanted to kick the door of a cop car but couldn't summon the strength in his leg. "Is it a trap? How did he know we were coming?"

"It was only a matter of time," said Christian.

"*Be advised: All units switch to melee only. I repeat. Melee only. There's hydrogen gas leaking from the vents.*"

"Are you fucking kidding me?" Charles exclaimed.

Cole couldn't help but smile and lift his gun over his shoulder onto his back. "More fun," he said. Each of them took the torches off their rifles and slid out their knives.

Owen put his gun in his holster, same as Henry. The squads and SWAT units did the same. A few men switched on their safeties intending to use their rifles as glorified bats.

Dennis unclipped the torch from his rifle. Sophie followed him in hesitance passing the leading squad. He turned right at the glow-sticks and stopped facing the corner. "What's this?" He asked, pushing against the wall on the right. "The blueprint showed left and right turns here."

Sophie shined her light at the edges of what was supposedly the right passageway. "Are you sure?"

"They've changed the layout." Dennis hit the wall with his palm.

The squad leader aimed his torch down the left passage without stopping. "Is it supposed to be like this?" He called back.

Dennis pushed past the rest of the squad to get to the front.

The squad leader had his light on a concrete wall in the middle of the hallway. "Was that supposed to go lead somewhere?" He asked Dennis.

"Yes. And this isn't supposed to be here." Dennis shined his own torch at the right turn a few metres before the wall. He pressed his comms which let out buzzing and humming. "Hello? Dawson you copy?"

"What could be doing that?" The squad leader asked.

"Jammer?" Sophie suggested.

"Or something in the walls." Dennis looked down the next hallway. It was wide like an empty room with closed doors on all four walls.

"He's splitting us up. Eye's open, keep your safeties on." Said one of the captains. Owen considered each of the five passageways they had arrived at. Two of them stood out as poorly constructed yet led deeper into the factory all the same. The squads divided into each revealing more splits and corners. Just as Owen decided on the fourth passage, the sound of clunking stone came from the middle. The lead man's foot sank with a square of the floor for no more than a second. It continued to slide down even after he pulled away. When it stopped, more sliding began beneath the floor, harder and heaver, then more up the walls. Turning gears and sliding hydraulics were brought to life with escalating momentum. Each squad stopped at the ready hearing the echoes of it come back through the halls as it spread throughout the factory.

A deep and distant click led to another which led to another. Something was pulled which released something which swung. Cole stood like a deer in headlights shining his torch on the blank walls.

"Hold up. You hear that?" Dennis asked. The squad leader pointed to their right.

"I hear machinery," said Sophie. She aimed her ear at the wall and concentrated her senses. A far more audible metal click started off a tight twisting somewhere on the second floor. Twisting turned to winding, turned to humming. The humming oscillated with rising frequency and pitch. Small clangs preceded crashing stone from all ends of the factory. Dennis recognized the wobbling of taught cables throughout the mechanism.

"The ceilings fallen blocking the way back." One of the men reported from behind. Dennis attempted to ignore it all and directed them through the doors down the middle.

Cole picked up his pace, checking corners with a brief peek before advancing. Hayden kicked down the first closed door they found, snapping something at the handle which turned the weight back on the door, slamming it in his face. Deck helped him try to push it open again but it was as firm as the rest of the wall. Cole recoiled when something stroked his face. A string hung from a dusty bulb on the ceiling. "Leave it." He warned.

Owen held his torch firmly while Henry pulled the handle down. It squealed as it turned yet did not open the door. Henry jiggled it in confusion. The handle did a full rotation and hung loosely on the door. Owen rotated it twice more and released it in reflex when the door fell away from its hinges and slammed loudly on the ground.

Sophie waited for the soldier to kick down the door before going past. He thrust his heel next to the lock and broke the door in millimetres before flying backwards off balance. Dennis used his shoulder to break it more, yet it moved no further. Sophie barged in front of him and pulled the handle back. The door swung out easily with nothing more than plain brick wall behind it. Dennis rotated his shoulder painfully and moved on, cursing under his breath.

Cole noticed the fishing wire that crossed the hallway at ankle level because now he was looking for it. It glinted in his torchlight for the others to see. When he stepped over it, a gentle click above him send a jolt down his spine. Deck shined his torch above Cole's head showing a little black motion sensor. Unit zero stood motionless and quiet, listening out for anything being triggered. After a minute, Cole waved his hand furiously under the sensor making it click again and again. When nothing happened, he nodded with a seething sigh and marched down the hall furiously. Deck and the other's hopped over the wire and followed at his adrenaline-packed pace.

"Slow down." Deck whispered, turning a corner after him.

Cole stopped suddenly with his hand out. Bentley walked around for a closer look at the web of shimmering tripwires blocking the rest of the passage. Their journey of constructed serendipity would have to continue down an empty corridor to their left. Cole didn't wait to evaluate the tripwires. He strode left with his torch on the broken corners of a four-way intersection up ahead. The left passage at the intersection was clear besides the comically oversized axe hiding in the ceiling. The right passage was bright from reflections off the barbed wire that circle it to the other end. The forward passage was obstructed by obstacles of angled hurdles and low hanging bars. Cole led them forward down the path of least resistance. Not by choice, but by obligation.

Meach's flashlight wavered over a red stain coming from the foot of a door. Cole and Deck stood back between two hurdles to light it up with their own flashlights. Blood seeped from every edge in the doorframe. Deck gestured for Bentley and Charles to breach it. Before Charles finished turning the handle, the door thudded into him with copious amounts of blood streaming out. Bentley and Cole leapt forward to help slam it. Bentley shook his arms splattering blood on the already soaked ground. Some of the blood from the door seeped down his neck forcing involuntary shakes and shivers. Hayden aimed his torch at Cole so he could wipe at the blood that fell across his chest and thigh. Two more doors slammed somewhere beyond forcing the unit to duck down for cover behind the hurdles.

"The rooms are red herrings," said Bentley.

"He's taunting us again, Cole." Charles cringed at the blood pooling around his boots.

"So ignore them." Cole commanded. He pulled himself to his feet and bolted down the hall. Closed doors, traps, and triggers redirected him down a singular path into the depths of the factory. Their run was soon forced to halt in a passage devoid of visibility, where the floor had fallen away and the walls were fractured and wrecked. Cole judged the distance to safety on the other side.

"Come, we'll give you a push," said Deck.

Hayden stepped back and lined up to jump between Cole and Deck, who stood on the edge ready to give him a push at the last moment. Charles gave him and initial push, then at the peak of his sprint, Hayden leapt with Cole and Deck shoving him from behind. The air rushed past his ears and dried his eyes. He landed with over a metre to spare. His boots hit the floor hard making it drop a little. The oddity of the sequential metal clunk gave it away. Hayden whipped around in shock but the others lost their footing as well. Both sides dropped inward giving them zero reaction time. The floor beneath their feet fell to the floor below forcing them down the middle like a slide. Cole kicked his feet out to prevent himself falling into the hole between himself and Hayden. Each of them held onto what they could, their torches fallen and missing. They felt at their surroundings getting a stronger hold of each other. When the second floor fell, they had nothing holding them up. They grabbed and clawed at everything within reach but were inevitably consumed by the rabbit hole.

Distant crashing amplified Owen's hearing such that the melody became more apparent. Through the decrepit foundations it called to him like a personal siren. The wedding theme played as though from a record, scratchy and off key.

"Owen? Don't!" Henry called. Owen had already run ahead and barged through a door to his calling. Henry pushed through just in time to see Owen clench his fists and barge through the next door across the room. Like a trick of the light, Henry's flashlight outlined Owen and then reflected back at him from a sheet of metal. Where there was a door there was now an industrial sheet of hardened steel fallen from a slit in the crooked doorway. Owen caught a glimpse of brass before the weighted slam sent a shock up his spine. He could hear Henry banging on it. They called out to each other but the sound barely passed through. Owen put his own weight into sliding the sheet but it remained solid and stubborn.

"Don't move!" Henry shouted from the other side. Owen understood. He knew Henry would try find his way, but the Phantom would not so easily let them reconnect. He made the path for Owen, and it was his alone.

Owen clenched his fists harder and stretched his arms. He grabbed the record player and threw it down the path that was laid out for him, stepping on it as he proceeded. There were no diversions or distractions, only that of the melody playing throughout the void. An audio-hallucination playing from Owen's mind into his owns ears.

"**What brought you down this path?**"

Owen stopped. The voice came from nowhere yet filled the hallway entirely.

"**It's not me you're looking for.**"

Owen kept walking with his flashlight up but the hallway was as blank and unkempt as every other.

"**I know what you want. I want to give it to you.**"

The voice spoke softly, secretively, even personally. "Where are you?" Owen asked uncertainly.

"**Let's talk.**" Said the Phantom.

An elevator in the far corner of the factory screeched like a crying banshee. Cacophonies of yelling and slamming ensued ubiquitously. "MOVE! MOVE! MOVE!" The squad leader shouted and pushed past Dennis and Sophie. The walls behind them closed in on the squad forcing them apart. Dennis helped a couple of the soldiers get out of the way. Sophie had her eye on the pneumatics that had pushed the walls and locked. An echoing crash from the elevator shaft left the factory quiet enough to hear the aftermath. Men on all floors yelled and banged with forceful confusion.

Unit zero's ephemeral recovery from the fall realigned them within disorientating darkness. The flashlights that didn't crack cast jagged shadows from beneath the bed of debris. They re-established security by checking their corners. Rusted railings and decaying machinery hid much of the room. Cole stood by the only door. He bust it open as soon as Meach's light shined on the handle. Dim red lamps led the way down a makeshift passageway with tall walls. Meach used his flashlight to help the others recover while Cole and Charles investigated the trail of lamps. Their eerie glows showed narrow paths left and right that curved out of sight.

Charles went ahead with a flashlight and Cole followed. He already had an idea of what to expect but wished quite desperately he was wrong. The more they followed the lamps, turning corners and peeking around bends, the more his idea solidified.

"Now he has us in a literal maze." Charles shook one of the flimsy walls.

"No, come on. We're not playing his games." Cole led him back to a corner curve and ran into it with his shoulder. The piece bent back slightly but not enough. Deck came in with a kick, attracting the attention of the others. They beat at the wooden wall and charged with all their weight. Its sides split away and hung loosely on the screws that kept it in place. They kicked the weak spots until the wood splintered from the screws and fell back with a loud echoing slap. From the outside, the maze looked like a nocturnal playground construction. Pillars at regular intervals indicated they were on the main factory floor. Cole wasted no more time and led them out a door back into the bulk of the building.

Without vents, rooms, or alternate corridors, Owen had far from an abundance of options. "You don't know what I want." He said, investigating the cold, black passageway.

"Do you believe that? After I showed you what they did?"

Owen looked up and down the hallway in search of the voice's origin. "Why did you show me?"

"You deserve to know."

"Where's Caitlin?" Owen found himself back in the focus of the moment.

"Safe and sound. They will find her soon. Now ask the other question that's been on your mind."

Owen's focus clouded with defiant emotion. Subconscious conflict within him resolved before he could be aware of it. Consciously, his guard would appear lower with the progression of the conversation until the Phantom was convinced. "How did you know they tampered with the evidence?"

"You did your investigation… I did mine."

"Why did they do it? Were they payed?" Owen saw an opening through the window of an emergency exit door.

"You know why. You need to ask the right questions."

"Who paid them?" He pushed the handle of the emergency exit and walked out into a large loading bay.

"You know who, you want their names. I can give you something better…" The Phantom's voice filled the loading bay to every corner of the high ceiling.

"What's that?" Owen circled left with his back to the wall while reaching for his gun.

"Their location."

Owen stopped again. "What do you mean?" He asked,

feeling his heart beat against his ribs.

"**I told you I want to give you what you want: The location of the killers.**"

"You can't possibly know where they are." Owen exclaimed.

"**The same way I can't know that they tampered with evidence? Or that the blunt weapon they used was a crowbar?**"

Adrenaline reached Owen's heart and spread to every capillary in his body. His hand rested on the back of his belt unconsciously. "Wh-Who told you that?" He asked breathlessly.

"**The killers did.**"

"You're lying..." Owen pulled out his gun and began searching the loading bay.

"**You were in Morocco on an operation that would turn out inconclusive. She was home from work, it was still evening in her time zone. Your neighbours said they heard a scream and called the police-**"

"You read the case file that means nothing!" Owen called out.

"**The case file mentions the black car they escaped in. In actuality it was a dark blue.**"

"Bullshit." Owen sped up to cover more ground, his legs surging with energetic rage.

"**You were looking for a local contact but got the call from your home...**"

"YOU'RE NOT PROVING ANYTHING!" Owen shouted as loud as he could. His throat throbbed at the frequency of his heartbeat.

"**They distracted you out of desperation...**"

Owen saw an envelope underneath the large entrance doors. He kept his gun up aiming at nothing in particular and knelt down to pick it up.

"They even took some evidence of their own in case you didn't get the message…"

The envelope had a small printed picture inside. Owen recognised his old living room. The cream coloured couches. Stripy carpet in the middle. The corner of a framed photo on the wall from their trip to the Cayman Islands. A cowering figure shaded under the sweet glow of the living room light, kneeling with a distraught expression, tears drowning her eyes and streaming down her cheeks. The last photo of Helen Lynn alive. Owen caved over with tears blurring his vision. He let the photo fall to the floor and knelt in front of it with his hands out on the dusty concrete. It wasn't like the crime scene photos that took him months to be able to look at. At least in those she felt nothing. She was at peace. For the first time, he could see traumatizing fear in her cute dimples. Her agony glistened in her eyes. The way she knelt helplessly for the photo, looking into the lens like she could see him. Like she was silently calling and begging him for help. Old wounds ripped open. Owen's body reacted instinctively. He could feel his protector-urge to run out and find her. The phantasm of her longing pulled at him like a muscle that was still contracting during amputation. A taught pain that could not be released because it was no longer attached.

"They distracted you because they couldn't tie the loose ends you were about to find." The Phantom stepped out from the shadows behind him. **"They needed to buy more time. So they sent thugs to your house… to force you back home."**

Owen choked and sobbed over the photo that was now damp with his tears.

"Apparently, the thugs weren't even meant to kill

her, because then you would have no need to return. It made them vulnerable to investigation. That's why they had to pay for the evidence tampering."** Phantom stood behind him, watching him gasp for air.

"Who- ordered- the hit?" Owen asked hoarsely. The doors of the loading bay opened in front of them.

"I've told you enough already. It's time to show you."

Owen looked up to see a pair of headlights and a license plate. The cold night air came rushing in from around the car.

"They sent you to therapy because they thought there was something wrong inside your head… that you might snap… but you just developed a higher appreciation for *effective* justice." The Phantom helped Owen up. **"Her death was not your fault."**

Owen swayed on his feet. He got a better look at the car when spotlights from outside lit up its subtle dark blue colour. Soldiers surrounded him with their weapons raised. Their torches merged in a blinding row. Owen knelt down and grabbed the photo off the floor. He scrunched it as small as he could and held it tightly in his fist while reaching for his ID.

A snap like the crack of a whip wrapped something around Henry's legs. He tensed up and prevented his face from hitting the ground at the cost of bruises up his forearms. Every passageway seemed to be directing him further away. He had run ahead to find the room that trapped Owen but the factory span him in infinite circles that could only lead in the opposite direction. They were supposed to have the factory locked down already. Pressing his communicator only caused it to scream static into his ear.

Dawson's radio buzzed and hissed with a signal from Henry's comms. Despite his indefatigable attempts, the Colonel wasn't getting through to anyone either. He elected to respond to the commotion by sending in reinforcements, but they all returned ten minutes later claiming the hallways to be blocked a few metres in.

They need a Knight to save them

The writing was painted with the same black from the reception. Dennis turned his attention to a light coming from the end the long hallway, oscillating between bright and dim. Cold, clean smelling air chilled his nostrils. Unknown horrors havocked the factory beneath their feet.

Sophie placed her steps cautiously. The floors and walls swayed and creaked noticeably. Beyond the corner, a light swung on the ceiling, illuminating a comprehensive number of arrows that had been painted on every surface, all pointing and accumulating around a single open doorway. Dennis took a wide arc to peek in as he got closer. A half open door somewhere in the darkness hinted at a seated silhouette. Dennis checked his corners. Sophie then aimed her flashlight while he pushed the door open all the way. The outlines of bodies hypnotized him, tunnelling his vision.

Sophie heard muffled calls in the next room around the same time Dennis discovered the sacks tied to the chairs.

"It's not them," he said, pulling one of the sacks off its chair.

"There's someone here!" Sophie strode into the next room. The man Shook his head and yelled against the duct-tape over his mouth. His wide eyes slowed her down but she still crossed the threshold, causing metal sheets to fall and lock. Dennis called her name from the other side. Only too late she noticed the hole in the ceiling. A camouflaged rope snapped from the walls launching the man up by his ankles. Sophie managed to grab his chin but let him slip away to avoid injuring his neck. He disappeared through the hole to be dragged across the floors above. Intrinsic recalculation and muscle memory sent Sophie kicking down the next door to chase after him. She followed the sounds of sliding and muffled cries all the way to an office room where she stood helplessly listening to it disappear upwards. The only way for her to go was left into an open section of offices. Whilst looking in, her light became lost in a greater glow that diffracted around her figure. She ducked and span, squinting at the light in pale shock. It was coming through the window of the neighbouring room from the office on the other side where a man stood facing the back wall.

Henry knew he wouldn't find his way back. Owen was probably as lost as he was somewhere in the depths of the factory. The concerning factor that built his anxious apprehension was the lack of commotion. As he ventured through new sections of the building, he heard less and less of the yelling, banging, and crashing. He expected to see the torchlights of a squad reflect in the windows, but it was only his own refracting through them.

Motion crossing the bottom of his torchlight made him double back and take cover behind a pillar. A regular black and white soccer ball rolled across the floor and into a room on his left. He took an offensive stance and arced right to look for the source, but the pillar from which it came offered no answer. Henry shined his light in every direction, determined to find something before panic stirred. The path of the ball led into a small room on the end of a row of offices. He kept an eye out while walking backward toward the room, then speedily glanced inside with a flash of his torch. Something on the ball caused him to double take without thinking. A single outlying strip of tape was wrapped around it. He surveyed the rest of the open area and backed inside. Then using his foot, he turned the ball over to read the writing on the tape.

For James. Merry Christmas.

Henry had to read it twice, slowly, to make sure he read it right. It had been too long since he checked his surroundings. The Phantom's powerful voice paralyzed him milliseconds before the signal to turn around reached his body.

"**Don't. Face forward.**"

Henry's body tensed between fighting and obeying. The Phantom was an unknown distance behind him, and held the visual advantage. Though Henry had the luxury to wait for a better opportunity.

"**I was hoping you wouldn't come.**" The Phantom conciliated. "**I don't want you to get hurt.**"

Henry thought quickly. "Nobody has to get hurt," he said, calming himself with subtle breathing techniques.

"**I wish you were right, Mr Busher. So much so that went through the effort of setting up this offer in preparation for your arrival…**"

"What offer?" Henry asked passively.

"**Your boy is seven, correct?**"

Henry felt a cold sinking down his arteries. "Yes," he said. His chest rose tightly against his bullet-proof vest.

"**It isn't fair to him. You work hard, you earn a living to provide for him and the court doesn't see that as important as his mother spending a couple of hours with him at home?**" Phantom said vehemently. "**He's in school most of the day. She works during that time as well, just not as much as you, and legally that means she deserves custody?**"

"What's it matter to you?" Henry interjected.

"**It pisses me off.**" Phantom spoke out solemnly. "**They don't see you as a father, they see you as an income. A monthly paycheque. James needs more. He deserves more. I've seen what she's like as a mother...**"

"You made that case about her neglect. I remember." Henry squinted as the Phantom suddenly switched the light on.

"**Keep facing forward.**" Phantom said firmly. "**She's an unfit mother. James is lucky to have you. He needs you. I want him to grow up with a father. Just walk away, Henry. No harm need be done.**"

Henry's heartbeat had slowed to normal. His uneasy feeling dissipated behind distraction. Given his disadvantage it was an offer worth considering. On the other hand, it was a chance, however small, to end the Phantom.

"**The National Guard has me surrounded... I have no escape.** *You're no good to him dead.* **Go. Take him far away from here.**"

"I can't."

"**You can.**"

Henry felt something at the tip of his fingers. He took the paper dubiously and skimmed through them under the office light. It was a file with his name on it. Inside were extracts printed under the Department of Justice and contact information for attorneys, accompanied by details and photographs incriminating his ex-wife as a negligent mother. Henry flipped through them confoundedly.

"**Come, time for you to go.**"

Sophie watched incredulously as the Phantom held the door for Henry. Whatever the Phantom had been looking through, Henry took with him as he left. And just as the Phantom was about to follow, he looked past the glass, directly at Sophie, and switched off the light. Sophie lost her breath. She stood catatonic in front of her shadowy reflection when her head was thrust into the glass leaving it shattered in a web pattern. Her hair was then pulled back with equal force. She fell back waving her arms for balance she couldn't find. A slim, voluptuous figure stood over her, eye's sparkling.

"Sophie Mercer," the Lady Danger said complacently, "You shouldn't be spying on your friends."

Sophie kicked at the Lady's knees but she pulled Sophie's foot and twisted it. Sophie spun herself in synch and delivered a kick to the Lady's arm. She then pushed herself up straight and held her fists up in a defensive stance. The Lady smirked excitedly and stretched her aching arm.

Sophie walked backward into the open space and concentrated on the Lady's outlines. She followed Sophie with a care-free stride and engaged with a back-hand swipe. Sophie blocked it with her forearms, bruising them with disproportionate pain. A metal frame, as dark as the room, was attached up the Lady's right arm and over her shoulder. Sophie rubbed the bruise on her forearm while backing away unconfidently, but the Lady wasted no time. She reengaged with well-placed jabs forcing Sophie further back in order to block successfully.

Sophie hopped back and kicked Lady's abdomen, following through with a solid left hook before grabbing her in a headlock. She felt her grip get closer to the Lady's throat when her weight was lifted from the ground. Lady held her breath and walked backward to slam Sophie against the boarded windows. Then she swung an elbow in her side, and flipped her over her shoulder.

Sophie span herself back into balance with scarcely enough time to dodge more of the Lady's swift kicks. She didn't have trouble backing away given the distance Lady kept between them. Right-hook counters incurred a secondary reflex counter from the Lady followed by a dizzying hit from her framed arm. Sophie kicked away, shaking off the sharp pains across her face. The Lady refused to let her circle left. She would step right, keeping Sophie in her centre, and circle the opposite way. Feeling blood and saliva drool from her mouth, Sophie quickstepped right to left and grabbed at the Lady's frame. Lady had next to no reaction but instead pulled Sophie into a knee-thrust and winded her with a tackle using her framed shoulder. Sophie's back ricocheted off the corner of a pillar letting her head slide narrowly against it. The Lady's right shoulder collided with the pillar forcing the two of them apart. Sophie had fallen to her back again, but the Lady staggered with perplexed discontent. Her head turned uncertainly to look around so Sophie slid forward to swipe a kick at her feet. Lady unforeseeably hopped over it with ease and punched Sophie's head to the ground. On top of being bewildered by the Lady's peripheral vision, Sophie's already dark vision became static with black spots.

    The Lady giggled and laughed maniacally. She stood over Sophie and knelt down, sitting hard on her stomach. Her punches broke away at the integrity of Sophie's forearm defence until the blood from her nose splattered out between them. In her desperation, Sophie swiped the Lady's hands away and swung at her head. The Lady laughed. She grabbed Sophie's right hand but choked as the left hook connected below her eye. Seizing her opportunity, Sophie used her right arm to subdue the Lady's counters and swung with her left, connecting every hook until the Lady jumped away, spitting blood on the empty floor.

    Sophie's knees wobbled lifting her weight. She angled her hips and shoulders to try again but the Lady span herself elegantly, sideswiping through Sophie's block and sending her diving to the concrete floor.

"If it were up to me I would've killed you already..." The Lady said fiercely, blood bubbling between her numb lips.

Sophie coughed the blood from the back of her throat. The rest of it blocked her nose. She aimed her face down to let it all drain while drawing painful breaths.

"But, I'm not allowed to, so..." The Lady vanished momentarily and began dragging something over.

Sophie fought against the stinging in her abdomen and sat up to see. The Lady kicked her shoulder down, dislocating it, and tied a hook around her ankles. Sophie screamed. As she drew in breath, she saw the Lady smirk sadistically and pull something from the ceiling.

The hook jerked Sophie away so rapidly that her own diaphragm pressed hard against her lungs. She could hardly hold her head up sliding with alarming speed. It dragged her around a corner, her torso rebounding off the wall, and accelerated. She saw a glint of the cable lead up an empty elevator shaft and gripped the hook with both hands. Her fingers ached against the pulling force. She felt her legs lift into the air slightly as she neared the end. By shuffling her feet, she wedged her heel into the loop of the hook and loosened it enough to pull her other foot free. The force of the cable pulled the rest of the loop off the end of her foot and zipped up the elevator shaft, clanging and rattling against the sides. Sophie caught her breath weakly, rubbing at her ankles.

To let himself snowball through so many deflections turned his stomach over with repugnant disappointment. Played with, mocked, embarrassed, and now shamed. Cole took on the mission as a challenger but the Phantom turned him into a toy. A lesser threat. His impact having no more affect than a thorn in the Phantom's side, to which he barely turned his head. Only for Cole to discover that he was one of many who tried and failed to slow the Syndicate down. Now the Phantom had him locked in a cage match, left to navigate his mazes like a rat in a lab. No interference, however, from commanding officers. Thus, the rules change.

Cole followed the sound in the walls. His ear glided millimetres away. There was something of a chain, turning on gears or axils that led into hidden depths. He reached a point where the chain turned over and looked about the surfaces.

"Kick it down." He demanded, stopping by a single door.

"Prepare for a trap," Charles warned.

Hayden leaned his weight into a kick that cracked the wood around the lock. Bentley stepped in and took a two-step run-up. The lock partially broke from the wood leaving the door loose.

"One more then back out the way." Said Deck.

Meach thrust himself into a drop-kick, breaking the door open and falling out the way of any triggers. As soon as the door swung into the closet-sized space, a goofy clown decoration sprung up to chuckle at them. Cole grabbed its head and ripped it out into the hallway. Then he pounded at the backboard with the hilt of his rifle. Deck was able to squeeze in and do the same. Once the nails in the backboard were mostly out, they switched to using their shoulders. The hallway echocd with hollow pounding that switched to synchronized thudding. Cole's exhilaration from the backboard breaking away pushed him to kick it down and jump into the room. The Syndicate must have made the box around the door to prevent anyone from seeing the machinery, which they could now see down to the bone. Cole's hesitation was dangerously short lived. The Grenade was in his hand with his finger in the pin before the other's had time to crouch into the room. He could see the neighbouring room past chains and pneumatics that led up to the next floor. Under the floorboards between the rooms was a dense spot of angled gears that served as a turning point for many of the larger connections running beneath the factory.

"Fire in the hole!" Cole shouted. He dropped it with brief rigour and kicked away to leap out behind the others. They could feel it in the air and the ground more than they could hear it. A single, deep, thud-like explosion, followed almost simultaneously by a loud, hollow pop from the residual traces of hydrogen igniting. Cole elated from the delectable melody of grinding and scratching that played through the smoke.

Every alternative Dennis exhausted left him apprehensive but more determined. The sandbags that were made to look like people had no effect on his certainty. Caitlin and Joel were in there with him. Somewhere behind the diversions, their conditions depended on what the Phantom wanted to show him.

Dennis' heightened senses picked up on a negligible resistance beneath his left heal. It all happened second by second. A high-pitched snap released wires on either side of him that fastened around his ankles. A square piece of the ceiling dropped a few metres behind making him twitch painfully against the taught wires, verging on a total loss of balance. He stole a glimpse of the void-black hole in the ceiling when kneeling down to cut the wire. A light electric shock travelled up the blade and into his fingertips. His grip on the knife held strong and remained when his hand jerked away. Supplemental cables were triggered to snap up from the floor. Dozens of them whipped under his chin, arms, and legs, forcibly lifting him to his feet. Others came from above and either side, locking against one another with Dennis trapped at the epicentre of their stress.

A hand came down from the hole and grabbed at the ceiling. Its fingers dug into the fracturing plaster and held onto something inside. Dennis choked against the cables to angle his head. He descried the Phantom's hood looming down from the hole with his second hand penetrating the ceiling. Parts of the plaster cracked and fell amongst raining dust. The Phantom slinked out of the hole, his glossy eyes observing Dennis' distress.

Dennis pulled against the cables. His teeth clenched. He fought against the agonizing tension digging into his vest and protective padding. The Phantom reached out to pull himself further. His thick boots stuck implausibly to the ceiling letting him crawl along it insidiously. Dennis twisted his wrist to shine the edge of his light on the Phantom, whose unwavering eyes constricted.

Phantom held the outer-most wires that held Dennis in place and pulled to goad him until he cried out. In one swift spin, his boots unstuck and dropped, cracking the fractured floor on impact. He then subtly released the magnetic soles from the bottom of the boots while straightening up. Dennis attempted to swipe at him but the web was unfaltering. Succulent trepidation grew within Dennis' exasperation. His wide eyes leaked fragrant fear which the Phantom indulged in with deep, sated breaths.

A thud, too loud and heavy to be one of his own, wrenched the Phantom down from his high. The grenade was distant and compacted but unmistakable.

Dennis' struggling ceased. His emanating fear lessened with the spreading calamity in the walls. While the Phantom tracked the damage attentively, Dennis' weight dropped from the cables giving him the manoeuvrability to shove his elbow into the Phantom's chest.

Phantom staggered but grabbed Dennis' elbow and wrist to prevent him from turning all the way around. He then kicked behind his knee and ducked aside from Dennis' backward head-butt.

Dennis dropped to his knee. His throat closed under the python-grip of the Phantom's arm but he turned enough to kick away from one of the walls.

Phantom revolved to slam Dennis to the floor but Dennis rotated his hips and planted his feet to twist out of the headlock. He barely made it out before the Phantom struck a left punch and followed through with two rapid right jabs.

Phantom capitalized on Dennis' momentary concussion by grabbing him by his vest and sending him ricocheting off a wall. He then took a key out of his pocket and flicked it to the ground in front of him. **"Your officers are through there."** He said, letting Dennis compose himself. He pointed to the hidden door at the end of the hallway and jumped up to pull himself through the hole before Dennis could engage.

Smoke hazed his intricate network of passages. He passed over dead hydraulics and hissing steam pipes. The electric cables overhead led to the server room where the Lady was likely evaluating the damage.

"Where was it?" He asked using a wired communicator on the passage wall.

"Bottom floor in the old kitchen storerooms, I don't see anyone." The Lady responded.

Phantom used the railing to pull himself efficiently through the passages, at times ducking or jumping through kinks. He reached the smoke-filled passage above the old storerooms and put on his modified goggles. Dials on the pipes indicated a total loss of pressure. He unlocked the trapdoor and checked the room before dropping in. There was a charred crater of warped metal in the floor network. Any hydrogen in the room would have been ignited by the naked flames. He assessed the damage looking for possible access points for the grenade.

A presence pounced from the box covering the door. Phantom jounced to evade but Cole's knee still collided with the side of his face. His mask took the hit allowing him to respond with an uppercut. Cole had already moved aside and forced him back with a swipe of his knife. Phantom sensed the back wall get close and engaged to avoid being boxed into the corner. Cole blocked with his forearms. Deck's attack forced Phantom to redirect his energy into a defensive stance. The Phantom then pushed his block against Meach's subsequent attack and dodged a kick from Cole. Charles and Hayden circled around him while Bentley guarded the door. Cole, Deck, and Meach persisted in simultaneous attacks to his head, chest, and legs.

Phantom blocked the most threatening attacks whilst taking the rest of the punches. He stepped back from sweeping kicks, protected his neck and lower ribs with his arms, and let the internecine punches rebound off his mask. Meach and Cole shifted to attack on the sides for higher impact rates. Phantom was shaken in every direction by the concatenation of vengeful strikes. He felt his back press against a wall and the impacts of their jabs sink deeper into his protective padding. Dense heat began growing out from his chest. A monstrous rage, electrified by the sense of powerlessness screaming in his head, surged through every muscle fibre and pushed the pain of a dozen bruises into overdrive. His left hand caught a right hook from Meach and redirected it to collide with the incoming hilt of Cole's gun. Deck responded with a straightforward kick which the Phantom punched to the ground. Phantom then kicked off

Deck's knee and pulled Meach's head into a knee thrust, cracking his skull. Meach flew back before Hayden could grab him. Phantom brought his elbow down on Deck's outreaching arms and launched a jaw-breaking uppercut that burst blood from Deck's mouth. Cole charged with another tackle. Phantom planted his feet firmly and lifted Cole with him as he fell back. Cole ducked into a disorientating roll and rose to be met with the Phantom's forearm. The impact cracked his nose and drove his head back with a speed akin to whiplash.

Charles swung his rifle but the Phantom leapt to his feet much faster than anticipated. The hilt whacked his side allowing him to pin it under his arm and pull Charles in. The Phantom then rammed his steel mask down on Charles' head.

Hayden jumped onto the Phantom and swung his weight. They fell to the floor together, Hayden locking his arms around the Phantom's neck. Bentley waited for the Phantom to be lifted to his knees and charged knee-first at his head. Phantom contracted his abdomen and whipped Hayden over his head and into Bentley's knee. He rose to a right hook from Bentley and a side-swiping pull from Cole. Letting his impetus travel with Cole, he kicked from the ground and span over. Cole reached out but the Phantom back-handed his arms and face as he exited his spin. Hayden and Bentley circled him beside Cole. Phantom felt the pneumatics behind him with his left hand and held one down to pull himself over it. He slid head-first over the machinery and into the next room. Bentley bolted through the box and sprinted to the next door. The Phantom burst out, shoving Bentley into the opposite wall and knocking him out. Cole and Hayden hurdled over his limp body and chased after the fleeting silhouette.

The Phantom sprinted through his maze with practiced pace. He led Cole and Hayden down a preselected emergency-route to a tight right turn where he doubled back and accelerated. His calculated drop-kick sent Hayden flying into the far wall. Making sure to grab Cole in a headlock at the same time, Phantom fell to the floor letting Cole's momentum lift his own feet out from under him.

Cole's vision flashed black, by which time the Phantom was on his feet and leaving. He got up and leaned into acceleration, nearly reaching the Phantom who scurried out of reach.

Phantom led Cole up two broken flights of stairs, dodging a squad of soldiers to get to the room with the hole in the floor. Cole pushed passed the soldiers who were helping each other out of a revolving wall trap. Phantom lined himself up and jumped into the hole with Cole closing in. He fell to the floor below and kicked down with his boots to break through it. Cole skidded in hesitation. Two floors below, the Phantom rolled swiftly into a run.

Caitlin and Joel were the only things on Christian's mind. Their voices, their faces. The certainty of his uncertainty nullified all comfort of Dennis' determination and capability. His glazed eyes sank into focus on the empty space where Dawson once stood. Captains relayed antagonistic commands under the moonlight like howling dogs. Every sight aimed at the front entrance and advanced in unison. Christian opened the car door, amplifying the sounds of chaos. He got out and jogged to see the origin of the threat.

Emerging from the front doors, dark born from the dark. Glints of steel in the torchlights. Searchlights from a helicopter cast shadows down the smooth, hooded figure. Bloodied, empty hands suspended passively at shoulder height. Beneath the hood, over the shimmering mask, wide eyes gravitated towards Christian. The Phantom dropped gracefully to his knees and put his hands behind his back, allowing the many approaching soldiers to push him to the ground and lean their weight on him.

Christian hovered into the open. He let himself draw closer to the dense crowd of officers and officials. Dawson called to him from behind and jogged with a slight limp to catch up. The crowd moved as one. A pitch-black hood rose in the centre above the heads and helmets. Christian stood with his feet rooted into the ground. A few of the officers attempted to usher him out of the way to no avail. Dawson growled back at them to separate around Christian, cutting the throng down the middle. Phantom strode forward eagerly, pulling the marines who held his arms. Christian locked on his gaze with equal determination. A dozen rifle barrels followed the Phantom's every move. He stepped up to Christian, stopping at arms-length. Dawson made the commands on Christian's behalf, halting the arrest. Three marines held the Phantom in place. His hands were cuffed behind his back and his ankles were chained together. He overlooked Christian with contentment sparkling in his eyes and a grin peaking over his metal mask. "**Detective Christian Taylor...**"

Christian contemplated him blankly. "What do I call you?" He asked simply.

The Phantom's misty breath leaked from the thin wire grids in his mask. "**You have your name for me.**"

"Where are they?" Christian asked faintly. They focused on each other's faces. Every microscopic twitch or muscle contraction. The shapes of the curves and tendons. Expansion of the iris. Lift of the unblinking eyelids.

"**Dennis has them.**" Phantom assured, his expression blank and expecting.

Christian kept his own expression blank, marshalling his thoughts. "Why surrender?" He asked simply.

"**What choice do I have?**" Phantom countered.

Their minds connected within a closed line of acknowledgement. Parallel trains of thought skipped stations to keep up with one another. The Phantom had prepared for their arrival and let himself become surrounded. Rudimentary logic dictated his intention to be in custody, his least desirable state. Christian figured there could be threats to be pacified in exchange for his freedom. But then why let himself be captured in the first place. There was always a point to his torments. Ethics with forced distortions. The Phantom watched Christian eliminate the many possibilities, eagerly awaiting his conclusion with yearning curiosity. Even if he had a scheme to force his freedom under moral constrictions, there was no guarantee they would be allowed to follow through. It could force insubordination, and by extension, criminal treachery in avoidance of the Phantom's worst tribulations. All to make a point. He wasn't above it.

The Phantom could believe his Syndicate capable of his recapture, but for what purpose. If not a point he would try to prove, which he already did multiple times, then he would be in search of something he desired. Something he wanted. Something they had. Law enforcement protocol was as obvious as it had always been. It was his medium of predicting and manipulating. He wanted to be taken in, and he knew exactly what that entailed.

"What are you trying to prove?" Christian asked suddenly.

"**I don't need to prove anything. I've already taught you everything...**" Phantom said deeply, "**...You did not learn.**"

"Your lessons were lost in your delusions. You can't preach morality you don't have." Christian retorted.

"You're so very confident your linear ideals are unquestionable. Why, then, are you allowed to be free? Do you consider yourself innocent after playing my games?"

"Those were tainted circumstances spoilt by your own infliction."

"**The precursory circumstances weren't real but your reality inside them was.**"

"If you only have one option then it's not an option. You think your point can still be accurate if you yourself are the only prerequisite?"

"**The cause does not matter, the effect is always the same. I know because I too had to make those very same decisions myself on behalf of the very same principles.**" Phantom admitted.

"Why put us through that as well?" Christian asked, equally as dejected.

"**I wanted you... to understand.**"

The Majors behind Dawson were restless. "Chris..." He said, drawing Christian's focus back to the immediate.

"Have you ever had to let a killer go?" Christian asked. The Phantom's melancholy expression lifted leaving him stony. His obsession with necessity denied him from proving a point he was never forced to learn. By process of elimination, he could only have alternate plans for escape, if he planned to at all. There was something they had that he wanted and he wanted to be taken to it. His expression became forcibly inexpressive in light of his unravelling.

"Where is it you want to go?" Christian asked provocatively.

Phantom's bright green eyes burned. His pupils dilated unconsciously. "**Isn't it obvious?**" He riposted.

Ambiguity was his only defence. Christian was a

talented reader but the Phantom must have had a history of learning not to be read. The advantage, however, remained with Christian. The Phantom's mental conditions, patterns of psychosis, were Christian's studied specialty and the very reason for his involvement in the first place. And so, the clash of minds began. A collision of cognition. A duel of wit.

The first place they would elect take him would obviously be their headquarters. The Phantom knew that, and he knew that they would take him elsewhere because they too, knew that he knew that. Christian had already accounted for it, and was already considering taking him anyway to shake the Phantom's prediction of blatant recalculation. For so long the Phantom must have prepared and considered every permutation of the outcome. Therein lies the Phantom's final maze trap; the logical recursion of expectation, prediction, and counter-coordination. Every choice Christian could make had its own equal and opposite counter the Phantom could have in place, each of which could be accounted for. The cycle was possibly but improbably infinite. The Phantom could only account for so many of Christian's tactical retaliations, but such a point was lost among the many iterations of potential recourses. Christian's only choices were to level the playing field - To be truly... unpredictable. Or to draw out the Phantom's machination using his one and only advantage.

"Is it the CIA?" In real time, only a couple of seconds passed, hosting the unperceivable psychological sparring.

"He already knows his way around." Dawson gritted his teeth.

Phantom hardened his stony expression. His silvery-steel mask covered the bottom half of his face so the truth would have to come from his eyes.

Christian angled his head and torso in a mesmerizing

motion to force the Phantom's muscles to work naturally so that he could maintain his harsh gaze, and by extension, his focus. "The CIA headquarters?" Christian scanned every microscopic reaction in the Phantom's face. He could not hide the dilation of his pupils. Christian waited until he blinked to speak again. "Or maybe you want to go to a city precinct?"

No reaction. Phantom had dealt with worse than city cops, there was also the defensive capability to consider.

"FBI?"

Phantom's pupils dilated again. There was a slight widening of his eyes more akin to a diversion.

"Not FBI, not CIA, England?"

Phantom tilted his head millimetres down.

"We can't do that." Dawson whispered in Christian's ear. Phantom tilted his head and shrugged only enough for Christian to tell.

"No state prisons, perhaps a military installation…" Christian suggested, his gaze still locked with the Phantom's as it had been since they stood up to each other.

And there it was - the direction Phantom had been leading him. Phantom's pupils dilated and remained so. Energy was being redistributed from the muscles around his eyes. Suppression.

"I don't know any but I'm sure the major can name a few."

The Phantom's central focus flickered to the major for a fraction of a second.

"Yeah how about area fifty-one?" Dawson spoke over Christian's shoulder but was cut off quickly. The more significant the installation the more obvious. It was then that Christian remembered something, from where he did not know. To know your enemy is to be on the offensive, to know yourself is to be on the defensive. Phantom had used this to be on the offensive on several occasions. His greatest offensive tool, deception, now lay in Christian's hands.

"Take him directly to the CIA with full military escort," Christian backed away but continued to watch the Phantom, who looked disbelievingly between Christian and Dawson. "Make sure all channels of intelligence are aware of his custody there. We will secretly transfer him to area fifty-one first thing tomorrow morning."

"I wasn't being serious, that's not what it's for." Dawson pressed.

"Excuse me-" The major asserted himself to interject but Christian whispered something in his ear to pacify him. The major then relayed the order while the Phantom watched perplexedly.

"Keep only the Phantom's custody at the CIA official. And redirect all of this to act as reinforcement in and around the building." Christian gestured to the National Guard's offense of tanks and squads while walking back to the car.

"But we're sending him to fifty-one? That was a joke." Dawson asked, limping a step behind Christian.

"We're going to pretend like we are. Keep it off record. Need-to-know. All that classified shit." Christian hushed.

"You know him... his Syndicate will find out anyway." Dawson said under his breath.

"Exactly." Christian adjusted his glasses. "Do it."

The Phantom was taken to an armoured convoy. He suppressed his exuberance and cooperated wordlessly all the way. Christian would be the architect of their final stand. The cards were laid out on the table, all that remained were those in their hands. The fate of the future no longer bet by fools. Tricks and deceptions twisted and entwined in knots of uncertainty.

Growing permutations of potential realities weaved slowly and fixed into place with each revealing moment.

The games are changing.

Printed in Great Britain
by Amazon